THE WAY OF FIRE

Hawkeye spoke but could not be heard above the shouts and cries for revenge. He tried to get the attention of the chief, but Skenendowa had turned away and was looking at his people. The old man glanced back at the two whites tied to the posts, then lowered his head and walked off, disappearing into the mob.

"Kahonwah!" Hawkeye called. "Don't do this! Don't—!"

The young warrior spun around and struck Hawkeye across the cheek, stunning him.

"The—the woman—" Hawkeye said, shaking his head to clear it. "Let her go. . . ."

Stepping forward, the brave grabbed his chin. "Die like a warrior, white man, not a dog. Then perhaps I will let you taste the lead of your rifle before we feed you to the flames."

Hawkeye turned to Astra, who looked up at him with fear and resignation. As he struggled for words to bring her comfort, he felt something scrape his leg—a branch dropped at his feet by a young brave who leered up at him and scurried away. Others surged forward. . . .

Also by Paul Block

DARKENING OF THE LIGHT

Song of the Mohicans

A Sequel to James Fenimore Cooper's
The Last of the Mohicans

by

Paul Block

BANTAM BOOKS
NEW YORK · TORONTO · LONDON · SYDNEY · AUCKLAND

SONG OF THE MOHICANS

A Bantam Book / April 1995

All rights reserved.
Copyright © 1995 by Paul Block and Ethan Ellenberg.
Cover art copyright © 1995 by Robert Hunt.

ISBN 0-553-56558-3

Published simultaneously in the United States and Canada

PRINTED IN THE UNITED STATES OF AMERICA

RAD   0 9 8 7 6 5 4 3 2 1

"Kawanio che keeteru"
"I am master wherever I am"
—I<small>ROQUOIS</small> <small>SAYING</small>

Foreword

America in 1757 has become a battleground. The two great European powers of England and France have spread their empires across the North American continent, and now they face each other in a bitter war for supremacy in the New World. Yet neither England nor France is the original owner of the vast, well-watered, and largely untamed forests of the Northeast. Dozens of indigenous tribes still live there, struggling to protect their ancestral homelands from the encroaching whites, even as they continue to make war against one another to the beat of ancient feuds and animosities.

A kaleidoscope of people is caught in the maelstrom. Bewigged and powdered French officers, fresh from the battlefields and opera houses of Europe, find themselves marching alongside Iowas from the banks of the Des Moines who wear nothing but loincloths, practice cannibalism, and speak a dialect so strange that no one can interpret their words. American rangers and militiamen, many of them farmers on leave from terrified families left to fend for themselves in the wilderness, serve next to British troops from the darkest of London's slums or from the glens of Scotland, marching in kilts to the sound of the pipes. French priests and trappers, Indian warriors and sachems, English merchants and ministers, a ragtag assortment of slaves, settlers, and adventurers . . . all find themselves engulfed in the struggle.

Such is the world of *The Last of the Mohicans.*

At the close of James Fenimore Cooper's novel the Mohican brave Uncas is killed by the Huron warrior

Magua, who in turn is shot by Nathaniel Bumppo, a woodsman and scout known to all as Hawkeye. The next day, a funeral ceremony is held among the Leni-Lenape, or Delaware Indians, presided over by the sage Tamenund. As Cooper concludes his novel Uncas's father, Chingachgook, addresses the gathering:

> "Why do my brothers mourn!" he said . . . "why do my daughters weep! that a young man has gone to the happy hunting-grounds; that a chief has filled his time with honor! He was good; he was dutiful; he was brave. Who can deny it? The Manitou had need of such a warrior, and He has called him away. As for me, the son and the father of Uncas, I am a blazed pine, in a clearing of the pale-faces. My race has gone from the shores of the salt lake, and the hills of the Delawares. But who can say that the Serpent of his tribe has forgotten his wisdom? I am alone—"
>
> "No, no," cried Hawkeye . . . "no, Sagamore, not alone. The gifts of our colors may be different, but God has so placed us as to journey in the same path. . . . He was your son . . . and it may be that your blood was nearer—but if ever I forget the lad who has so often fou't at my side in war, and slept at my side in peace, may He who made us all, whatever may be our color or our gifts, forget me! The boy has left us for a time; but, Sagamore, you are not alone."
>
> Chingachgook grasped the hand that, in the warmth of feeling, the scout had stretched across the fresh earth, and in that attitude of friendship these two sturdy and intrepid woodsmen bowed their heads together, while scalding tears fell to their feet, watering the grave of Uncas like drops of falling rain.
>
> In the midst of the awful stillness . . . Tamenund lifted his voice to disperse the multitude.
>
> "It is enough," he said. "Go, children of the Lenape, the anger of the Manitou is not done. . . . The pale-faces are masters of the

earth, and the time of the redmen has not yet come again. My day has been too long. In the morning I saw the sons of Unamis happy and strong; and yet, before the night has come, have I lived to see the last warrior of the wise race of the Mohicans."

Who are these Mohicans of whom Chingachgook and Tamenund speak and James Fenimore Cooper writes? In the third chapter of *The Last of the Mohicans*, Chingachgook describes to Hawkeye how his people originally came from far to the northwest and eventually dominated a vast region along the Atlantic Ocean. But then:

"The Dutch landed, and gave my people the fire-water; they drank until the heavens and the earth seemed to meet, and they foolishly thought they had found the Great Spirit. Then they parted with their land. Foot by foot, they were driven back from the shores, until I, that am a chief and a sagamore, have never seen the sun shine but through the trees, and have never visited the graves of my fathers."

Hawkeye asks what became of the Mohicans who were pushed back into the land of the Leni-Lenape in the northern Hudson Valley, to which Chingachgook replies:

"Where are the blossoms of those summers! —fallen, one by one: so all of my family departed, each in his turn, to the land of spirits. I am on the hill-top, and must go down into the valley; and when Uncas follows in my footsteps, there will no longer be any of the blood of the sagamores, for my boy is the last of the Mohicans."

But did the Mohican line truly end with Uncas and Chingachgook? While Cooper's characters are fictional, the Mohicans, or Mahicans, did indeed exist, and some fought with the British during the events depicted in the novel. But the Mohicans did not die out, as Chingachgook predicted. At that time they made their home in the village of Stockbridge in western Massachusetts. But in 1784 they relocated to Oneida Lake, New York, only fifty miles from Cooper's home, and were still living there when *The Last of the Mohicans* was published in 1826. Today several hundred of their descendants live on a reservation in Shawano County, Wisconsin, where they go by their official name: the Stockbridge Indians.

My interest in the novels of James Fenimore Cooper had its roots in a childhood love of Davy Crockett and anything on television having to do with "cowboys and Indians." Later I was enthralled watching television broadcasts of such movie classics as *Drums Along the Mohawk*, starring Henry Fonda, *Stagecoach*, starring John Wayne, and of course the 1936 version of *The Last of the Mohicans*, with Randolph Scott. It was not until I was in college in the early 1970s that I became interested in the literature behind many of these classic television shows and movies, and this led eventually to a career writing westerns and historical novels.

A special love for James Fenimore Cooper and *The Last of the Mohicans* developed quite naturally during the past decade. First I began visiting the Farmers' Museum and Fenimore House, which are located in Cooperstown, New York, on the site of the Cooper family's farm. Then I found myself living and working just a few miles from Stockbridge, the former home of the Mohicans. And five years ago I married a woman from Oneida, New York, and became familiar with the region where the Mohicans lived during Cooper's day. I also spent increasing time in the Lake George region, where the novel is set. Finally I fell back in love with the story after seeing Michael Mann's 1992 movie starring Daniel Day-Lewis and Madeleine Stowe. That led me to reread the book and start wondering what Hawkeye and Chingachgook might have done after the deaths of Uncas and Cora Munro.

In exploring that question in *Song of the Mohicans*, I have tried to be as accurate as possible in depicting the events of 1757 and life on the frontier of upstate New

York. While I have endeavored to provide a realistic portrait of the way of life of the Mohicans, Oneidas, and other Native American tribes, I have done so within the limitations of story and within the framework already laid out by James Fenimore Cooper. When faced with conflicts between Cooper's book and historical sources, I generally have relied on the latter, except in those instances where doing so would alter the background given in *The Last of the Mohicans*. And while the Mohican and Iroquois words used in this book are authentic, these were not written languages, and many variant spellings can be found. Furthermore, since several distinct Iroquois dialects exist, I have by necessity drawn upon a number of them.

If you are interested in reading more about the Mohicans, the Six Nations of the Iroquois, or the conflict between England and France as it was played out in upstate New York in the 1750s, a bibliography of some of my research sources is included at the back of this book.

Those who have seen the most recent film treatment of *The Last of the Mohicans* but have never read James Fenimore Cooper's novel may not realize that it is the dark-haired Cora Munro who dies at the end of the story, rather than her fair-haired younger sister, Alice. And it is not Hawkeye to whom Cora is attracted, but Uncas. During their funeral, the Delaware women speak of the future that Cora and Uncas will share in the next life.

Perhaps Cooper was being sensitive to the prejudices of an audience that might reject the notion of any kind of relationship between a white woman and a Native American brave when he chose to describe Cora as having almost Indian features:

> *The tresses of this lady were shining and black, like the plumage of a raven. Her complexion was not brown, but it rather appeared charged with the color of the rich blood, that seemed ready to burst its bounds.*

His explanation for her being so much darker than her blond, blue-eyed half sister, Alice, is that Cora's mother was a West Indian "whose misfortune it was, if you will . . . to be descended, remotely, from that unfortunate class who are so basely enslaved to administer to the wants of a luxurious people."

As James Fenimore Cooper's novel draws to a close, Cora has been given a Christian burial atop "a little knoll, where a cluster of young and healthful pines had taken root, forming of themselves a melancholy and appropriate shade over the spot." Uncas lies nearby, buried in a shell of birch bark "in an attitude of repose, facing the rising sun, with the implements of war and of the chase at hand, in readiness for the final journey." Alice is safe in the arms of her beloved, Major Duncan Hayward, and has been reunited with her father, Colonel George Munro (the actual commander of Fort William Henry was named Monro). Chingachgook and Hawkeye continue to mourn the death of Uncas—the last of the Mohicans.

Chingachgook's final words to his son are in the form of a song:

> A low, deep sound was heard, like the suppressed accompaniment of distant music, rising just high enough on the air to be audible. . . . It was succeeded by another and another strain, each in a higher key, until they grew on the ear, first in long drawn and often repeated interjections, and finally in words. The lips of Chingachgook had so far parted, as to announce that it was the monody of the father. Though not an eye was turned towards him, nor the smallest sign of impatience exhibited, it was apparent, by the manner in which the multitude elevated their heads to listen, that they drank in the sounds with an intenseness of attention, that none but Tamenund himself had ever before commanded. But they listened in vain. The strains rose just so loud as to become intelligible, and then grew fainter and more trembling, until they finally sank on the ear, as if borne away by a passing breath of wind.

Perhaps his song is answered, not by Uncas, but by other Mohicans who have survived the years of war and disease. This novel imagines what may have happened if Chingachgook and Hawkeye heard that call and went in search of the *Song of the Mohicans*. . . .

Song

of the

Mohicans

Chapter I

"Who comes hither, among the beasts and dangers of the wilderness?"
—*The Last of the Mohicans*, Chap. IV

*T*wo men stood in silence at the edge of a rock bluff that protruded two hundred feet above the floor of a narrow mountain pass. The sun lay hidden behind the eastern peaks of the Adirondacks, but already the deep azure canopy was yielding to the first streaks of orange and yellow. The air was crisp and still, as if the world had arrived at the edge of summer and was holding its breath before yielding to the harsh winter winds. The only sound that broke the dawn was the frenetic gabble of nine Canada geese who seemed to be arguing over the correct location of some favored pond or brook as they circled the sheltered valley. Their quest was made all the more difficult by heavy fog that had settled among the mountains during the night. It formed an unbroken blanket that stretched in all directions only inches below where the men were standing, as if a churning sea had been lapping at the edge of the bluff and had congealed into the softest of white down.

The taller of the men shifted slightly, gripping his hunting rifle higher on the barrel and leaning into it as though it were a staff. He glanced at the geese passing above, then turned his head to search the northern reaches of the pass. His companion held his gaze fixed on the eastern horizon, his shorter military rifle resting snug under his right arm, its barrel angled toward the ground.

The two men were as unalike in appearance as they were in stature. The tall, lean one looked to be in his mid-thirties and was the younger by perhaps half a dozen years. He wore a wool hunting shirt of forest green fringed in yellow, and a pair of buckskin leggings gartered above the knees and laced down the sides with thongs of deer sinew. Tucked behind a belt of wampum was a long-bladed knife, and hanging at his sides on crossed shoulder straps were a powder horn and a leather pouch. His moccasins were beaded with Indian designs, but he wore his brown hair long and loose in the fashion of white frontiersmen.

The shorter man was as muscular as he was compact, with full-formed limbs and an expansive chest that looked as if it would burst his red hunting shirt with each inhalation. His breechclout and buckskin leggings were decorated with white beads and porcupine quills, and the ankle cuffs of his moccasins were folded down and faced with beaded red velvet. His wampum belt held both a tomahawk and knife, and across his chest was a necklace of eagle talons. His head was closely shaved, leaving at the top only a long scalp lock, from which a single eagle's plume hung over his left shoulder.

Though both men had ruddy complexions, the shorter man was naturally so, while his younger companion's skin had been burnished by the sun, which did not mask his European heritage and features. His family had come into the wilderness by choice, and hard years had marked his face with a rugged beauty and grace rarely found in the settlements that pushed against the edges of the frontier. The older man's birthright to the wilderness, on the other hand, was an ancient one, for his people had once dominated a region that stretched along the salt lake—the white man's Atlantic Ocean—from the place where tidal currents no longer affect the Hudson River to a river twenty suns' journey to the south. His people were the children of the Leni-Lenape and fathers to the Ojibwa, Ottawa, and Potawatomi. They were the Mohicans, and he feared that he was destined to be the last of their race.

"I remember a morning such as this in my youth, Chingachgook," the younger man said in the Mohican dialect of the Leni-Lenape tongue. "It was on the heights overlooking the lake known as Glimmerglass. The sky was just as clear and blue, and the clouds had dropped down upon the face of the earth, turning the mountains into islands amid a sea of white." He turned to his friend. "Perhaps this is what the world looked like when your grandfathers crossed the great waters."

Chingachgook swept his left arm in front of him and intoned, *"Muhheconnuk."*

The young man nodded thoughtfully. He had often heard Chingachgook, sagamore of the Mohicans, recount the story of how his ancestors first came into this land. In a time beyond reckoning, they had emigrated from a place in the northwest where their former country was connected to this one by a string of islands on a great body of water affected by tides. In remembrance, they named themselves Muhheconnuk, which meant "great waters constantly in motion, either flowing or ebbing," and also used the name for the tidal river, later named the Hudson, along which they made their new home. From this term, the white settlers had derived the name Mohicans.

"Old Man has spread his white robe to drive away Young Man," Chingachgook continued, nodding sagely. "Old Man's hair is long and white. His lodge is made of ice. His footsteps turn the earth as hard as rock. His breath makes the lakes solid and the rivers stop flowing. His only friend is North Wind, and they smoke their pipes around a fire that gives no heat." Lowering the butt of his rifle to the ground and leaning against the barrel, he looked up at his companion. "I tell you this, Hawkeye, so that you will understand that at the end of their day, all things must wither and die."

Hawkeye was surprised to hear the sagamore speak so freely—especially about matters close to his heart—for he knew that Chingachgook was speaking not of the legend of how winter replaces summer, but of his son, Uncas, who had been killed by the Huron warrior Magua and laid to rest only a few days before. Hawkeye had been proud to have killed Magua and prouder still to have called Uncas friend.

Reaching forth, he grasped the older man's forearm, saying, "But we are told that Young Man does not die. He goes into hiding in the south, where he gathers strength before returning to claim his land and drive Old Man and North Wind away."

"Old Man has struck and hardened my heart. It may never warm again."

Hawkeye was about to reply, but Chingachgook raised a hand to silence him and cocked his head as if listening to something.

"A deer?" Hawkeye asked as he tried to make out the faint snapping noises that drifted up through the fog, which was just beginning to rise in thin wisps off the valley floor.

The Mohican shook his head. "A man."

"Could the Hurons be following us?"

"It is a white man; no red man would crash through the brush like that." He paused, listening intently, then added, "He is being pursued by red men, but whether they are Hurons I cannot say."

Hawkeye heard now the faint cry of an Indian war party entering the valley from the north. Much nearer, the sound of snapping branches was accompanied by the gasping breath of a man on the run.

Removing the stopper from his horn, Hawkeye primed the pan of his rifle and covered it, then poured a measure of powder down the barrel, following it with wadding and a ball from his leather pouch. As he set the ball with the ramrod he nodded toward the valley below. "We'd best find out if he's a Frencher or friend."

Chingachgook had also loaded his rifle, and the two men shouldered their traveling packs and set off down the winding trail that led from the outcropping. The maple and oak were still in full leaf, though the willows had begun to fade from green to yellow, and the combination of forest brush and fog provided adequate cover as the men descended toward the valley floor. The heaviest fog had lifted to the tops of the trees, but the morning mist limited their sight to no more than twenty yards, so they moved cautiously down the rocky deer trail toward an Indian path that traversed the pass.

Hawkeye felt Chingachgook tug at his sleeve and dashed behind a tree alongside the trail. He heard the gasping breath of a man climbing toward them; he sounded hurried, even panicked. If this man was indeed being pursued by Indians, he would have good reason to be in a panic, for he was still a half day's hike from the nearest white settlement, Fort Carillon, the French fortress at Ticonderoga. And the man was either lost or desperate, for he had veered off the main path and was scrambling up this little deer trail, which would lead him only as far as the bluff, halfway up the mountainside, where he would face certain capture or death.

Hawkeye raised his long rifle, Killdeer, and pulled the hammer to full cock. Sighting down the barrel, he eased his finger against the trigger and waited for the man to appear. What emerged from the fog seemed more spectral than human, with the features of a young man but the wild, ghastly aspect of an apparition. He was completely naked, his smooth, hairless body crisscrossed with lacerations from his run through the trees, his long hair and straggly beard golden blond and matted with sweat. He wore only a gold chain and locket, which swung against his chest as he stumbled breathless up the trail, his gaunt arms flying in all directions and his head jerking from side to side on a neck as thin as a reed. Most striking of all was the deep, straight wound that ran from beside his right eye to his jaw. It was not bleeding but was open and raw. It might have been the work of a blade, though it looked more as if a musket ball had dug a furrow along his cheek.

"Be you Frencher or English?" Hawkeye called, stepping out in the trail and training the barrel of his rifle on the stranger's chest.

With a gasp, the man staggered to a halt, his pale blue eyes widening with shock and surprise. He opened his mouth as if to speak, then glanced beyond Hawkeye and saw the imposing figure of an Indian warrior emerge from the trees. Raising his arms in front of him, he dropped to his knees.

Taken aback, Hawkeye lowered the muzzle slightly and repeated his question. The man clasped his hands together and began to babble in a harsh, guttural voice that Hawkeye thought might be French—until he recognized it as a prayer in English for deliverance or a quick death.

Uncocking the rifle, Hawkeye stepped forward, grasped the kneeling man's shoulder, and demanded in a quiet but firm voice, "To your feet, soldier! What is your company?"

As if on instinct, the man struggled upright and muttered, "New York Militia, sir!"

"Provincials." Hawkeye nodded. "Late of William Henry?"

The wild light in the man's eyes was testimony to his presence at the fort at the southern tip of Lake George during its recent surrender and the subsequent massacre of the English prisoners. Roving bands of French-allied Indians had disregarded the terms of surrender, which promised that the English would be delivered unharmed to nearby Fort Edward, and had butchered and scalped upward of one thousand of them, with the French and Canadian escorts making little effort to intercede.

"I served with Colonel Munro as well," Hawkeye said to reassure the man, at the same time slipping a blanket from his pack and wrapping it around the naked man's shoulders. "So did my friend Chingachgook."

The man calmed somewhat but kept glancing behind him.

"Who chases you?"

"M-Montcalm's Indians," the man stammered in reply, naming Louis Joseph, the Marquis de Montcalm, the French general who led the assault on Fort William Henry.

Hawkeye considered asking which tribe was pursuing him. If they were allied with Montcalm, they could be Leni-Lenape or one of the tribes of the West: Ottawa, Ojibwa, Mississaga, Potawatomi, Menomini, Sauk, Fox, Winnebago, Miami, or Iowa. Or they might be one of the so-called mission tribes, Christianized by the French: Abenaki, Huron, Nipissing, Algonquin, Micmac, or Malicite. They might even be one of the Six Nations of the Iroquois—the Mohawk, Oneida, Seneca, Cayuga, Onondaga, or Tuscarora—for while most Iroquois fought for the English, a few small bands had been converted by the French and joined the other mission tribes. Knowing that few whites could tell one red man from another, Hawkeye simply asked, "How many?"

The man shrugged, then looked around in agitation. "Where are the other rangers?" he asked.

Realizing the man thought he was one of Rogers' Rangers, Hawkeye shook his head. "I have served as a scout when called upon, but today my friend and I travel alone."

"Just two of you? But—but we'll be slaughtered!"

"Not if the good Lord wills otherwise and Killdeer remains true." He hefted his rifle.

Chingachgook stepped forward and made several hand signs to Hawkeye, who nodded and whispered to the stranger, "Your pursuers have turned onto this trail—a half dozen by the sound of them. You'd best be coming with me."

"Where?" the man asked, but Hawkeye was already heading up the slope toward the rock bluff, and Chingachgook had disappeared from sight. There was nothing for the man to do but follow, and he did so with understandable haste, scrambling up the path and making more than enough noise to signal the Indians that they were on the right trail.

Hawkeye did not waste any effort silencing the man. He realized there was no point in trying to fool the war party, so he turned his full attention to reaching the outcropping as quickly as possible. If anything, the clamor the man was making would keep the Indians thinking they were pursuing only one person. And if they knew the region, which Hawkeye was certain they did, they would realize this trail led to a place of no escape, and they might slow their chase.

The stranger must have thought the trail led to freedom, for he moved with renewed strength and agility, clambering over the boulders that littered the steep final hundred yards to the bluff. When he joined Hawkeye on the long, narrow outcropping, he looked around to see which way the trail went but discovered only a sheer drop on one side and a smooth vertical wall on the other. The Indian named Chingachgook was not there, and the scout stood calmly at the edge of the bluff, peering down into the thinning fog.

The man started to speak, but Hawkeye hushed him with a raised hand, then motioned for him to come over. "There!" Hawkeye whispered, pointing the barrel of his rifle toward the forest below.

First one and then a second Indian could be seen passing through an opening in the trees. They were followed in quick succession by three more, each wearing the paint of an Oneida warrior.

"Mingos," he told the stranger, using a common term for a member of any of the six tribes that made up the Iroquois League. He stepped back from sight and asked, "Are you certain they were on the side of the Frenchers?"

"Yes," the man said, and Hawkeye nodded, realizing that this must indeed be one of the bands that had broken off to join the mission tribes, allied with France.

"Wait here," he told the soldier. Checking the flashpan of his rifle to make sure there was still a full charge, he moved quickly and silently down the slope and took up a position behind a large boulder near the head of the trail. The war party would have to slow down when it rounded the bend below and started up this steepest part of the trail. Taking a final glance around the side of the boulder, he calculated how close he could allow the first man to come before opening fire. Then he pulled the hammer of his rifle to full cock, sat back on his haunches, and waited.

Less than a minute later the five Oneidas emerged from the woods and started up the incline. Gauging their locations by sound alone, Hawkeye tried to determine how spread apart they were. When the lead man was no more than forty feet away, Hawkeye sprang up from his hiding place, shouldered Killdeer, and fired. The ball caught the Oneida in the middle of the chest, hurling him back off his feet, his musket discharging into the trees as it clattered to the ground. The others hastily raised their own muskets, but by the time their first shot rang out, Hawkeye had ducked behind the boulder and was calmly reloading. A second shot ricocheted off the boulder, and he waited for the next, certain he had seen three muskets, and one man armed only with a bow and arrow.

Realizing that if he waited any longer, they would have time to reload, Hawkeye darted to the opposite side of the boulder and rose slightly, swinging up the barrel of his rifle. The man now in the lead was hidden behind a rock, but the next man in line was standing in plain view, his musket searching for the ambusher. Catching sight of Hawkeye, he jerked the barrel toward him. The two guns rang out simultaneously. The Oneida's musket ball went wide, nicking the corner of Hawkeye's hunting shirt. But the scout's rifled barrel sent its fatal contents straight on the mark, picking off the brave in the middle of his forehead and flopping him backward onto the trail.

Of the three remaining men, the nearest one had reloaded and took a wild shot, which shattered a corner of the boulder to Hawkeye's right. He then drew his tomahawk and sent it whirling only inches from Hawkeye's head. When the scout recovered his balance and looked back around, the Indian had his knife in hand and was bounding toward him. There was no time for Hawkeye to reload, so he grasped Killdeer's warm barrel and wielded it like a club. The two more distant Indians came charging up the trail as well, putting aside their muskets for tomahawk and knife.

Hawkeye swung the rifle and warded off the first knife thrust. The Indian shifted the blade to his other hand and darted to one side, scrambling a bit higher on the trail so as to put himself alongside the scout. His companions were only a few yards away when the air was split by the crack of a rifle, dropping one of them to the ground, a lead ball in his back. The other brave spun around and saw Chingachgook standing in the middle of the trail only a few feet away. Forgetting the remaining brave and the scout, he gave a piercing cry and leaped at the Mohican, tomahawk raised high.

Chingachgook's sudden appearance momentarily distracted the brave who faced Hawkeye, enabling the scout to draw his own knife from his belt and move in on him. Hawkeye's first thrust grazed the man's stomach. Eyes widening with rage, he gave a furious howl and swung his blade wildly, forcing Hawkeye back against the boulder. He made a desperate lunge at Hawkeye's chest, but the scout managed to grasp the man's wrist and bring his own knife into play, laying a long gash across the man's side. The Indian grimaced but did not back off, grabbing the wrist of Hawkeye's knife hand with one hand and jamming the tip of his own blade ever closer to Hawkeye's throat.

The man shouted something that Hawkeye did not understand, but his cry was cut off by a wrenching thud that jerked the Indian to the side. His muscles went slack, and he dropped to his knees and then sprawled face forward down the trail, a tomahawk buried in his back. Ten feet farther up the trail, the militiaman stood with his legs spread wide, his right arm still extended from having released the brave's own tomahawk at him.

Hawkeye's eyes met the soldier's for the briefest of moments, then he spun around to help his friend with the last of the Indians. But Chingachgook already had the brave on the ground and had managed to wrest his tomahawk from him. Raising it over his head, he brought it down in a vicious arc, nearly decapitating the man. He wiped the weapon on the man's buckskin breeches and stuck it behind his own wampum belt, then drew his knife, grasped the man's scalp lock, and make a quick, clean cut.

As Hawkeye walked up to where the soldier was standing, he heard the man mutter, "Savage . . ."

"If you're referring to this day's dark business, then yes, savage it has been—and I thank you for seeing that it didn't end poorly for me. If you mean *that* "—he nodded toward where Chingachgook was lifting the scalps of the other Oneidas—"then you don't understand the nature of the red man. My friend Chingachgook wears his scalp lock as a challenge to his enemies, and the day he falls to knife or 'hawk, he prays they lift it and release his spirit to the world to come. There is no great honor to be gained in dying in bed with one's scalp intact."

The militiaman said nothing but pulled the small blanket more tightly around him and followed Hawkeye down the trail to where the Mohican was waiting. Chingachgook started to offer the stranger the scalp of the brave he had tomahawked, but Hawkeye waved him off. Apparently the customs of the whites were as peculiar to Chingachgook as Indian ways were to most white men, and he shook his head in disbelief and tied the tuft of hair beside the others hanging from the barrel of his rifle.

"Now tell us how these Mingos came to be chasing you," the scout said, pouring a charge of gunpowder down Killdeer's barrel. "But first you should know who we are. My given name is Nathaniel, but my friends call me Hawkeye and my French enemies La Longue Carabine, by which they do me no great honor, there being little likeness between the gifts of Killdeer and those of a common military carbine. My friend is Chingachgook, sagamore of the Mohicans and a sworn enemy of Montcalm and any Mingo devils at his side."

The stranger shook Hawkeye's offered hand. "Sergeant Clifton Reginald Wharton of the New York Provincial Militia, of late attached to Fort William Henry."

"Where you received that wound?" Hawkeye asked, indicating the gash on the man's cheek.

"I took a French musket ball defending the northwest bastion."

Hawkeye examined the wound more closely. "You're fortunate the angle was not more direct. If you'll allow it, my friend can use Indian ways to attend to that." He grinned. "The sagamores know how to listen to plants. Many a wound of my own has been eased by his poultices of slippery elm and black alder."

Wharton looked uncertainly at Chingachgook, who was standing nearby, then gave a hesitant nod. The Mohican opened the pouch at his side and removed some dried leaves and shaved bark, which he proceeded to chew into a gummy paste. Wharton winced slightly but held himself steady as the Mohican smeared the concoction over his cheek.

"Taken captive during the massacre, were you?" Hawkeye drew his ramrod and set a ball atop the charge in his rifle barrel.

The man's lip quivered slightly—not from the salve but from the memory of that day. He nodded.

"A black day it was," Hawkeye commented. "And a black stain it shall leave on the reputation of the Marquis de Montcalm. He offered generous terms of surrender to Colonel Munro but failed to back them with the force of arms. He took charge of all our sick and wounded, yet stood aside and let his heathens slaughter them in their beds. And when the massacre began during the march to Fort Edward, the French detachment of escorts raised neither weapons nor alarm."

Chingachgook finished ministering to the man's wound and stepped back.

"We knew that as many as two hundred were carried off by the Indians," Hawkeye continued. "Do you know anything of their fate?"

"I was one of six being held by a war party of ten braves. They seemed in no rush to ransom us to the French in Montreal, and when we turned away from Lake Champlain and headed west, we feared they were taking us to our deaths."

"How did you escape?"

"They spent much of last night drinking rum, and just before dawn they made me take off my clothes and were going to have some sport with me. They were arguing—I guess over how to torture me—and I managed to break free into the woods and give them the slip. But they soon picked up my trail."

"You were the only one to get away?"

"Yes. But I'm not alone in these woods. Yesterday the war party caught a militiaman on the loose, and he told us that many more have managed to escape, thanks to the stores of rum the savages took from Fort William Henry."

Reaching out, Hawkeye touched the gold locket around the sergeant's neck. "How did you manage to hold on to this? It's not like a Mingo to pass up such a bauble."

For the first time Wharton smiled. "One of them spoke some English—that one over there." He indicated one of the corpses. "When he tried to take it from me, I told him it possessed great magic." He flipped open the locket's cover, which was ornately engraved with leaves and tendrils. Inside was a lock of fiery red hair. "Either they believed me or were waiting until I was dead and the power passed, for they left it alone."

Chingachgook stared in wonder at the locket. He spoke briefly to Hawkeye, who nodded and told the sergeant, "My friend believes the Mingos must have thought it the scalp lock of some great warrior." He spoke again with Chingachgook, then said, "Five braves lie dead on this trail, leaving five behind. Are they far to the north?"

"No more than an hour."

"They may have heard our rifles and will be expecting their men to return with you or your scalp. It will not go well for your comrades when they fail to return." He laid his hand on Wharton's shoulder. "But if you've got your wits about you and are keen for a bit of revenge, perhaps we three can repay a portion of what those Frenchers allowed to happen—and free your comrades in the doing."

The young sergeant looked down at the loaded long rifle cradled in the scout's arm, then over at the Mohican, whose silent, unwavering expression bore testimony to his resolve. Touching a finger to the scar on his cheek, Wharton drew in a breath and nodded. "I'll take you to where those bastards are camped. And when the first blood is drawn, may it be from this militiaman's hands." He raised his fist and smacked it against his palm.

Chapter II

"Judge not too rashly from hasty and deceptive appearances," said the lady, smiling.
— *The Last of the Mohicans*, Chap. II

It was Astra Van Rensselaer's twenty-second birthday, and she was determined to look her finest at the party her father was hosting for her. She had already washed her long red hair with the perfumed soap imported from their family's hometown of Rotterdam, and her lady's maid, Clarice, had just finished curling it and putting it up in ribbons. She removed her heavy wool robe and handed it to Clarice, then stepped in front of a body-length cheval glass in the dressing room of their house on the Hudson River, just south of Albany.

"I think I'll wear my new gown *à la Française*," she said, pulling her white linen shift tighter around her waist and examining her figure. "And the whalebone stays." She wanted to look her trimmest, and for that her whalebone corset with its twenty-inch waist was far superior to her regular corsets stiffened with wood or metal.

While Clarice was assembling the items, Astra moved to the dressing table and placed her right foot on the bench. She took up one of a pair of white silk stockings, slipped it on, and pulled it up over her knee, tying it in place with a ribbon garter. After donning the second stocking, she stepped back to the cheval glass and adjusted the angle of the pivoted mirror. She viewed herself dispassionately, as if her body were merely a canvas on which she must work. And for the most part she was pleased with what she saw, though she knew that some might consider her a bit too tall to make a suitable match. But it was not her height that inhibited most men but her eyes, as lustrous and flashing green as cut emeralds. They were the eyes of a woman who knew what she wanted and always succeeded in getting it.

Coming up behind Astra, Clarice slipped the stays around her waist, waiting as her mistress adjusted her bosom and held the front of the corset in place. The young maid deftly laced the cords through the eyelets at the back and, with Astra holding on to a chair, pulled them toward her.

"Tighter," Astra insisted, letting out her breath to narrow her waist even further.

Clarice shook her head but did as requested, drawing the cords until the edges of the corset touched, then quickly tying them.

Astra turned back to the mirror and nodded approvingly. The corset produced the desired effect, pulling her shoulders back and shaping her upper body into a cone. The effect would be heightened by the next article of clothing, which Clarice was already fitting in position. The panniers were a pair of whalebone hoops held in place by a linen collar fastened around the waist with a drawstring. They would form the exaggerated hips and small bustle fashionable among the higher classes. Clarice also tied a hanging pocket just under the hoops, which could be reached through side slits in the outer skirt, petticoats, and panniers.

After putting on a flounced underpetticoat, Astra stepped into the first of three items that made up the gown. This heavier formal petticoat was made of the same white silk taffeta as the rest of the gown, since the outer skirt was cut so that it would hang open in front to reveal the undergarment. With some effort, the two women pulled it over the panniers and fastened it around Astra's waist. Next Clarice tied the stomacher over the corset. It formed the bodice of the gown and was covered with gilt lace tendrils. The outer skirt, which like the petticoat was brocaded with undulating flowers and leaves to mirror the stomacher, had half-length sleeves with lace ruffles that hung to her wrists.

It took several minutes for Clarice to pin the gown in

place, and then Astra donned a pair of brocaded silk shoes and made a final examination of herself in the mirror.

"Do you think Becky would approve?" she asked, not expecting Clarice to answer, since the maid had never met Astra's childhood friend, Rebekka Brower, who had married at the age of sixteen and gone to live on the frontier. "Yes," she answered herself, smiling at her reflection. "Most definitely yes."

"You look beautiful, Juffrouw Van Rensselaer."

"Well, good enough, at least, to keep Father from any suspicions." Turning, she fixed the maid with the full force of her gaze. "You understand what you are to do, Clarice?"

"Yes, *juffrouw*. Everything will be ready as you directed."

"Good." Smiling, she came forward and took the younger woman's hands. "And you must start by calling me Astra."

"I will, Juffrouw Van Rensselaer."

"Astra," she corrected.

Clarice blushed. "Yes, *juffrouw*."

Astra shook her head and sighed, then squeezed her maid's hands. "You'll do just fine. Now, it's already past noon, so run downstairs and tell Father that I'm coming. And not a hint to him of our little secret."

Curtsying, Clarice scurried from the room and disappeared down the hall. Astra waited a moment, then turned to follow. Hesitating at the doorway, she looked back a final time at her image in the mirror.

"Our little secret," she whispered with no trace of a smile, then walked from the room.

Hendrik Van Rensselaer was in his element, circling the formal drawing room and making light conversation with the guests who had gathered to celebrate his daughter's birthday. Rather than wearing his usual powdered wig that tied at the back, he had on a peruke with oversized curls that flowed down his shoulders. The buckles of his shoes were pure gold, and his blue full-dress suit was elaborately embroidered with red and gold flowers, denoting his stature as one of Albany's wealthiest Dutch citizens.

Hearing the butler answering the front door, he walked over to the foyer entrance and saw his close friends the Ten Eycks coming in. "Willem, Elsa, *goeden dag!*" he exclaimed, his hands raised in greeting as he strode across the foyer.

"*Goeden dag,*" Elsa replied, smiling demurely as Hendrik bowed to her.

"*Hoe gaat het?*" he asked, pumping Willem's hand.

"*Heel goed, dank jou. En jou?*"

"*Goed* . . . very good!" He signaled the butler to take their overcoats. "I'm so pleased you could attend."

"We wouldn't miss Astra's special day," declared Elsa, who looked to be a decade older and a few pounds heavier than her fifty-year-old husband. "After all, we've known her since she was born—since her poor mother died. Where is the darling *juffrouw?*" She looked beyond Hendrik through the drawing-room doors.

"She'll be down to join us in a moment. But please, you must come greet our friends."

As Elsa entered the drawing room Willem halted and gripped Hendrik's arm. "Have many sent their regrets?"

"A few."

"It is understandable, given the news from the north."

"I considered postponing the affair, but I do so hate to disappoint Astra. And I'll be leaving for New York tomorrow with no guarantee when I shall return."

"Then may I assume that news is good regarding Pieter?"

Hendrik frowned. "We have had no word of him these past two weeks."

"None?" Willem looked surprised. "His name hasn't been posted?"

"Not among the rescued." Hendrik's smile returned. "*Ja,* but neither among the dead."

"Thank God our Ernestus isn't with the militia. How are you and your daughter bearing up?"

Hendrik puffed himself up proudly. "Pieter's an adventurer, like his father. He shall return in his own good time with tales of colonial bravery and French deceit." A slight glint came into his normally cold blue eyes. "And of Indian atrocities. Have you seen Major Putnam's report?" When Willem shook his head, Hendrik reached into his coat pocket and unfolded a piece of paper. "It was posted this morning." Thrusting it into Willem's hands, he stabbed a finger at a paragraph near the bottom. "You must read this part here."

The section in question recounted the conditions Major Israel Putnam discovered upon reaching Fort William Henry just after the French had burned it to the ground:

> *The fort was entirely destroyed; the barracks, outhouses, and buildings were a heap of ruins—the cannon, stores, boats, and vessels were all carried away. The fires were still burning —the smoke and stench offensive and suffocating. Innumerable fragments of human skulls, and bones and carcasses half consumed, were still frying and broiling in the decaying fires. Dead bodies mangled with scalping knives and tomahawks, in all the wantonness of Indian barbarity, were everywhere to be seen. More than one hundred women butchered and shockingly mangled, lay upon the ground still weltering in their gore. Devastation, barbarity, and horror everywhere appeared; and the spectacle presented was too diabolical and awful either to be endured or described.*

"We'd heard rumors," Willem said, shaking his head in dismay. "But this is really beyond belief. Astra must be desperate with worry about her brother."

"Oh, we Van Rensselaers are steady in the face of adversity." He clapped his friend on the back and led him into the drawing room.

Rather than a scene of gaiety, the gathering resembled a wake, with talk dominated by the recent events at the fort just sixty-five miles to the north, at the head of the lake the French had called Lac du St. Sacrament and the English had recently renamed Lake George. News about the fort's capitulation and the subsequent massacre of the English troops had been trickling into Albany during the past two weeks, accompanied by wild rumors that an enormous French force was poised to attack Albany and even New York City.

An air of gloom permeated the room. In fact, the most animated person was Hendrik Van Rensselaer himself, this in spite of the uncertainty about his son, who could be lying dead somewhere or perhaps had been dragged off into the Canadian wilderness by the Marquis de Montcalm's Huron, Abenaki, and Nipissing warriors.

Hendrik paused in making his rounds to speak to Clarice, who entered the drawing room and cautiously approached. Nodding and dismissing her, he walked to the doorway and watched the stairs until he saw his daughter descending. Then he turned and raised his hand for silence.

"We shall now be honored by the arrival of the young *juffrouw* for whom we have gathered this day. It was *tweeëntwintig*—twenty-two years ago today, on the twenty-third day of August in the year of our Lord 1735, that *mijn vrouw,* my dear departed Margaretha, brought her into this world, and it has been a far better one because of it. So may I present *mijn dochter,* Astra Van Rensselaer!"

Facing the doorway, he touched his forehead, then swept his hand low in a grand flourish, completing it just as Astra entered the room to the applause of the assembly and shouts of "Congratulations!" and *"Gefeliciteerd!"*

The young woman immediately began circling the room, accepting congratulations here, smiling at a compliment there, until she had greeted all fifteen of the guests. If she was at all concerned about the fate of her older brother, Pieter, she did not let it show. In fact, if anyone happened to mention the recent troubles to the north, she immediately changed the subject, saying that there had been far too much brooding in Albany of late and that today they must put such thoughts from their minds.

At one point after she had been speaking to the Ten Eycks for a few minutes, her father came over, wrapped his arm around her, and said, "You'll excuse me, Willem, Elsa, if I steal my daughter away for a moment?"

"But of course, *mijnheer,*" Willem declared.

Steering Astra across the room to a secluded corner, Hendrik turned her toward him. "You are enjoying yourself, *ja?*"

"*Ja, mijn vader.* It's a delightful party."

"Then you no longer are angry with your *vader*?" He gave a mock pout.

"How could I stay angry at you?" She leaned close and kissed his cheek. "And you were right, of course. It's good for everyone to forget, if only for a few hours."

"But of course I'm right!" he blustered. "Were he here, Colonel Munro himself would agree."

For a moment Astra thought he was going to say Pieter's name, but he had forbidden anyone in the household to use it and only mentioned it himself when an outsider brought up the subject. She was disappointed but forced a smile. "If you're really intent upon raising everyone's spirits, then how about playing the *glassspiel* for them?"

"Not tonight, my dear. This party is for you; no one wants to see an old man making music."

"An old man? You're barely fifty, and I know everyone would love to hear you play."

"Not another word about it. Tonight is your night, not mine. I'm only sorry that Ernestus couldn't be here to celebrate your day with you. They told you all about Ernestus, didn't they?" he asked, indicating the Ten Eycks.

"They mentioned that he was in New York."

"*Ja,* and making quite a name for himself. I'll be doing some business with his firm while I'm there." He folded his arms and waggled his right finger, an affectation he assumed whenever he wanted to drive home a point. "You know, *mijn dochter,* young Ten Eyck has always been fond of you. I'm certain that if you showed him some encouragement, it could blossom into more."

Normally Astra would rebuff any suggestion of a match between herself and the self-involved Ernestus Ten Eyck, but today she smiled demurely and said, "Perhaps you should suggest he call on me when he's next in Albany."

"Really? *Met plezier!*" Hendrik declared. "And when he does, you must wear this." Slipping a hand into his jacket pocket, he removed a small rectangular box, which he handed to her. "Go ahead." He gestured for her to open it.

Untying and removing the blue ribbon, she lifted the top and gazed in wonder at the cameo brooch. "But this is . . ." Her finger traced the features of her mother's face carved in ivory.

"*Ja, jouw moeder*—Margaretha. I had it made for you last time I was in New York." He took it from the box and pinned it to his daughter's gown near her heart.

"*Oh, Vader, dank jou!*" She wrapped her arms around his neck and kissed him.

Her eyes welled with tears as she watched him cross the room and fall back into easy conversation with the visitors. She loved him so much—especially at moments like this when she could see the tender, caring man he once had been. And that was why it hurt so much to know that he had changed—was changing a little more each day—one moment sentimental and giving, the next fierce and terrible. And so very cold and dispassionate.

It frightened her, almost as much as the knowledge that later that very night she was going to hurt him, perhaps as much as Pieter had done. It was a topic they avoided these past two weeks—not the mystery of Pieter's fate but the circumstances that had driven him to defy his father and join the militia. It was something Hendrik could neither understand nor abide, and he had practically disowned his son when Pieter announced earlier that summer that he was leaving the family banking business to enter the provincial forces. When Hendrik realized his son would not be dissuaded, he contrived to purchase a commission as an officer for him, and he had been humiliated when Pieter refused the appointment and secretly ran off to join as a lowly militiaman. They had not heard from him since.

Astra watched her father circle the room, chatting amiably with the men and flirting with the women. With all the women except one, that is, for Marthe Cryn was not like the others. An attractive brunette of forty-five, Marthe was the wife of Colonel Reinold Cryn and the lover of Hendrik Van Rensselaer. Her long-standing affair with Hendrik was common knowledge to everyone in the room—even to Colonel Cryn, a provincial militiaman who was serving with General Webb fifty miles away at Fort Edward.

Two hours later, when the last of the guests were heading to their carriages, Astra was not at all surprised that her father was going to escort Marthe home. In fact, he did so almost every night that the colonel was on the frontier, and Astra had counted on tonight being no different. She thanked Marthe for coming and said good night to Hendrik, knowing he would not return until the next morning, when he would be sailing down the Hudson to New York City.

By then it would be too late, she thought as she hurried upstairs and struggled out of her gown. She already had composed a letter explaining that she was visiting friends for the day and wishing him well on his trip. By the time he discovered the truth, it would be too late to stop her.

Astra put on a modest riding dress without the bulky hip panniers, then donned a hooded cloak and hurried downstairs. Leaving the letter on the silver card tray in the foyer, she headed back through the house and out the kitchen door. Waiting in the yard was Clarice, who held a pair of Narragansett pacers, each with a leather travel bag lashed to the back of the saddle. Taking the reins of the larger sorrel, Astra adroitly hoisted herself onto the sidesaddle, then waited until Clarice had somewhat more awkwardly done the same atop her bay.

"Atta girl," she said to the sorrel, slapping the reins against its neck. She turned and smiled at her maid, who was doing her best to stay in the saddle. "Are you coming, Clarice?"

"Yes, *juffrouw*," the young maid replied hesitantly, imitating how her mistress was working the reins.

"I told you . . . from now on you must call me Astra."

"Astra," Clarice repeated, smiling as her horse settled into a gentle lope behind the larger sorrel.

"Much better. Now, if anyone stops us, we are merely friends on our way to lend assistance to the unfortunates at Fort Edward."

"But why do we have to pretend?" Clarice asked, bringing her horse alongside Astra's.

"Because they wouldn't allow a woman of social standing to go traipsing through the woods on a desperate mission such as ours. But a couple of commoners will be allowed through without question."

Clarice blushed. "Are there really women such as that?"

"Do you mean camp women?" She laughed. "Clarice, you're such an innocent. Wherever soldiers go, the camp women are not far behind. So just follow my lead, and we'll soon be safe within the walls of Fort Edward. Someone there will know of Pieter . . . and what's become of him."

Clarice started to sob gently, and Astra pulled her horse closer so that she could reach out and touch the younger woman's hand.

"There, my dear. It will be all right, I promise you. Nothing is going to happen to us."

"It . . . it's not us I'm worried about. It's . . ."

"Yes, Pieter."

"And Mijnheer Van Rensselaer. He won't even allow us to mention your brother's name. And when he finds out what we've done, he'll—"

"You let me worry about my father. His moods can be dark, but underneath it all he loves his son. And by the time he gets back from New York, we'll already have been there and back, and we'll have Pieter home safe and sound with us. What can he do then?"

She looked over at Clarice and saw that the young woman was less than reassured. Masking her own uncertainty and fear, she continued down the winding drive to the carriage road that ran alongside the west bank of the Hudson River. Pulling to a halt at the edge of the road, she shifted on the saddle and glanced back at the gray and black stone mansion with its sloping hip roof and narrow peaked dormers.

I'm doing the right thing, aren't I, Becky? she asked her absent friend, but she felt only a cold shiver in response.

Whispering the single word *good-bye* under her breath, she turned away from the house and started out onto the road. Slapping the reins, she urged the horse into a canter and headed for the Great Carrying Place on the Hudson River, where Fort Edward had been built two years earlier to protect the portage roads that led to Lakes George and Champlain. She rode north toward Fort Edward and her brother.

Chapter III

"I know, from often seeing it, that they have a craving for the flesh of an Oneida; and it is as well to let the bird follow the gift of its natural appetite."
          —*The Last of the Mohicans,* Chap. XVIII

The heavy bank of honeysuckle shrubs rustled at the edge of the forest clearing, and a branch moved to one side, revealing the painted face of an Oneida warrior. But this was no ordinary brave, for his hair was blond and was worn loose, rather than shaved into a scalp lock. Most striking of all were his eyes, as pale blue as a robin's egg, yet burning with an almost white heat.

A second warrior appeared beside the first, painted the same but with brown eyes and hair. He was joined by a third, the only one with the traditional scalp lock and dark features of an Indian. The three were Sergeant Clifton Wharton, Hawkeye, and Chingachgook. The Mohican sagamore had painted them in the Oneida style, and they had donned some of the clothes of the braves they had killed. It was a disguise that would fool only the most unobservant Oneida, but it might buy them a few seconds when entering the encampment where the half-dozen white captives were being held.

"They're right where I left them," Wharton whispered, letting the branch slip back into place.

Hawkeye tapped him on the shoulder and motioned him deeper into the woods. He had seen enough of the activity in the clearing to determine that the five remaining Oneidas were using the absence of their companions to dip into the remaining supply of rum, but he did not want to tempt fate by any incaution on their own part.

"Will we wait until dark?" Wharton asked, keeping his voice to a hush.

"No. They'll soon be missing their friends, and there's nothing like a touch of fear to sober up a Mingo. We'll strike now, before the spirits leave them." His grin was confident but humorless.

Four muskets had been taken from the dead braves, which when added to the scout's Killdeer and the Mohican's military rifle gave them two guns apiece. But the Indian weapons were twenty-year-old trading muskets that had been notoriously inaccurate even when new. And the clearing was a large one—more than two hundred yards across—which meant that they would have to get closer to the Oneidas before they could bring their guns into play with any hope of success.

Each man checked his charges, and then Hawkeye showed Wharton how to hold two of the muskets side by side but staggered slightly so that sparks from one flashpan would not ignite the neighboring charge. They would have six shots between them, and with almost that many Oneidas in the camp, they would have to make every shot find its mark.

The three men reviewed their plan, and then Hawkeye gripped Chingachgook's forearm, took up Killdeer and one of the muskets, and led Wharton through the trees, circling toward the far side of the clearing as silently as a cat stalking its prey. The militiaman did his best not to make any noise, and the few snapping twigs were masked by the sound of a small but lively rivulet that ran along one edge of the clearing. Keeping the water between them and the Oneidas, Hawkeye brought Wharton to a point close to where the white soldiers sat, tied back-to-back in twos around a pair of trees. They were clothed but barefoot, without any jackets or blankets to protect them from the late-summer chill.

Signaling Wharton to wait there until the attack began, Hawkeye moved on alone. The Oneidas had only two packhorses between them, and he had to be especially careful as he approached where they were hobbled. He would use them as a shield when he emerged from the

trees and hoped he would be able to sneak close enough to
his intended targets—two braves seated on the skin of a
bear gambling on the deer-button game. They took turns
tossing six deer-antler buttons, which had been blackened
on one side. Whenever five of the six landed showing the
same color, the player was allowed a quick swig from the
keg of rum they both jealously guarded. If all six turned up
the same, several generous gulps were earned.

Hawkeye took up a position at the edge of the trees
and surveyed the scene. The gamblers were about a third
of the way across the clearing. Beyond them, near the center of the clearing, two more braves were seated at a central campfire sharing a keg of rum, the one with a scalp
lock telling stories and making boasts that set his long-
haired partner alternately laughing or arguing. They
would be the targets of Chingachgook, whose appearance
gave him the best chance of getting close to them. The fifth
Oneida was guarding the prisoners, and he alone was not
drinking, though his wobbly stance indicated he had already consumed his fair share. He would be left to Sergeant Wharton, who had been instructed not to make his
move until after the gunplay began.

When one of the gamblers earned a pull from the keg,
Hawkeye stepped into the clearing at a point behind the
packhorses where he was hidden from view. At this signal,
Chingachgook emerged from the trees across the way and
started toward the campfire. Hawkeye edged closer to the
animals, taking care not to spook them, then shifted to
the right so that he would come around them near where
the gamblers were seated.

Chingachgook was halfway to the campfire and still
had not been noticed when a keening yell rent the air,
drawing all eyes to the woods near the captives. To Hawkeye's amazement, Clifton Wharton came barreling out of
the bushes, giving a poor imitation of an Indian war
whoop as he charged across the brook.

"Fool!" Hawkeye muttered at the militiaman's pre-
mature appearance. But there was no time for recrimina-
tions, for the gamblers were already snatching up their
muskets to race to their comrade's defense.

Raising Killdeer and the Indian musket to his right
shoulder, Hawkeye sighted down the long barrel of the

hunting rifle, tracking the forward gambler, who was only twenty yards away. Holding his breath, he squeezed the trigger, sending flint against frizzen and setting off the powder in the flashpan. The charge ignited, the rifle kicked against his shoulder, and the brave pitched headlong into the grass. This caught the attention of his partner, who swung his musket around, firing at the same instant that Hawkeye pulled the trigger of his second weapon. When the acrid gun smoke cleared, Hawkeye alone was standing.

The battle was not over, for only one of Chingachgook's bullets had found its mark, and he was now in a desperate hand-to-hand struggle with the remaining Oneida at the campfire. Hawkeye dropped the Indian musket and began to reload Killdeer when his attention was drawn to a movement to his left. Apparently the musket had not fired true, for the brave was only wounded and had crawled to where his partner's loaded and primed weapon lay. As the man rose to his knees and brought the barrel up, Hawkeye dropped his powder horn and rifle and snatched the knife from his belt. In one smooth motion he spun toward the brave, drew back his arm, and released the blade. It flipped twice through the air and buried itself in the neck of the brave, who clawed at his throat, the musket discharging into the dirt as it fell. With a gurgling death rattle, he landed facedown in the grass.

Hawkeye knelt beside Killdeer and finished reloading. Glancing to his left to confirm that Clifton Wharton had dispatched the Oneida guard, he raised the rifle and trained it on the long-haired brave battling with Chingachgook. They were no more than fifty yards away— normally an easy shot for Hawkeye—but they were so entangled that it was impossible to be certain they wouldn't move at the very moment he fired, with the Mohican taking the ball intended for the Oneida.

Steadying Killdeer, Hawkeye trained the weapon on the Oneida's back and gauged the time it would take for the flash in the pan to travel down the priming hole and set off the main charge. He waited until they were locked in position, feet firmly planted and free hand gripping the other's knife hand. He held his breath and eased back the trigger. There was a puff of smoke as the powder in the pan flared, then a muffled boom. But as the gun kicked against his shoulder the Indians shifted position, and the lead ball sailed harmlessly by, plowing into the ground just to the right of its intended mark.

Hawkeye was reloading when the most curious thing happened. Chingachgook had managed to disarm the Oneida, and he slashed out with his knife, tearing open the man's hunting shirt and laying a bloody gash across his chest. The Mohican was about to finish the job with a thrust of the knife when suddenly he stayed his hand and just stood there. The young brave took a few steps back, looked around frantically, and broke into a run for the trees. Chingachgook made no effort to stop him, and when Hawkeye raised Killdeer and sighted on the fleeing Oneida's back, Chingachgook turned and waved his arms, signaling him not to fire. Hawkeye hesitated, then pulled the trigger, purposely aiming a few inches to the right so as to send the brave on his way all the faster. A moment later he was into the trees and gone from sight.

Hawkeye raced to where the captives had been held and discovered that Clifton Wharton already had them untied and was wiping the Oneida war paint from his face, his mates cheering and clapping him on the back. It was apparent by their reaction to Hawkeye that they thought him an Indian loyal to King George II, but Wharton announced, "Our savior, my good friends, is a scout known to his Indian friends as Hawkeye and his French enemies as La Longue Carabine."

Many of the soldiers had heard of Hawkeye, and some had even seen him in action at the battle of Fort William Henry, and they eagerly pumped his hand and offered their thanks.

"Your gratitude is more rightfully due my Mohican friend, Chingachgook." Hawkeye nodded toward where the sagamore was standing near the body of the brave he had shot.

The soldiers set about gathering their boots, uniform jackets, and supplies. Hawkeye, meanwhile, noticed that Chingachgook was still staring at the spot where the Oneida had escaped into the trees. Sensing something was wrong, he took leave of Wharton and the soldiers and strode across the clearing.

"What troubles you, friend?" he asked as he approached.

Chingachgook neither moved nor showed any trace of emotion as he placed a fist against his chest and uttered a single word: "Unamis . . ."

Hawkeye knew that his friend was referring to the small blue tattoo emblazoned on his chest—the symbol of Unamis, the Turtle, indicating his status within the Mohican nation. His son, Uncas, had worn the identical sign.

"What do you mean?" Hawkeye asked.

In the Mohican tongue, Chingachgook said, "He was wearing the sign of Unamis upon his breast."

"But he was an Oneida," Hawkeye replied, also in Mohican. "Are you certain?"

Slowly Chingachgook turned to his friend, and there was a trace of tears in his eyes. "*Hugh!* How can this be? The unchanged race of my people is no more. The last of the children of Unamis died with the passing of Uncas."

"Perhaps it was only a design—a totem of power."

"Was not Uncas the last?" the sagamore asked. "Is it possible that by my own hand I almost brought to an end the line of the Mohicans?"

"Yours is the symbol of a chief and sagamore of your people, and you and Uncas are truly the last in that long line," Hawkeye told his friend. "There must be some trickery at work here. How else could a Mingo have come to sport the sign of Unamis?"

Chingachgook just stood there in silence, staring toward the trees.

"Come," Hawkeye said, gripping his friend's shoulder. "There is nothing more for us here."

Chingachgook started to follow, then halted, reached to the ground, and picked up a single eagle's feather that had fallen during the hand-to-hand struggle. Unfastening the plume that hung over his left shoulder, he let it drop to the earth and, in its place, tied the eagle feather of the young Oneida brave.

Chapter IV

"In the woods, in the air, O, I hear
The whoop, the long yell, and the cry:
In the woods, O, I hear
The loud whoop!"
—The Last of the Mohicans, Chap. XXXI

By early evening Hawkeye, Chingachgook, and the seven soldiers were within a few miles of Fort Carillon on the banks of Lake Champlain. It had been a slow march, with the Mohican taking extra precautions to see that they did not leave a trail easily followed by any friends of the Oneida he had allowed to escape. And there was the ever-present risk of running into stray bands of hostile Indians. But they had seen no signs of Indians or French troops in the region, which led Hawkeye to wonder whether Montcalm had abandoned Carillon for winter quarters in Montreal or was massing his forces for a renewed attack against the English, perhaps at Fort Edward or even Albany.

The soldiers, armed with the muskets of the Oneidas, followed Hawkeye to a secluded cave near the base of Mount Hope, where they would hide while the scout and his Mohican companion climbed the heights and surveyed the area. The highest ranking among them was Lieutenant Leslie Rowland, a grenadier in the Forty-eighth Regiment of Foot. But the other soldiers—three English regulars and two provincial militiamen—did not appear to hold him in particular regard and looked for leadership to Sergeant Clifton Wharton, whom they credited with having led the rescue mission against their captors. While Hawkeye took a less generous view of Wharton's precipitous role in the attack, he had to acknowledge that the man was fearless in battle, and so he encouraged the soldiers' impression of the militiaman as an accomplished Indian fighter.

The lieutenant did not seem overly pleased by the status being afforded a mere sergeant—and a colonial provincial, no less. He was particularly irked when the soldiers took to calling Wharton by the nickname Cap'n Yellow Beard. But none of these men had been under Rowland's command before their capture, and he apparently thought it wise to let them have their fun. Instead he took out any frustration he was feeling on Hawkeye, who as a volunteer scout ranked even lower than the provincials, and he pestered Hawkeye continually about whether the Mohican could be trusted not to lead them into an ambush.

At the cave, while the lieutenant made a big show of organizing the men into pairs to keep watch at the entrance, Hawkeye conferred briefly with Wharton. Then he joined Chingachgook on the trail up Mount Hope, which rose just west of Carillon and commanded a view not only of the fort but of the portage between Lake Champlain and Lake George. Formerly the trail had been a narrow Indian path, but since construction of the fort had begun two years earlier, it had been widened into a military road so that troops and artillery could be placed atop the mountain in times of attack.

Though it did not appear as if the Mount Hope battery was currently manned, the two men were exceedingly cautious in their approach to the summit. When they neared the top, they took to the woods and headed around to the north side, creeping forward until they came in sight of the area cleared the previous summer by the French. Some crude earthworks had been put up, facing south toward the portage road, but there were no guns in position. At first they thought the battery completely unoccupied, but then Chingachgook gripped Hawkeye's arm and pointed to the right. There at the far end of the earthen wall was a small log shack, and through the open rear door they could see someone moving about.

"Lookout sentry," Hawkeye whispered, his guess confirmed when a soldier emerged, walked out along a walkway cut into the wall, and stood gazing into the valley below. He wore the uniform of the Royal Roussillon: black tricorne hat, white woolen leggings with brass side buttons, pale blue jacket with navy collar and cuffs, and white leather belt and bandolier.

Easing the knife from his belt, the Mohican drew a finger across his throat. Hawkeye nodded and signed that Chingachgook should circle to the left and dispatch the soldier while he approached the shack from the right, in case anyone else was on hand.

The sun was dropping behind the mountains as the scout slipped out of the woods and made his way toward the log building, protected from sight by the earth glacis, into which the structure had been built for protection from cold, wind, and attack. Crawling along the sloping outer side of the hard-packed wall, he came to a position almost directly over the shack, where he waited and tried to listen to the sounds within. There was some scuffling of a person moving around but no voices whatsoever; most likely there were only two sentries, one inside and the other out upon the wall.

Hawkeye peered over the top of the wall to see if Chingachgook had finished his task. To his surprise, the Indian was nowhere in sight and the sentry was walking back toward the building. Ducking from view, Hawkeye waited until the man pulled open the door and stepped inside. Rising to his knees, he saw Chingachgook at the far end of the wall, holding up his knife and shaking his head at having missed his prey.

Hawkeye raised Killdeer and signaled the Mohican to keep out of sight. Moving right up beside the shack, he eased himself to the ground, hugging to the log wall and listening to the activity within. There were two voices, both speaking French, which the scout did not understand. Confident that they were the only soldiers on hand, he ducked below the window, moved around to the rear door, and yanked it open, thrusting Killdeer inside.

The two soldiers were seated at a small table playing cards, and they jumped with a start at the sudden appearance of the frontiersman. One reached for a musket propped beside him against the wall, but Hawkeye centered Killdeer's barrel on the man's chest and barked, "Don't move!"

The soldier understood the scout's intent, if not his words, and he pulled his arm back and kept his hands in full sight. His younger partner, meanwhile, was already removing his belt and letting his sword drop to the floor.

"Mon Dieu!" the older man exclaimed as Chingachgook came around Hawkeye and gathered up their muskets. His mate looked particularly distressed and on the verge of collapse, cringing involuntarily as the Mohican snatched the sword from the floor and carried the weapons outside.

"Do as you're told, and you just may live to enjoy another of your Frenchified feasts," Hawkeye warned them, shaking his head at their apparent lack of comprehension. "Either of you speak English?"

The final word seemed to make sense to them, for they both shook their heads brusquely. The older one started to speak, but Hawkeye cut him off with a wave of his rifle.

"Save that for someone who can make sense of your babble," he declared, lowering Killdeer as Chingachgook returned and trained his own rifle on them.

Hawkeye spoke to Chingachgook for a moment, then headed from the cabin. Moving quickly along the walkway, he halted at a spot where he could see Fort Carillon to the east. The last of the sun was spilling through a gap in the Adirondack peaks, slanting across the valley floor and lighting the French fortifications. The fort was a star-shaped structure constructed of logs laid horizontally and reinforced with earth. It was large enough for a permanent garrison of four hundred men, who lived in a series of stone barracks. Work had already begun on covering the outer walls and bastions with stone, and additional protection was ensured by an outer abatis of felled trees and sharpened branches to entangle any foot soldiers who dared approach.

The French flag could be seen flying over the Place of Arms, the central parade ground where the soldiers practiced their drills, and a steady stream of smoke rose above the northeast bastion, which housed the bakery. It was obvious that the fort was still fully manned. But what in-

terested Hawkeye most was the broad meadow between
the fort and Mount Hope. It was here that bivouac tents
had been set up earlier that summer to house the eight
thousand troops with which the Marquis de Montcalm
had laid siege to Fort William Henry. But today the only
sign of the bivouac were the outer fences and scarred
ground. Equally telling was the absence of all but the
smallest bateaux and canoes at the dock on the south side
of the fort, where the La Chute River carried the waters of
Lake George down into Lake Champlain. Apparently
Montcalm had suspended any further actions and sent his
forces north to Montreal for the winter.

Hawkeye took a final look at the region known to the
Indians as Cheonderoga, or "Three Rivers," and improp-
erly called Ticonderoga by the Europeans. The name came
from the confluence of what appeared to be three separate
bodies of water but in fact were two, only one of them
being a river. But Lake Champlain was so narrow at this
point that, north and south of the inlet of the La Chute, it
appeared to be separate river branches.

There was no noticeable activity on the portage road,
which circumvented the unnavigable La Chute rapids and
falls. The road marked the quickest route to Lake George
and the English forts to the south, but it was prone to
attack by marauding Indian bands. Furthermore, once
they reached Lake George, they would have to steal or
build boats in order to take the shorter water passage, and
though Hawkeye knew that he and Chingachgook could
outpaddle any pursuers, he did not have such faith in the
foot soldiers they had rescued. Instead, they would take
the longer but safer land route that ran along the west side
of the lake.

Returning to the shack, Hawkeye saw that his Mohican friend had tied the prisoners' hands behind their
backs.

"Shall we take them with us?" Chingachgook asked
in his native tongue.

"Yes—they may be able to tell General Webb something of Montcalm's plans."

"But when they're found missing, the fort will send a
rescue party on our trail."

Hawkeye glanced around the shack. "They have

enough supplies here for a week. They may not be missed soon, and when they are, it will be assumed that they deserted. Only the winter garrison remains at the fort, and they'll not search hard for a pair of sentries."

He gathered enough of the clothing and supplies to make it appear as if the soldiers had struck out on their own, then ushered them outside. Shouldering Killdeer and the French muskets, which were far superior to the Indian muskets back at the cave, he headed out in front, as Chingachgook led the prisoners down the trail.

They were about a quarter mile from the base of the mountain when the keening wail of an Indian brave pierced the air. The war whoop was echoed first by the mountains, then by other voices that took up the cry, which was punctuated by a burst of musket fire.

Spinning around, Hawkeye saw that Chingachgook had already dragged the prisoners into the woods and was tying them to a tree. Leaving the unloaded French muskets propped beside the trail, the scout took off at a run, checking Killdeer's priming charge as he raced toward where the soldiers were hiding.

The gunfire was muffled, as if coming from within the cave. But after a few rounds it trailed off and finally ended. The whooping did not, however, and Hawkeye could only fear the worst. He had not heard any return fire, and he wondered if this Indian band might be armed with only traditional weapons. But he took no heart in that, since a bow and arrow in the hands of a skilled warrior was far more effective in close action than a slow-loading musket.

Turning off the trail, Hawkeye crashed through the underbrush on the most direct route to the cave, hoping the noise would convince the Indians they were under attack from the rear. He veered to the right and left, both to protect himself from ambush and to confuse the Indians as to how many were coming. He heard someone following just off to his left and knew it was Chingachgook close on his heels.

A rustling of branches ahead caused Hawkeye to dive to one side, just as a bowstring twanged and a streak of white shot through the trees, an arrow thunking into the bark of a birch. The shaft was still quivering when Killdeer sang out, the bullet tearing into the underbrush at the pre-

cise spot where the arrow had emerged. There was a gasping scream, and a brave crashed headlong through the
leaves and lay unmoving on the ground.

Hawkeye rose to his knees and was pouring a charge
of powder down Killdeer's barrel when a second warrior,
in the war paint of an Abenaki, came leaping out of the
same bank of bushes, knife raised in one hand, tomahawk
in the other. Wielding the rifle like a staff, Hawkeye
warded off the first blow of the 'hawk. But the brave
landed on top of him, knocking him backward onto the
ground. He managed to grab the man's left wrist, pushing
the knife away from his face while avoiding the 'hawk
flailing wildly in the man's other hand.

The Abenaki swung down with the 'hawk, but the
scout rolled to the side, knocking him off balance and
sending the hatchet blade thudding into the earth beside
Hawkeye's ear. With a final furious shove, Hawkeye threw
the brave clear. But the Abenaki scrambled to his feet,
shifted the knife to his right hand, and sprang at him
again. In one smooth motion, Hawkeye wrenched the
tomahawk from the ground and hurled it through the air,
catching the brave in the center of the chest. He staggered,
then dropped to his knees. The knife slipped from his
nerveless fingers, and he fell onto his side, blood trickling
through his lips.

After reloading Killdeer, Hawkeye continued through
the woods, fearing the worst. During the fight with the
Abenaki, he had heard Chingachgook's gun fire several
times, and when he finally reached the small clearing in
front of the cave, the Mohican was already there. The only
sign of the war party were two braves lying dead near the
entrance. Signaling that he would approach so that any
surviving soldiers would not mistake Chingachgook for an
enemy, Hawkeye called out to the men and stepped from
the trees. He was greeted by a return cry, and he and Chingachgook went running into the cave.

Inside, all was chaos. Of the seven soldiers, one was
dead, and Clifton Wharton had been shot through the
chest with an arrow. But apparently their guns—and the
sudden appearance of the scout and the Mohican—had
driven off the Abenakis.

"What happened?" Hawkeye asked, hurrying over to

where Wharton was lying, his eyes bleary and his face pale from the loss of blood.

Standing nearby, trembling with excitement and fear, Lieutenant Rowland sputtered, "They came out of nowhere! Aye, a dozen at least! I—I told him to stay in here. . . ." He nodded toward the sergeant, whom Hawkeye cradled in his arms. "Damn fool had to make his play. Got himself shot, and that other fellow, too."

"And saved your scalp," Hawkeye said derisively, paying no more attention to the officer, who was nervously peering out into the gathering darkness.

With the assistance of a couple of the soldiers, Hawkeye carried Wharton into the thin light at the cave entrance. Kneeling beside them, Chingachgook cut open the Oneida shirt Wharton was still wearing and examined the wound. The arrow had pierced his chest and quite probably his lung just to the left of his heart and was protruding from his back. It could not be removed with the arrowhead in place.

"Rest easy, Cap'n," Hawkeye told the militiaman. "We'll have that thing out of you in a moment."

Wharton forced a smile and grunted through clenched teeth, "Wouldn't a p-poultice do?"

Hawkeye held him steady as Chingachgook grasped the shaft at the point it emerged from Wharton's back. Gripping it firmly with both hands, the Mohican suddenly jerked his right hand, snapping off the arrowhead.

Wharton groaned but did not cry out. His eyes fluttered closed as he slipped lower in Hawkeye's arms and stammered, "W-was th-that all? Hardly felt it."

"We're all but finished," Hawkeye lied, thankful that the man was on the verge of unconsciousness. He looked up at Chingachgook and nodded.

Coming around to the front, the Mohican gingerly took hold of the fletched end of the shaft. He nodded twice, and the third time he placed his moccasin against the sergeant's chest and pulled. Wharton gave a strangled cry, and Hawkeye had to keep him from bolting upright. The arrow held a moment, then slid free, releasing a stream of blood that Chingachgook immediately set about stanching.

Wharton's eyes rolled back, then reopened as he

struggled to remain conscious. Lifting his right hand, he gripped the Mohican's sleeve. "They go in a m-mite easier than they come out," he muttered. His head lolled to the side, and his eyes closed.

Chingachgook leaned close to Wharton's lips. Looking back up at Hawkeye, he shook his head.

"Dead?" Rowland gasped, his face blanching.

Lifting the gold chain over Clifton Wharton's head, Hawkeye lowered him to the ground. He flipped open the locket and touched the lock of hair pinned to one side, and as he snapped it closed he noticed words engraved on the back. Unable to read them, he ran his fingers over the letters, then opened the leather pouch at his side and started to slip it inside. But a hand grasped his wrist, and Chingachgook told him to wait a moment. He drew the scalping knife from his belt and reached for the sergeant's hair.

"No!" Rowland lunged at Chingachgook, but Hawkeye jumped to his feet and intercepted him. "That savage is scalping—"

"Quiet!" Hawkeye shouted, shaking the man into silence. Looking back at Chingachgook, he gestured for him to proceed.

Ever so tenderly, the sagamore of the Mohicans grasped Clifton Wharton's blond hair and cut off a small lock. Sheathing the knife, he tied a knot in the hair to hold it together and handed it to Hawkeye, who placed it inside the locket.

"Take the sergeant to the back of the cave, wrap him in his blanket, and cover him with rocks," Hawkeye told a soldier who was standing nearby. "The same with that poor fellow." He indicated the other dead man.

Stepping forward, Rowland grabbed the soldier's arm to hold him back. "We've got to bury those men."

"There isn't time." The scout signed to Chingachgook, who nodded and headed from the cave to retrieve the prisoners they had left on the trail.

"Then we must take them back with us," the lieutenant said in the most official tone he could muster as he looked between Hawkeye and the four remaining soldiers.

"That would slow us down. And by now the Abenakis will be at Carillon, raising the alarm."

"Do you think they'll come after us?" one of the other soldiers asked.

"Not tonight. Those Jack-a-dandies won't come out from behind their walls until sunrise."

"What about the Indians?"

"When they see the Frenchers won't be roused, they'll come seeking revenge. By then we'd best be long gone."

"Yes . . . we'd best be on our way," Rowland muttered as he strode to the cave entrance and peered outside. Turning back to the other soldiers, he looked almost confused, then suddenly blurted, "Drag those bodies to the back of the cave, and be quick about you!"

Chapter V

At first their progress was slow and guarded, as
though they entered with reluctance amid the
horrors of the spot.
　　　—*The Last of the Mohicans,* Chap. XVIII

The morning after her twenty-second birthday found
Astra Van Rensselaer several miles north of the hamlet of
Half-Moon, where she and her maid had spent the night at
a wayside inn. From here it would be a long day's journey
of thirty-five miles to the bend in the Hudson River known
as the Great Carrying Place, where Fort Edward guarded
the portage roads that led into French-controlled territory.

Astra and Clarice passed few travelers on the road,
the massacre at Fort William Henry having effectively
halted all but military traffic. It was when they were nearing the section of river known as Still Water that they were
overtaken by a company of two dozen scarlet-coat English
regulars, who came galloping up the road from the direction of Albany. Signaling Clarice to let her do the talking,
Astra reined in her horse and waited for the officer in
charge to approach.

Raising his hand, the officer drew the company to a
halt and, accompanied by a second officer, rode over to
the women. He doffed his hat and swept it in front of him
as he announced, "Colonel James William Hall, Forty-
eighth Regiment of Foot—" he grinned and gave a slight
nod "—fortunately not of foot today but of hoof, returning to my regiment at Fort Edward. This is Major
Horace Trevlayne of General Webb's staff. May I ask the
pleasure of your acquaintance?" His smile seemed warm

and genuine, and everything about his appearance inspired confidence. He was not wearing a wig but had pulled his brown hair to the back of his neck, and his features were much darker than most Englishmen, causing Astra to wonder if he might have seen service in the West Indies.

Astra was about to give a fictitious name when the man named Trevlayne boldly declared, "Why, Colonel Hall, we have the honor of addressing the daughter of the Dutch patroon Hendrik Van Rensselaer. Miss Astra Van Rensselaer, is it not?" His smile was equally confident but laced with what might be a touch of English arrogance, heightened by his almost pure white wig, which would have looked almost feminine had his features not been so strong.

Stunned at being recognized, Astra glanced at Clarice, then turned back to the major, whose dark eyes flashed with amusement. "Yes," she finally replied, giving up all thought of pretense. "This is my maid, Clarice. But my father is no patroon—only a simple burgher who runs a modest banking company. The Albany patroon is a cousin, and a distant one at that."

"I stand corrected." He bowed to each of the women.

"I don't recall our ever having met, Major Trevlayne."

"We weren't introduced, but I was in attendance earlier this year when General Webb hosted the Pinkster Ball."

Astra thought a moment. "Horace Trevlayne . . . you had just arrived in the Colonies, hadn't you? You served with distinction during the war for Austrian succession."

"Your memory serves you well."

"Not as well as yours, it seems, Major."

"You women are far from home," the colonel put in, steadying his horse. "It wouldn't be that you're making the journey alone to Fort Edward?"

"My brother has been serving with the militia, but we've no word of Pieter's whereabouts since the trouble at Fort William Henry. I had hoped that this visit might provide a firsthand accounting."

Trevlayne looked at her with curiosity. "But surely your father—"

"My father is in New York." She cut him off, smiling politely but silencing him with her gaze.

Trevlayne turned to the higher-ranking officer. "Colonel, seeing as how we're also bound for the fort . . ."

"But of course." Hall again doffed his hat to the women. "Ladies, if you would be so good as to fall in beside the major, we'd be honored to escort you to Fort Edward."

As they crested a knoll just before sunset Astra rose up on the saddle and peered over the bank of low pines that lined the road, craning her neck for a better view. She imagined great geometric earthworks and a star-shaped outer wall of stone or heavy timber, protecting an inner fortress of barracks and storehouses, all filled with the clamor of men and horses practicing their drills in precise and orderly formations on the parade ground under the shadow of the encircling walls.

What Astra saw bustled with activity, indeed, but in far more motley surroundings. There was a large nondescript stone building that served as a storehouse, surrounded by a few wood shacks and dozens of tents, all perched amid what appeared to be hastily dug breastworks. Dotting the fortifications were an assortment of cannons and fieldpieces that appeared to be pointing in no particular direction, as if they had been flung out upon the earth and left where they had landed. Such were the battlements and buildings that made up Fort Edward.

The soldiers made no better an impression. There were thousands of them, mostly provincial militia that had poured into the fort upon learning of the fall of William Henry. Here and there among the homespun and buckskin were pockets of scarlet—the English regulars of the 42nd Highlanders, the 35th, 44th, and 48th Regiments of Foot, and the 60th Royal Americans. They filled the fortifications and spilled out across the surrounding fields, forced to bivouac under the stars without enough tents, blankets, or kettles to go around.

Slumping back in her saddle, Astra rode in silence the final mile to the fort, paying no attention to the commotion she and Clarice caused as they passed through the outer breastworks and approached the small cluster of buildings at the center of the fortifications. At first the surroundings barely registered in her mind at all. It seemed a riot of red and blue uniforms, of fringed buckskin jackets and Indian loincloths and leggings. But slowly the scene took form, and she began to see order amid the chaos: troops lined outside the mess tent, waiting for their bowls of potato-and-leek soup; men seated around a campfire, cleaning muskets and sharing the latest news from home; stretcher bearers scurrying in and out of the hospital tent, carrying in the next moaning victim for the surgeon's knife and carting away the covered corpse of the last.

Most striking of all was the odor. Astra was accustomed to the smell of open sewers, but nothing in her experience on the streets of Albany had prepared her for the stench of a military encampment, and she had to cover her nose with a handkerchief to keep from being sick. Along with the smell of human and animal waste was the odor of putrefying flesh from a pit at the western end of the fort, where cattle, chicken, and pigs were slaughtered. A sickening mixture of blood, mess-hall slop, and excrement ran in ever-converging rivulets through the ditches and walkways of the camp and spilled into the nearby Hudson River.

Astra was so transfixed by the sights around her that she did not notice when the company pulled to a halt in front of the log cabin that served as headquarters. Major Horace Trevlayne had to call her name twice before she realized he was standing beside her Narragansett sorrel and offering his hand to help her down. Accepting it, she slid to the ground and allowed herself to be ushered into the quarters of General Daniel Webb.

The two women stood off to the side as Colonel Hall and Major Trevlayne presented themselves to the general, who rose from his desk and returned their salute. Coming forward, Trevlayne handed him a sealed letter, which the general placed on the desk but did not open. Then Hall introduced the guests, and Webb bowed to each in turn.

"It is so delightful to see you again, Miss Van Rensselaer," he declared, beaming at her. "I trust your father is well?"

She came straight to the point. "It is my brother I've

come about. Pieter is serving with the New York Militia, and we've heard no word of him these past two weeks."

Webb nodded sympathetically. "There were twenty-two hundred men with Munro when Fort William Henry capitulated. Hundreds died, and hundreds more are wounded and still to be accounted for. Every day survivors straggle in to our fort. It is no surprise that a particular militiaman is not yet upon the lists. What *is* surprising is that his sister would make so arduous and uncertain a journey, at no small risk to herself and her companion." He gave a half bow to Clarice.

"Surely someone here has word of Pieter. That is why I've come."

"But if everyone missing a brother or son or husband were to come in search of their loved one, surely you can see what a strain that would place upon our resources."

"But I am not everyone, General Webb."

"Surely you are not."

"Then I may stay and seek my brother?"

The general returned to his desk and sat down, a faint smile playing upon his lips. "It is quite unprecedented. We occasionally entertain the wife of an officer, and of course we are visited by laundresses and the like who follow every army. But an unmarried gentlewoman such as yourself . . ."

"I will interfere in no way. I'll scarcely be noticed."

He chuckled. "Ah, but you've already been noticed, I daresay."

"Perhaps that is for the good," Colonel Hall put in, removing his gloves and folding them behind his belt. "With so many sick and wounded, it would lift morale to see a lady such as Miss Van Rensselaer."

"Yes," Astra said, seizing upon the idea. "And Clarice would be available to assist in any manner you see fit. All we would require is a small tent of our own and permission to go about the camp making inquiries."

The general thought a long moment, then finally rose and nodded. "It would be unconscionable to send you back upon that road unescorted, and since there will be no company going to Albany until later this week, the only sensible plan is to provide you with shelter. But there will be no talk of a tent. I'm certain a room can be arranged in one of the officers' barracks."

"I'd be delighted to give up mine," Trevlayne offered.

"The major is welcome to share my quarters," Colonel Hall added.

"Then it's settled," Webb declared with a clap of his hands. "You shall have the hospitality of Fort Edward until an escort is available to see you home. As for inquiries, I shall have my sergeant assist in any way possible. Perhaps when you return to Albany, you can carry news not only of your brother but of many another brave defender of Fort William Henry." He turned to Colonel Hall. "Colonel, if you would be so good as to escort the ladies to Major Trevlayne's quarters. I'd like to speak with the major for a moment."

Hall saluted, and the two women thanked the general and took their leave.

When they were alone, General Webb sat down at his desk, broke the pair of seals on the letter the major had given him, and read the contents, nodding and frowning periodically. Finally he closed it and placed it on the desk in front of him.

"A nasty bit of business this could prove to be," he said, shaking his head. "I assume you've read the letter?"

"It was sealed," Trevlayne reminded him.

Webb's smile was conspiratorial. "Come, Major, you weren't assigned this post because you'd allow a mere seal to blind your eyes. It's precisely because I know I can never trust you that I have such complete faith in you. Please, sit down, and we'll get to the heart of the matter."

"You honor me with such faith." Trevlayne grinned as he took the seat indicated.

"Then what do you make of this report from Loudon?" Webb asked, referring to John Campbell, the Fourth Earl of Loudon, who was commander in chief of the English forces. Loudon was usually headquartered in Albany but was presently in New York City, whence he had forwarded the letter.

"An Indian prophet?" Trevlayne sneered, his tone dripping with disdain. "I've been in these godforsaken Colonies less than a year, and already I've heard of a half-dozen such prophets. And still their messiah has not come.

Nor will he, as long as King George remains their Great Father."

"It is unimportant whether or not there *is* a messiah. That prissy King Louis could be the Second Coming, for all I care. The danger is that the Iroquois may believe such a man exists and is walking among them in the form of this man they call the Oneida Prophet." He picked up the letter and shook it in his fist. "Especially if this charlatan is preaching alliance with the French."

"We don't know that."

"Our reports say that he counsels neutrality, which sounds like the work of French infiltrators. First turn them away from the Crown, then woo the heathens to their own damnable cause. They've already got the Hurons, Abenakis, and most of the western tribes. If they turn the League of the Six Nations against us, we're finished on the frontier. We might as well retreat down the Hudson and raise our defenses on the streets of New York."

"The Iroquois hate the Hurons and all the rest of Montcalm's Indians," Trevlayne noted. "They've stood solid behind us all these years."

"Not as solid as we'd like. So many have gone west to join the tribes of the Ohio that their numbers here are not what they once were. The majority haven't taken up arms against us, 'tis true, but many have refused to take the field for our cause unless their own lands are threatened. And a few Oneidas and Mohawks—three hundred warriors, I'm told—have been won over by French lies and have joined the Caughnawaga mission near Montreal. They refuse to fight their fellow Iroquois, but the Frenchies have sent them on forays against our border posts, and some have even entered into illegal trade with those treasonous burghers in Albany—that young lady's father among them, no doubt."

"It's only a handful. For the most part we've kept the league under our flag."

"Thanks to Johnson," Webb said, referring to General William Johnson, who as superintendent for Indian affairs had worked for years to win the support of the Iroquois, even going so far as to take a Mohawk wife. "If they ever lose trust in him . . ." He shook his head. "It wouldn't take much to steal their allegiance. It's just not in the nature of a red man to see the grander scheme."

"Then you think we should send a delegation to meet with this Oneida Prophet?"

"We don't know where he is—or if he even exists." Rising, Webb crossed to the window and looked out upon the grounds. "But yes, if there's a way to win him and his followers to our cause, we should seize it. If not . . ." He turned and slapped fist into palm. "If we're going to approach this so-called prophet, we must have the full support of the Crown's representative. I'll prepare a response for you to bring to Loudon when he returns to Albany. But for now we must keep this entire matter in the strictest of confidence."

"You can count on my utmost discretion, General."

"I'm sure that I can." He dismissed the major with a wave of the hand, but as Trevlayne headed to the door, he called after him, "One other thing . . ."

"Yes?" The officer turned and looked back at him.

"Regarding Miss Astra Van Rensselaer . . . her father is a man with some influence in Albany. Make certain you've covered your flanks before laying siege to hers."

Horace Trevlayne returned General Webb's knowing smile. "You can count on my utmost discretion."

Chapter VI

"Seek you any here? . . . I trust you are no messenger of evil tidings?"
—*The Last of the Mohicans,* Chap. II

By the time Lieutenant Leslie Rowland of the 48th Regiment of Foot made his report to General Webb at Fort Edward, the story of his heroism at Mount Hope had grown, while that of his fellow comrades had diminished to an equal extent. To hear Rowland tell the tale, the backwoods scout and his Mohican companion had not captured the pair of French soldiers. Instead, he himself was responsible for that act of daring, for he had organized the reconnaissance mission and overseen the attack on the small French lookout post, which by now had grown in magnitude and in the number of its defenders. As for the Abenaki ambush, it was Rowland who had led the counterattack, boldly plunging from the cave with musket in hand, heedless of the risk in which he was placing himself in order to protect the men under his charge. Sergeant Clifton Wharton was merely an unfortunate victim who might still be alive today if he had paid more attention to Rowland's commands.

Had Hawkeye been on hand to hear the grenadier's fanciful account, he might have been moved to set the record straight. But he was more concerned that the rescued soldiers were cared for adequately and the French prisoners treated with some measure of respect. As for making a proper military report, he was only too happy to leave such formalities to the lieutenant and did not much care if he and Chingachgook received due recognition. He was

especially disdainful of the lengthy written reports that
military officers were so fond of creating—and fabricating.
He had no use for the lies that flowed from the feather of a
goose's wing and often remarked that he trusted but one
book, the words of which were too simple and plain to
require much schooling. That was the book of God, written not by religious scholars but by his own hand in the
wilderness of his creation.

As Hawkeye walked away from the small stone building that had been placed in service as a prison for the
French lookouts, he noticed a circle of soldiers taunting
someone in their midst. Even before he saw the object of
their ridicule, he knew it was Chingachgook. He pressed
through the crowd to the Mohican, who stood motionless,
his arms folded around his rifle, his eyes fixed on no particular point as if gazing into the future or the past.

"Hey!" an English regular shouted when the scout
pushed roughly past him. "You a friend o' Scalp Lifter,
here?"

"Don't he know the Injun camp is down at the river?"
another put in.

"Look at him," a third voice cried out. "As stiff as a
dead man." He jerked his thumb toward Chingachgook's
chest. "You still breathin'?"

"Get some rum in him and that tongue'll loosen right
up." The militiaman thrust a jug toward the Mohican,
who did not react as Hawkeye slapped it away.

"What? Prefer French brandy?" the man asked,
laughing.

"Look under his breechclout!" someone shouted.
"See if he's got the same what them Forty-second Highlanders got under their skirts!"

One of the soldiers took up the challenge and jabbed
a stick at Chingachgook as though to raise the flap of cloth
that hung over his wampum belt. He was met by the butt
of Killdeer, which crashed down on his hand, cracking the
stick and quite possibly several of his fingers. With a yelp
of pain, the man pulled back, then turned to leap at Hawkeye but found himself facing the barrel of his rifle.

"Back off," Hawkeye said without emotion, his eyes
directing the words to the entire crowd.

No one moved at first, but then one of the soldiers

said, "Forget him," and tugged at the shoulder of the injured man. Slowly the others stepped back and began to disperse.

When at last they were alone, Chingachgook said in the Mohican tongue, "You change the will of the Great Spirit when you take on another man's fight."

"Perhaps it was his will that I do just that," Hawkeye replied.

"*Hugh!*" the Mohican exclaimed. "You bend words like a white man."

"And what would you have done had I not interfered?"

"I would have waited until they angered me."

"And then?"

"I would have pulled the trigger." Chingachgook's expression remained impassive as he started toward the river.

After they made their camp in a stand of pines beside the Hudson, Hawkeye took up his rifle and headed through the fort compound to the headquarters building. Stepping onto the porch, he opened his leather pouch and withdrew the gold chain and locket that he had taken from the neck of Sergeant Clifton Wharton. He was about to knock on the door when it suddenly opened and Lieutenant Rowland emerged, accompanied by a second officer. Rowland was dressed in a crisp scarlet uniform, loaned him by a fellow officer, and he held his high-crowned grenadier's hat under his left arm.

"Good evening, Hawkeye," Rowland said brusquely, eyeing him suspiciously.

"Lieutenant," Hawkeye replied with a nod.

He started to move past them, but the second officer raised a hand and asked, "Are you the scout known as La Longue Carabine?"

Hawkeye looked the man up and down. He was dressed in the uniform of a major but wore a rather foppish white wig more suited to an armchair general. Masking his disregard for such affectations, the scout said somewhat curtly, "My father named me Nathaniel and my friends call me Hawkeye. Only my French enemies would

dare name me after a weapon such as their Canada carbine."

"Then that must be Killdeer." The man smiled in admiration at Hawkeye's hunting rifle.

"You've heard of Killdeer?"

"It is as legendary among the officers as the reputed
skill of its owner. Excuse me, I didn't introduce myself.
My name is Major Horace Trevlayne, of late attached to
General Webb's staff." He offered his hand, and Hawkeye
noted that his grip was firm and sure.

"Are you here to report to the general?" Rowland put
in, looking a bit disconcerted that his account of the recent
events might be contradicted.

"I'm content to leave reports to officers such as yourself. I'm here only to deliver this." He held the locket aloft.
"It belonged to Sergeant Wharton. I'd like to see that it
goes to his family."

"Might I look at it?" Trevlayne asked. Taking the
locket, he opened it, then turned it over and examined the
inscription on the back. "You say this belonged to a sergeant?"

"Clifton Wharton," Rowland interjected. "He's the
militiaman I mentioned in my report. He wore that thing
the whole time we were with the Indians."

"Oh, yes, the one who got himself killed when you led
the charge from that cave," Trevlayne said, his tone betraying that he had taken the lieutenant's account of his
own heroism with more than a grain of salt. Turning back
to Hawkeye, he closed his hand around the locket. "I'll see
to this, if you don't object. General Webb will want it
taken care of as quickly as possible."

"Thank you," Hawkeye replied.

"Are you bivouacked here at the fort?"

"I'm with a Mohican. We're camping at the pine
copse beside the river." He pointed in the direction from
which he had come.

"If you'd like quarters in the fort—both of you—I'm
sure I can arrange—"

"No, thank you. We'll sleep better under the stars."

"Of course. Now, if you gentlemen will excuse me, I'd
like to see to this matter at once." Trevlayne turned back
to the building. "You'll be with your regiment, Lieutenant

Rowland?" he asked, and the grenadier nodded. "Good. I'll send for you if anything more is needed." With a half salute, he opened the door and disappeared inside, leaving the two men on the porch.

The lieutenant looked awkwardly at Hawkeye, then muttered, "Good day," and strode off across the compound.

Restraining a smile, Hawkeye replied under his breath, "And good day to the hero of Mount Hope."

Astra Van Rensselaer dropped down on the bed in the room she was sharing with Clarice in the officers' barracks. "I simply will not sit here any longer listening to General Webb's sergeant drone on about why he hasn't been able to turn up any information about my Pieter. No, I'll not be put off another second. I intend to march out there and interview every soldier in that hospital tent—in the entire fort, if need be." Jumping up, she grabbed her shawl from the bedpost and threw it around her shoulders.

"Do you think that's wise, *juffrouw*?" Clarice asked somewhat hesitantly.

"Wise? Good Lord, girl, it's about the only thing that makes sense around here."

"But I've been out there the better part of the day, and I don't think you realize what such an undertaking entails."

"So now *you're* trying to protect me as well? You'd think I'd never seen a sick man before."

"Many of the soldiers are delirious with fever. But it's not just that. It's the horrible wounds . . . the terrible suffering."

"And my brother may be lying there among them."

"But I've been at the bedside of most every one of them," Clarice pointed out. "He isn't there."

"But some are bandaged so totally that you couldn't even see their faces. Isn't that so?"

"Yes, *juffrouw*, but—"

"Then he might be one of them."

"But if I couldn't recognize—"

"A sister knows her own brother." Pushing past the young woman, she yanked open the door. "I'm going over there, and you and that sergeant won't stop me any longer." She marched down the corridor and out the front door, Clarice snatching up her shawl and hurrying after her.

Hiking the hem of her skirts a few inches, Astra strode briskly across the compound, paying no attention to the curious stares of the soldiers. Word had spread quickly through the fort that a pair of women had arrived from Albany the previous evening. While the presence of women was not unusual—in fact, there were more than a hundred working women currently on hand, and an equal number had reportedly been killed at the massacre of Fort William Henry—these new arrivals were reputedly unattached ladies of some standing. As the stories grew Astra was transformed from the daughter of a Dutch businessman into a titled aristocrat, and Clarice became a cousin whom Astra was taking on a tour of the Colonies. As for rumors that she was searching for a missing militiaman, some claimed he was her brother, others a secret lover who had come to New York to escape the wrath of her father, a nobleman living in Holland.

"Which way is the hospital?" she asked one flustered provincial, who averted his eyes and pointed toward a large tent a hundred yards away. "Thank you," she said, turning to leave but then looking back at him and asking, "Are you with the New York Militia?"

He shook his head and muttered, "Massachusetts, ma'am."

She was already on her way, moving quickly across the muddy ground, pausing only to inquire whether one or another of the soldiers was with her brother's militia and perhaps knew of him and his fate. When at last she reached the first in a series of tents that housed the wounded, Clarice came up beside her and asked, "Are you sure you want to do this?"

"I must," she declared.

"Then I will come with you." Clarice held open the flap of the tent and followed her inside.

There were no beds, only straw pallets that lay end to end the length of the tent, with narrow aisles between each row. More than a hundred men crowded the large single room, many of them with heads completely bandaged, others with stumps where limbs had once been. The smell of suppurating flesh made Astra gag. The appalling sight of so many suffering men—their labored breath and piteous moaning—brought tears to her eyes.

"Come, let us go," Clarice urged, taking her mistress's arm to lead her from the dreadful place.

"No," Astra said, pulling free.

Give me strength, Becky, she prayed, calling on her friend as if she were a guardian spirit. Rebekka had always been the strong one, having been raised in the rugged Helderbergs just west of Albany and then marrying Jakob Brower and accompanying him deeper into the wilderness. Now Astra prayed that a portion of Rebekka's strength would support her.

She walked forward into the room, starting down the nearest row. The first soldier she came to was little more than a boy—fourteen or fifteen, perhaps—his neck swathed in blood-encrusted strips of cotton. His eyes were closed, and she stooped down and stroked his cheek. The skin was cold, rigid to the touch, and she jerked her hand back, realizing with a start that he was waiting only for someone to cart him off to the burial ditch.

Across the aisle, another man was tossing from side to side, groaning in pain. His head was wrapped in gauze, and a poultice on his side covered what appeared to be a musket wound. "Pieter?" she said, knowing he probably could not hear her and that even if he could, he was unable to reply. "It's going to be all right," she soothed, kneeling beside him and caressing his arm.

"Do you know Lieutenant Morgan?" a man asked, and Astra looked up to see a gray-bearded man in a blood-stained jacket. "Dr. Miles Whitworth, surgeon of the Massachusetts Regiment," he introduced himself. "Is the lieutenant an acquaintance?"

"No," she replied, standing. "My name is Astra Van Rensselaer, and this is my friend Clarice."

"Yes, we met earlier." He bowed to each of them. "She told me of your mission."

"I'm searching for my brother, Pieter, of the New York Militia."

"I'm sorry, but I don't know him." Whitworth gestured toward the bandaged soldier. "Thomas Morgan—he fought valiantly at the lake."

"Were you at Fort William Henry also?"

"Yes, and it was a nasty bit of work. The lieutenant was fortunate not to have been wounded there."

Astra looked down at the man lying on the pallet, swathed in gauze. "I'm afraid I don't understand."

"This is from the massacre afterward. He is one of the lucky ones." Seeing her confused expression, he explained, "Most of the men badly wounded during the siege did not survive. If they were too sick or injured to walk, they were turned over to the French surgeon and placed in huts on the fort grounds. But I'm afraid he was unable or unwilling to protect them from the Indians. Among my own regiment were seventeen wounded, and though the surgeon placed sentinels on duty, they left on the morning of the tenth. Immediately thereafter, the Indians dragged the poor men out of their huts and killed and scalped them with their tomahawks. French soldiers and officers were no more than forty feet away but didn't come to their aid." He shook his head bitterly. "Yes, the lieutenant is one of the lucky ones. That wound in his side will heal, and if infection doesn't set in, a wig should cover where a patch of hair once stood."

Astra stared in shock at the bandage covering his head, her eyes widening as she looked out across the floor and saw so many of the same wounds. "Do you mean . . . ?"

"Yes. Many were scalped alive, and some like the lieutenant may live to tell the tale. Now, if you'll excuse me, there are wounds that need dressing." He smiled at Clarice. "Thank you again for your assistance." He gave a final bow and continued down the aisle to where an orderly was tending to one of the men.

Clarice saw that Astra had backed a few feet down the aisle and was gazing out across the scene as if in a trance. *"Juffrouw,"* she said, and when there was no response, she spoke again.

"Yes?" The word seemed distant and disconnected.

"If you have no need for me, I will stay and help the surgeon."

"Yes . . . of course," Astra replied, hardly noticing as Clarice curtsied and headed across the tent.

Just then Lieutenant Morgan gave a particularly pained moan, and Astra reached instinctively for him. But as his head lolled to the opposite side, she saw that the entire right side of his bandage was encrusted with blood. Her hand drew back, and she felt herself about to gag. Turning, she hurried back down the aisle and yanked aside the tent flap. Slipping outside, she breathed in the foul air, which seemed far fresher now, and tried to block out the groaning cries from within the tent.

She was just recovering her equilibrium when she noticed Major Horace Trevlayne approaching across the compound. Steadying herself, she forced a smile and returned his wave.

Coming up to her, Trevlayne removed his hat and bowed crisply. His dark eyes seemed strangely impassive, and his tone was cautious and formal as he said, "I'm afraid I bring sad news, Miss Van Rensselaer."

"Pieter . . ." The name escaped her lips in a sigh.

"His was a hero's death."

A dark veil descended upon her, and she felt her knees tremble and give way. The dreadful moaning poured out of the tent and swirled around her, pulling her down into a vast pit, into the burial ditch of a thousand lost souls. She felt the earth closing over her, sealing her in bitter cold blackness. The cry grew muffled and weak, till in the faintest of whispers it carried his name into the silence and was gone.

She was unaware of time as she lay suspended between darkness and light, between all and nothingness. But then the veil parted, and a soft light intruded in her consciousness. It grew brighter—harsh, even—and brought with it the sound not of moaning or music but of a man.

"Astra . . . Miss Astra . . ." he repeated over and over.

Blinking her eyes against the light, she saw a familiar face and tried to recall who it was. And then the name eased through her lips: "Horace . . ."

"Rest easy," he urged, placing a comforting hand on her shoulder.

She tried to make out her surroundings and saw a lantern beside where she was lying. For a moment she thought herself in the tent of the wounded, but then he said, "You're in your room—my room—in the officers' barracks. Just rest easy and don't try to get up."

"I . . . I fainted."

"It must have been a shock. I shouldn't have blurted it out like that."

It all flooded back to her then, and she asked, "My brother . . . is he really gone?"

Trevlayne nodded, and she began to sob.

An hour later, Astra had composed herself and was seated in a chair beside the bed, awaiting the return of Major Trevlayne, who at her insistence had gone to fetch the man who had confirmed her brother's death. Pale but alert, she occasionally dabbed at her eyes with a handkerchief.

Hearing a knock on the door, she looked up and called, "Is that you, Major?"

"Yes."

"Please, come in." She wiped her eyes a final time and folded the handkerchief in her hands, summoning a smile as Trevlayne entered the room. "Has he come?" she asked.

"Yes. But are you sure you don't want to wait until tomorrow?"

She shook her head emphatically. "Please ask him in."

Stepping back, Trevlayne ushered another soldier into the room and announced, "Miss Astra Van Rensselaer, this is Lieutenant Leslie Rowland of the Forty-eighth Regiment of Foot."

"Miss Van Rensselaer," the lieutenant said, bowing stiffly.

"Major Trevlayne tells me you were with my brother when he died," she began, not waiting on formalities. "You *are* certain it was Pieter, are you not?"

"I knew him by the name Clifton Wharton, but yes, it was your brother."

"How can you be sure?"

Trevlayne came closer and answered, "Because he was

wearing this." He reached into his pocket, then held forth his hand.

Astra's eyes misted as she took the gold locket and turned it over, running her finger over the words *Voor Mijn Zoon, Pieter. Margaretha Van Rensselaer.* Reaching to her breast, she touched the locket that always hung around her own neck, identical in every respect but for the first part of the engraving, which on hers read *Voor Mijn Dochter, Astra.*

"I know a little Dutch and thought it strange that a man named Clifton Wharton would carry a locket engraved 'For my son, Pieter,'" Trevlayne told her, "so I took the liberty of checking with some of the New York militiamen at the fort, and one of them explained that your brother had secretly joined under an assumed name. Apparently he didn't want any influence being used on his behalf."

"I didn't know," she whispered. "I should have guessed." She opened the locket, and her eyes welled with tears when she saw that it contained not only her mother's red hair but a blond lock that undoubtedly was her brother's. Forcing calm into her voice, she said to the lieutenant, "Did he say anything? About his family, perhaps?"

"We weren't able to speak much when we were in the hands of those savages, and when we did, it was only in generalities, I'm afraid. But he did say that he had a sister he cared for deeply. I understood there was some sort of disagreement with his father. But Sergeant Wharton—I mean Van Rensselaer—carried no anger with him to the grave. When he died, it was with clear heart and mind."

"And it is true that Pieter died a hero?"

Rowland looked over at the major a bit uncomfortably, apparently having already been forced to confess at least a portion of the truth of the events at Mount Hope. Turning back to the young woman, he nodded and said with what passed for heartfelt conviction, "A more valiant hero I did not see on the fields of Fort William Henry. He was serving on the watch when the heathens attacked, and he braved their withering fire to give the rest of us time to enter the fray. It is a sad truth of military strategy that he who first engages the enemy can do the most to effect victory but all too often does so at the greatest personal cost."

Astra again felt herself on the verge of breaking down, but she steeled herself and declared, "I want to see my brother. Will you take me to him, Lieutenant Rowland?"

"But . . . but Miss Van Rensselaer—" he stammered, looking quite flustered. He glanced over at Major Trevlayne, who placed a comforting hand on Astra's shoulder.

"I'm afraid that isn't possible," he told her.

"But I must see him. I must bring him home—"

"He isn't here. I mean . . . they were not able to bring his body back with them. Isn't that so, Lieutenant?"

"I wanted to." Rowland rubbed his hands together nervously. "But that scout, he was too afraid, and he put the fear in our men. Refused to lead us back to Fort Edward if we didn't leave the dead behind. I would have said to hell with the coward, but I don't know those woods— none of us do. Only that scout and his heathen companion did. And of course there were the men to consider, and my prisoners."

"Lieutenant Rowland captured two infantrymen of the Royal Roussillon," Trevlayne put in. "They were privy to a wealth of information, and it was incumbent upon the lieutenant to get them here as quickly as possible."

Astra raised a hand. "I understand, Lieutenant, and I harbor no ill will. But I must find my brother and bring him home. Can that scout you mentioned take me there?"

"I'm afraid not," Trevlayne said. "Your brother lies buried near Ticonderoga in the shadow of Fort Carillon. It would be suicide to try to recover his body."

"Surely you can help me," she implored, gripping the major's arm. "He's my brother . . . my father's only son."

"And he's a sergeant of the provincial militia who fell in action and was given a soldier's burial on the field of battle. I am certain that he was proud to have saved so many of his comrades and would be equally proud to know that he is interred on the very ground he hallowed with his life."

Astra lowered her head in acceptance and defeat.

"I think we should let Miss Van Rensselaer rest now,"

Trevlayne told the lieutenant, leading him from the room. "Perhaps tomorrow you can make a copy of your report, and she can bring it home for her father."

Standing in the doorway, Lieutenant Rowland gave a smart salute, then headed from the barracks.

Reentering the room, Trevlayne cautiously approached the chair where Astra was sitting. "I'm sorry our efforts have borne such bitter fruit. If there were any way I could alter the outcome . . ."

"It is not your fault," she whispered. "You really have been most kind."

"Perhaps in the future I can be of more congenial service to you and your family." He bowed and withdrew, closing the door behind him.

For a long time Astra just sat there without moving. Finally she walked over to the bed and lay down upon it. "Pieter . . ." she sobbed into the pillow. "Oh, my dear, dear Pieter!"

Chapter VII

"The white man may, and does often, forget the burial-place of his fathers; he sometimes ceases to remember those he should love and has promised to cherish; but the affection of a parent for his child is never permitted to die."
—*The Last of the Mohicans*, Chap. XI

Hawkeye leaned close to the fire and stirred the embers. As the light flared brighter Chingachgook sat upright, turning his head from side to side. "*Hist!*" he exclaimed in a low voice. "Someone comes!"

The scout strained to listen and finally discerned the sound of someone approaching through the trees from the direction of the fort. He assumed it was only one of the soldiers, but to be safe he took up his rifle and cocked the hammer.

"Who goes there?" he called, training the barrel on the footpath that emerged from the trees. He glanced to the side, but already the Mohican had disappeared into the darkness, tomahawk and knife at the ready in case of trouble.

A shadowed figure stepped into the clearing, and from its great girth, he thought it might be a bear. But then with a start he realized it was only a woman, her girth merely the effect of the peculiar bone hoops that filled out her black dress, a fashion rarely seen upon the frontier.

"Who are you?" he demanded, standing and taking a step toward her.

"No one to fear, I assure you," she replied in a soft, tremulous voice, raising a hand toward him.

Realizing he still had the rifle trained on her, he lowered the muzzle and uncocked the hammer. As she stepped into the light and pulled back the hood of her cape, he saw that her hair blazed as brilliant a red as the fire.

"Are you the scout who brought two French prisoners to the fort this morning? The one known as La Longue Carabine?"

"Who wants to know?"

"My name is Astra Van Rensselaer, and I am from Albany."

"And why are you seeking this Longue Carabine?"

She gave a disarming smile. "May I approach? I assure you, I carry no weapon."

Hawkeye returned a wary smile as he motioned her forward. "A woman's weapon is not always visible, yet it can down its prey with twice the cunning of my long rifle." He showed her to a tree trunk that was lying near the fire. After she made herself as comfortable as possible, he sat down on the ground a few feet away.

"I seek no prey," she told him. "Only a friend."

"And what friend is that?"

"The scout who brought in those prisoners was on hand at a cave near Ticonderoga when a pair of militiamen fell during an Indian attack. That scout is the one I seek, and when I inquired around the fort, I was given the name La Longue Carabine and directed to this place. Are you not he?"

"Indeed, I'm that scout, though my friends call me Hawkeye."

Astra looked around the clearing. "And you travel with an Indian? A Mohican, I believe?"

"The sagamore sees us, even when he cannot be seen." Turning, he called Chingachgook's name, and the chief slipped silently into view, moving close to the fire and taking his place on the ground near Hawkeye.

"I don't wish to take up your time, Mr. Hawkeye—"

"We have no use for titles in the wilderness. Hawkeye alone is sufficient."

"Hawkeye," she repeated. "I will speak directly, if I may." She slipped her hand through an opening in her skirt and withdrew a small leather pouch. "I would like to hire your services, along with those of your Mohican companion."

"Hire?" His tone sounded almost disdainful. "We are neither porters nor guides. For what would you hire us?"

"To take me to that Ticonderoga cave."

"*Hugh!*" gasped Chingachgook. Hawkeye himself was too stunned to reply.

"I know it seems an odd request, but I must find my brother and bring his body back to Albany."

"Your brother died at the cave?"

"He was the one you knew as Sergeant Wharton, but his real name was Pieter Van Rensselaer. He entered the militia under an assumed name so that no influence would be used on his behalf." She reached to her neck and lifted a pair of chains, revealing the gold lockets given her and Pieter by their mother. "You may have seen him wearing this. If you'd like, you can read my mother's inscription to him."

She started to unclasp the chain, but he motioned that it was unnecessary. "Your brother showed it to me. The hair inside matches yours."

"It belonged to my mother, Margaretha. Pieter must have put his own lock alongside it. Now this is all we have left of him—of either of them."

"It is your brother's hair, but he wasn't the one who put it there."

"He wasn't?" she said in surprise. "Did you—?"

"No. It was my friend, Chingachgook."

Astra looked beyond him to where the Mohican was staring into the fire, his expression betraying no sign of emotion. "If you will thank him for me . . ."

"You may do so yourself. He speaks our language."

Leaning forward, she said somewhat hesitantly, "Thank you for your thoughtfulness."

Fixing her with a solemn gaze, he nodded.

Astra turned back to Hawkeye. "Pieter was my only brother. I can't leave him lying in some unmarked cave, and I don't want to return home with only this lock of hair to show his father. Will you take me to him?"

Hawkeye looked into the flames, then back at the young woman. Drawing a deep breath, he replied, "I'm sorry, but I cannot."

"Why?"

"It would not serve your brother's memory to cause the death of another Van Rensselaer. How would your father feel to learn that not one but both of his children are lost? And on such a reckless errand."

"Do you call recovering the body of a loved one reckless?"

"Traveling through the thick of Montcalm's Indians to the heart of his stronghold is not only reckless but a fool's errand."

"Then I am a fool," she declared. "But a fool with a purse of gold." She shook the pouch so that he could hear the coins.

"Many a man has purchased his own death with coins such as those."

"This one journey could provide you with wages for a year."

"I have never worked for wages, nor do I wish to leave this earth before my appointed hour."

She eyed him closely, as if gauging his sincerity. Finally she took another approach. "They told me you were not a man to frighten so easily."

He gave a sharp laugh. "Only a man who already walks among the dead can afford the luxury of being without fear. The rest of us would do well to keep a good measure of it at close hand."

"But not so much as to doom us to inaction."

"Your brother gave up his life not because he was fearless but because he did not shrink from taking action when it was needed. But he'd be the first to tell you that a journey through enemy country merely to ease the minds of those he left behind would not only be a fool's errand but an insult to his memory." He shook his head. "Chingachgook and I will not be a part of such folly."

Astra looked back and forth between the two men. "There is nothing I can say to convince you otherwise?"

"I'm sorry," was Hawkeye's reply.

She stood. "Then I will have to find someone who does not think me so foolish."

"You mustn't," he implored, rising and facing her. "These woods are no place for a woman, especially with Montcalm's Indians about."

"I appreciate your concern, and I truly thank you for the kindnesses you showed my brother. But I am intent on my mission, even if I must throw myself on the mercy of the Marquis de Montcalm himself."

"It will not be Montcalm from whom you'll be begging mercy but his Huron and Abenaki varlets."

"That really is no concern of yours," she replied and turned to leave.

"*Shh!*" he hushed, moving to block her passage.

"What?"

He gestured for her to be quiet, then called something in Mohican to Chingachgook, who was already on his feet. In an instant the chief had snatched up his weapons and disappeared into the trees.

"Could be Abenakis skulking around," he whispered, leading her away from the fire.

"But we're at the fort."

"They fill the woods as far south as Half-Moon."

Hawkeye was checking the charge of his rifle when an ululating cry pierced the night, followed by the rustling of branches and the whoosh of something spinning through the air. He pulled Astra behind him just as a tomahawk thudded into the tree trunk only a few feet away. Raising Killdeer to his shoulder, he trained the barrel on the woods, pulling the hammer to full cock. Just then a shrill scream was heard, followed by the cawing of a crow. When the crow cried out a second time, Hawkeye cautiously uncocked the hammer and lowered the rifle to the ground.

"It is finished," he declared and turned to Astra, whose face was blanched with fear. Gripping her shoulder to steady her, he said, "It was an Abenaki, but Chingachgook has dispatched the intruder."

Just then the Mohican emerged from the edge of the woods, and in the flickering light of the fire a scalp lock could be seen dangling from his hand. Astra gasped, and Hawkeye turned her away from the sight.

"I'll escort you back to your quarters, but you must promise to give up any notion of traipsing alone through these woods. There will be time enough when the war is over to bring your brother home for a proper burial."

Astra nodded numbly.

"Good. Then we'd best be going before any more of those varlets return." He called back to Chingachgook, then led her through the trees toward the safety of the earthworks of Fort Edward.

Astra gently closed the door so as not to awaken Clarice, who was asleep on a mattress in the corner of their room in the officers' barracks. Leaning against the door, she listened to the receding footsteps of the scout named Hawkeye and felt a rush of fear and excitement course through her. She had heard enough about Indian ambushes and had met quite a few Iroquois during their periodic visits to Albany to trade pelts for guns and metal goods. But never had she been so close to a real life-and-death battle. And to see that Mohican come out of the woods brandishing the bloody trophy of his victory had both horrified and thrilled her.

She could only guess how many other men the scout and his Indian companion had dispatched. Theirs must be a brutal life, she told herself, to live so isolated an existence in the woods, to spend one's days apart from the comforts and civilities of society. Yet Hawkeye did not seem to have been brutalized by his environment. Indeed, he possessed a certain grace and rough charm, and he had spoken eloquently and convincingly. She guessed that he did not know how to read, but certainly that was no true measure of intelligence. And when it came to reading human nature, she sensed that he was as accomplished as any Albany burgher.

Astra's reverie was broken by the sound of someone knocking on the door. It took her by surprise; she had not heard anyone approaching down the hall.

"Who is it?" she called softly.

"Major Horace Trevlayne."

"Just one moment." She walked over to the bureau and fetched the candle lamp, which Clarice had left burning. When the young maid stirred and looked up at her, she whispered, "It's all right. Go back to sleep." Then she headed back to the door and pulled it open.

Doffing his hat, Trevlayne gave a courteous bow. "I'm sorry to disturb you so late, Miss Van Rensselaer, but I called on you earlier and was worried that something untoward might have happened."

"Why, good evening, Major." She lifted the lamp to better see him. "I went for a walk. But as you can see, I'm fine, and so is Clarice." She gestured toward the room behind her, indicating that her lady's maid was present.

"I would caution against wandering the grounds unescorted—especially after dark. This is a fort, but we are surrounded by hostiles who are far more brazen once the sun has set."

"I'll be more careful, thank you." There was an awkward silence, which she broke by asking, "Is that why you came?"

"Excuse me?"

"To warn about the Indians?"

"Why, not exactly," he replied, looking a bit uncomfortable. "Actually, I came to offer my services as an escort."

"To the cave?" she blurted, her expression brightening considerably.

"The cave? Good Lord, no. I mean Albany. I'll be leading a company in the morning, and the general and I thought it would be best if you accompanied us. This really is no place for a woman such as yourself, and now that you've found out about your brother . . ."

"I'd hoped to bring him home with me."

"I know. But you must realize how futile such a mission would be."

Astra lowered her head but did not reply.

"I hope you weren't trying to get that scout to take you there."

"Hawkeye?"

He seemed taken aback by the familiarity with which she used the scout's name, but he forced a smile. "I must confess that I saw him with you. I only pray that you haven't convinced him to take you into the wilderness—"

"I tried," she admitted. "But he said the same thing as you—that it's too dangerous and foolhardy an effort."

"He exhibits more sense than his kind usually do."

"I'm still loath to return home without Pieter."

"Then I shall make you a promise. If you and Clarice will agree to accompany me in the morning, I shall pledge to find your brother and bring him to Albany for proper burial just as soon as Fort Carillon falls into our hands."

"But that could be years away. By then—"

"No," he declared, shaking his head emphatically. He looked around as if to make sure no one was about, then motioned for Astra to step out into the corridor and close the door. When she complied, he withdrew a piece of paper from his jacket pocket and prepared to read it, saying in a conspiratorial tone, "We've had word from our commander in chief, the Earl of Loudon. He writes: 'I am on the way with a force sufficient to turn the scale, with God's assistance; and then I hope we shall teach the French to comply with the laws of nature and humanity. For the knowledge I have of the murders committed at Fort William Henry will oblige me to make those gentlemen sick of such inhuman villainy whenever it is in my power.' " He stuffed the message back in his pocket. "He means to take Fort Carillon while the bulk of Montcalm's forces are in Montreal for the winter."

"Will he succeed?"

"If he acts before hard winter sets, there's no reason why he should not. The French prisoners confirm that Montcalm and the bulk of his forces have departed from Carillon, leaving only a winter garrison of fewer than five hundred."

"And you will be on hand when the fort falls?"

"It is up to General Webb to make my assignments, but I can guarantee that if I'm not there that very day, I will accompany the general soon after. And then I shall visit that cave and see that your brother and his comrade are treated with more dignity than that scout afforded them."

"I don't want anyone put at needless risk, and indeed I do not desire that you should find yourself under the French guns at Carillon on my account, but I desperately want my brother to be given a Christian burial. And if indeed Carillon will soon fall . . ."

"Then you'll accept my offer and return with me to Albany? For if there's one thing on which that scout and I agree, it is that the northern woods are no place for a woman, nor for any but the most fortified of armies."

She knew that the major and the scout both made

perfect sense, yet her heart continued to pull toward Ticonderoga. Reluctantly, she acceded to the voices of reason—her own included—and she nodded. "Clarice and I will be pleased to have you escort us to Albany."

His smile was warm and generous. "I shall come for you and your maid at dawn." He took her hand, holding it a bit longer than propriety dictated before lifting it to his lips and kissing it tenderly. Then he turned on his heels and was gone.

For a long moment Astra just stood there, wondering at the swirl of conflicting emotions that coursed through her. Finally she shook her head as if to clear it, then disappeared into her room.

Chingachgook was seated cross-legged in front of the fire, cleaning his rifle, when Hawkeye returned and sat beside him.

"She was not frightened too greatly?" the Mohican said in his own language.

"Nothing that a good night's sleep won't cure," the scout replied. "I trust that all was quiet while I was gone." His lips quirked into a smile.

"I had to kill three more varlets." Chingachgook's tone was solemn, but his eyes betrayed a hint of merriment.

"Did their scalps look Abenaki this time? That last one was an Oneida if ever I've seen one. And rather dried out for having just been lifted." He turned to his companion and grinned broadly now. "I must say it was a nice touch. If she doubted that we were under attack, that scalp convinced her otherwise. But your tomahawk came a bit closer than I would have liked."

"Not as close as I intended." The hint of a grin passed across Chingachgook's face.

"Well, at least our little ruse should make her think twice before asking someone else to take her to Ticonderoga."

Chingachgook nodded, and the two men fell into a long silence, during which the Mohican filled the bowl of his clay pipe with a mixture of tobacco, sumac leaves, and red willow bark. Lighting it, he took a long draw, then handed the pipe to Hawkeye.

After they had smoked for a time, Chingachgook said, "Your thoughts are like these curls of smoke." When Hawkeye looked at him curiously, he added, "They blow to the north."

The scout nodded and took another draw on the pipe. "I am thinking about the man named Pieter. He threw a tomahawk like a Mohican and saved my life."

"Just as you first saved his." Chingachgook allowed the words to make their impact before adding, "And then he almost took that life away again by attacking the Oneidas too soon."

"He didn't know the ways of the woods but was trained like a redcoat—to stand in the open fields and fight."

"And die."

"Yes, and die. But he did so with bravery and honor."

Chingachgook nodded in agreement. When Hawkeye handed him back the pipe, he turned it upside down and tapped out the ashes. Standing, he looked down at his friend and said, "We must sleep if we are to leave before dawn."

"Leave?" Hawkeye replied, then realized that his friend had heard his thoughts. "Yes," he said, rising and heading over to where Chingachgook was already opening his bedroll. "It will be a long journey back to Ticonderoga."

Chapter VIII

"Life is an obligation which friends often owe
each other in the wilderness."
—*The Last of the Mohicans,* Chap. VIII

The sun was fading when Hawkeye and Chingachgook made landfall near the north end of Lake George. Hiding their canoe in the brush, they set off on one of the many Indian paths that circled the western side of the La Chute River, which connected Lake George and Lake Champlain to the northeast. A more direct route followed a portage that had been cut just east of the La Chute rapids, but the French usually kept an advanced post at the head of the carrying place, and the portage itself was used regularly by the various tribes allied with the Marquis de Montcalm. Instead, the scout and the Mohican followed a more isolated path through the rough forest country to a trout stream that carried enough water to conceal their tracks. Entering the stream, they cautiously made their way in the fading light toward where it emptied into the La Chute River not far from Mount Hope.

The two men were just finishing a particularly steep descent when Chingachgook threw his rifle to his shoulder and swung the barrel to his left. Hawkeye instinctively followed suit and found himself staring down the barrels of four small but effective muskets, wielded by warriors painted with the distinctive markings of the Abenaki. Spinning to the right, he discovered three more warriors holding him and Chingachgook under their sights.

Realizing that resistance meant death, the two men lowered the barrels of their rifles. They could only hope that these were not the same Abenakis who had attacked the cave, or if they were, that they did not recognize the scout or the Mohican.

"We come in peace," Chingachgook intoned in the Abenaki tongue.

Though Hawkeye had never learned Abenaki, it was in the Algonquian family of languages, which included Mohican, and he understood enough to follow what was being said.

Chingachgook looked from one warrior to the next, his gaze finally settling upon one young man whose paint indicated that he was leading this war party. "I would speak with your elders," he told the man.

"There are no elders here," the man replied, walking toward the edge of the stream but keeping his musket trained on the Mohican. "You will come with us." He motioned a pair of braves forward, and they lowered their guns and approached the two men to take away their weapons.

Hawkeye saw Chingachgook relinquish his military rifle, and he reluctantly handed over Killdeer. The braves then snatched their knives and Chingachgook's tomahawk.

As they climbed out of the stream bed they were surrounded by the Abenakis, who prodded them forward with their muskets. The group took off at a run toward the north, angling away from the La Chute and a little to the west of Mount Hope. Despite the gathering darkness, the scout recognized the region as the one through which he and Chingachgook had led the rescued soldiers.

The path they traveled wound through heavy stands of pine and maple and finally up a rise and out across a forested plateau. Presently they saw the flicker of campfires through the trees and soon came into a clearing where a band of perhaps fifty Abenakis had pitched a temporary village. Their arrival was greeted with quite a bit of excitement as they were led through the lodges toward the central fire. Women stepped away from their steaming pots of venison and succotash to whisper among themselves and point at the white frontiersman and the Mohican warrior. A few children ran back and forth in front of them, calling them names and tossing sticks and pebbles. The men of the village, who had been standing in clusters repairing their hunting weapons and conversing, now fell silent and eyed the two strangers with suspicion.

The leader of the war party brought them to the fire that was burning in front of the largest of the lodges. Taking the prisoners' rifles from the other braves, he carried them into the lodge. The braves sat down in a circle around the fire and were joined by other men of the village. Hawkeye and Chingachgook were left standing in the midst of the assembly, waiting for the leader to reappear and decide their fate.

When the man emerged from the lodge, he was not alone but had a woman at his side. Though she was old enough to be his mother, she was still in the full vigor of her years, and she leaned on a stick not because she was aged or infirm but because in the past she had sustained an injury to her right leg. Her hair was worn long and loose and was as raven as when she had been a young maiden, and her dark, expressive eyes flashed with what could be either humor or malice.

The woman gestured for the young man to take his place in the circle. Then she walked to where Hawkeye and Chingachgook were standing and examined first the white scout and then his companion. Nodding to Chingachgook, she intoned, "Muhheconnuk," then said in the Abenaki tongue, "By what name are you called?"

"Chingachgook," he said without looking at her.

"The Serpent!" she replied, for his name meant Big Serpent.

The well-known name passed in a hush through the seated assembly. Then someone whispered, "La Longue Carabine." It was taken up by one and then another, and all eyes turned to the scout at Chingachgook's side.

"He is the one your French father calls La Longue Carabine," Chingachgook confirmed.

"We have heard of the son of Unamis," the woman said, jabbing a thumb at the spot on his red hunting shirt directly over the tattoo of a turtle. "He is no friend of the Abenaki. He and La Longue Carabine fight for the English father and kill our people."

Some of the men started shouting now, calling for the prisoners to be flayed or made to run the gauntlet. The village women could be seen just beyond the light of the fire, gathering sticks and clubs with which to unleash their fury on these men who would bring death to their people. Hawkeye showed no emotion as he took in the scene, all the while calculating in which direction they might best make their flight. But when he glanced at Chingachgook, he saw that the Mohican seemed completely unconcerned and gave no sign that he even considered making a run for it.

"What have you to say?" the woman demanded, poking Chingachgook again.

"For ages beyond reckoning, our people have been friends," the Mohican began, staring straight ahead. "We are sap of the same tree. Yet we have allowed enemies to invade our lands and strike our tree asunder. We have sold our birthright for their trinkets and guns."

"It is a fine gun that you carry—the gun of an English slave."

"I am slave to no man," he replied solemnly.

"Are you not a dog to your English masters? Do you not lap at their feet and eat the scraps from their tables?"

The angry voices of the men grew louder, and several rose from the ground and shook their tomahawks or fists.

Chingachgook looked at the woman for the first time. "We do not pass through this land in anger, nor do we wish to take up arms against the Abenaki."

One of the men approached the Mohican, waving his tomahawk above his head as if to strike him. But the woman lifted her walking stick to bar his approach and gestured for him and the others to sit back down. Reluctantly they complied, muttering all the while that they would see the blood of this Mohican and his white friend before the night was out.

"Our men and women are angry because our chief and three of our bravest warriors fell to the guns of your English masters just three suns ago under the shadow of Carillon. Did you hear of this great battle?"

Hawkeye realized with a start that they were talking about the incident at the Mount Hope cave. Apparently they did not realize that he and Chingachgook had participated and even taken Abenaki lives.

"I know of no great battle," Chingachgook replied

truthfully, for indeed it had been little more than a skirmish.

"Many died, and all the English dogs were killed," she said, smiling. "And now we find you sneaking through our lands. How many English do you and this scout bring to kill our people?"

"We travel alone, in peace, through lands my people called home until the white man's guns and diseases found us in our lodges and cut us down. I am the last of my people. When you kill Chingachgook, you end the Muhheconnuk line forever."

"What is that to me?" she asked.

"When the French and English finish fighting each other and only one is left standing, he shall turn his wrath against all of his red brothers, and then you shall see what it is to be the last of the Abenaki." He glanced at Hawkeye, almost sorrowfully, then turned back to the woman. "It makes no difference whether the last of the Mohicans dies under the 'hawks of your braves or as an old man, shriveled under his robes. Do what you want with me. I ask only that you spare the life of La Longue Carabine."

The woman took a step back and stared at Chingachgook for a time, then hobbled over to the young man who had escorted her from the lodge. She whispered something to him, and he dashed into the lodge, emerging a moment later with their two rifles.

"We have heard of La Longue Carabine," the woman said, taking Killdeer and holding it aloft, its barrel pointed to the sky. Her eyes widened with excitement as she pulled the hammer to full cock and squeezed the trigger. There was a moment's hesitation as the sparks struck the old charge, then the powder ignited and the gun bucked in her arms. She grinned malevolently as the smoke curled around her. "It is said that La Longue Carabine can hit the eye of a turtle at one hundred paces. Let him show that this is true, and we shall let him live." She thrust the rifle at Hawkeye.

Cradling Killdeer in his arms, Hawkeye said to his friend, "Ask her what she would have me shoot."

"I understand your words," she said in the Mohican tongue. Suddenly she grasped the front of Chingachgook's shirt and ripped it open, baring the tattoo on his chest. "If you can shoot the eye from this turtle, we will let you leave unharmed."

At her signal, several warriors grabbed Chingachgook and dragged him across the clearing to an open space about fifty yards away. They held him by his outstretched arms while the young warrior leader came forward with a torch in one hand and Chingachgook's rifle in the other and held the flaming torch close enough to illuminate the tattoo on the Mohican's chest. Chingachgook made no effort to resist but stood calmly with his feet spread apart, the blue turtle rising and falling with each breath.

For a long time Hawkeye just stood looking at his friend, their eyes locked in silent communication. Then the scout pulled Killdeer's hammer to half cock and blew into the touchhole. He reached into the leather pouch at his side for a cartridge, one of a dozen he always carried but rarely used, preferring to load the gun directly from his horn so that he could better regulate the amount of powder that went into the barrel and the flashpan. But a cartridge had the advantage of speed, so he chose one and palmed a second.

The cartridge was made of strong paper wrapping and filled with powder, with one end sewn shut and the other tied to the small flash that projected from the lead ball as a result of casting. Gripping the cartridge firmly and keeping the second one hidden in his palm, he bit off the sewn ends of both and poured a small amount from one onto Killdeer's flashpan, then covered the pan. He lowered the butt to the ground and poured the rest of the first charge down the barrel, following it with the empty cartridge and ball. Pulling out the ramrod from under the barrel, he forced the ball down the grooved barrel, then replaced the ramrod and lifted Killdeer to his shoulder, all the while keeping the remaining torn cartridge hidden in his hand.

The Abenakis grew quiet as Hawkeye sighted down the barrel at the tattoo on his comrade's breast. One of the braves holding Chingachgook looked ready to let go of his arm and retreat to a safer distance, but the leader with the torch shouted for him to hold steady as he thrust his torch a few inches closer to the Mohican's chest. The older woman, meanwhile, seemed fascinated by the whole proceeding, and she backed a few steps from Hawkeye and circled toward his front so that she could better see his face and whether or not he had the will to kill his friend and save his own life.

"Pierce the turtle's eye and bring down the Big Serpent and you shall live," she taunted, raising a finger and pointing at Chingachgook.

Hawkeye raised his head and stared straight at her, and a fleeting shadow of fear crossed her face, as if in his eyes she had seen her own death. But then she moved her finger from the Mohican to the scout and said, "Now!"

Sighting along the barrel, Hawkeye found his target, held his breath, and ever so gently squeezed the trigger. There was a loud report and a shriek of pain and surprise as the lead warrior's legs gave way and he fell forward onto the torch, snuffing it out.

Already Hawkeye had poured the second charge down the barrel, and he flung aside the cartridge and ball and used the ramrod to jam the powder home with enough pressure to force some backward up the touchhole. Without removing the ramrod from the barrel, he swung the gun to his right, jerked back the hammer, and pulled the trigger. The entire operation had taken three seconds—just long enough for the Abenaki woman to let out a gasp of fear. And then the ramrod was blown out of the barrel like an arrow, piercing her right eye and shattering the back of her skull.

Hawkeye leaped through the ring of stunned warriors, swinging Killdeer like a club and knocking one man down to clear a path to the trees. As he sprinted across the clearing toward the dark forest beyond, he glanced over his shoulder and saw in the dim reflected firelight that Chingachgook had broken free and was making a run for the woods. He heard the crack of a rifle and recognized it as Chingachgook's; he prayed that it was the Mohican who had retrieved his weapon. The Abenaki braves started shooting now, but they were firing wildly, the bullets smacking into the trees all around Hawkeye. And then he gained the edge of the forest and disappeared into the darkness.

He knew that runners would be on their trail in a matter of seconds, and he gave the caw of a crow and was relieved to hear Chingachgook's return cry. A moment later the Mohican was at his side, brandishing not only his military rifle but a tomahawk he had managed to wrest from one of his captors.

The two men sprinted silently through the forest, aided in their flight by the relative lack of underbrush in this Adirondack forest and guided only by their keen senses and the thinnest of moonlight that filtered through the trees. They did not slow their pace until they had traversed several miles of rugged terrain, heading first back toward the trout stream and then circling around to the north and then east toward the lower valley of Lake Champlain. They could no longer hear their pursuers and were confident they were safe, at least until dawn. The Abenakis undoubtedly would assume the two men were trying to reach the English-controlled lands to the south and thus would concentrate their search on the region between their camp, the stream, and Lake George. By the time the warriors picked up the trail in the morning light, Hawkeye and Chingachgook would be many miles in the opposite direction.

It had grown somewhat brighter, the moon having risen higher in the sky, and as the forest thinned in the lowland country, they sighted the looming shadow of Mount Hope to the east. Quickening their pace, they made for its southern base and soon found their way to the cave. Hawkeye reloaded Killdeer, tamping the ball in place by tapping the rifle butt on the ground, since his ramrod had been sacrificed during the escape and the one on Chingachgook's military rifle was far too short. Then he moved close to the cave entrance and searched for any sign of human or animal occupants. Satisfied that no one was there, he gave a birdcall, and a moment later Chingachgook appeared at his side carrying a blazing brand. Together they entered the cave and made their way to the rear, where they were relieved to find the two makeshift graves undisturbed.

It took only a few minutes to uncover Pieter Van Rensselaer's body from beneath the rubble of rocks. It had been tightly wrapped in a pair of Indian blankets, and

Chingachgook used some of the lacing from the front of his torn hunting shirt to secure them in place. Then Hawkeye hoisted the body across his shoulders and Chingachgook took up their rifles, and the two men headed back into the night.

They knew it would be suicide to remain in the cave, for they had not had time to cover their trail and would be tracked there the next morning. And to try to follow the portage or river to their canoe at Lake George would likewise bring certain capture by the Abenakis, who undoubtedly were swarming across that region and might well have already found the boat. Instead they settled upon a bold but dangerous plan. Turning east, they made for Fort Carillon.

The French garrison was not expecting trouble in the middle of the night, nor had their outlying sentries warned of English forces approaching, so the few soldiers manning the walls were less than alert, spending their time talking, playing cards, or in some cases nodding off to sleep. It proved a simple matter for Hawkeye and Chingachgook to follow the base of the earthen glacis past the west wall, circle the fort entrance, and slip down to the dock at the confluence of the La Chute River and Lake Champlain. The riskiest moment came as they neared the storehouses and shacks that dotted the shore. But they proved to be unguarded, and a few minutes later Hawkeye was easing his burden into the hold of a small flat-bottomed bateau, while Chingachgook untied the vessel and leaped on board.

The water was calm, and the two men took up oars and headed south along the narrow lake, moving slowly so as to avoid detection from the fort. As they gained distance they rowed harder, the raked bow of the bateau slapping gently against the water. By dawn they would be twenty miles to the south and well to the east of Lake George, a region known to the Indians as Onderiguegon, or Conflux of Waters, which marked the head of Lake Champlain. From there it was twenty miles overland to Fort Edward. Then a final fifty-mile journey by land or along the Hudson River would bring Pieter Van Rensselaer—Sergeant Clifton Reginald Wharton of the New York Militia—home at last.

As Chingachgook leaned into the oars at the rear of the bateau, he called in Mohican, "Hawkeye, I will help you bring this soldier to his sister. But then there is something I must do."

"What is it?" the scout asked in his friend's language.

"At night when I am asleep and walking the land of the ancients, I see two faces. . . ."

Chingachgook fell silent for a long time, and finally Hawkeye asked, "Is one of them Uncas?"

"Yes."

"I see him, too."

"It is the second that troubles me. It is the face of the warrior I almost killed at the Oneida camp—the one who bore the sign of Unamis."

Hawkeye nodded thoughtfully. "And what does he say to you?"

Chingachgook drew in a breath and let it out in a single hushed word: "Father."

Hawkeye let the word settle on the night wind before finally asking, "Why would he call you that?"

"You did not see him. Beneath his paint, he was the image of Uncas, as if he was an older brother."

"But is such a thing possible?"

"There was a woman who walked beside me in my youth. We were to be man and wife, but she accepted the god upon a cross and took a white name—Hannah. She ran off with a Potawatomi who also had been infected by this white disease and went to live in his land where the sun falls at night. We never spoke of her again in our village."

"And you think she may have been carrying your child?" Hawkeye asked, and Chingachgook replied with his silence. "But the warrior we saw was Oneida, not Potawatomi."

"If a Mohican maiden became Potawatomi, perhaps Potawatomi became Oneida. But beneath his war paint he was a Mohican, as surely as I am one. Perhaps his mother marked him with the sign of Unamis so that one day he would know this truth."

The two men rowed in silence for a few minutes, and then Hawkeye said, "There is wisdom in your words, just as there is wisdom in the fate the Great Spirit decrees for each of us. What do you intend to do?"

"The path that now lies in front of me is clear."

"And where does that path lead?" Hawkeye asked, a note of concern edging his voice as he put up his oars and turned to look at the Mohican.

"After we bring this man to his home, I must strike out on the path of the Oneidas who carry the white man's cross. I must find the woman named Hannah and ask her if it was our child that I saw. I must find my son."

"You'll go to Caughnawaga? But that's in Canada. You could fall prey to the Frenchers."

"One red man is much like another to the French."

Hawkeye resumed rowing, pulling hard on the right oar to steer the bateau out into the center of the narrows. "We have walked together these many years, you and I and Uncas. I will go with you to Canada," he declared.

"You must not. While I may pass for a mission Indian in search of the white man's god, you will not be mistaken for an Indian or a Frencher. You have neither the skin nor the tongue for it."

"Still, I shall go with you. If there are any Mohicans in Canada, I will help you find them and bring them home."

"We will speak of this another day," Chingachgook told him. "When this journey is finished and the next is waiting to begin."

"Wherever that path leads, we shall walk it together, my friend."

"If the path is both of ours, then so it shall be," Chingachgook declared.

"So it shall be."

Chapter IX

"Thou sayest well . . . and hast caught the true spirit of Christianity. He that is to be saved will be saved, and he that is predestined to be damned will be damned. This is the doctrine of truth, and most consoling and refreshing it is to the true believer."

—*The Last of the Mohicans*, Chap. XII

Astra Van Rensselaer led her guest from the sitting room of her Albany home to the foyer, where he donned his red cape and swept his tricorne hat in a low bow.

"Thank you so much for your hospitality, Miss Van Rensselaer," Major Horace Trevlayne declared, accepting her hand and kissing it.

She felt herself flush when his lips brushed the back of her hand. As he looked back up at her she could not deny that he was handsome, with a full but firm mouth, an aquiline nose, and dark flashing eyes. And he certainly filled his uniform to good effect.

Suddenly embarrassed at how she was staring at him, she gave a nervous smile and said, "I should think that after such an adventure you could call me Astra."

"Adventure? I trust the journey from Fort Edward wasn't too arduous."

"Not at all. But there were a few moments just north of Half-Moon . . ."

"Ah, but those were Mohawks, and they fight for King George."

"So you said. But I confess that knowing who they were did not completely put my mind at ease."

"We were outnumbered, it is true, but they had hardly a musket between them. One volley from our ranks would have sent them scurrying back into the forest, had they proved less than friendly."

"It was a comfort to know that you were looking after us, Horace."

"It was certainly my pleasure." Again he kissed her hand. "But now I'm afraid that duty calls. I must report to army headquarters."

"Will you be in Albany long?"

"At least until our commander in chief arrives from New York City, which could be any day now. After that, I am at his disposal."

"Perhaps I will see you before you leave?"

"That would be a great honor. May I call upon you?" She blushed again. "I'd like that."

Opening the door, she joined him outside, where a sergeant was standing beside a pair of horses. Trevlayne strode to his mount, took the reins, and lifted himself into the saddle. As the sergeant mounted his horse Trevlayne doffed his hat in a final farewell, then said, "I almost forgot. I've something for you from General Webb." He reached into the leather saddlebag and withdrew a packet. Urging the horse a few steps forward, he held it down to Astra. "It's our most complete list of Fort William Henry's dead and wounded. We thought you might wish to turn it over to the civil authorities yourself."

"Yes. Thank you." Her voice was wooden and distant, but then she forced a smile and said with conviction, "I really mean it . . . thank you. You've been more than considerate, and I appreciate it." Clutching the packet to her breast, she retreated to the doorway.

"Good day, Astra." With a sharp kick against the horse's flanks, he set off at a trot down the drive, the sergeant following.

Astra watched him turn onto the carriage road and ride off toward Albany. As the dust settled and the sound of hooves was replaced by the gentle lapping of the Hudson River against its banks, she closed the door and returned to the sitting room. Spreading the skirts of her mourning dress, she dropped onto a green velvet sofa by the window and pulled the ends of the ribbon that held the packet closed. There were more than a dozen pages of names, each giving the man's regiment, town of residence, and age, along with a description of how he was injured and whether his wounds had proven fatal.

The entries were listed in the order that the information had been gathered, so she turned to the final page and started scanning from the end, until halfway up the page she saw the terse words. Her eyes welled with tears as her finger traced the cold block letters that constituted her brother's obituary:

> *Sergeant Clifton Reginald Wharton, formerly Pieter Van Rensselaer, age 26; New York Regiment; Albany; taken by French Oneidas the 10th of August, 1757; led escape of seven soldiers; killed the 23rd of August while organizing their defense against Abenaki attack near Mount Hope, Ticonderoga.*

Wiping her eyes with a handkerchief, Astra skimmed the pages, which listed more than three hundred names—English, Dutch, Irish—with homes in Boston, Hartford, Peekskill, or as far away as London and Liverpool. Each had a home and a family, many of whom had not yet learned of their loss.

Astra turned again to the final page and reread her brother's entry. She was about to close the packet when a name leaped off the page—a militiaman killed during the massacre whose death had only just been confirmed.

"Jakob . . ." she muttered in shocked disbelief, praying that it could be some other Jakob Brower. But there it was: German Flats, where he had taken his young wife after their marriage, and age twenty-four, two years older than Rebekka and Astra.

"No!" she cried out, crushing the papers in her hands and sobbing. "You can't have them both! I won't let you!"

Hawkeye led the small horse-drawn cart up to the last of the sentry posts guarding the road just north of Albany. He stood patting the horse's muzzle as a provincial militiaman sauntered over and began examining the cart and its cargo.

"What you got in there?" the soldier asked in a disinterested drawl as he jerked a thumb at the long wooden crate on the back.

Glancing back at the pine box, Hawkeye replied laconically, "Pieter Van Rensselaer."

"What?"

"Pieter Van Rensselaer," he repeated as he handed the man a folded piece of paper. "We've permission from Webb to bring his body home."

The soldier read the order of safe conduct, signed by General Daniel Webb, then walked up to the casket and rapped on the lid. He glanced over at the Mohican standing beside the cart, then returned to where Hawkeye was waiting. "Mingo?" he asked, nodding toward Chingachgook.

"No. Mohican."

The man seemed satisfied and handed the scout his papers, gesturing that they could proceed. "'Fraid I can't direct you to the poor fellow's house. Lots of Van Rensselaers in these parts. Most anyone in Albany should know which ones he belonged to."

"Thank you." Hawkeye pulled on the reins and continued down the road, leading the cart behind him.

An hour later, as the last rays of the sun spilled from beyond the ridge of the Helderbergs to the southwest, they passed Fort Frederick at the head of Jonckers Street and descended into Albany. They followed the broad, grassy street down toward the Hudson River, past the town hall and the market and the two churches that dominated the center of the city. The street was lined with overhanging trees and freestanding Dutch houses, each with a small plot of land and its own well and garden. Men were already gathering on the wide, spacious porches, lighting long clay pipes and discussing the day's events. As young men followed the cows home from the commons known as the Pastures at the south end of the city, the clanging cowbells drew maids into their yards, where they set up stools and buckets for the evening milking. Everywhere children scurried about or gathered on the porch steps with porringer bowls in hand as they awaited the evening meal.

The appearance of the scout and the Mohican caused quite a stir along the road. Indians were not uncommon in Albany, but they usually wore European clothing and confined themselves to the trading posts and taverns at the edges of town. Occasionally a band of warriors in ceremonial costume would visit the fort, and the citizens would gather on the hill to see them arrive with great fanfare. But few braves were so brazen as to march through the center of town in full dress, accompanied only by a frontiersman who by his outfit appeared to be half-Indian himself.

The bolder of the children ventured forth from the stoops for a closer look and were invariably called back by their mothers, who gathered the smaller ones behind the enormous folds of their skirts and ordered the bigger ones inside. The men put down their pipes and gazed with a critical eye on the strangers, satisfying themselves that there was no threat to the carefully controlled order of their community.

"Aepjen!" one of the more impertinent young men called to the Mohican as he drove his cow ahead of him up the street. Several of his companions chuckled, and others repeated the nickname, which meant "Little Ape."

Hawkeye did not speak Dutch, but he knew what was being said, for *aepjen* was a fairly common epithet that had been attached first to a particular Mohican sachem and then to any Indian of any tribe. If Chingachgook understood the word, he gave no indication but walked proud and erect with his eyes straight ahead.

They had just passed one of the churches and were nearing the bottom of the hill when a round-faced old man hobbled toward them from the side of the road. Pulling the pipe from between what was left of his teeth, he waved a hand at them and said quite jovially in English, "With the rangers, eh? Seen much fighting?"

"A fair amount," Hawkeye replied, choosing not to correct the man's impression that he was one of the rangers led by Captain Robert Rogers.

The man fell in step beside them. "Don't mind them." He waggled the stem of his pipe at the young men who had been calling names and taunting them. "I can see your companion is a Mohican and a friend. But ever since the massacre, it's not been safe for any Indian in Albany."

"We intend no trouble. We're here on army business."

The old man's eyes brightened. "Oh, and what might that be?"

Hawkeye was tempted to tell him that it wasn't any of his concern, but instead he asked, "Would you happen to know the way to the Van Rensselaer house?"

"And which one do you mean? John Van Rensselaer?"

Hawkeye shook his head. "The house I'm looking for is home to a young woman named Astra and her brother, Pieter."

"Ah, then it's Hendrik you're seeking. But I'm afraid you're too late to see his son, for the latest posting has Pieter among the dead."

"That's who we're carrying." He gestured at the box on the cart.

Realizing that it contained a body, the man came to a sudden halt and was almost knocked over by the cart. Resuming his pace, he was soon marching beside Hawkeye again. "Bringing him home to his poor family, eh?"

Hawkeye nodded. "Can you direct me to their house?"

"Why, of course. Everyone knows Hendrik Van Rensselaer, though I'm not certain he's back from New York yet. But you'll find his daughter there, all right."

Hawkeye hid his growing impatience. "Which way?"

"That depends on whether you prefer the back road or the one along the river."

"Whichever is more direct."

"Well, then, I'd advise heading along the river. Just turn south on Handelaer Street and keep going until you cross De Vysele Kill. That's the city limits, and most everything beyond it belongs to the Van Rensselaers. Not more than a mile farther will bring you to an open field and a small hill. Atop the hill is Hendrik Van Rensselaer's manor."

"Thank you." Hawkeye picked up the pace in hopes of leaving the old fellow behind.

"You'll not be able to miss it," the man called, coming to a halt and letting the cart pass. "It's the most somber of grays and looks out upon the river like it owns it."

*　　*　　*

It was almost dark as Hawkeye and Chingachgook walked up the drive toward the Van Rensselaer manor. Word had preceded them on horseback along the back road, and Astra was already waiting outside, a shawl pulled around her shoulders against the evening chill. When she caught sight of them, she hurried down the drive, exclaiming, "It's true! You've brought Pieter home!" The faint light of the rising moon glistened upon the tears in her eyes as she looked up at Hawkeye, who brought the cart to a halt. "But you said it was too dangerous."

"Your brother saved my life—many lives, in fact. I owed him a debt of gratitude, and when I saw how determined you were, I knew he'd want to lie nearby you if he could."

"Thank you!" she sobbed, unable to control her tears. "Thank you so very much!"

She reached out and grabbed his arm, and he instinctively drew back, frightened more by her touch than he would have been by a Huron war party.

"And thank you, too," she said to Chingachgook, holding her hands toward him in gratitude.

Turning to her, he said in English, "You are welcome."

With a servant leading the way, the two men carried the pine casket around the house to one of the outbuildings, where it would remain until it could be buried in the family plot the next day. Then Chingachgook went to tend to the horse while Hawkeye was ushered into the sitting room to meet with Astra. She joined him on the sofa, and it was clear from the moment he sat down that he was quite uncomfortable, not only by the plush surroundings but by being seated beside her. He was even more disconcerted when she placed her hand upon his.

"I want to apologize for presuming that I could bid you do my will with a purse of gold." She smiled sincerely. "What made you change your mind?"

She seemed to sense his discomfort and withdrew her hand. Hawkeye took the opportunity to rise and walk about the room, examining the ornate furnishings as he replied.

"I was never unwilling to go back for your brother, only unwilling to take you along into such country."

"Why didn't you tell me that at Fort Edward?"

Hawkeye paused in front of a lamp made of cut colored glass in the shape of a red rose. Leaning closer to marvel at how the light reflected through the petals, he replied, "You didn't strike me as a woman who would be content to be left behind. And it would have been cruel to make a promise we might not have been able to fulfill."

"You mean . . . Pieter might have been carried off by the Indians," she said with a shudder.

Hawkeye looked up at her and nodded. "It seemed wiser to see you safely on your way to Albany before setting out on what might have proved a futile mission."

"But it didn't, and for that I'm in your debt." She rose and walked over to where he was standing. "And I insist on paying back a portion of that debt. Tonight—and for as long as you remain in Albany—you and your friend shall be guests in our home."

Hawkeye looked up at her like a possum caught in a trap. "That is most kind, but unnecessary," he finally said. "We'll be fine at—"

"But I insist, as I'm sure my father would, were he here." She smiled demurely. "This is a very large house, and it's the least I can do to repay what my family owes you."

"Yes, but—"

"I simply will not allow you to refuse," she declared.

She proved herself equal to the task, and before Hawkeye knew what was happening, he was being escorted into one of the guest bedrooms. Chingachgook escaped such a fate, saying that he would not be able to sleep on a white man's bed and would be far more comfortable in the stables with their horse. Hawkeye would have preferred such an arrangement himself, but his Mohican friend had taken a certain amount of pleasure in joining Astra in her assertion that Hawkeye's place was in the house. Now the frontiersman found himself standing in the middle of a room that was twice as large as any Indian lodge, staring at the inordinately high and soft mattress of an enormous four-poster bed.

Hawkeye put down his rifle, which was fitted with a new ramrod he had obtained at Fort Edward, and was just removing his powder horn when a knock sounded at the door and Astra called, "May I come in?"

"Yes, of course." He took a few nervous steps back.

She opened the door and entered, carrying a candle lamp. "It really is quite early," she began, "and I've had the most delicious idea." The flickering light set her green eyes dancing almost mischievously. "I've been invited to a small gathering at the home of our neighbors the Ten Eycks. I hadn't felt in the mood for a party and turned down the invitation. But now with Pieter brought home, it seems like just the thing to raise my spirits. What do you think?"

"Yes, you ought to go."

"Wonderful." She strode across the room and opened a tall mahogany wardrobe. "These belonged to my brother; I'm certain one will fit you," she said, riffling through the row of men's suits.

"Me?" he gasped. "But—"

"I'll send someone up to help you get dressed." She spun around and was halfway to the door as she called back to him, "We should be ready to leave in an hour." And then she was gone, leaving him with his mouth hanging open in feeble protest.

Astra stood alone in the open doorway of the stone shed behind the manor house. She had told herself that she wouldn't come here—that she would accept the word of the servants that it was indeed Pieter Van Rensselaer whom Hawkeye and Chingachgook had brought home to her. She had wanted to have him laid out in the parlor but had been convinced it was not a good idea, given that several days had passed since his death. Still, she could not let him be placed in the ground without looking on his face one final time. Just to be certain. Just to say good-bye.

The pine box had been placed upon a pair of benches in the middle of the shed. As Astra took a cautious step forward the light from her lantern cast eerie shadows upon the walls and objects of the room, turning a pile of crates into a horse and a stack of garden tools into a man. She jumped with a start at what looked like the figure of an Indian wrapped in a robe and seated on the floor beside the casket, then let her breath out in a sigh, realizing it was probably nothing more than an old blanket draped over a chair. She stood transfixed, watching how the bobbing light appeared to make the blanket move, convincing herself that it was an illusion and not a face that she saw just above the blanket. But then the specter spoke in clear but somewhat broken English.

"You come see brother. . . ."

She gasped and almost dropped the lantern.

"It is Chingachgook," he said, rising from the floor.

"I—I didn't recognize you. I'm sorry."

"I go."

He started from the shed, but she raised her hand to stop him, saying, "May I ask you something?"

He looked back at her but did not speak.

"My brother . . . his last moments. Did he suffer?"

The Mohican shook his head solemnly. "He was great warrior. I would be proud to call him brother."

"I am," she whispered, choking back her tears. Walking forward into the room, she approached the casket and placed the lantern on top of it, then ran her hand over the rough-hewn pine. "He was more than a brother to me. After our mother died, he took care of me—protected me. My father, he was too . . ." Her voice trailed off, and she raised her hand to her eyes.

"It is said that when warrior dies, his spirit walks with person closest to his heart."

She gazed down at the casket and smiled. "Yes, Pieter walks in my heart." Lifting the lantern, she turned to Chingachgook. "Will you help me?"

He looked at her questioningly.

"I want to see my brother a final time. Will you open the casket for me?"

Chingachgook stared at her a long moment, as if gauging her strength of will. Finally he nodded and drew the tomahawk from his belt. Stepping up to the pine box, he slipped the hatchet blade under the corner of the lid and pried upward. Moving around the box, he worked each corner up until the nails came unstuck and the lid was freed. Grabbing it firmly, he lifted it off the casket and stood it against the wall.

Astra took a hesitant step forward, holding the lan-

tern out over the casket. She prepared herself for the shock
of seeing her dead brother's face but was surprised to find
the body encased in a shell fashioned of strips of birch
bark, tied with vines.

"I prepare him Mohican way," Chingachgook explained, leaning over and undoing some of the vines so
that he could peel back the birch. When he was ready, he
looked up at Astra, who drew in a breath and nodded.

The light from the lantern gave Pieter Van Rensselaer's face a warm, ruddy glow that made him appear almost alive. His blond hair had been parted in the middle
and brushed, as he had worn it in life, and he was dressed
in the uniform of a militia sergeant, which Hawkeye had
obtained at Fort Edward before completing the journey to
Albany. At his side was the musket with which he had
freed his fellow captives and defended them at the cave.
Astra had prepared herself for an odor, but she was surprised at the fresh scent until she noticed that the body had
been garlanded with herbs and flowers before being
wrapped in the birch casing.

Chingachgook came up beside Astra and said in the
softest of tones, "Is it true that in religion of the cross each
man's name is in book, and when he passes to next world,
book determines his fate?"

She looked up at him with surprise. "Yes, I suppose
it's something like that."

He nodded sagely. "If there is such book, your
brother among the saved."

He prepared to cover the body back up, but Astra
stayed his hand. Reaching to her breast, she removed the
locket her mother had given Pieter and placed it around
his neck.

"Good-bye," she whispered, stepping back as Chingachgook tied the birch bark over the body and replaced
the casket lid. Then with tears washing her cheeks, she
hurried from the shed.

Chapter X

"It is refreshing both to the spirits and to the body to indulge in psalmody, in befitting seasons," returned the master of song.
—*The Last of the Mohicans*, Chap. II

*H*awkeye struggled not to fidget as he sat beside Astra Van Rensselaer on the rear seat of the small calash carriage. Perhaps for the first time in his life he did not feel like Hawkeye or even La Longue Carabine but like Nathaniel Bumppo, and he wondered if his father had ever looked or felt as ridiculous as he did just now, all decked out in Dutch finery, his long brown hair tied at the back of his neck with a bright blue ribbon.

As if to belie his thoughts, Astra exclaimed, "You look wondrous," and nodded approvingly at him.

Hawkeye stuck a finger under the ruffled lace cravat that held his shirt collar closed. "Do the menfolk around these parts wear these things all the time?"

Leaning toward him, she patted the ruffles into place. "Only when they want to make a suitable impression on the ladies, which is precisely what you're going to do tonight."

"I'm not much concerned about impressions, Miss Van Rensselaer—"

"I insist that you call me Astra."

"Well, Astra, I'd rather make an honest impression than a good one. And for that, my buckskin leggings and shirt are far more suitable."

"In the forest, perhaps. But here in Albany, there's

nothing that makes a man like a blue silk suit." She ran the back of her hand along the brocaded flowers on his lapel.

"What makes a man in the settlements seems to be based more on appearance than substance."

"But you can tell so much about a person by his appearance."

"I can tell a varlet from a friend by the color of his paint, and a hawk from a gull by the set of its wings against the sky, but I haven't the learning to read the color of an Englishman's heart from the cut of his suit."

"Tonight you shall begin that education," she declared. "Your first lesson will be to observe the way the men wear the lace at their wrists. You see that I chose for you a shirt that reveals only the slightest ruffle."

He held up his arm and examined the lace cuff, which protruded slightly from the end of the coat sleeve.

"Very tasteful and not at all showy," she continued. "Quite masculine, yet neither coarse nor common. It bespeaks a man who is very sure of himself."

"What if there weren't any lace at all?" he asked.

"A man who does not know his way in life. Not a bad sort at all, but lacking a certain strength."

"And if the ruffle hangs below the hand?"

"The longer the lace, the less trustworthy the man."

He shook his head in confusion. "I'm afraid I don't understand. A bit of lace is better than none, but too much and the man becomes a scoundrel?"

She grinned. "It's a delicate science, to be sure. But so is tracking a deer. Don't you take into account more than just the direction of the trail, such as the depth of each track and whether the animal drags a hoof or leaves any other identifying marks?"

He acknowledged that it was so.

"And so it is with a man. It is not just the clothing he chooses or the length of his cuffs but how he carries himself. Tonight, watch for this sign: Any man who continually draws his hand in front of his nose, as if to admire the scent dabbed on his wrist, is a man so taken with himself that he can hold no place in his heart for another. He is a man who can be trusted only to break a woman's heart. And the young maidens who flutter about him, seeking to catch his eye, are like little birds waiting for their hearts to be stilled." She looked up as the carriage turned off the road. "Ah, but we are here."

The calash pulled to a halt in front of an imposing house that had been built entirely of pink granite. Masking his starched discomfort, Hawkeye climbed down and offered his hand, which Astra gratefully accepted, stepping from the carriage and taking his arm. Together they approached the house and passed through the open door, Astra nodding politely and giving the doorman their names as they entered the foyer. They were immediately ushered into the drawing room and announced as "Juffrouw Astra Van Rensselaer and her guest, Nathaniel Bumppo."

All eyes turned their way, and the host and hostess came over to greet the young couple.

"We did not expect you," Willem Ten Eyck said, kissing Astra's hand.

"But we're delighted you came," Elsa quickly added.

"As will Ernestus be." Willem glanced around the gathering of about four dozen people—a mix of Dutch burghers, English merchants, city officials, and even a couple of army officers. "He's around here somewhere. Arrived from New York less than an hour ago."

Elsa sidled closer to Hawkeye, smiling as she awaited an introduction.

"Willem, Elsa, I'd like you to meet Mr. Nathaniel Bumppo."

"You're not from these parts, are you?" Willem asked, shaking his hand and eyeing him with suspicion.

"I've been to Albany often enough, but only to visit."

"He's a scout for General Webb," Astra explained. "He was with Pieter at the end and was kind enough to bring him home to us."

"Pieter is back?" Elsa gasped.

"His remains," her husband snapped a bit testily. Turning back to Hawkeye, he again pumped his hand. "Then we, too, are in your debt, Mr. Bumppo."

The scout winced slightly and said, "Few people call me that. I prefer Hawkeye."

"Hawkeye? How . . . descriptive." Willem smiled politely.

"Oh, Astra, this is so wonderful," Elsa gushed, taking her arm. "Do you know who's here?—"

"Shh!" Willem snapped, shaking his head brusquely. "Let it be a surprise."

"What kind of surprise?" Astra asked, noticing the looks passing between them.

"Willem is right." Elsa patted the younger woman's hand. "You'll soon enough see."

Just then a voice called, "Astra!" and a young man in a light-brown powdered wig pushed through the crowd. He was in his late twenties and was dressed in a rather smart salmon-colored velvet suit with long swallowtails and brass buttons. His white silk shirt had a preponderance of ruffles at the throat and long lace cuffs that seemed to pour from the coat sleeves. "Astra, *wat mooi*!" he declared as he came over and gave a low bow, adding a slight nod to Hawkeye.

"You're too kind, Ernestus," she said, averting her eyes.

"But you *are* beautiful." Taking her hands, he raised them with a flourish, nodding in admiration at how she filled her black silk gown. "As beautiful as a black tulip." Turning to Hawkeye, he offered his hand and said rather perfunctorily, "Ernestus Ten Eyck."

Before Hawkeye could speak, Willem interjected, "*Mijn zoon*, may I introduce a gentleman friend of Astra's who goes by the name of Hawkeye."

Ernestus's eyebrows arched with incredulity. "I'm pleased to make your acquaintance, Mr. Hawkeye."

His father chuckled. "Not 'Mister.' Just Hawkeye."

"A most curious appellation."

Hawkeye's jaw tensed as the other man looked him up and down with apparent disapproval. "It was given me by the Mohicans," he explained.

"Indians?" Ernestus said aghast. "What have you to do with them, might I ask?"

"Hawkeye is a scout," Astra put in.

"A scout?" He made little effort to conceal his amusement. "A well-heeled one, at that," he added with a wave of the hand and a flourish of lace at his wrist.

Hawkeye forced calm into his voice. "Miss Van Rensselaer was good enough to loan me something of her brother's."

"Ah, I see. Then this is not your *native* garb." His grin was smug and self-assured. "That would explain why you look so . . . discomfited."

"Why, Hawkeye looks perfectly delightful." Astra gave her escort's arm a gentle touch of reassurance.

"Oh, I agree completely. He's the image of a gentleman. But there are signs . . . small things only another man would recognize. Aren't I right, Hawkeye? You're feeling a sense of—" he waved a hand, searching the air for the right word, then said in an affected French accent, "*maladresse . . . absurdité.* Yes, that is precisely how I would feel were I to find myself running around the forest dressed like a heathen. But of course I would never allow myself to be cajoled into such a foolish situation."

Hawkeye realized he was clenching his fists and was surprised at how sweaty they were. He had been calmer confronting a party of Huron warriors. Reaching up, he undid his cravat and let it hang loose around his neck. "If you mean I look absurd, then you'll get no argument from me. As for your donning 'heathen' garb, I reckon you'd be right to avoid such foolishness. After all, you may be the image of manliness in your Dutch finery, but there's nothing like a breechclout to take the real measure of a man."

Astra suppressed a giggle. Even Ernestus was amused, and he bowed to Hawkeye. "You've proven your wit as sharp as your eye." Turning to Astra, he said, "I don't recall you or your father ever mentioning Hawkeye. Where did you meet?"

"Just recently at Fort Edward."

Ernestus nodded, and from the way he narrowed his eyebrows with displeasure, it was apparent he already knew about her recent mission there. Clearly not wishing to pursue the subject, he again addressed Hawkeye. "I take it you are on friendly terms with the Indians."

"There are some I'd call friends, others I wouldn't care to turn my back on—same as the English."

"And the Dutch," Astra added with a grin.

"Yes, but we Europeans and colonists alike have certain rules of engagement—far more civilized and predictable, wouldn't you say?"

"There are rules in the forest as well, and I daresay there's quite a bit our people could learn from studying the ways of the red man."

Stepping between the two men, Astra slipped her hands through their arms and declared, "Let's not argue about such things. We're here to enjoy ourselves."

As she started to lead them away Willem called after them, "Now, Ernestus, don't be telling her about our unexpected guest. Let it be a surprise."

Hawkeye allowed himself to be escorted through the room. Much to his consternation, he was the object of much attention, especially from the half-dozen unattached young women, who knew all the available men in Albany and were interested in anyone new who came into their midst. They were especially intrigued to discover that he was a frontiersman, and though that might rule him out as a suitable match, it did not keep them from admiring how striking he looked in his suit. If they noticed his discomfort, they probably attributed it to his being of a reserved, taciturn nature, and it only served to add to the aura of mystery that surrounded him.

Hawkeye was greatly relieved that there was no music or dancing. Though he had participated in quite a few Mohican celebrations, their dances were far less formal than the ones he had seen in the white settlements, and he had no desire to provide men such as Ernestus Ten Eyck with any further reason to make sport of him. It was difficult enough to figure out the proper way to eat the various hors d'oeuvres that were served by a small regiment of liveried servants.

Hawkeye was maneuvering a stuffed clam off its shell and into his mouth when a raven-haired young woman managed to catch him alone and commented, "Astra looks unusually radiant, given the loss she's suffered."

Quickly swallowing the morsel, he glanced over to where Astra was talking with Ernestus, then gave the woman an uncomfortable smile. "She's had a few days to adjust."

"When I lost Rutger—my husband—it was weeks before I came out of the house. No, I don't believe anyone ever really adjusts to the loss of a loved one, don't you agree?"

Hawkeye thought of Uncas, who had been like a brother to him, and nodded. "I reckon that's true."

"Then it must be Ernestus who's put the blush back in her cheeks. Or perhaps you." She held out her hand. "We haven't been introduced. My name's Christina Gerritsen, and you must be the frontiersman they call Hawkeye."

"Mrs. Gerritsen." He gave a stiff bow, then awkwardly took her hand and lifted it partway to his lips.

"You don't mind my calling you Nathaniel, do you?"

"It's my given name."

"Better yet, I'll call you Natty, for that's precisely how you look tonight."

"As you wish, Mrs. Gerritsen."

"Christina . . . I insist."

"Christina, then."

"He's really quite smitten, you know." She indicated Ernestus, who appeared to be hanging on every word Astra said. "He has been for the past five years."

"And Miss Van Rensselaer?"

"Oh, Astra is a strange one, all right. Perhaps it's because all the girls are after Ernestus that she pays him so little mind. I must say, I've known her since we were children, and she's always been something of a puzzle. It may be her mother. I've heard that Margaretha was a bit of a rebel. Perhaps that's where Astra gets her brazenness. To think of her going alone to Fort Edward. But then, it was to be expected."

"I'm not certain I understand."

"Didn't she tell you about Rebekka?" When he shook his head, she continued, "Rebekka Hirsch was a friend of Astra's. Her father was a tenant farmer up in the Helderbergs on Van Rensselaer land. When they were younger, Hendrik used to let Astra spend her summers up there, but in time he decided that Rebekka's family was too common and, well, vulgar, and he tried to break off their friendship. They saw each other now and again, but it wasn't the same, and in time Rebekka married a fellow named Brower and moved deeper into the wilderness. I believe Astra's gone once or twice to visit."

"And you think this Rebekka was a bad influence?"

"That's not for me to say. But ever since, she's been a bit high-strung and independent. Don't you agree?"

"I wouldn't know about that."

"Perhaps you like that in a woman." She placed her hand on his forearm and fixed him with her dark-eyed gaze. "Or do you prefer a woman who's more compliant?"

"That all depends on what she's complying with."

"Or whom." She let her touch linger a moment, then gave his arm a slight caress before withdrawing her hand. "Astra tells me you're not accustomed to our fashions, though I must say they suit you. Would you mind if I . . . ?"

Before Hawkeye realized what was happening, she had taken the ends of his open cravat and was tying it in place around his collar. Feeling his face redden, he stood as still as possible while she tightened and adjusted it. When she finished, she let her hands rest on his chest a moment, and he became aware of the rushing beat of his heart. Finally she removed her hands and nodded admiringly.

"Yes, it suits you marvelously."

Disconcerted by the intensity of her gaze, he looked down at his gold-embroidered waistcoat and blue silk knee breeches and muttered, "Hardly the outfit for a man of my profession."

"I'm sorry she dressed you up. I would have preferred to see you in buckskin. It's so much more graceful."

He chuckled. "I'm not sure graceful is the word I'd use to describe myself—in buckskin leggings or silk stockings."

From behind Hawkeye, a woman said, "Has Christina been behaving herself?" He turned and was relieved to see Astra standing there; Ernestus was nowhere in sight.

"We're getting along famously," Christina replied. "Aren't we?" Again she touched his arm, but only for a moment, then gave Astra a conspiratorial grin. "You should have told us you've been entertaining a gentleman such as this. Does Mijnheer Van Rensselaer approve?"

"Hawkeye arrived just this afternoon. And no, my father is still in New York and doesn't know. But he would insist that I do no less for a man who has done our family such service—and a friend of Pieter's."

"Of course. Just promise that you won't keep him

locked away so the rest of us don't get a chance to impress him with our charms. That is, unless he's already spoken for." She turned to Hawkeye. "Are you spoken for, Nathaniel?"

"I, uh . . ." he stammered, looking quite uncomfortable.

"Never you mind, Christina." Astra took Hawkeye's arm as if to lead him away. "This is one gentleman who won't be spoken for easily."

"Not even by you?" Christina pressed.

"Why, Hawkeye is like a . . . a brother to me." She smiled up at him. "Yes, a brother."

"Then it's all right if your friends take an interest? Perhaps even pay a social call?"

"If you women don't mind," Hawkeye interjected, "I'd prefer to make up my own mind whether or not I'm spoken for. And as for social calls, Mrs. Gerritsen, I'm afraid that won't be possible. Chingachgook and I look to be leaving in the morning."

"No," Astra blurted. "I mean, you only just arrived. You must wait—at least until Father returns home."

Hawkeye saw the fear in her eyes and realized with a start that she had been quite serious about considering him a brother. It might have been something about his personality or mannerisms that reminded her of Pieter, or simply because he had been with Pieter in his final hours and had brought him home. But she had latched onto him as the brother she once had, and perhaps that was why she was not allowing herself to grieve.

"You mustn't leave tomorrow," she insisted. "Tell me that you won't."

"I . . . I have to check in at Fort Frederick in the morning. After that I'll know where and when I have to go."

"Then we'll have no more talk of leaving—at least until after you've visited the fort."

"It sounds as if Nathaniel is spoken for by the British army," Christina put in.

"With the Frenchers pressing at our back, there aren't many who don't have to answer to a British uniform," he acknowledged.

"You mean like that one?" Christina asked, nodding

toward the entryway, where a man dressed in the scarlet coat of a British officer was just entering the drawing room.

Astra stared at him as if transfixed, her lips mouthing his name as the doorman announced: "Major Horace Trevlayne."

Hawkeye turned and saw a man who carried himself without any trace of self-consciousness—a man who looked as if he would be equally at home on the battlefield, in an Indian village, or among the gentry of London or New York.

The major spoke briefly with Willem Ten Eyck, who nodded and then escorted him to where Astra was standing. As Trevlayne bowed to her, Willem said, "Major Trevlayne tells me you are already acquainted. May I introduce Mrs. Christina Gerritsen and Mr. Nathaniel Bumppo?"

"The pleasure is mine," Trevlayne said, taking Christina's hand. "And good evening to you, Hawkeye. I didn't realize you were from Albany." His expression was friendly but wary, and it was apparent that he was taken aback at encountering the scout in such surroundings.

"He isn't," Astra put in. "He brought Pieter home this evening."

"You did?" Trevlayne looked quite astonished.

"He went all the way back to Ticonderoga—the same morning we left for Albany. Wasn't that thoughtful?"

"Yes, indeed," the major replied, his dark eyes betraying an edge of displeasure. "Does General Webb know?" he asked Hawkeye.

"We stopped at Fort Edward on our way here. The general provided us with a horse and cart."

"Then congratulations are in order," Trevlayne declared, forcing enthusiasm into his voice. "I had thought to do Miss Van Rensselaer such service after Fort Carillon falls, but sometimes these matters are better handled by a frontiersman alone in the woods."

"He wasn't alone," Astra put in. "His Mohican friend was with him."

"By alone, I meant that he was the only white; an Indian doesn't really count," he replied quite flippantly.

"Indeed he does," Hawkeye countered. "None know the region of the lakes better than Chingachgook."

"Then you were smart to take him."

"In truth, he took me."

"Major Trevlayne," Christina said, stepping closer. "I believe we've already met. Were you at the Pinkster Ball?"

"I was. And if I'm not mistaken, you're married to a soldier. Roger Gerritsen, I believe?"

"Rutger," she corrected. "He passed away some years ago."

"I'm sorry . . . I'd forgotten. But I'll not forget the dance we shared."

She blushed. "I didn't think you'd remember."

"But of course I do—just as I recall that Miss Van Rensselaer was far too occupied with the other gents to entertain a dance with me, which we'll have to remedy at the next ball I attend." He gave Astra a knowing smile. "Now, Mrs. Gerritsen, you must be truthful with me. Did I acquit myself well enough on the dance floor to have earned a second go-around with you?"

She gave a mock pout. "Not if you're going to be dancing with just about anyone and everyone."

"I make this solemn vow tonight. If you ladies will afford me the honor, I shall divide all the dances between you two alone."

"But Major Trevlayne, that would be most improper," Christina said with a saucy grin. "I'd be delighted. But of course, Nathaniel will have to promise me the other half."

Hawkeye could feel his collar closing around him like a noose. "I'm afraid I'm not much for dancing."

"Then Astra and I will have to teach you. Won't we?"

"Yes, of course," Astra replied somewhat distractedly.

Hawkeye sensed that the attention of both women had shifted to the handsome English major, and he wondered if it was the man or the uniform that attracted them. He was relieved to no longer be the focus of their fascination, yet there was something disturbing about the officer. He was smooth and confident, to be sure, yet there was nothing overbearing or effete about him. He certainly was not one of those affected men Astra had described during their carriage ride. For that, one need look no further than Ernestus Ten Eyck, who just now reentered the room.

"Ladies and gentlemen," Ernestus announced, raising his arms until the room quieted. "Tonight we've a special treat. While in New York, I had the good fortune to accompany our good friend and neighbor Hendrik Van Rensselaer to the studio of a noted piano maker who has been working with Mr. Benjamin Franklin of Philadelphia on refining an instrument that is becoming all the rage in Europe. Surely many of you have heard Hendrik play his *glassspiel.*"

"And take a generous nip or two from them!" a man called out. His comment drew a round of laughter as folks recalled how Hendrik would arrange eighteen crystal glasses on a cloth-covered board and fill them with various amounts of liquid, then play songs on them by running a moistened finger around the rims. When he had to tune a glass, he would either add more liquid or drink a bit of it, which invariably led his friends to tease that they were filled with spirits rather than water.

Waving his hand for silence, Ernestus continued, "In this modern age, it has taken the likes of the noted Mr. Pockrich of Ireland and our own Mr. Franklin to take the simple *glassspiel* and perfect it into something that I daresay will soon grace all the better parlors of our Colonies, as it already is doing in the manor homes of Europe. And tonight I would like you to hear one of the first such instruments produced on our own shores."

He motioned to a pair of servants, who threw open the doors that led into the formal ballroom. Almost immediately a single tone poured from the room, as pure and liquid as a mountain lake. As it grew louder and fuller a deeper note sounded at a distance and ever so slowly expanded, until it rolled under and embraced the first tone. The two notes became three, all with a rich intensity that vibrated in every cell of the listeners. The chord shifted to a minor key and was joined by a line of melody that danced lightly an octave higher, an old Dutch hymn that was both melancholy and exceedingly sweet.

"Mevrouws en mijnheers," Ernestus continued, "may I present Hendrik Van Rensselaer, performing on his glass armonica!"

As the guests entered the ballroom, Willem Ten Eyck moved alongside Hawkeye and Astra and said, "Hendrik agreed to come home for our party, and Ernestus convinced him to bring his new instrument straight from the dock. Ernestus says that he's played it the past two days almost without stopping."

Hawkeye followed Astra as she made her way through the crowd huddled at the far end of the ballroom, where they were ogling the curious instrument. As they pressed to the front he spied an imposing man with broad shoulders and an equally broad, ruddy face who was seated behind a wide, waist-high cabinet of polished mahogany. The top of the cabinet was open, and his hands were moving left and right inside the contraption as his head lolled back and forth to the swaying tones of the music. His gaze was transfixed on what his hands were doing, and he seemed unaware that he was surrounded by people.

Circling to the right, Hawkeye noticed that Hendrik Van Rensselaer's feet were working a pair of treadles, which turned a horizontal spindle inside the cabinet, on which a series of narrow glass cylinders had been mounted. They spun like a row of wheels with their edges up, the cylinder on the left being the largest in circumference and the ones to its right getting progressively smaller. As they rotated they passed through water troughs at the bottom, moistening them, so that when Hendrik pressed his finger against each one, it produced a clear tone, forming a two-octave scale. The layout of the cylinders resembled a piano, with clear crystal being used for the white keys and dark blue crystal for the black sharps and flats. And he played it much like a piano, his left hand forming chords of two or three notes while his right produced the melody, with subtle shadings of volume and timbre being created by the amount of pressure he employed.

From the faces of the crowd, it was obvious that whereas his friends had merely tolerated his crude *glassspiel,* they were mesmerized by the armonica, which combined the richness of an organ and the clear, fluid tones of a flute. When he finished and lifted his hands from the instrument, there was a long hush, and then the assembly burst into cheering applause. He basked in it, and Hawkeye saw how he beamed with pride as he looked from face to face, until at last his gaze came to rest on his daughter.

"Mijn dochter . . ." he said in a hush, opening his arms to her. But as he rose and started toward her, he stumbled and almost fell but was steadied by Ernestus.

"Vader!" she exclaimed, rushing to embrace him. Others also gathered around, but Ernestus waved them away so that Hendrik could catch his breath.

"I'm all right," Hendrik insisted, pushing himself away from his daughter as she fussed over him. "The ride up the Hudson has unsteadied me, is all." He straightened his gray wig, then stood with one hand braced on the armonica, the other rubbing his belly.

"Is your stomach upset?"

"All the way up from New York on a boat—wouldn't anyone be unsettled?"

"Perhaps if he'd gotten a bit more fresh air," Ernestus put in with a lighthearted smile. "Your father spent the entire journey in the captain's wardroom, playing his new amusement."

Hendrik frowned. "You commanded a performance tonight, and I couldn't very well do so without a bit of practice."

"And practice you did!" Grinning, Ernestus turned to the others. "The music accompanied us all the way to Albany, and it attracted quite a crowd. We had everyone from settlers to savages lining up along the shoreline to find out what kind of boat had such an angelic voice."

"Enough about me," Hendrik gruffed. He turned to Astra. "The Ten Eycks told me where you've been." His unwavering expression made it clear that he did not approve of what she had done.

"I had to go. I had to find out about Pieter—"

"We'll discuss it at home," he said sternly, cutting her off with a wave of the hand. He winced, and his hand went back to his stomach.

"We'd better be going, then," Astra insisted.

"I suppose you're right. I'll just say good-bye to Willem and Elsa and wait for you outside." He turned to Ernestus. "In the morning I'll send my man for the armonica." With a bow, he walked over to where the Ten Eycks were standing, and the three of them started from the ball-room, Hendrik pausing now and then to accept compliments from the guests.

As soon as he was gone, Astra turned to Ernestus. "Has Father been like this long?"

"Just since last night. A bit too much travel, no doubt. He'll be fine after a night's sleep in his own bed."

"I'm sorry I didn't introduce you," she said to Hawkeye.

"You've other things on your mind just now."

"There'll be time to get acquainted during the ride home."

"Perhaps this isn't the moment," he suggested. "You ought to be alone with your father. I can find my own way back."

"I'd be happy to arrange for one of our carriages to bring you," Ernestus offered.

"That won't be necessary," Major Trevlayne put in, coming up beside Hawkeye. "I'll be leaving shortly and would be delighted to drop you off on my way to the fort."

"Would you?" Astra said eagerly.

"It would be my pleasure."

"Thank you, Major," Hawkeye told him.

"It will provide an opportunity for us to talk. I'd like to hear more of your exploits at Ticonderoga. But if you'll excuse me for a moment, I will show Miss Van Rensselaer to her carriage." He gave Hawkeye and Ernestus a brisk bow and held out his arm for Astra, who let him escort her from the room.

"It looks as if we've been left to fend for ourselves," Ernestus said with a grinning shrug.

Hawkeye was trying to think of a reply when Christina Gerritsen came up to them and shook her head in dismay, saying, "Has Miss Astra lost her senses, to go off and abandon two fine gentlemen such as yourselves?" Stepping between them, she took Hawkeye by the right arm and Ernestus by the left and gave each a smile. "I'll just have to do my best to entertain you by myself."

"You are too kind, Mevrouw Gerritsen," Ernestus declared with a flourish of the hand, in which he swept his ruffled cuff suspiciously close to his nose. "Wouldn't you agree, Hawkeye?"

"Of course he does," she said, not giving him time to answer. She squeezed his hand knowingly. "Nathaniel is a most agreeable man."

Chapter XI

"I have heard it said that there are men who read in books to convince themselves there is a God. I know not but man may so deform his works in the settlement, as to leave that which is so clear in the wilderness a matter of doubt among traders and priests. If any such there be, and he will follow me from sun to sun, through the windings of the forest, he shall see enough to teach him that he is a fool, and that the greatest of his folly lies in striving to rise to the level of One he can never equal, be it in goodness, or be it in power."
—*The Last of the Mohicans,* Chap. XII

"*Y*ou're being quite unreasonable," Astra declared, turning away from her father in the calash.

Hendrik Van Rensselaer's left hand balled into a fist. "Unreasonable? Do you call it reasonable to go running off on a fool's errand? And with so much French and Indian trouble afoot . . . ? Well, do you?"

Her eyes ablaze with anger, she grabbed his hand and exclaimed, "Your son is dead! Pieter is dead! And all you care about is that I disobeyed your instructions!"

"I told you never to mention that name to me!" He jerked his hand free and pounded it against his leg.

"You said I couldn't talk about my brother. Well, I don't have a brother anymore! You drove him away!"

"His impertinence drove him away. His intolerable stubbornness."

"Just like his *vader*." She said the word as if it were poison.

"You think I want him dead? My only son? I wanted him alive, at my side, ready to take over—" He choked back the words.

"Father," she said a bit more softly, reaching for his hand but again being rebuffed. "What you wanted was for him to be just like you. But Pieter never was. He was . . . just Pieter."

"He was a failure."

"Don't say that."

"He was. He had no sense for business, and even when I relented to his ridiculous notion about joining the military, he proved too much a coward to serve as an officer."

"That isn't true. He just didn't want everything handed to him because of his name."

"A common soldier. Can you imagine the embarrassment of having one's son—a Van Rensselaer, no less—serving as nothing more than a common soldier?" He shook his head bitterly. "No, it wasn't idealism that made him run off and change his name. It was cowardice, nothing less."

"Pieter wasn't a coward. If you have any doubts, you can talk to Hawkeye when he—"

"Enough talk of that Hawkeye fellow," Hendrik snapped. "It's bad enough for you to have gone traipsing through the woods with nothing but a lady's maid to protect you, but to befriend a common scout and invite him into our house—and when I'm not even home? And then to parade him around at the Ten Eycks' party? What were you thinking? Didn't you realize the talk that would follow?"

"No one said anything untoward."

"Not to your face. But I don't doubt we're now the object of ridicule and scorn."

"That isn't true, Father."

"You . . . you've made us *laughingstocks*!" he sputtered, gritting his teeth and spraying out the words. He raised a fist at her, then suddenly gasped and doubled over.

"Father!"

She grabbed him by the shoulders and felt his body

stiffen with a spasm. After a few moments the attack passed, and he straightened up, his muscles relaxing.

"Is it worse?"

He waved off her concern with a flick of the hand. "I'm fine."

"You don't look fine." Even in the thin, flickering light of the calash lamp, she saw how pale he had become. Leaning forward, she called to the driver, "Turn back to Albany. Take us to Doctor—"

"No!" he blurted and roughly pulled her back onto the seat. "*Neen!*" he repeated in Dutch when the driver looked back at him. "Continue home."

"But you look awful," she said, then repeated the word in his native language to stress how strongly she meant it: "*Afschuwelijk.*"

"*Een indigestie.* That's all."

"But you never have trouble with your stomach. This may be something more, and Dr. Coeymans—"

"Enough! I'll not be treated like a child!" He folded his arms over his chest, his forehead furrowed in anger.

"All right, Father, but you're to go right to bed. You need your rest."

He frowned but did not respond.

Hawkeye was seated beside Major Horace Trevlayne, who expertly worked the reins of the carriage he had hired for the evening. Their conversation was awkward at first, and Trevlayne was particularly cool and formal. But as Hawkeye recounted his journey to Ticonderoga the major appeared to relax and even grew a bit jovial.

"First you face the Abenakis, then you slip right under the noses of the French. And they say it takes a British general to spin a good yarn."

Hawkeye stiffened. "I assure you, Major, I've told exactly what occurred. I've no interest in adding adornments."

"Good God, don't take offense. I didn't mean to suggest you were exaggerating, but when you've been a soldier as long as I have, you can't help but become a bit jaded. I'm sure it happened exactly as you stated, and the reason I'm convinced of that is because an English officer would have said he dispatched half the Abenakis to their Makers and sent the whole French fort scurrying back to Montreal. And he certainly wouldn't have given credit to his Indian scout."

"Chingachgook is no white man's scout—he goes where he pleases and bends to no man."

"Then you're fortunate he's chosen to walk alongside you." Trevlayne shook his head and grinned. "But I must say, I'd love to have been there when you recounted your story to General Webb."

"There was no reason to. What Chingachgook and I did was for the woman, not the army."

"You didn't tell him?" the major said, looking incredulous.

"Only that we'd been to Ticonderoga and retrieved the body."

Trevlayne chuckled. "Then surely I believe your story —every word of it—for only an honest man or a fool would have done what you did and not sought any credit." He glanced over at Hawkeye. "And something tells me you're no man's fool."

"I'll take that as a compliment."

They rode in silence for a time, following the Hudson River south toward the Van Rensselaer estate. When Trevlayne again spoke, his tone was familiar and almost conspiratorial. "The Van Rensselaer woman . . . what do you make of her?"

Hawkeye eyed him suspiciously. "I'm not sure I know what you mean."

"She's a strong-willed filly—her trip to Fort Edward attests to that. But do you think she's an experienced one as well?"

"I'm certain I wouldn't know," the scout replied curtly.

"But you wouldn't mind finding out."

"That's hardly the sort of thing two gentlemen should be discussing—"

"Now, don't play the innocent with me, Hawkeye. I'm just trying to learn the extent of your involvement with the woman. I mean, if you've set your cap for her, I'll certainly honor your claim—after all, you're sleeping right in her house. But if not, I just want you to know I have a prior interest, and anything you can do or say to advance my cause would be most appreciated and reciprocated in kind."

"I doubt you need any assistance from me."

"Don't discount your influence with the woman. I've seen how she looks at you—almost as if you were a brother." He emphasized the word, as if to make a point. "That *is* what she said—that you were just like a brother to her? Christina Gerritsen mentioned it." Trevlayne's lips formed a sly smile as he glanced over at Hawkeye. "Yes, I'd say Christina has taken quite an interest in you. And I don't doubt that if you show her a bit in return, you'll find her response to be far more intimate than a sister's."

"Thanks for the advice, but I'm afraid I don't share Mrs. Gerritsen's interest—if indeed she has any."

"I just thought we might be able to assist each other where the women are concerned." He slapped the reins against the horse's back. "No matter. I'm content to press my own case with Astra, seeing as how her involvement with you is no more than brotherly."

"Yes, but a good brother is always ready to protect his sister's virtue."

Trevlayne gave a droll laugh. "It's neither her brother nor her virtue that I'm worried about. It's her father!" Snatching up the whip, he snaked it out over the horse's head and gave it a snap, setting the animal into a brisk trot.

When Astra arrived home with her father, she was secretly pleased that Chingachgook was not on hand and that Hawkeye was following with Major Trevlayne. Given her father's dark mood, she preferred to put off any further discussion of her trip to Fort Edward or Pieter's fate until Hendrik had rested and was feeling better. She did, however, tell him where the casket was being kept, and she was not at all surprised when he did not profess any interest in seeing it.

Hendrik went off to his bedroom on the second floor, still looking a bit unsteady, and Astra assumed she would not see him until the next morning. However, when Hawkeye arrived a short time later and she prepared to go outside to greet him, she was dismayed to see her father coming down the staircase to the foyer. He was no longer wearing a wig but had tied his graying brown hair at the back of his neck. And he had changed from his suit to a brocaded silk banyan, an informal dressing gown popular among the wealthier class.

"Is that the army scout you were telling me about?" he asked, intercepting her at the foot of the stairs.

"Yes. Major Trevlayne offered to bring him from the party."

"You wait here," he said brusquely, heading for the front door.

Outside, Hawkeye had just climbed out of the carriage, and he shook the major's hand and thanked him for the ride.

"It was my pleasure," Trevlayne replied. "I'll be at Fort Frederick the next few days. You mentioned at the Ten Eycks' that you'd be visiting there tomorrow?"

"General Webb asked me to give the Earl of Loudon my impressions of Fort Carillon's winter defenses."

"I'll see you at the fort, then." He kicked off the brake and started the carriage back down the drive.

When Hawkeye turned toward the manor, the door was just opening, and he found himself confronted by Hendrik Van Rensselaer. "I presume you're the one they call Hawkeye," the Dutchman said, not bothering with preliminaries as he strode down the steps and presented himself with little more than a curt nod of the head. "My daughter told me what you did."

"That's quite all right," Hawkeye replied, not sure if the man's comment was meant in gratitude.

"If you're expecting some kind of recompense, you should know that my son left here of his own accord, and I won't be held accountable for his debts."

"I assure you, payment was the farthest thing from my mind."

"Good." Just then the door opened again, and Astra came outside. Hendrik glowered at her, then said to Hawkeye, "One other thing. My daughter can be a bit impulsive—I'm afraid she got that from her departed mother. She should have considered consequences before inviting a stranger to stay under our roof while I was away. But now that I'm home, I suppose there's no harm for one night."

"I'll get my things and leave at once," Hawkeye replied, restraining his growing anger.

"No need for that. The Van Rensselaers won't be accused of putting a man out in the middle of the night. You were planning to leave in the morning, I assume."

"We'll be gone before daybreak," Hawkeye said emphatically.

"We?" The Dutchman looked questioningly at his daughter.

"Chingachgook and me," Hawkeye went on, unaware that Astra had not yet informed her father about their other guest.

"I forgot to tell you," she lied. "A friend of Hawkeye's helped him bring Pieter home."

"Friend? What kind of friend?" he demanded of Hawkeye with a scowl.

"Chingachgook is a Mohican."

"A savage?" Hendrik said aghast, spinning back toward his daughter. "You let a savage in our house?"

"Chingachgook isn't a savage, and he isn't even in our house," she snapped. "He's in the stables."

"Don't you know what they do, girl? I won't have a heathen skulking around my property, that's for damn sure!"

"But he saved Pieter's life."

"Then who's that lying in a box out back?" he shot back, shaking his fist in the direction of the stone shed.

"*Father!*" she gasped. "How could you!"

"I'm not the one who opened our doors to strangers and savages! You'd think I'd raised you with a bit more sense."

"They're not strangers. They're friends of Pieter's . . . and of mine."

Hawkeye took a step toward them. "I think it would be best if Chingachgook and I left tonight."

"You can't," Astra blurted. "It's too late, and it wouldn't be Christian of us." Turning to her father, she implored, "Tell him it wouldn't be Christian."

"What do heathens know of Christianity?" Hendrik

brayed. "And as for this . . . this woodsman, I doubt he's set foot in a church in a lifetime of Sundays."

"It's true that Chingachgook is no Christian," Hawkeye acknowledged, removing the suit jacket Astra had insisted he wear. "As for me, I know there is one God, and he may well have died upon a cross for my sins. But I'm not one for spending my Sundays convincing myself that he did." After neatly folding the jacket, he gave it to Astra and proceeded to undo his cravat. "It may be that a man becomes so blind in the cities that he cannot plainly see what is so clear to strangers and savages. But he need only spend a single day in the wilderness to see God's hand at work in everything and everyone, heathen and Christian alike." He handed Astra the cravat, then bowed stiffly to Hendrik. "If you'll excuse me, sir, I shall gather my things and be off at once." He turned to Astra. "Chingachgook and I thank you for your hospitality." Striding up to the door, he pulled it open and disappeared inside.

Astra stood glowering at her father, who met her gaze with an equally withering one. When she finally spoke, it was only to mutter, "How could you?"

"It's better this way," he replied.

"You should be ashamed." She turned her back on him and followed Hawkeye inside.

A half hour later Hawkeye was dressed again in his comfortable buckskins, and he and Chingachgook were preparing to leave the Van Rensselaer property. "Where shall we spend the night?" he asked in Mohican as they hoisted their rifles and packs and started from the stables.

"On our way here we passed a copse of pine trees along the Muhheconnuk near the beaver creek."

"The one that old man called De Vysele Kill?"

Chingachgook shrugged. "He spoke the tongue of the white men who came here before the English, and they did not teach it to my people. We know it only as the beaver creek."

"Then the beaver creek it is," Hawkeye declared, pushing open the stable doors and stepping outside. "And tomorrow we'll get a good breakfast at Fort Frederick and be on our way." He started down the dark drive.

"Where will you go?" Chingachgook asked, matching his younger friend's pace.

"With you, of course."

"I told you that I must go north to see if there are any more of my people in the Canadas."

Coming to a halt, Hawkeye placed a hand on Chingachgook's forearm. "I have always wanted to see the Canadas in winter."

"This is not your path to walk. Your people are spreading like the grass across the mountains and forests. It is my people who are no more."

"My people are your people. My path is yours."

"It will be a dangerous one for a white man to walk."

"Before the French made war against the English and red brother turned against red brother, you told me of times when the Hurons came down from the Canadas to visit your council fires. Did they not swear that they suffer far greater than the Mohicans when Old Man turns the land white?"

"The Hurons are a boastful people who make themselves dogs to their women."

Hawkeye grinned. "This is so. Though I have seen the Canadas only in summer, it did not seem much colder than here. The time has come for me to visit in winter and see if the Hurons speak the truth or are merely yelping like dogs."

The thin moonlight revealed a smile that touched only the Mohican's eyes. Clasping his friend's arm, he declared, "So it shall be."

The two men were again starting down the walk when they heard hurried footsteps and turned to see Astra approaching from the house, her face illumined by a candle lamp.

"I will wait for you ahead," Chingachgook said in Mohican, then silently disappeared into the night.

"I'm glad you haven't left yet," she said as she came up to Hawkeye. She threw back the hood of her cloak and looked around. "Where is Chingachgook?"

He gestured in the direction of the river, and she nodded, choosing not to pursue the matter.

"Are you all right?" he asked.

"Yes, but I had to see you before you left. I'm so

ashamed. My father isn't feeling well, or he never would have said those things."

"Don't feel embarrassed on my account. I'm really more comfortable out here—like this." He looked down at his woodsman's garb.

"You were so kind to humor me tonight. I know you didn't want to dress up like that, and it was probably wrong of me to insist. But you did look so very elegant. It reminded me of when I used to go out with my brother." She gave a light laugh that was edged with sadness. "You really don't look anything like him—he was shorter and so fair-haired. But somehow you remind me of him."

He saw her shiver slightly. "You'd best get back inside. It's a bit chilly out here."

"I'm not cold. It's just . . ." She shook off the thought.

"Well, Chingachgook must be wondering where I am," he said awkwardly.

"Yes." She took a step back, then asked, "Where will you go from here?"

He shrugged. "Fort Frederick in the morning. After that, it's back to the forest, I suppose."

"And you're certain you'll be all right tonight?"

"We'll be fine," he assured her.

"Then good night. And thank you, Hawkeye."

"It was nothing."

"No, it was something very special that you did for me . . . and for Pieter. Even for my father. He'll come to his senses as soon as he's feeling better, and he'll be sorry for not thanking you himself."

"Good-bye, Astra."

"If you're ever back in Albany, you must promise to visit me."

"I will."

She turned to leave, then looked back at him. "If you see Major Trevlayne at the fort, will you thank him for me as well?"

He nodded.

She stood there for a long moment, as if afraid to let him go. Finally she muttered, "I . . . I wish . . ."

"What is it?"

She started to speak again, hesitated, then suddenly

walked back to him, leaned close, and kissed his cheek. As he stood there looking both sheepish and stunned, she ran back to the house. He watched the lamplight dim and finally flicker out as she passed through the entryway and shut the door behind her. Shaking his head in wonder, he turned toward the river . . . and almost barreled into Chingachgook, who stood there with his legs spread apart, his rifle cradled in his arms. There was no hint of a smile on his face, but Hawkeye could see it nonetheless in his heart.

The sagamore nodded toward the house and said a single word: *"Muhheconnuk."*

Hawkeye looked at him suspiciously, then realized Chingachgook had not been referring to the Mohican people or the Hudson River when he had spoken the word meaning "great waters constantly in motion, either flowing or ebbing."

"Let's go," the scout said with a frown as he shouldered Killdeer.

"Are you sure you would rather not be sleeping between sheets tonight?" Chingachgook asked in Mohican.

"Her brother," Hawkeye replied a bit testily. "She said I remind her of her brother."

"Oh, yes—her brother with eyes like robin's eggs and hair as pale as straw, and yours as brown as mud." He chuckled. "If you are her brother, Hawkeye, then perhaps I am her father."

"Let's go." Hawkeye pushed brusquely past him and headed down the drive.

"Muhheconnuk," the sagamore repeated, shaking his head solemnly as he fell into step beside his friend.

Chapter XII

Six Delaware girls . . . strewed sweet-scented herbs and forest flowers on a litter of fragrant plants, that, under a pall of Indian robes, supported all that now remained of the ardent, high-souled, and generous Cora. Her form was concealed in many wrappers of the same simple manufacture, and her face was shut forever from the gaze of men. . . .

. . . Seated, as in life, with his form and limbs arranged in grave and decent composure, Uncas appeared, arrayed in the most gorgeous ornaments that the wealth of the tribe could furnish. Rich plumes nodded above his head; wampum, gorgets, bracelets, and medals, adorned his person in profusion.

—*The Last of the Mohicans*, Chap. XXXIII

Astra removed her cloak and draped it over the foot of the bed. She was just unfastening the bodice of her dress when she heard someone entering the room, and she turned to ask Clarice to help her with the hooks at back. But it wasn't her lady's maid standing in the doorway but her father, still dressed in his banyan and with an oil lamp in his hand. He frowned at her, then strode into the room and placed the lamp on the dressing table near where his daughter was standing. When he looked back up at her, she saw the sweat beaded on his brow.

"You really should be resting." She kept her tone low and even.

"*Ja, mijn dochter.* And you?"

There was a harsh edge to his voice that frightened her, but she forced herself to remain calm as he walked to the bed and lifted the hem of her cloak, then let it slip back through his fingers.

"And you?" he repeated. "Where have you been off to, after I told you to stay inside?"

"I just went out for a moment to—"

"I know where you've been!" he brayed, spinning around and shaking his fist. "I saw you!"

"I was only saying good-bye."

"I already said all the good-byes necessary."

"They were my guests, and—"

"They're a couple of fortune hunters, no doubt. And you—*mijn dochter!*—had the effrontery to invite them into our house! Then when I run them off, you slip out for a final assignation!"

"Father! How unspeakably cruel! I did nothing but—"

"You're just like your mother! When I found her, she was nothing more than a well-paid whore, and she died no better! Now you!"

Stunned, Astra just stood there, her eyes welling with tears. She had never heard Hendrik speak so crudely about her mother, nor had she seen such violence in his eyes. When he raised his fist again and took a step toward her, she held up her hands and backed across the room.

"Are you afraid?" he railed, a smirk touching his lips. "You ought to be. I'll be damned if you'll turn your back on the likes of Ernestus Ten Eyck just so you can present me with the get of some thickheaded woodcock."

"You're crazy," she muttered, shaking her head in disbelief.

"Crazy? I'll show you crazy!" He stormed over to where she was standing and grabbed her arm, twisting it viciously. When she tried to put up her other hand to defend herself, he slapped her hard across the cheek. She cried out in pain, her body stiffening, and he smacked her again. She went limp, and he hauled her across the room and threw her onto the bed.

"Just like your mother!" he raved as he loomed over her, his broad face mottled red, his hands balled into fists.

"Only she learned to submit—something you've yet to master."

A voice cried out, "*Mijnheer!* No!" and he spun around to see Clarice in the doorway.

The young woman rushed toward the bed, but he intercepted her, grabbing her by the shoulders and shaking her brutally. She started to scream, growing more hysterical as he shook her. He threw her backward onto the floor, cursing as she lay whimpering at his feet.

Astra clutched her stinging cheek and forced herself not to cry as she struggled to sit up on the bed. "Get out of here," she seethed, staring up at her father with hatred. Hendrik seemed on the verge of striking her again, but she did not flinch as she rose to her feet and gestured toward the door. "Get out!"

He glowered at her for a long moment, then hissed almost beneath his breath, "Don't ever disobey me again." Glancing down at the sobbing woman on the floor, he shook his head in disgust and walked around her, disappearing down the hall.

Astra was immediately at Clarice's side, embracing her and whispering that everything would be all right.

Marthe Cryn clutched a candlestick and raised the hem of her cream silk nightgown as she descended the stairs of her modest Dutch home near the foot of Albany's Jonckers Street. "I'm coming!" she called as the pounding on the door grew louder.

She reached the first floor and saw Helga enter the foyer from the rear of the house, where the maid's room was located. Waving her away, she hurried over to the front door and threw the bolt lock, then jerked the door open a crack. Peering outside, she saw a dark figure standing on the porch.

"It's me!" the man blurted as he pushed the door open wide and strode inside.

"Good heavens, Hendrik, whatever are you doing here?" she asked, shutting the door behind him.

"He isn't home, is he?" Hendrik Van Rensselaer barked, looking around the foyer before turning to Marthe.

"Reinold?" She shook her head.

"Good."

"You look a fright." She helped him out of the coat that covered his banyan, then took his arm and led him into the small front parlor. "When did you return from New York?"

"Why weren't you at the Ten Eycks' tonight?" he demanded, dropping onto the sofa and pulling her beside him.

"Is that what you woke me up to ask?" she said, incredulous.

"Just tell me."

"If you must know, I was feeling tired. And I didn't expect you back until next week."

"There isn't anyone here, is there?" His eyes raised suspiciously toward the second floor.

"Hendrik Van Rensselaer! Is that why you came here? You think I've taken a lover?"

"Another lover," he corrected her.

"If you don't trust me, then march right upstairs and see for yourself! And when you've finished making a fool of yourself, you can take yourself home and not bother coming back anymore."

"I trust you. It's just . . ."

"What is it?" she asked, her tone softening. "What's wrong?"

"I . . . I had a fight with Astra."

"At the Ten Eycks'?"

"No, at home afterward."

"What about?"

He shrugged. "I'm not sure I know." He leaned forward slightly and held a hand to his forehead.

She reached up and touched his cheek to comfort him, then pulled her hand back in surprise. "Hendrik, you're burning up!"

"I'm all right," he insisted, pushing her hand away when she tried to feel his forehead.

"You're not all right. How long have you been ill?"

"I told you, I'm not," he snapped. He stood and walked away from her. "It's just indigestion, is all."

"Is that what you were fighting about?"

"Fighting?" He looked at her in confusion.

"You and Astra. You said you had a fight."

"Oh, yes. Astra . . ." He shook his head and started to pace back and forth in front of her. "She's being so willful. So obstinate."

"This is about Ernestus, isn't it?"

"I had such hopes. And then, outside in the lamplight, I saw her kiss him."

"But that's wonderful!"

"Not Ernestus. Another fellow. A common army scout she found up at Fort Edward."

"She's just a bit rebellious. I'm sure in time she'll come to her senses and—"

"No!" he blurted, shaking his head more in frustration than anger. He came to a halt in front of the sofa and stood staring at his hands, squeezing them into fists and then opening them back up again. "That's not the problem."

"Then what is? You're not making sense."

"It's me. I . . . I struck her."

"Astra?" she said in surprise.

He just lowered his head, his chest heaving with emotion.

"My God . . . is she all right?"

"I've never hit her before," he muttered, dropping to his knees in front of Marthe. "Never." He looked up at her, his eyes begging for her understanding and forgiveness.

"You haven't told her yet, have you?" she said, knowing the answer without a reply. "You have to tell her. She will understand."

His eyes welled with tears, and he dropped his head onto her lap and began to sob.

"I forgive you," she whispered. "But you must tell her what's wrong." She smoothed back his matted hair. Bending over him, she wrapped her arms around his back and ever so softly hummed an old Dutch lullaby.

Major Horace Trevlayne rose from the bed and walked over to where he had tossed his clothes. As he pulled his shirt over his head and fastened the collar with his cravat, a pair of arms slipped around his waist, and a woman pressed her naked body against his back.

"Must you go so soon?"

He had been pleased by the hunger of her lovemaking and was not surprised that she would want him again. He did not try to mask his smug grin as he turned in her arms and admired her full, inviting figure. But when he gazed into Christina Gerritsen's eyes, he saw something he had not expected, and it made him cringe inwardly.

"I—I must get back to the fort before I'm missed. The Ten Eycks' party ended hours ago."

"When will I see you again?"

"I'm not sure when I'll return to Albany," he replied quite truthfully, though he would have said the same thing even had he known.

"You'll write, though." It was as much a plea as a statement.

"Where I'm going, there won't be the means of posting a letter." Seeing her disheartened expression, he lightly pressed her chin. "Don't frown, *mijn mevrouw*. I'll be back soon enough."

"Don't go," she cajoled. "Not yet. I . . . I don't want to be alone."

Her hands moved down his chest and eased under his shirt. He felt her fingers take hold of him, firmly, urgently, her eyes pleading for him to possess her. He knew that she wanted more from him than just his body; he knew also that she would settle for whatever he gave. Lifting her off the floor, he carried her back across the room.

"You love me, don't you?" she whispered as he lowered her onto the bed. "I love—"

He stilled her voice with his lips.

Along the banks of the Hudson, Hawkeye pulled his blanket up over him and lay back against the ground, gazing at the stars winking through the pine branches overhead. In the distance an owl hooted, and farther off he heard the howl of a dog. He knew that in the houses of Albany and in the lodges and longhouses of the Leni-Lenape and the Huron and the Iroquois, men were lying beside their women, some sleeping, some talking, others taking pleasure in each other.

He had known women in his life, yet they were truly a mystery to him. He was not above spending the night with a willing maiden—white or red—but he shrank at the thought of a woman joining him on his path. That would mean children and an end to wandering, and he did not know if he would ever be able to settle down to such a life. It was better, he thought, to continue walking this path he had chosen. Though its pains and pleasures might seem more narrow, they were familiar and would never abandon or disappoint him. No, he told himself, he would remain a man apart.

Hawkeye was shaken from his reverie by Chingachgook, who said in Mohican from his bedroll several feet away, "It was good when the lodges were filled with children and the deer ran like fish spawning in the streams."

"You are thinking of the former times among your people?" Hawkeye asked.

"Ever since we sent Uncas on his final journey, my thoughts return often to the days before we were visited by white man's wars and diseases."

"It may not be over for your people. If we came upon one brave, perhaps there are others to be found."

"With my own hands I almost killed what may be the last of the children of Unamis, and now I may never find him again," the sagamore grunted in reply.

"You must not think so darkly."

"And you must not bind your future to that of an old Muhheconnuk warrior. It is time for you to take a woman and make children so that your line will not end, as mine has done."

"What woman would have me? A woman of my father's race would not understand my ways. And a red woman would see them all too clearly and would not want such a man."

"Many are the women who have wanted you, my son." He used a Mohican word that indicated he considered Hawkeye as much a son to him as Uncas had been. "The maidens do not call you Long Rifle because they admire that gun you sling across your back." He chuckled at his joke.

"And you, Chingachgook, would make many a Leni-Lenape woman swoon. Doesn't your name mean Big Serpent? And what serpent do you think they mean? No, you are not yet too old to take a wife and bring new Muhheconnuks into this world."

"Those days are done for me. I am content to live out my years as the Great Spirit chooses. But you are at the beginning of life's journey, when a warrior must take a wife and raise a family."

"Why are you saying this tonight? Is it because of that woman back there? She thinks of me as a brother, not a husband."

"She is a white woman. She does not understand her own heart."

"And you do?"

"Like you, I am a hunter and a warrior. I know it is the animal who does not see the trap that ends up in its jaws."

"And which one of us is the prey? Her or me?"

"Let us go to sleep," Chingachgook replied. "You will need your rest if you are to have enough strength to chew off your own foot."

Astra's legs jerked, and she gripped her bed pillow as if it were a great branch on which she was clinging. She did not know how she had fallen into the river, but the current was too strong for her, and she cried out as it threatened to drag her under. The hard, twisted wood responded, embracing and pulling her from the churning waters.

She was standing beside the Hudson, and a young brave was holding her hands. As he released them and took a step back, he intoned a single word: *"Muhheconnuk."* She narrowed her eyes, tried to see him more clearly in the swirling fog. He had the same features as the sagamore named Chingachgook but was younger and taller, and his chest was emblazoned with a striking blue turtle. She remembered Hawkeye speaking about another Mohican—Uncas, he had called him—and she whispered the name as she moved toward him. He lowered his gaze, turned, and disappeared into the mist.

"Hawkeye!" she cried out, alone and frightened, suddenly so very cold.

"Slut!" a voice shouted, and she turned to see her father striding toward her along a cliff at the very edge of the river, a wailing baby in his arms. He shouted the word again, not at her but at the child, as he held it high above his head, out over the rocky precipice.

"Don't!" she shrieked, running toward him. But she did not seem to get any closer and could only watch in horror as he flung the infant off the cliff, dashing it upon the rocks at the very edge of the river.

"Slut!" he raged again, raising his fists as she ran into his arms. He locked her in his grip, shaking her, cursing and blessing her. And then his lips were upon hers, and she pulled back with a start. But it was not her father, and she broke away from him, shaking her head in disbelief, stammering his name: "P-Pieter!"

Her brother's features tightened with pain, with some indescribable fear, and he held a hand toward her, his eyes begging her forgiveness. She reached out to him, and as he drew her back into his arms, she was overcome by the heady smell of leather and musk. She looked up into his pale blue eyes—those eyes so very dark and intense—and she reached up and stroked Hawkeye's long brown hair. She knew that she was safe in his arms, and she wanted him to kiss her again. She arched her neck, her lips parting, yearning to feel the touch of his mouth, the power of his hands and loins.

"Astra . . ." he said in a hush, but when she opened her eyes, it was not the scout but the major who held her in his embrace. His grip was so sure, so knowing, and she was frightened by his strength. She felt him pressing down upon her, his passion hungry, overcoming her resistance, devouring her, filling her with the most exquisite pleasure and pain.

"No!" she gasped, breaking free of him, stumbling backward, teetering at the very edge, tumbling over the precipice. She was hurtling through the air, arms and legs flailing, soundlessly screaming, waiting for the touch of cold stone that would be her final embrace.

Slowly her body relaxed as she floated through the mist. She felt the firm press of earth against the soles of her bare feet, and then the world settled into form around her. She was in a forest—brilliant green and suffused with a faint shimmering light. She looked down and saw that she was naked, yet she was not embarrassed, even when she heard a voice call her name and turned to see a man and woman beckoning her. It was the young brave with the sign of the turtle, dressed in a loincloth and bedecked with wampum and bracelets, a beaded gorget around his neck and a headdress of rich plumes nodding above his head. The woman at his side was not Indian but darkly featured, with flowers and tendrils adorning her simple native dress and the long tresses that fell across her shoulders.

Like Astra, both were barefoot, and they walked hand in hand along a narrow trail among the trees, drawing her deeper into the forest. She followed unafraid, somehow knowing that they meant her no harm and would not lead her into danger. Presently they came to an open meadow, and in the meadow was a small Indian village, with tipis, lodges, and even a few longhouses. She did not attract any attention as she passed among the people, which surprised her, since she was not wearing any clothing. But then she glanced down and saw that she now wore an outfit similar to the woman's, and her long red hair was braided with daisies.

They led her to a lodge at the center of the village and gestured for her to enter, pulling aside the skin that served as a door. She stepped through and saw a circle of men and women seated around a central fire. Her two guides entered behind her and took their place among the circle, motioning for her to join them.

As she approached she looked from face to face. At first they appeared unfamiliar, but on closer inspection she realized that she recognized first one and then another. They did not look exactly as she remembered them, but she knew that one was her friend Rebekka Brower's husband and another was her own brother, Pieter. A particularly attractive woman looked up at her and smiled, and in the woman's eyes Astra saw the reflection of her mother. There were others she knew as well, all having passed on from their life upon the earth, all looking familiar yet somehow different than they had in life.

Have I died? she thought, and without words they told her, smiling, that she had not.

She wanted to ask where she was and why she had come, but before she could fashion the words, Jakob Brower stood and held forth his hands. She moved closer and saw that he was holding an infant child. *Tell her we are well,* she heard him say, though his lips never moved. *Tell her not to be afraid. . . . Ease her journey home.*

She looked down at the infant, then back up at Jakob, who smiled and closed his eyes. She felt momentarily dizzy, and when she regained her senses, he was gone, along with the child. The only ones left were her brother and mother and the two guides. Her brother was seated on the far side of the fire, and he rose and walked toward her, his lips fashioning the words *thank you* as he stepped into the fire, filled with light, and receded into the flames.

"Mother!" she called, searching desperately for the woman she had never seen before yet had recognized instantly. Margaretha was no longer seated at the fire, but her voice was near, as if sounding within her.

"Mother! What shall I do?" Astra beseeched her.

Follow your path, the voice intoned.

"But what about Father? He'll—"

Follow your path.

She looked around frantically but saw no one—not even the lodge . . . only the dancing flames of the central fire. In it were the images of the man and woman who had brought her there. She reached a hand toward them, and they smiled and shook their heads, as if to say that it was not yet her time. The woman raised her hand in greeting and said, *There is another guide who will take you west. He will lead you to your destiny.*

The images faded until there was only the light, and then it, too, dissipated and finally winked out. Astra was left standing alone in the darkness, naked, shivering with the cold and with fright.

Chapter XIII

"As I am journeying thitherward myself; I concluded good company would seem consistent to
the wishes of both parties. . . .

". . . I have therefore decided to join company, in order that the ride may be made agreeable, and partake of social communion."
—*The Last of the Mohicans*, Chap. II

*H*awkeye left Chingachgook waiting outside the
grounds of Fort Frederick while he went in to make his
report to the Earl of Loudon. As he approached the headquarters he was intercepted by Major Horace Trevlayne,
who hurried across the parade ground from one of the
buildings that served as an officers' barracks.

"Hawkeye!" he called, waving to the scout as he approached. "You've come to see the Earl of Loudon?"

"Yes." Hawkeye lowered the butt of his rifle to the
ground and leaned upon the barrel.

"Have you met the earl?" When Hawkeye indicated
he had not, Trevlayne glanced around to make sure he
would not be overheard, then confided, "Lord Loudon is
an irascible Scot with a hot temper. He's both lazy and
inefficient, always in a hurry but never ready. On top of all
that, he's a fool, which explains why he's our commander
in chief. When he heard about what happened at Fort William Henry, he swore to strike back at Fort Carillon before
the snows set in, but now he's backed down completely.
Would rather winter in front of a warm fireplace."

"Webb's no better—nor the French generals. From
what I've seen, they're all fools."

"I suppose so," Trevlayne agreed. "But Loudon's *our* fool, and we've got to make the best of it."

Hawkeye nodded, then picked up Killdeer. "I'd best be going in. I'd like to get this finished as quickly as possible and be on my way."

"Where are you headed?"

Choosing not to mention his plans to go to Canada, he shrugged and said, "Things will quiet down until spring. Chingachgook and I will likely take to winter quarters."

"Might you be interested in a bit of adventure?"

Hawkeye's brow arched with suspicion. "What kind?"

"Let's go inside. The earl is expecting us."

"Us?"

The major grinned. "He asked me to be present. Come along—I'll tell you all about it inside." He ushered Hawkeye ahead of him, and the two men mounted the steps and entered the building.

The Earl of Loudon was a tall, round-faced man with large brown eyes, an equally large nose, and a white powdered wig with curls that fell just below his ears. He was wearing a red jacket faced with white, a red waistcoat, and a dark green tartan kilt with matching knee-length socks and buckled shoes—the uniform of the Highland Regiment. Looking up from his paperwork as the two men entered his office, he motioned them to a pair of seats.

"Lord Loudon," Trevlayne began when the earl indicated he should proceed, "this is the scout sent by General Webb."

Loudon raised one eyebrow as he examined Hawkeye, then glanced down at some papers on his desk. "Nathaniel Bumppo?" he said, tapping the papers.

"He's called Hawkeye," Trevlayne quickly said.

Loudon looked back up at the frontiersman and commented without a trace of humor, "How quaint."

"The Indians prefer names that mean something," Hawkeye said, uncomfortable with having another man speak for him.

"We're hardly savages here."

Hawkeye chose not to answer but simply waited while the earl went back to consulting his papers.

"A courier arrived from Fort Edward last night," Loudon continued. "General Webb says you've been up to Carillon and brought back French prisoners."

"Two, from the outpost atop Mount Hope."

"Did you get a look at their defenses?" Loudon asked without enthusiasm.

"There weren't any to speak of. I'd estimate between four and five hundred regulars on hand. The rest of the force has already retired to Montreal."

"Ripe for the picking, I'd say. Too bad our own troops are so decimated by war and disease." The earl shook his head bitterly. "How Shirley let things get into such a state, I'll never comprehend." He referred to General William Shirley, whom he had replaced as commander in chief the previous July.

"Then you won't be moving on Ticonderoga?" Hawkeye asked.

"We'll take Carillon, by damn!" He pounded a fist against the desk. "Come spring, those Frenchies will pay for their deceit at Lake George!" Rising, he walked to the window and stared out to the north.

There was a long, heavy silence, which Major Trevlayne finally broke by suggesting, "Perhaps we should tell Hawkeye about your idea, Lord Loudon."

"Yes, of course." He returned to the desk and stood beside it, his hands resting on the fur sporran that hung at the front of his waist. "We've had troubling reports from the west. The Oneidas may be wavering in their support of the Crown, and if they shift their allegiance to the French, the rest of the Six Nations could follow."

"The Oneidas?" Hawkeye said. "What makes you think that?"

"We know of French visits to their villages near Lake Oneida."

"But the French have sent delegations many times to each of the Six Nations. Why should the Oneidas listen to them now?"

Nodding, Loudon sat back down and tented his fingers in front of him. "What do you know of the Oneida Prophet?"

Hawkeye looked at him with confusion. "Oneida Prophet?"

"You haven't heard of him?" Loudon asked, and the scout shook his head. "Not many have. He sprang up out of nowhere, and he's already attracted quite a few followers. He foretells some sort of apocalypse for the whites and that a new world is coming for the heathens."

"The Mingos are always looking for a savior," Hawkeye said, his voice betraying a hint of disdain. "But what has this prophet to do with the French?"

"We're not sure. But he's preaching that the Iroquois should not take up arms in our defense."

"Does he counsel them to fight against us?"

"Not that we can be sure."

"That's what we must find out," Trevlayne interjected.

Hawkeye looked back and forth between the two men, his eyes narrowing with understanding. "And you want me to go out to Lake Oneida and find out whether this prophet is friend or foe."

Trevlayne leaned toward him. "I'll find that out. We just want you to take me there."

"You?" he said in surprise.

"Major Trevlayne has met with the Iroquois during their visits to Albany and understands our interests with them," Loudon said. "He's most qualified for such a mission."

"Meeting with a delegation of Indians here at Fort Frederick isn't the same as traveling to the frontier to see them on their own ground. The woods between here and Lake Oneida may not be the friendliest."

"But that's Mohawk land, and they're our Iroquois allies," Loudon pointed out.

"It may be Iroquois land," Hawkeye acknowledged, "but there are no signposts in the forest. And with the French riling up the Indians all along the frontier, there's no telling who we might encounter. There are plenty who would consider the scalps of a company of English regulars to be fitting trophies for their medicine shields."

"There will be no company of soldiers," Trevlayne declared. "I plan to make the trip alone—just myself and a guide."

"That would be more sensible," Hawkeye agreed, his expression revealing that he was not used to a military officer who was so astute. "But are you sure you want to make such a journey without a company of rifles to back you?"

"I'll be satisfied with one—your Killdeer." The major gave Hawkeye time to consider the proposal, then asked, "Will you do it? Will you take me to Lake Oneida?"

"I would want a third man to accompany us."

"Chingachgook?" Trevlayne said, nodding to indicate that he had already expected Hawkeye to make the request and was in agreement. "But will a Mohican be willing to travel so deep into Iroquois land?"

"Chingachgook is not afraid of the Mingos. But whether he's willing to make the journey I cannot say. If he is, then I will serve as your guide."

"I'd like to leave at dawn tomorrow."

Hawkeye stood from his seat. "I'll talk it over with Chingachgook and let you know within the hour."

The two soldiers rose and shook Hawkeye's hand. As the scout turned to leave, Trevlayne started to follow, but Loudon signaled for him to remain behind.

The commander in chief walked Hawkeye over to the door, shook his hand again, and thanked him for considering the assignment, then ushered him out and closed the door. Turning back to his junior officer, he asked, "Do you think he'll go for it?"

Trevlayne considered the matter for a moment, then gave a hesitant nod. "He'll do it because he knows that he's the only one who can."

"He's that much a patriot?" Loudon said with disbelief.

"No. But he's that sure of himself."

"What about the Indian?"

"The Mohican will go where his friend goes."

"I hope you're right."

"I'll start packing my things. We should only require one canoe."

"And plenty of ammunition."

"Of course. But it will be stealth that carries us through the land of the Mohawks—which is why I've chosen Hawkeye for this mission. If it comes to fighting, I fear we won't have a chance to make Lake Oneida."

"It's not making the village of the Oneida Prophet

that concerns me but your getting out of there alive." Returning to his desk, he opened the top drawer and removed a sealed letter, which he handed to the major. "This contains the details of your mission. Go ahead, read it."

Trevlayne broke the seal and unfolded the paper. As he read the contents his expression hardened, and at length he drew in a breath and nodded. Closing the document, he handed it back to Loudon.

"Are you still willing to take on this assignment?"

"It's what I'm trained to do."

"Fine." The earl held the letter over the chimney of his desk lamp. It started to smoke, then caught fire. When it was almost fully aflame, he dropped it on the floor and stamped it out with his shoe.

"What about Hawkeye?" Trevlayne asked.

"He's not to know the true nature of your mission."

"He'll find out soon enough. What if he tries to stop me?"

Loudon shrugged off the concern. "Do whatever you want. One military scout is of no great importance to the Crown—nor is his Mohican friend."

Trevlayne's jaw set with determination, and he nodded. "One other thing, though. What if I find out this Oneida Prophet is no threat to us?"

"Your mission remains the same. A religious fanatic can be just as dangerous an ally as a foe."

Trevlayne saluted and headed for the door.

"You're confident you can carry this off?" Loudon called after him.

"Oui, monsieur," Trevlayne said in perfectly accented French, turning and smiling at his commander in chief. "Not only will there be one less messiah to worry about, but the Oncidas will be convinced that a *saboteur français* was responsible for his death."

"I will go with you to the land of the Oneidas," Chingachgook said in Mohican.

"Good," Hawkeye replied, surprised that the sagamore had agreed so quickly. "But are you certain you want to do this?"

"The brave that I saw was with Oneidas from the Canada mission. All the mission Indians will be taking to their lodges until spring; my journey to the north can wait. Perhaps at Lake Oneida I can find out how one of their braves came to bear the sign of Unamis."

Hawkeye walked up to his friend and clapped him on the shoulder. "Once the major is safely back at the fort, I will travel wherever your moccasins lead."

Chingachgook abruptly turned and looked across the compound. Following his gaze, Hawkeye saw a soldier and a woman standing in the shadow of one of the buildings, looking their way. The soldier pointed in their direction, and the woman started toward them. As she stepped from the shadows the light caught the locks of red hair that showed beneath her straw hat, and Hawkeye realized with a start that it was Astra Van Rensselaer.

Seeing that she had been recognized, Astra raised her hand in greeting. But she did not smile as she approached. In fact, she kept her head low, shaded by the brim of her hat. When she came up to them, it was readily apparent why.

"Who did this to you?" Hawkeye demanded, wincing at the sight of the purplish bruises on her cheek.

"It's unimportant," she replied, averting her eyes.

"What kind of father would strike his daughter?" He handed Chingachgook his rifle and started to reach for her, then awkwardly held back.

"It's nothing . . . really." She looked up at him, a faint smile on her lips. "That's not why I came." She reached into the pocket beneath her skirt and produced a small leather pouch. "At Fort Edward I tried to hire your services, and though you turned me down, you proved yourself a better friend than many have been. This time I want you to reconsider my request and serve as my guide." She held forth a pouch of coins.

"We've already been to Ticonderoga."

"It's not there that I wish to go."

"Where, then?"

"A place called German Flats. Have you heard of it?"

"Of course. It's a Palatine settlement west of here on the Mohawk River. Why do you want to go there?"

"That's where my friend Rebekka lives. Her husband

was among the dead at Fort William Henry. I don't think she even knows, and I want to be there when she finds out."

"German Flats is at the edge of the wilderness. Few whites venture that far."

"I visited her last year," she replied, a touch of rebuke in her voice. "And I plan to see her again."

"If you're concerned that she doesn't know about her husband, I can bring her your message. Chingachgook and I leave in the morning on a journey that will take us near German Flats. But there's no reason for you to go."

"I *have* to go. And if you won't take me, I'll find someone who will."

"But that makes no sense. Even if I take you there, how will you get back?"

"I'm not coming back."

He saw the determination in her eyes and just stared at her in disbelief.

"There's nothing for me here in Albany," she went on. "Pieter's gone, and my father . . . he doesn't really need me. It's time I found my own way in the world."

"At German Flats? It's nothing like Albany."

"I can't say that I'll stay in German Flats, but it's a beginning. Rebekka has a baby boy, and I can help her around the place. In time I'll know what I must do."

"It's a hard life on the frontier, Astra. An exceedingly hard life. Not at all suited to a woman of luxury," he added bluntly, gesturing at the finely tailored black silk dress that she wore as a mourning outfit.

"Do you think that's all I am? A woman of luxury? I spent much of my youth on the farms of the Helderbergs."

"That's patroon land and nothing like you'll encounter on the frontier."

"Help me, Hawkeye," she entreated, touching his arm. "I mean to do this, whether or not you will."

He shook his head in frustration. Finally he let his shoulders slump, and he sighed. "We'll be leaving from the fort at dawn. We'll drop you off at German Flats, and on our way back we'll see if you're ready to come home."

Astra leaned forward and impulsively kissed his cheek. "I'll be back before dawn," she promised, her smile warm and genuine.

Regaining his composure, he nodded at her hooped skirt and said, "I'm afraid our canoe won't be wide enough for an outfit such as that."

"Don't worry—I'll be ready to travel." Looking beyond him, she said good-bye to Chingachgook, then headed back across the compound.

Hawkeye turned to his friend, whose expression remained impassive but whose eyes flashed with amusement. "Don't say a word," he warned the Mohican, snatching back his rifle. "Not one word."

Chapter XIV

"Whence comes this discord! Has hell broke loose, that man should utter sounds like these!"
—*The Last of the Mohicans,* Chap. VII

*C*larice jerked upright on her bed. The scream had been so powerful and terrifying, as if a man were being gutted alive. *A dream?* she wondered, listening in the stillness of the dark manor house for any sign that someone else was awake or moving about. Deciding that it had been some sort of horrible nightmare, she shivered and lay back down, pulling the blankets around her.

And then it sounded again—a low bellow at first, then a shuddering roar that seemed to shake the entire building. It was a cry of anger and of terrible pain, and it ended with the wrenching shout, *"Astra! No!"*

Fearful that her mistress had come to harm, Clarice leaped out of bed and snatched her robe from the bedpost, struggling into it as she ran barefoot from her room behind the kitchen. Dawn was just breaking, and in the faint light that spilled through the windows, she saw the large wooden island at the center of the room. Dashing around it, she made for the door, throwing it open and hurrying down the hallway toward the stairs.

A lamp was burning at the front of the house, and as she raced into the foyer she almost ran right into Hendrik Van Rensselaer. He was in the middle of the foyer in his slippers and dressing robe, a sheet of paper in his hand and a look of such rage and desolation on his face that she cringed with fear.

Seeing her in the doorway, he crushed the paper in a

trembling fist, his eyes widening as he hissed, "You bitch! Why didn't you tell me?"

She just stood, frozen with terror.

"Why?" he blared, advancing toward her with the fisted paper raised in front of him.

"I . . . I—"

"Bitch!"

He struck Clarice full on the cheek, knocking her back against the jamb. Her legs gave way beneath her, and she slumped to the floor, whimpering more with fear than pain. As she lay there on her side he threw the crumpled paper at her. She waited for another blow, but instead Hendrik turned on his heels and stormed up the stairs.

The young maid felt her head getting woozy, and she fought not to lose consciousness as she pulled herself to a sitting position. Her numb cheek began to sting now, and she gingerly touched it and felt the bruise rising. Forcing back her tears, she reached for the paper and smoothed it open. In the flickering light of the foyer lamp, she read the message Astra had left for her father:

Mijn vader:

I hoped things would be better if I found Pieter safe and healthy, but such was not to be. Yesterday I watched as he was buried beside Mother, and I am content that he is at peace. Now it is time for me to find my own peace.

No longer can I abide your dark moods and the uncertainty of knowing if or when you will lash out at me again. I am sorry if I have disappointed you, for indeed I disappoint myself. Now I must take measures to change those things about myself of which I do not approve, and I begin by leaving Albany and setting out on my own.

After laying Pieter to rest yesterday morning, I made arrangements to leave Albany, and by the time you find this letter, I will be gone. Do not try to bring me back, for if you do, you will lose me forever. If you do not interfere, I will write in the coming weeks and tell you where I am and how I am doing.

I am sorry that I must hurt you like this—it is not my desire. But I do not love Ernestus Ten Eyck, and I cannot be the person you want me to be. I see your anger and disappointment every time you look at me, and I cannot bear to be the cause of such pain—to you or to myself. Perhaps with me gone, you can find the peace you so desperately need and deserve.

I love you, Father, and hope that in time you will forgive me.

—Astra

In his second-floor room, Hendrik Van Rensselaer sat on his bed, pressing his palms against his temples. The headaches were coming more frequently, just as Dr. Coeymans had predicted. The diagnosis had been cerebral syphilis in the tertiary stage, and no matter how much of the doctor's ointments he dabbed on his sores or little blue mercury pills he ingested, nothing seemed to halt the progression of the disease.

The pain swelled behind his right eye, and his vision fogged over. He waited for it to pass, then pulled himself to his feet and shook his head to clear it. The incessant throbbing made everything so confusing—made it so difficult to think. And now he had to think clearly. He had to drive the pain away.

Hendrik stumbled over to his armonica, which had been placed in the bedroom when it had arrived from the Ten Eycks' house. Dropping heavily onto the bench, he opened the cabinet, placed his feet on the treadles, and watched the glass cylinders moisten with water as they began to spin. Dipping his fingers into a basin at the front, he gingerly touched the tips of his right thumb and middle and little fingers to the C, E, and G cylinders to produce a C-major chord. Shifting his middle finger to the blue cylinder to the left, he turned it into a minor chord, which grew in richness and volume as the spindle increased in speed.

His left hand made a companion chord. His fingers began to tingle, and the feeling climbed his arms and spread across his back. The sensation thrilled him, and he felt the chords pulsing inside his head, overriding and deadening the pain. He had been told that some players found the friction and timbre of the vibrating glass cylinders to be extremely enervating or to cause nervous irritability. But it was precisely these qualities of the armonica that so soothed Hendrik—especially when his illness was flaring up, as it had been doing with increasing strength and frequency. It was true that he was often left debilitated and sick to the stomach after playing, but as long as it cleared his head of such agony, that seemed a minor inconvenience.

Hendrik played a series of slowly shifting chords. As the throbbing in his head grew duller he was able to focus his thoughts more clearly. And what he found himself thinking about was his daughter and the letter she had left for him on the foyer calling tray. She probably hadn't expected him to find it so soon, but his headache had awakened him, and he had donned his robe and gone wandering through the house in the early hours of the morning.

He doubted that she had actually left Albany. After all, where would she go? he asked himself. There were no boats leaving for New York at this hour, and even if that was her intended destination, what would she do once she got there? No, he told himself, she had probably gone to the home of one of her friends in town and would stay away just long enough to upset him.

"Yes," he whispered. "That's what she's done." And he would force that little wench downstairs to tell him where her mistress had gone—even if he had to beat it out of her.

He pressed the spinning cylinders ever more forcefully, causing one of them to squeal and sending a piercing shiver up his spine.

Clarice had just returned to her room when she heard the first chord of the armonica begin to play. At least she knew what Mijnheer Van Rensselaer was doing, and she grew somewhat calmer as she placed her mistress's letter on the dresser and lit a lamp. It was then that she saw the second letter, this one lying on top of the dresser and bearing her name.

She quickly broke the seal and opened it. The message was similar to the first one, except that it revealed that Astra had gone to the German Flats home of her friend Rebekka Brower. She apologized for leaving without saying good-bye and said that she had placed a gift in the top dresser drawer and that she hoped Clarice would use it to begin a new life of her own.

The young woman jerked open the drawer and snatched up a leather pouch that lay on top of her folded undergarments. Loosening the drawstring, she turned it upside down and counted the gold coins that tumbled out. Thrilled, she scooped up everything in the drawer and dumped it onto her bed, then began emptying the other drawers. She did not know precisely where she would go, but it would be far away from Albany.

New York, perhaps, she thought with a smile.

It was when she was stuffing her possessions into a large straw valise that she realized the music had ended. The house was eerily silent once again, and it terrified her. The air closed in around her, and she felt the breath catch in her throat.

Clarice forced herself to turn around, and she gasped. Hendrik Van Rensselaer was standing in the doorway, a leather strap dangling from his fist.

The canoe was of Mohawk design, with a stylized eagle painted on each side of the high-peaked prow. It was almost twice as long as the usual twelve-foot, two-person canoe and had a somewhat flatter bottom for increased stability. Hawkeye would have preferred a faster, round-bottom canoe, but with four occupants and several packs of supplies, safety was the primary consideration, and so he and Chingachgook had chosen this one from the small flotilla maintained by the army at their dock on the Hudson River.

The scout was at the bow, taking long, steady strokes on the right side as they headed up the Hudson toward the inlet of the Mohawk River. He matched the rhythm of Chingachgook's paddle at the stern as the Mohican drew it through the water and gave a slight outward twist at the end of each stroke to keep the vessel heading straight. Between them, Major Horace Trevlayne and Astra Van Rensselaer knelt among the canvas packs, conversing about the conditions they might encounter between Albany and German Flats.

Hawkeye noted that Trevlayne was being particularly solicitous to Astra, which did not surprise him, despite how vociferously Trevlayne had objected upon finding out that she was coming along. When she had showed up at the fort just before dawn and Hawkeye had explained the situation, Trevlayne had taken him aside and argued that such a journey was not suitable for a well-bred woman and that her presence would only slow them down. The major had finally been convinced by Astra herself, who repeated her assertion that she was going to German Flats with or without their aid.

The morning was quite warm and humid, and Hawkeye was pleased that Astra had taken his advice to be practical in her choice of clothing. Gone was the long, hooped mourning gown, and in its place she wore a blue jacket with a fitted bodice over a rather plain skirt of striped holland linen that had been shortened to just above the ankles. To protect herself from the sun, she sported a wide-brimmed straw hat covered in cream silk and tied below her chin with light blue ribbon. The effect was both subdued and captivating.

By contrast, Major Trevlayne was easily visible for miles, all decked out in scarlet and polished brass. Perhaps suitable on the field of battle, Hawkeye thought, where soldiers needed to identify their fellowmen amid the flashing gunfire and smoke. But for slipping through Indian lands undetected, a British uniform was not the preferred outfit. When Hawkeye had pointed this out, Trevlayne had replied that there was plenty of time to don forest green after entering the real wilderness beyond German Flats.

A scarlet peacock, Hawkeye thought, gazing over his shoulder at Trevlayne, who was seated with his back to the bow. Glancing beyond the major, he caught Astra's eye, and when she smiled at him, he quickly turned away.

Hawkeye tried to concentrate on the task at hand. Still, he could not help but overhear the conversation between Astra and the major, and he had to fight the temptation to interrupt.

"The Mohawk contains an annoying series of little rapids and even a waterfall or two," Trevlayne was saying, "so there will be several portages before we reach German Flats."

"Will we have to hike very far?"

"They're easily bypassed by land. But don't be concerned; I'll assist whenever you need a hand."

I'm sure you will, Hawkeye thought and immediately found himself wondering why he would let the man's idle chatter bother him so much.

"Thank you," she replied. "I really don't mind walking, but my shoes may not be the most practical."

"Ah, but they are certainly the most attractive." Trevlayne gave a light chuckle. "If need be, I'll carry you over the most difficult places."

Hawkeye covered his groan by stabbing the paddle into the water harder than necessary.

"I'm quite certain I'll be able to manage, Horace, but thank you."

"Not at all, Astra. . . ."

Hawkeye cringed at hearing her use Trevlayne's Christian name. Even worse was the almost suggestive tone with which the major had said "Astra."

"Do you think we'll have any trouble from the Indians?" she asked.

"I shouldn't think so. This is Mohawk land, and they're allied with us," Trevlayne reassured her.

"Yes, but we hear stories in Albany about Mohawk atrocities."

"Most such reports are grossly exaggerated. The only real trouble comes from the tribes stirred up by the French. On the whole, the Mohawks have proven a trustworthy and peaceable lot. I've dealt with them often enough at Fort Frederick to know how to handle the situation should we run into any."

Unable to bear it any longer, Hawkeye put up his paddle, twisted around, and commented, "You know how the tribe got the name Mohawk, don't you, Major?"

"Mohawk?" he asked, turning toward him. "I can't say that I do."

"To the Algonquins they were the Magkwah, and the Mohicans called them Mquoh—the bear that devours any-

thing that falls into its hands. Before they joined the Iroquois League and took the name Kanyenkehaka—the
People of the Flint—they called themselves Mohawk,
which means Eaters of Live Food, which is their way of
saying 'cannibals.' They used the name long before any
French were here stirring things up." Seeing Astra's
shocked expression, he added, "Sorry, Miss Van Rensselaer, but I wouldn't want you thinking this journey is just a
jaunt down the Hudson. It's true that the Mohawk are our
allies, but all the Mingos are a crafty lot, and they've well
earned their fierce reputation. So I suggest we keep our
eyes open and our arms at the ready, for they might just
consider a lone canoe as too sure a prize to pass up."

"Yes, that would be sensible," Trevlayne agreed, nodding thoughtfully. He turned back to Astra. "I just didn't
want to frighten you needlessly."

"You're most kind," she told him. "Both of you," she
added to Hawkeye.

Chingachgook called out something to Hawkeye in
Mohican, and he nodded and said to the passengers,
"We're approaching the first portage." Facing forward
again, he dipped the paddle into the water and pulled for
shore.

Hendrik Van Rensselaer raised the mug of rum to his
lips and took a deep draft, then smacked it down on the
counter. Leaning back against the counter, he surveyed
the room. The Proost Huis was rather small and dark, the
least reputable of the waterfront drinking establishments
on Albany's Handelaer Street. It wasn't quite noon, and
the place was deserted except for an elderly drunk snoring
on a bench in the corner and a younger dark-haired man
with a straggly brown beard who was nursing a bottle of
whiskey at one of the plank tables near the window. The
fellow, who looked to be in his thirties, occasionally
glanced up at Hendrik but did not pay him much attention.

The only other person in the room was the taverner,
Nicolaas Lendt, and Hendrik turned to him now and said
in a low voice, "Is that the one?" He nodded in the direction of the man at the table.

"*Ja, mijnheer*. Name's Marcus Dent—Irish, I think. Kicked out of the militia, he was. Would you like me to introduce you?"

"No need."

Hendrik tossed a coin onto the counter and motioned for a refill, then picked up the mug and headed across the room.

"Mr. Dent?" he asked, approaching the table. "Marcus Dent?"

The man's dark eyes narrowed. "Who's asking?"

Smiling broadly, Hendrik sat across from him at the table. "I'm Hendrik Van Rensselaer. Perhaps you've heard of me?"

"Van Rensselaer? Who hasn't?"

"Good. Then I'll not waste time on formalities. I've been told that you're a man who knows how to get things done."

"What kind of things?" Dent asked suspiciously.

"I've a job that needs to be taken care of. But it would require more than one man—perhaps half a dozen."

"Ah, you've got rents that need collecting from the tenant farmers?"

Hendrik shook his head. "I leave that to my cousin John."

"I've worked for him before, you know."

"Yes, which is why I've sought you out." Leaning forward, Hendrik lowered his voice. "This is a much more delicate matter, because it involves my daughter. The fool girl's been convinced to run off to German Flats, and I want her brought back."

"Against her will, I take it. And against the wishes of her beau."

"There's no beau, but there are some men who might try to stop you."

"How many?"

"Three. One is a British major by the name of Trevlayne. The other two are a scout and his Indian friend."

"Which scout?"

"He goes by the name Hawkeye."

Dent's eyes widened, and he drew in a breath. "La

Longue Carabine . . . and the Indian would be that Mohican he travels with, right?"

"Yes."

"It would take at least six men, but that's no problem, provided you're willing to pay."

"I'll pay. You just bring my daughter home."

"How long ago did she leave?"

"Just this morning. I've made inquiries, and it seems they left at dawn in a single canoe."

"Good. We can set out this afternoon on horseback and overtake them before they reach German Flats."

"You'll do it, then?" Hendrik asked.

Dent's thin lips drew back in what passed for a smile. "It would be my pleasure, Mr. Van Rensselaer."

"And you won't have any trouble rounding up the men for the job?"

Dent waved off Hendrik's concern. "It won't take but an hour to round them up. They're good lads, all, and've helped me in the past when the farmers were a bit slow with their rents."

"Are you sure you can handle Hawkeye and the others?"

"For the right price, I can handle anyone."

Hendrik watched Dent's eyes closely as he withdrew his purse and laid several gold coins on the table. When he sensed that he had offered enough, he pushed the money across to him. "Are you still interested?"

"Aye," Dent replied, grinning as he scooped up the coins and stuffed them into his pocket.

"Bring my daughter, Astra, home safely to me and I'll double that purse."

"You'll have her."

"Safe and sound," Hendrik repeated. "If I find out that any of your men have laid a hand on her . . ."

"They won't," he promised. "But what about them others?"

"The officer is of no concern to me. But the scout and his Indian friend . . . I'd sleep a bit better knowing they won't be coming back."

"You'll be sleeping like a baby." Dent's grin widened. "Just like a baby."

Chapter XV

"My nostrils are offended; they scent the blood of a coward."
—*The Last of the Mohicans,* Chap. XXIV

*H*awkeye and Chingachgook chose a spot to spend the night sheltered in a copse of pines near one of the many small rapids that made travel up the Mohawk River so tedious. The canoe was turned upside down to form a shelter for Astra Van Rensselaer, while Hawkeye and Major Trevlayne spread their bedrolls on either side of the canoe. Chingachgook spent the night at some distance from the others, on a low rise from which he could look down upon the river and survey the surrounding area.

The night passed without incident, and just after dawn Chingachgook returned to the campsite and helped the men repack their supplies. Afterward, Astra served a cold breakfast of dried meat, biscuits, and jam, which she laid out on a linen cloth. Then the group boarded the canoe and set off once again on their journey.

At midmorning, as they were rounding a fairly wide bend in the river, they had their first encounter with the Mohawks. Astra was writing in her journal, and she looked up with a start to see four braves in a pair of canoes heading downriver toward Albany.

"Don't worry," Trevlayne whispered as he and the other men checked the charges in the rifles.

She nodded and sank a little lower in the canoe, trying to breathe calmly as she watched the others. Hawkeye handed his paddle back to Trevlayne and gestured for him to keep paddling. He smiled at Astra, but her moment of reassurance faded when she saw him raise Killdeer's barrel and rest it on the gunwale so that the Mohawks would see they were armed.

"Keep a steady stroke," Hawkeye said to Trevlayne, his fingers tightening around Killdeer as the canoes drew closer.

Astra could hear Chingachgook's paddle dipping in and out of the water, and she felt a pang of fear when the sound stopped, though she dared not turn around to see what he was doing. Then he called out something, apparently in the Mohawk tongue, for the approaching braves seemed to understand. They started to backpaddle, bringing their canoes to a halt in the middle of the river and waiting for the larger canoe to draw alongside.

Astra felt their eyes boring in on her, and she noticed that Hawkeye did not ease his grip on Killdeer. There was some more discussion back and forth between Chingachgook and the Mohawks, and then one of the braves gestured toward Astra in what she could only interpret as a threatening manner. All four were armed with short-barreled muskets—not too effective at a distance but deadly in the close quarters of the river—and the braves at the front of the canoes had their guns at the ready, while the steersmen kept theirs across their laps, continuing to work the paddles.

Suddenly the brave at the bow of the nearer canoe started to bring his musket into play, and Hawkeye instantly had Killdeer shouldered and trained on the man. There was a long, heavy silence as the two groups eyed each other, and then the steersman started to laugh and motioned for his partner to put down his gun. Chingachgook spoke to the steersman, who appeared to be the leader of the group, and then Hawkeye said to Trevlayne, "Toss them some tobacco."

The major rummaged through one of the bags and came up with a tied packet, which he held up for the Mohawks to see. The steersman brought his canoe closer, and Trevlayne threw the tobacco to him.

"Thank you, Yengeese," the man said in barely discernible English. Then he shouted something to his men, and they took up their paddles and set off down the river, passing from view around the bend as quickly and silently as they had appeared.

Astra heard her breath escape in a long sigh and realized she had been holding it ever since the Mohawk brave had threatened with his musket. And her hands were shaking, so much so that she had to clutch the fabric of her skirt to steady them.

"Is everyone all right?" Hawkeye asked, turning to look at her.

"Yes . . . f-fine," she stammered, forcing a smile.

"Then let's get away from here." He took the paddle from Trevlayne, and a moment later the canoe was gliding upriver against the current, the bow gently slapping the water.

Three hours later Astra had all but forgotten the encounter with the Mohawks and was beginning to enjoy the ride again when suddenly the early-afternoon quiet was shattered by the explosive pop of gunfire as first one and then several muskets opened fire from the trees lining the right bank of the river. Almost immediately, Trevlayne fell backward onto the floor of the canoe, clutching his left arm and groaning with pain. Astra saw Hawkeye grab his rifle as she dropped below the edge of the gunwale and crawled around the bags to where the major was lying, his arm soaked in blood. Following his directions, she quickly set about improvising a tourniquet from a strip of cloth she tore from the hem of her petticoat.

A few feet away Hawkeye brought Killdeer into play, ducking low as he aimed at a point in the trees where he had seen the flare of a muzzle flash. He squeezed the trigger, and the loud recoil set the canoe rocking. There was a scream in the distance, and Astra glanced over the gunwale to see a body come tumbling through the underbrush. To her amazement, it was not an Indian but a white.

"Rest easy," she urged the major, who was trying to pull himself up.

"My gun—" he gasped, motioning toward where it was lying.

Just then Hawkeye snatched up the major's rifle and fired at the ambushers while Chingachgook got off his first round. There was sporadic return fire as the two men ducked down and reloaded, with two shots piercing the bark sides of the canoe only inches from where Astra was kneeling.

Chingachgook called out to Hawkeye, then tossed him his rifle. The scout used all three guns to provide cover, firing smoothly and efficiently, while Chingachgook took up the paddle and brought the canoe across the river to a small island.

The gunfire ceased as they slipped around the sheltered side of the island. Hawkeye quickly jumped from the canoe, Killdeer in his right hand and Trevlayne's rifle in his left. He was joined by Chingachgook, and they took up positions among some scrub brush near the water's edge.

"There!" Hawkeye blurted, waggling the barrel of his gun toward a group of trees across the river. Several men could be seen scurrying about, moving upriver so as to position themselves directly across from the island. It was a long shot for most weapons, but Killdeer had an effective range almost double the usual rifle. Raising the rear sight, he picked out a man in a red shirt, carefully following him as he darted through the underbrush. When the man paused to load his gun, Hawkeye squeezed the trigger, catching the man in the belly and knocking him off his feet.

Hawkeye quickly reloaded, but already the attackers were in retreat. He sent another shot after them and a moment later heard the sound of hooves as horses plunged through the brush.

Chingachgook grasped his arm, pulling him away from the water's edge, and the two men ran back to where the canoe had been beached on the far side of the island. Trevlayne had already been helped ashore by Astra, who had removed his jacket and shirt and was dabbing at the wound with a wet cloth.

"I'm all right," the major said as they came over.

"I think it passed through," Astra told Hawkeye, pulling the cloth away so he could examine the wound.

"Yes," he agreed, poking gently. "A nasty gash, but not too deep."

He spoke to Chingachgook, who was already preparing a poultice, then turned back to the others. "The Mohicans can heal wounds that would be fatal in the hands of a military surgeon. Just do as he says." He started toward the canoe.

"Where are you going?" Astra called after him.

"To find out what kind of sneaking cowards could throw so much ammunition at us yet only once strike their mark."

Placing his rifle in the bottom of the canoe, he pushed it out into the river and leaped on board.

When Hawkeye returned to the island, he gathered the group together, smoothed out a patch of ground, and used a stick to draw a sketch of what he had found.

"This is the river, and here's our island. Over here, about a hundred yards from the riverbank, is a wagon road that leads all the way back to Albany. There were six men on horseback, and now there are four, with the two extra horses in tow. The two we shot were left where they lay—here and here." He drew a pair of Xs to indicate where he had found the bodies.

"Are you sure that four remain?" Trevlayne asked.

Hawkeye nodded. "There were six horses, and I found boot prints of six men where they dismounted downriver, and four sets up here where they got away. One of them's wounded, though—I'd say in the arm."

"How ever could you tell?" inquired Astra.

"He was able to walk by himself, and the bloodstains were generally a few inches to the side of his left boot prints. If it was his body, the blood would have run along his leg. My guess is he was carrying his musket in his right arm, and his wounded one was left hanging."

"Where did they go?" Chingachgook asked in English.

"They didn't make any effort to cover their trail. They took to the wagon road and headed west." He extended the line of the wagon road he had drawn in the dirt and stabbed the stick into the ground at a point to the west.

"But that's where we're headed," Astra pointed out.

"Which is why we should reconsider what we're doing." He turned to Trevlayne. "They're likely lying in ambush up ahead. I don't take to the notion of putting Miss

Van Rensselaer in any additional danger, and you should give that arm some time to heal."

"My arm will be fine."

"And I don't intend to let a few highwaymen send me scurrying back to Albany," Astra insisted. "They're probably long gone by now."

"They weren't highwaymen. They came hunting us, and I doubt they'll give up so easily."

"How do you know they were after us?" Trevlayne asked.

"That fellow over there"—Hawkeye gestured toward the spot across the river where the second ambusher was shot—"lived long enough to admit that someone hired them to kill us."

"Who?"

Hawkeye shrugged. "Died before he could say, though I think he would have. He didn't seem too pleased to be left by his mates, lying there gut-shot."

"Did he say anything else?" Astra asked.

"Just the word *dent*. Does it mean anything to you?"

She thought a moment, then slowly shook her head. "Perhaps it's a name."

"Could be," he agreed. "Ever hear of anyone called that?" he asked the major. "Perhaps someone who doesn't want to see you reach the Oneidas?"

"Dent . . . Can't say that I have."

"Well, whoever he is, he wants us dead. And I don't intend to give him that pleasure."

"By heading back to Albany?" Trevlayne plucked the stick from the ground and scratched away Hawkeye's sketch. "I've got my orders, and they don't include turning tail at the first sign of trouble."

"Normally I'd agree, but with your arm shot up and a woman in tow . . ."

Chingachgook came over to Hawkeye and knelt beside him, whispering in Mohican. Hawkeye frowned but finally nodded in agreement and said to the others, "My friend has an idea we could try, if you're game."

"What is it?" Trevlayne asked.

"Miss Van Rensselaer," Hawkeye said, turning to her, "have you ever paddled a canoe?"

*   *   *

A half hour later they were moving up the river again, this time with Hawkeye as the steersman and Trevlayne at the bow, his left arm in a sling and his right balancing a rifle against the gunwale. Seated near the center amid a pile of bags that would serve as a shield should they encounter more gunplay, Astra was paddling as hard as she was able.

Chingachgook watched them for a moment from the shelter of the trees near where the ambusher had been gut-shot. He checked the charge in Major Trevlayne's military pistol and stuffed it behind his belt. Gripping his rifle firmly in both hands, he took off at a run to the nearby wagon road that paralleled the river. Turning left, he set a steady pace, following the hoofprints of the riders.

As he ran he continually checked the tracks for signs that the horses were slowing their pace. The trail was fairly easy to follow, since the riders were not suspecting trouble from land and had made no effort to obscure their marks. And even though there were other hoofprints and wagon tracks, most of the horses that had passed this way were unshod Indian ponies moving at a walk rather than a gallop. His task was made still easier by the presence of a Narragansett among the ambushers' mounts. A small but hardy breed, the Narragansett had developed a peculiar natural gait, moving its side legs in unison.

Periodically the road topped a rise, and Chingachgook was able to see the river through the trees. Each time, the canoe had fallen a little bit farther behind, allowing him to catch a moment's breath before continuing his run. He had gone more than two miles before he saw signs that the riders were reining in their mounts. He quickly darted into the trees beside the road, moving more cautiously as he listened for his quarry.

Hearing the splash of a horse entering the water, he slipped through the trees to the riverbank. He pushed aside the underbrush and glanced to the left, confirming that the canoe was still out of sight around a bend. Then he looked to the right and saw a horse and rider emerging from the water on the far side of the river about two hundred yards upstream. The man quickly dismounted and led the animal into the forest. Returning a minute later, he raised his musket as a signal to his mates on Chingachgook's side of the river, then retreated into the protection of the trees.

The Mohican was pretty sure that only one man had crossed the river, but he would have to get closer to be certain. Just then the canoe emerged from around the bend a hundred yards away. The river was fairly narrow along this stretch, and Hawkeye was steering the canoe near the opposite bank to keep as far as possible from the muskets of the ambushers.

Chingachgook waited until the canoe was halfway to him, and then he gave two sharp cries of a crow, followed after a pause by a third. He saw Hawkeye's back stiffen, and he repeated the cry once more. The scout lifted his paddle from the water and waggled it somewhat in front of him and to the left, indicating the opposite shore ahead. Chingachgook replied affirmatively with a single birdcall and saw Hawkeye immediately steer toward the center of the river. The Mohican then took up his rifle and headed for where the ambushers lay in wait.

Major Trevlayne heard the cry of the crow but paid it no attention as he surveyed the trees along the northern bank of the river, looking for any sign of the ambushers. He held his rifle balanced on the gunwale, steadying it with his good right arm, ready at a moment's notice to pull back the hammer and fire.

He felt the canoe shift direction and realized they were heading back into the center channel of the river. Just then Hawkeye called to him, "Keep a lookout on the left."

"The left?" he said in surprise, twisting around toward the scout.

"That crow you heard was Chingachgook warning that some have crossed to the left bank."

Trevlayne shifted the barrel of the rifle to the left gunwale and pulled the hammer to full cock as he scanned the trees on that bank of the river. He saw no movement, either there or on the north side.

"When they start firing, you leave off paddling and duck among those bags," he heard Hawkeye direct Astra.

As they continued up the river Trevlayne noticed a small finger of land that jutted into the water about a hundred yards ahead and to the right. Realizing it was a good fording place, he carefully scanned the forest directly across from it on the opposite side. He noticed some branches rustling, and he called back just loud enough for Hawkeye to hear, "There's something in the bushes directly across from that spit of land. It's too far for my gun, but perhaps with that hunting rifle of yours . . ."

There was a short pause, and then Hawkeye abruptly announced, "We're heading for shore." He steered the canoe toward the south bank. "No sense in running a gauntlet," he added when Trevlayne looked back at him in confusion. "And it just might draw them out of their holes."

A minute later the canoe nosed up onto the riverbank, and Trevlayne clambered over the side and pulled the prow onto land with his one good arm. He helped Astra climb out, then grabbed his rifle from inside the canoe. He waited until Hawkeye had also disembarked, then led Astra away from the riverbank. As they gained the safety of the trees he looked back, expecting to see the scout right behind them. Instead, Hawkeye had pushed the canoe back out into the current and was leaping on board.

"Damn fool!" Trevlayne yelled, racing back to the water's edge. But Hawkeye was already in the middle of the channel, Killdeer propped against the gunwale as he paddled furiously upstream.

Hawkeye's move indeed drew the attention of the men hiding along the river. The one on the left bank showed himself first, stepping out from his cover and raising his musket to his shoulder. Convinced the distance was too great, Hawkeye let him aim and fire, and there was a tiny splash where the bullet struck the water about twenty yards in front of the canoe. Then he saw a muzzle flash on the opposite bank, followed almost immediately by the percussive pop of the gunshot. It was followed by two more shots a few feet away. All three fell short of their mark and confirmed that the remaining men were on the north bank.

As Hawkeye swiftly drew the paddle through the water, he saw the first man hurriedly reload, raise the musket, and fire again. This time the bullet pierced the prow of the canoe and sank into the bags piled in front of the scout. Dropping the paddle at his feet, he hefted Killdeer, thumbed back the hammer, and sighted on the back of the man, who was dashing for cover. A shot rang out from the opposite side, but Hawkeye ignored it as he calmly squeezed the trigger and fired. The man was just ducking into the bushes when his body stiffened and he fell headlong to the ground.

Hawkeye heard the crack of a rifle and recognized it as Chingachgook's. Snatching up the paddle again, he made for land.

Chingachgook had crawled to within fifty yards of the ambushers when the first shot rang out from across the river. Almost immediately the three men hiding along the riverbank opened fire, and the Mohican was able to pinpoint their locations. As they reloaded he jumped up and sprinted through the trees toward them.

The nearest man must have heard him coming, for suddenly he rose from his hiding place and swung his musket around, searching for the intruder. Chingachgook darted to one side just as the gun fired, and the bullet went wide. Chingachgook quickly raised his rifle and returned fire. The man clutched his chest and staggered backward into the bushes, blood spurting from between his fingers. He stumbled but managed to keep his footing as he tried to draw a pistol from his belt. Chingachgook, however, was already upon him, and in one smooth series of motions he knocked aside the pistol with his rifle barrel, drew his knife, and sank it into the man's belly, twisting it and jerking it free. With a horrified gasp, the man fell to his knees, then went tumbling down a small incline into the water.

The gunfire drew his comrades, who came crashing through the underbrush, muskets at the ready. There was no time to reload, so Chingachgook dropped his rifle and yanked the pistol from his belt, thumbing back the hammer as he spun to his right to face his attackers.

The lead man emerged from a bank of bushes about ten feet away. His eyes locked on the Indian's, and they fired almost simultaneously, Chingachgook's bullet catching him in the leg and throwing his shot high. The Mohican reached for his tomahawk to finish him off, but the man's partner hurtled out of the bushes, firing his musket as he came. Chingachgook staggered as the ball creased his right side. He went down on one knee, clawing at the handle of his 'hawk.

Before Chingachgook could draw his weapon, the gunman barreled into him, spilling him onto his back. The man stood over him and raised the musket, then swung it like a club at the Mohican's head. Throwing up his arm, Chingachgook deflected the blow, taking the brunt of it with his wrist. He felt his hand go numb and managed to roll clear just as the fellow tried to hit him again.

Springing to his feet, Chingachgook tried to draw his tomahawk, but his fingers would not close around the handle. The man came at him, swinging the musket wildly, forcing him to jump from side to side to evade the blows. Suddenly Chingachgook leaped at his adversary, knocking the musket aside with his deadened right hand as he jerked the 'hawk from his belt with his left.

Dropping the musket, the man clawed at the 'hawk and managed to grab hold of it. But the Mohican kneed him in the groin, doubling him over. Then Chingachgook jerked his hand free and brought the 'hawk down in a vicious arc, the edge of the blade sinking several inches into the man's skull. His knees buckled, and he fell dead.

Chingachgook looked around but saw no sign of the fellow he had shot in the leg. Planting his foot on the dead man's back, he yanked upward on the handle of the 'hawk, and it slipped free. He was about to wipe the blade on the man's shirt when he heard the trampling sound of someone coming at a run, and he spun around and raised the 'hawk, almost releasing it before recognizing Hawkeye. The scout glanced at the two bodies, then looked around for the third.

"He was shot," Chingachgook said in his native tongue, clapping a hand against his left leg to indicate where.

His comment was punctuated by the sound of horse's hooves in the distance, and Hawkeye took off at a run toward the wagon road.

The Mohican tried to clench his right hand to get the feeling back in his fingers. The numbness began to change into a painful sting, which extended up his arm and into his chest. He felt strangely dizzy as the pain swelled, burning down the entire length of his side. Dropping to one knee, he remembered the musket shot he had taken. He looked down and saw the jagged rip and the blood soaking through his shirt.

Chapter XVI

"I would I had a thousand men, of brawny limbs and quick eyes, that feared death as little as you! I'd send them jabbering Frenchers back into their den again, afore the week was ended, howling like so many fettered hounds or hungry wolves."
—*The Last of the Mohicans,* Chap. XIV

After tending to his wound, Chingachgook insisted he was fit enough to travel, but Hawkeye decided it was better they rest before moving on. He scouted ahead and chose for their camp a sheltered glen about a mile upstream, then transported the rest of the group and their supplies there. Returning by canoe to the place of the attack, he double-checked the tracks and signs until he was convinced that the remaining wounded ambusher had hightailed it to Albany and was no longer a threat. Finally he gathered the bodies of the dead, stripped them of guns and ammunition, and dumped them unceremoniously in a shallow pit. He covered them over, then loaded their weapons in the canoe and returned to the encampment.

When he arrived at the glen, about a hundred yards south of the river, he found Astra changing Major Trevlayne's bandage. Chingachgook's poultice seemed to be working, and there was no sign of swelling or discoloration around the wound. The Mohican had already made a low fire, and Hawkeye sat beside it and checked the condition of the recovered muskets, cleaning and readying each for future use.

Every now and then he noticed Astra glance over her shoulder at him, her expression troubled and angry. He had an idea what was bothering her, and he considered broaching the subject but remembered the advice Chingachgook had often given him when he was younger: "There is no enemy more vexing than a woman's rage."

It was clear that she wanted to say something but was holding back. It was equally apparent that the major knew precisely what was going on and was enjoying Hawkeye's discomfort. In fact, he seemed intent upon increasing the heat by commenting, "That was quite a play you made back there, Hawkeye. I confess I didn't expect it."

The scout kept his head down as he continued to work on the muskets.

"Yes, it certainly was," Trevlayne went on, scratching his chin.

Suddenly Astra dropped the end of the bandage and whirled around to confront Hawkeye. "What exactly did you think you were doing?" she blurted.

"Me?" He looked sheepishly at Chingachgook as if uncertain which one of them Astra was addressing. The Mohican's expression remained impassive, though Hawkeye could read the delight just below the surface.

"Don't play the innocent with me," Astra chastised. "You know what I'm talking about. What did you think you were doing? Trying to protect me?"

"'Tis a noble pursuit," Trevlayne put in, grinning.

Astra did not share his humor, and she grasped the bandage and gave it a yank.

Wincing, Trevlayne said, "You'd best surrender while you can, Hawkeye."

The scout put down the musket he was working on. "It made no sense to give them varlets three targets to shoot at."

"So you tripled the risk of getting yourself shot? And you think that made sense?"

"But I wasn't shot," Hawkeye replied a bit feebly.

"And what if you had been?" She shook her head in frustration. "A dead hero is of no use to anyone, let alone himself."

"I wasn't trying to be a hero, just—"

"You were being reckless, plain and simple. We had a plan—we all agreed to it—and then you went and changed it without a word to anyone. We might have been able to help, you know."

"You did help. You *are* helping."

"I'm not going to anymore—not if you're intent on treating me like a child. I will not be coddled, Mr. Nathaniel Bumppo."

It was Hawkeye's turn to wince.

"And I will not have Major Trevlayne tricked like that on my account." Again she jerked the bandage.

Trevlayne gave a sharp sigh. "Surrender to the woman, Hawkeye. My arm can't take much more of this."

Realizing that she was hurting him, Astra blushed and quickly loosened the bandage.

"Perhaps the major is correct," Hawkeye said, shrugging in resignation. "I surrender, Miss Van Rensselaer. Please accept my apology."

Her frown softened, and finally she nodded.

"Speaking of plans," Trevlayne said to change the subject, "when might we reach German Flats?"

"Midday tomorrow. We'll stock up on supplies and set off for Lake Oneida the next morning." He turned to Astra. "It will take at least a week, maybe two, to get out there and back. There are about three hundred settlers at German Flats, so you should be in no danger while we're gone."

"Unless you consider the Palatines a danger," Trevlayne commented.

"What do you mean?" she asked as she tied off his bandage.

"Just what I said." He slipped his arm into a sling. "Those Germans are not to be trusted. Is your friend a Palatine?"

"Rebekka? Her father was, but her mother was Dutch."

"And her husband?"

"Jakob? Yes, I think the Browers are German—I never gave it much thought."

"If this Jakob was living at German Flats, you can bet he was a Palatine—and no great lover of the English."

"Then why did he sacrifice his life at Fort William Henry?"

"He was with the militia." Trevlayne made it sound

almost disreputable. "Most of them fight for the Colonies, not the Crown. Wouldn't be surprised if they take up arms against the king one day, given how they feel about us."

"I've nothing to worry about from the Palatines, then. I'm Dutch, not English."

The major smiled. "That's probably why General Webb warned me about you."

"Whatever do you mean?"

He chuckled. "Let's just say that we English are almost as wary of the Dutch as we are of the Germans."

"I assure you, there's no need to be concerned about me."

"I wasn't being serious, Astra. But I was when I warned you about the Palatines at German Flats. It's no secret that the French have been trying to woo them for quite some time now. If they could win over the settlers along the western frontier, along with the Oneidas and maybe even the Mohawks, they might well be able to push us back to New York City."

She turned to Hawkeye. "Is that true?"

"I'm afraid so. But you should have nothing to worry about at the settlement. As you said, you're a Hollander, and Rebekka Brower is a close friend."

"What about you?"

"We've nothing to fear, either. I've been through German Flats numerous times, and though the settlers may not look kindly on the English, they hate the French even more."

"Enough of this troubling talk," Astra said with a slight shudder.

Standing, she scooped up the remnants of the old bandage and tossed them into the fire. She watched for a moment as the flames flared up around the bloody cloth, then walked over to where their supplies were piled. Retrieving her bedroll, she spread it open not far from the fire.

"We're supposed to be getting some rest, and that is precisely what I intend to do. I suggest you gentlemen do the same."

Turning her back on them, she lay down and pulled the blankets up over her.

*　　*　　*

"Jakob!"

Rebekka Brower bolted upright on her bed. The air was cold; the fire had gone out.

"Jakob?" she repeated, hugging herself against the chill. And then she remembered: Her husband had been with the militia at Lake George, and she still had no word as to his fate.

Rebekka slipped out of bed, wrapped her shawl around her shoulders, and padded over to the fireplace. Picking up the poker, she stirred the embers until they were glowing red, then tossed some kindling on top. They crackled to life, and she added several larger pieces. The flames shot up, casting warm light through the room.

Pulling the shawl more tightly around her, she crossed to the dresser and placed her hand atop her prized possession, a silver-and-brass pendulum clock that her husband's family had brought with them from Stuttgart. Leaning close, she could just make out the hands in the thin light. Two fifty-five in the morning—she had been asleep only three hours. Dawn was still several hours away, and she would have a busy day tending the animals and putting up the last of the vegetables. And the roof needed repairing. She had hoped to leave it for Jakob's return, but the nights were getting colder, and when he got home there would be plenty of other things for him to do in preparation for winter. She would take care of the roof and perhaps surprise him by finishing that fence behind the hog pen.

Rebekka removed her shawl and climbed back under the blankets. Thinking how much she missed her husband, she reached over and touched the little bundle that lay where he usually slept.

"Stefan . . ." she cooed, not wanting to wake their son, who had just turned three months old. He looked so much like his father, with strong hands, a full head of dark hair, and an easy smile. He had Rebekka's brown eyes, though—warm, large, and inquisitive. And he was growing so quickly that she doubted Jakob would recognize him when he returned.

Closing her eyes, Rebekka listened to Stefan's shallow, steady breathing as she tried to fall back asleep. She felt herself beginning to drift off when she was awakened by a cry. Rolling toward her son, she muttered, "Shhh

. . . rest easy. . . ." and listened to see if he needed to be nursed. But the sound came again, and she realized it was in the distance and growing louder, like the noise of an approaching mob.

She was on her way to the window just as a brilliant flash lit the predawn sky, followed by an explosion that rumbled through the room. *A gun!* she thought. *No, a cannon!*

Stefan burst into tears, and Rebekka rushed back to the bed and gathered him in her arms. Stroking his head to calm him, she returned to the window and looked out. There was another flash of cannon fire, which came from the direction of the west picket fort, one of three the community had built to provide refuge in case of an Indian attack. But Indians did not have cannons, and neither did the settlers; these had to be French or English.

Placing her crying son back on the bed, she hurriedly donned some clothes and a heavy coat. She got additional blankets, wrapped them around her son, and carried him out into the main room, where an old musket and a powder horn stood propped beside the door. She put Stefan down on a chair and frantically began loading the musket, spilling quite a bit of powder in the process. She was not a very good marksman, so she filled the gun with shot, which would be brutally effective at close range.

Reaching up to the hook beside the door, she snatched the cloth sling that she had improvised for carrying Stefan while working in the garden. Tying it around her neck and waist, she lowered him into it, making sure his hands and feet did not protrude from the blankets. Then she raised the door latch, tucked the musket under her arm, and headed into the night.

From off to the west, the cannons were joined by musket fire and the sounds of people yelling. She also heard sporadic firing to the north, probably near the second picket fort, so she turned to the east and ran through the middle of her vegetable garden toward the remaining fort.

Rebekka had just crossed onto the neighboring farm of Johan Jost Petrie, who served as magistrate of German Flats, when she heard a crackling sound in the direction of their barn. Then a woman screamed, and with a whoosh the barn burst into flames. As they darted higher and illuminated the surrounding fields, she saw that they were swarming with silent, shadowed figures.

With a gasp of terror, she dropped to her knees, clutching Stefan to her and rocking him so that he would stop crying. The light brightened as the Petrie house was put to the torch, and she was able to see that the raiders were converging on the last of the picket forts, which stood just beyond the farm. Realizing she would find no refuge there, she started to turn back to her own house only to see flames dancing across the roof.

"Qui vive?" a voice shouted from the direction of the Petrie homestead. She knew enough French to translate it as "Who goes there?" When she heard a gunshot in reply, she prayed that Johan had killed the murderous Frenchman.

Clutching Stefan and the musket, Rebekka rose from the ground, crouching as she headed south toward the river. There was a line of trees about fifty yards away, and if she made it there unseen, she might find a place to hide along the riverbank until the raid had ended.

She was about halfway to the trees when she stumbled and fell to her knees. She started to rise but heard a movement behind her, like someone running, and she raised the musket and swung it around, praying it was one of the Petries. Instead she found herself confronted by a ghostly demon, his face flashing brilliant white in the firelight. The breath caught in her throat as she saw his scalp lock and the beaded gorget on his chest. This was no demon but an Indian warrior, painted for war.

The brave pulled up short at the sight of the musket barrel trained on him. He held a tomahawk, and he grinned malevolently as he drew it back to throw. Instinctively Rebekka pulled the trigger, and the brave's eyes widened with shock as the pellets shattered the beads on his chest and tore through his neck. He flung the 'hawk but without strength, and it fell harmlessly a few feet away, covered with the blood that was spurting out of him. He landed facedown in the dirt, his body twitching with its last death throes.

Rebekka gagged and forced herself not to look. Leaving the musket where she had dropped it, she wrapped her arms around Stefan and staggered to her feet. She turned toward the trees and ran directly into the arms of another brave. He grabbed her by her hair and forced her to her knees, while a second Indian came rushing up and yanked Stefan from her arms. She pleaded with them, screaming over and over to leave the child alone, as they pulled her back to her feet and started dragging her away. She twisted her head around and caught a glimpse of the brave jerking Stefan's blankets off of him and tossing him to the ground. The last thing she heard as they forced her into the trees was her baby's hysterical screams. They ended abruptly, and the world went silent and black.

Chapter XVII

"Here has the cunning Frenchman been posting a
picket directly in our path," he said; "redskins
and whites; and we shall be as likely to fall into
their midst as to pass them in the fog!"
　　　　　—*The Last of the Mohicans*, Chap. XIV

*T*he first sign that something might be wrong at German Flats was the smell of scorched earth, which reached Hawkeye and his fellow travelers soon after they broke camp and took to the river. From the acridness of the smoke, Chingachgook believed that it was not just wood but also black powder that had burned during the night.

It took several more hours to reach the place of battle. As they rounded a final bend in the river, they paddled cautiously toward a row of blackened pilings that poked out of the water amid the burned-out hulks of canoes and flatboats. This was all that remained of the once impressive dock the community had built along the northern bank of the river. Several warehouses and businesses had stood along the riverbank, but they were nothing more than smoldering piles of rubble.

Hawkeye looked in concern at Astra, whose eyes were wide with shock. Major Trevlayne had already moved close to her in the canoe, so the scout returned to the task at hand, bringing the vessel in among the pilings to an open area along the beach. As soon as the bottom struck ground he climbed out and lifted the prow, pulling it ashore. Telling the others to wait where they were, he hefted Killdeer and sprinted up the embankment.

What greeted him was a scene of total devastation.

Sixty or more buildings had once dotted the surrounding valley, and now they were sixty columns of smoke. Dark mounds littered the fields, and as Hawkeye focused on them he recognized the stiffened carcasses of hogs, cattle, and horses. There were other bodies as well, and he knew that those were the residents of German Flats.

Hawkeye made a quick circuit of the area, examining for signs of what had taken place. When he returned to the dock area, he found Astra and Trevlayne standing on shore and Chingachgook nowhere in sight.

"I think he heard something," Trevlayne explained, gesturing west along the riverbank with his rifle. "He went up that way."

Hawkeye nodded.

"What did you find out?"

The scout looked in concern at Astra, who forced a half smile and said, "I'm all right—really I am."

"It was the French—there's no doubt of that. Several hundred troops, accompanied by Indian war parties—Huron, Abenaki, and some others. They struck in the middle of the night when folks were in their beds. Most who made it outside were still in their nightclothes."

Astra's body went rigid, but she forced calm into her voice as she asked, "Were there any . . . ?"

"Survivors?" Lowering his gaze, he shook his head. "At least not that I found."

Trevlayne tried to put his arm around her, but she pulled away. "I want to see her," she said without emotion.

"Your friend?" Trevlayne's expression was incredulous.

"I want to see her house," Astra went on, turning to Hawkeye. "Please take me there."

"I don't think—"

"You'll take me there. Now."

Chingachgook reappeared from among the trees that lined the river, and Hawkeye walked over to meet him. Returning to where Astra and Trevlayne were waiting, Hawkeye repeated the Mohican's news.

"Chingachgook found the Frenchers' trail. They're on foot, heading to the northwest. It looks like they've taken prisoners."

"What was it he heard before?"

"Just a fox." He chose not to describe what the fox was feasting on.

Astra pointed toward the northeast. "Her house was over there." She started in that direction, and Trevlayne moved as if to stop her, but Hawkeye caught his arm and signaled to let her go.

Keeping close behind, the three men followed her through the ruins of what had been the center of the town and out across the fields. The settlers had lived in close proximity to one another, sharing the grazing land, and it was only a half-mile walk to the Brower farm. Astra finally came to a halt in front of the charred remains of a farmhouse. The stone foundation and chimney were intact but were buried under the twisted, blackened beams of the roof, which had collapsed in upon the structure. The fire had burned unevenly, smothering itself before fully consuming the house.

"Is this it?" Hawkeye asked, coming up beside Astra, who lowered her head and nodded.

Handing his rifle to Trevlayne, Hawkeye waded into the wreckage, avoiding hot spots as he picked through the rubble for any indication of Rebekka Brower's fate. Chingachgook, meanwhile, began a careful search of the surrounding grounds.

Hawkeye came upon the remains of a cradle, but there was no sign of the child or its mother. If they had been inside the house when it was put to the torch, it was not likely they could have gotten out alive. He also found, half-melted, what had once been a beautiful pendulum clock, its hands stopped at precisely thirteen minutes past three. Eventually he gave up his search and returned to where Astra and Trevlayne were standing. Seeing his forlorn expression, Astra broke down in tears.

Hawkeye heard the squawk of a crow and turned to see Chingachgook waving at him from near a line of pine trees at the far end of the field. Taking his rifle, he headed there at a run. When he was about ten yards away, he spied an object on the ground. A few yards closer and he recognized it as an infant. The little boy had been stripped of any clothing or blankets and brutally hacked to death with a tomahawk.

Hawkeye had seen much violence on the frontier, but he had to steady his stomach against the horrible sight. When he looked up at his friend, he saw that the Mohican's eyes glistened with tears.

"I tracked the mother's footprints from the house," Chingachgook said in Mohican. "A Huron came up on her over there." Pointing to a place a few yards away, he handed Hawkeye an arrow he had found. It was fletched in the Huron style. "She must have shot him. Later he was dragged away."

Hawkeye examined the ground and saw the moccasin prints and the bloodstained, matted grass where the brave had fallen and been carted off. He also saw the prints of a woman's shoes and the spot where she had struggled with other Hurons.

"Two braves took her away—to the northeast," Chingachgook continued, then motioned toward the house.

Hawkeye turned and saw that Trevlayne and Astra were approaching.

"I will mark their trail and see what they have done with the woman," Chingachgook said.

As the Mohican hurried off, Hawkeye went to intercept the others.

"What is it?" Astra said in concern as he approached.

"Don't go there," he told her.

"Rebekka?" she gasped, throwing her hand over her mouth.

"No . . . her child."

"Stefan!" she cried out, plunging forward. But Hawkeye grabbed hold of her. "I must! I must see if it's him!"

"He's gone. There's nothing to be done."

"But . . . but maybe it isn't—"

"It's him. The footprints lead right from the house."

Astra began to sob, and Hawkeye pulled her close and sheltered her in his arms. After a while she calmed somewhat and stammered, "Wh-what about Rebekka? Is she . . . is she . . . ?"

"We don't know. Chingachgook is following her trail."

"But who . . . ?"

"Hurons—allied with the French."

"My God!" She buried her face against his chest.

After she calmed down somewhat, Hawkeye led her back to the house, Major Trevlayne following. Making a seat of sorts from some of the rubble, he sat her down, and slowly she regained her composure. Eventually Chingachgook returned and spoke with Hawkeye for a few minutes, then headed back across the field to bury little Stefan's body.

"We've reason to hope your friend is still alive," Hawkeye told Astra, kneeling in front of her.

"Why?" she said numbly.

"She was taken by two braves, who were joined by at least two more. Chingachgook tracked them far enough to determine that they left the area with three prisoners, your friend Rebekka among them."

"But by now she could be—"

"No." He cut her off, standing. "If they were going to kill her, they wouldn't have bothered to take her. It's likely she and the others will be held for ransom or—" he hesitated, then decided it was best to speak plainly "—or as one of the bounties of war."

"She's being dragged off to wherever they're from?"

"The Canadas. Yes, it's possible. We know that they didn't join up with the French."

"How can you be sure?" Trevlayne asked.

"Chingachgook tracked them long enough to confirm they're headed to the northeast, into the heart of the Adirondacks. The French are on their way to the northwest, probably to Fort Frontenac."

"We've got to get her back!" Astra blurted, rising from her seat.

"Which is what I plan to do."

"But how?" Trevlayne asked. "The nearest British forces are at least two days away. And it would be suicide for the four of us to go traipsing off into the Adirondacks."

"I know, which is why I intend to go alone."

"Alone?" Astra said in disbelief.

"That's often the best way to work in the woods."

Trevlayne nodded in agreement. "What about Chingachgook?"

"He'll stay with you. If something should happen to me, he'll see you through to the Oneida village."

"And what about Astra?"

Hawkeye turned to her. "If you want, Chingachgook will first take you back to Albany."

"But my mission," Trevlayne exclaimed. "I'm under orders. I must make Lake Oneida before snowfall."

"And I've no intention of going back to Albany without Rebekka," Astra put in. "I'll wait right here for you."

"I thought as much," Hawkeye said with a hint of a smile. "But with French Indians crawling through Mohawk land, you'll be safer if Chingachgook takes you deeper into Oneida country. He speaks the Oneida tongue and knows their ways; they'll give sanctuary to him and anyone with him."

"She'll come along with us?" the major asked in concern.

"We're certainly not going to leave her here."

"Of course not. But—"

"Then it's decided. You two and Chingachgook will go ahead. I'll go after Rebekka, then follow."

"But we'll have the canoe," Trevlayne pointed out.

"One of those canoes back at the dock must be serviceable. Before you set out, Chingachgook will patch one up and hide it for me."

Astra touched Hawkeye's arm. "Is there really a chance she's still alive?"

"If she is, I'll bring her back."

As Chingachgook finished scraping away the soft earth and burying the little boy, he wondered if he could say anything more to convince Hawkeye not to go alone after the captured woman. He had already argued that it would be better for the two of them to hunt the Hurons while the major and the red-haired woman made camp nearby. After all, the village was completely destroyed, so there was not much likelihood that either the French or their Indian allies would return. It was true that the soldier had been wounded, but he was healing well, and there was no reason he couldn't look after the woman. Hawkeye, however, had insisted that at least one of them remain behind, saying that they had an obligation to protect Astra and to see Trevlayne through to the Oneida village and back.

The woman, Chingachgook thought, smiling ruefully. Undoubtedly Hawkeye was less concerned about her coming to harm at the hands of the French or the Indians than at the major's. Chingachgook had pointed out that Hawkeye could be the one to remain behind but had been forced to admit that his own wound might slow him down enough to allow the Hurons to escape.

After he finished burying the child, the Mohican returned to the dock and started inspecting the half-sunk canoes while the others visited the grave to say a few words over the boy. Picking out a small canoe that was in fairly good condition, he emptied it and carried it to a small copse of trees along the riverbank, where he would hide it after making repairs. A few minutes later they all gathered again at the dock, and Hawkeye checked his ammunition and filled his pack with a two-day supply of food. He also carried a small bedroll, his rifle, and a brace of pistols tucked behind his belt.

"Shall we wait at the Great Carrying Place on the Mohawk River?" Chingachgook asked in English, indicating the point where the river was no longer navigable and they would have to continue by land.

Hawkeye shook his head. "I don't know how long I'll be or what I'll find when I catch up to them. Rebekka Brower could be hurt, and I may have to take her to Albany." He hoisted his pack and clasped his friend's arm. "I'll find you," he promised.

"I will protect the woman for you," Chingachgook said in Mohican.

Hawkeye said good-bye to Astra and the major and set off at a sprint across the fields. He had only gotten about fifty yards when he heard Astra calling to him. Holding up, he waited as she approached.

"There's something I want you to tell her," Astra began. "I . . . I had a dream. It was about her husband. He was holding their little boy, and he wanted me to give her a message." She gazed beyond him, across the fields, her eyes fixed on some distant memory.

He delicately touched her arm. "What is it, Astra?"

"He said . . . 'Tell her we are well. Tell her not to be afraid. Ease her journey home.'" Lowering her head, she began to cry.

Hawkeye hesitated, then stepped closer and took her in his arms.

There was only an hour of sunlight left by the time Chingachgook completed repairs to the canoe and hid it among the trees for Hawkeye to use when he got back. He discussed the situation with Trevlayne, and they agreed it would be best to continue upriver to some less open area before making camp for the night.

A few minutes later they were on board their canoe and had pushed away from the riverbank. As usual, Chingachgook served as steersman, while Trevlayne, despite his injury, paddled at the bow. As they moved against the current, Chingachgook saw the major wince with each pull of the paddle, yet he neither complained nor slackened his pace. Even though there was something about the soldier that the Mohican did not trust, he could not deny that this was a man of courage.

The river grew increasingly narrow, and before long they came upon a small set of rapids. After completing the portage, Chingachgook decided that they should make camp. He hid the canoe among some bushes, then used a leafy branch to remove all trace of their footprints from beside the rapids. Afterward, he led them deeper into the forest to a sheltered cove against a rocky hillside, where they would be protected from wind and intruders.

As dusk settled he returned to the canoe to gather some additional supplies and to erase all sign of their passage to the cove. He chose the necessary items and was just emerging from the bushes when some inner sense made him turn with a start. There, to his right, was an Abenaki warrior with an old trading musket leveled at his chest. He started to bring up his own rifle and expected the man to fire, but instead he heard a rush of air and felt a sharp crack as something smashed against the back of his skull, knocking him senseless to the ground.

*   *   *

"He's been gone a long time," Major Trevlayne commented as he strode across the narrow cove, then paced back again, his rifle crooked under his right arm.

"You saw how painstakingly he wiped away our tracks at the river. He's just being cautious." Astra was seated on a broad, flat boulder, and she patted it and said, "Why not sit down for a bit."

"How do we know he hasn't abandoned us?"

"Chingachgook? He'd never do that."

"Perhaps not with Hawkeye around. But now? There's nothing to keep him here."

"There's his word."

"The word of an Indian?" He shook his head with disdain. "They don't think as we do."

"How do you know?"

"That's my point. You can never know with an Indian." He sat beside her and leaned the rifle against his lap.

"Well, I trust him."

"I hope it's well placed."

There was an awkward silence, which she finally broke by asking, "How's your arm?"

He was no longer using the sling, and he lifted his left hand and clenched it into a fist. "Just a bit sore, is all."

"You should rest it some more. Tomorrow you must let me paddle—at least part of the time."

The hint of a smile played across his lips as he unclenched his fingers and rubbed his palm with his right hand. "There's nothing wrong with this arm that couldn't be healed by the touch of a woman." He turned to her, his eyes glistening in the fading light. "A woman like you, Astra."

"But, Major—"

"*Shhh!*" he suddenly hushed, cocking his head as if he had heard something.

"What is it?"

He raised a hand to silence her. Picking up the rifle, he listened some more, then leaned toward her and whispered, "Someone's coming."

She heard it, too, now. "It's just Chingachgook," she said and started to rise, but he pulled her back down. She was about to object, but he pressed a hand to her lips.

Thumbing back the hammer to full cock, Trevlayne rose from the boulder and took a few steps forward. Trees surrounded the cove, and the light was getting quite thin, so he couldn't see anyone, but as the sound grew louder he became convinced that there were more than one person approaching. He turned, grabbed Astra by the arm, and pulled her deeper into the cove, where they could seek refuge among the larger boulders at the base of the hillside.

They had gone only a few steps when a voice shouted, *"Arrêtez! Arrêtez!"*

Trevlayne swung his rifle around and saw several men in the white uniforms of French grenadiers come rushing into the cove. He trained the barrel on the lead officer, and the man pulled up short, his men following suit.

"Monsieur," he said, continuing in English, "if you do not lower that barrel, my men shall open fire, and the poor mademoiselle shall be dead."

The English major looked back and forth across the line of a half-dozen soldiers, each of whom had his musket trained on the two of them.

"If you are expecting help from the Indian, I am afraid he is *indisposé.*"

There was a rustling sound, and then two Indians dragged the unconscious Mohican into the cove.

"So you see, there is no point in—how do you *Anglais* put it?—ah, yes . . . in resistance."

Trevlayne could feel Astra huddled close behind him. "I'm sorry. . . ." he whispered to her, his shoulders slumping as he lowered the barrel of his rifle.

The French officer shouted a command, and several of his men hurried forward and took charge of their prisoners.

Chapter XVIII

"A Huron!" repeated the sturdy scout, once more shaking his head in open distrust; "they are a thievish race . . . you can never make anything of them but skulks and vagabonds."

—*The Last of the Mohicans,* Chap. IV

*H*awkeye peered through the leaves at the woman lying faceup in the high grass beside the trail. She was motionless, and he knew she was dead even before he pushed aside the curtain of brush and approached. She had light brown hair, like Rebekka Brower. But when he checked her right ankle, he noted that it was swollen, and from the footprints he had been following, it was clear that one of the other captives had a sprained right leg. This woman had been stripped of her clothing, so he could not confirm that her shoes had made those prints, but her foot size was about right. Furthermore, she was quite flat-chested and did not appear to have been nursing a baby.

There were marks on her throat, and the cause of death appeared to be strangulation. Apparently her sprain had gotten worse, and the Hurons had decided not to carry her. And there were signs that she had been assaulted sexually, which greatly troubled Hawkeye. It was quite unusual for a woman—even a captive one—to be raped, and if this woman had been, her abductors might well be under the influence of liquor provided by the French.

Hawkeye examined the woman's flesh and slipped his hand under her arms. The body was still quite warm, and the blood had not yet begun to pool, indicating that she had been killed only recently. Standing and looking down at her, he nodded and allowed himself some grim satisfaction. He had been chasing the war party for almost four hours and had assumed he was at least another four hours behind them, and now he had reason to hope he was much closer. But with dusk at hand, it was unlikely he would catch his prey before daybreak.

Leaving the woman where she lay, Hawkeye stepped back out on the trail and resumed his run. Darkness was closing in, and he knew he must find a place for the night. It promised to be quite mild, so he decided to make camp on high ground, which in the morning might afford a view of the region ahead. Turning from the trail, he climbed a hill and found a rocky bluff that stood above the trees.

He put down his rifle and supplies and was just clearing a place for his bedroll amid the boulders when the harsh cawing of a crow caught his attention. For an instant he thought it was Chingachgook following his trail, but careful listening revealed that it was a real bird and not the Mohican or any other human. But the cry was so pained and eerie that he thought the poor animal must be on the verge of death.

The cawing stopped, replaced by the sound of pecking. In the fading twilight, Hawkeye began a circuit of the bluff, looking for the animal. As he approached a boulder-strewn slope the frenetic squawking returned, and with it the flapping of wings. Easing his way down the slope, he came around one particularly large boulder and saw the large black bird on the ground. It looked up and saw him as well, and it beat its wings to make a hasty retreat. But it rose only an inch or so and then was pulled back down again.

As Hawkeye edged closer he saw that the crow's right claw was wedged among the rocks. Apparently it had landed, perhaps searching for food, and the rocks had shifted, trapping it.

"Easy, now. . . ." he said, cooing gently as he moved toward the bird, trying not to dislodge the stones and perhaps crush the poor thing. He raised his hands ever so slowly and held them out, but the movement served only to frighten the crow further, and it started pecking at its leg.

Realizing the bird had been trying to free itself by

pecking off its own claw, Hawkeye hurriedly untied the leather thongs at his collar and pulled his wool hunting shirt over his head, holding it open between his hands as he moved in on the crow. The bird began to flap frantically, and just when it looked as if it would tear off its own leg, Hawkeye dropped the shirt over it.

The bird became wild with fright, and Hawkeye had to wrap the cloth tightly around it to stop it from flapping. Slowly it grew still, perhaps sensing that it was defeated. He kept whispering to it, urging it to be calm, holding it steady as he wedged his own foot among the rocks and slowly pushed the uphill boulder away.

Suddenly the bird's claw came free, and Hawkeye fell backward among the rocks but managed to hold on to the crow, which was all wrapped up and tucked tightly against his chest. He unpeeled the cloth, until the bird was able to poke its head out. It must have realized that it had been saved from one trap only to land in another, and it cocked its head and looked up at Hawkeye, as if gauging how best to extricate itself from this new predicament.

The scout grinned at the bird. "Don't worry, little fellow. We'll have you on your way in no time."

He opened enough of the shirt to reveal the damaged claw, which looked as if it had been scraped raw but not otherwise hurt. Deciding it was best to let nature take its course, he stood, lowered the animal to the ground, and cautiously pulled the shirt all the way off.

The crow took an awkward hop to test its claw. Looking back up at him, it dipped its head almost as if in gratitude, then spread its wings and lifted from the rocks. It circled twice overhead, cawing contentedly, then flew down off the hillside and into the forest below. There was very little light left, and the black bird quickly passed from sight, but then it reappeared down among the trees as a small glowing orb. For a moment Hawkeye wondered if it had been a real crow or perhaps some kind of spirit bird, until he realized that the light was not the bird transformed but was the glow of a campfire, no more than a mile to the north.

"Thank you," he whispered, scrambling back up the slope to where he had left Killdeer.

* * *

Hawkeye moved silently through the dark forest, drawn by the occasional flicker of light through the trees. It was a brighter fire than caution would dictate, which further reinforced his belief that the Hurons were drinking —if in fact this camp belonged to the party he was hunting.

The forest had grown so black that he had to be careful not to walk into the trees, and on numerous occasions he found his path blocked by heavy underbrush or some other obstacle he had not seen in the darkness. But he made slow, steady progress, covering the mile in just over an hour. As he drew closer he could hear the sounds of laughter and an occasional stray word in a language he didn't understand, but which sounded like Huron. He listened for the women and worried they might already be dead.

Hawkeye covered the last hundred yards on his hands and knees, using the noise of the Hurons to mask his approach. Soon the campfire came in sight, and he could make out a pair of braves dancing around it, poking playfully at each other in their reverie. At first he did not see the women, then glimpsed other figures in the shadows beyond the fire. Circling slowly to his right about twenty yards, he took a position behind a large tree and rose up on his haunches, peering around the trunk.

From this angle he could clearly see the activity around the fire. Two braves had one of the women stretched out on the ground, her dress torn from her. She was bloody and apparently had put up quite a fight, but she was no longer able to resist as one of them held her arms and the other raped her. The second woman was still clothed and lay on her side a few feet away, a gag around her mouth and her wrists bound in front of her. The two remaining braves continued to prance around the fire, laughing and shoving each other—perhaps arguing over who would have the woman first.

Hawkeye knew he must act at once if there was to be any hope for the women. He already had loaded his weapons, and he drew the two pistols and pulled their hammers to full cock, then tucked them back into his belt. As he cocked Killdeer the rasp of metal caught the notice of one of the dancing braves, and he pushed his comrade away and stumbled toward the trees from which the sound had come. He called something to the others, and though Hawkeye did not speak the Huron language, he could tell that the man's voice was slurred from the effects of alcohol —French brandy, no doubt.

Easing his knife from its sheath, Hawkeye waited for the brave to get close to the trees. Just then a bird cawed from somewhere high in the trees, and the brave halted and looked up. His face was completely shadowed, but Hawkeye could read the expression of his body and knew the man was debating whether or not the crow had made the earlier noise. He seemed satisfied, and when he glanced back over his shoulder and saw that his friend was huddled over the bound woman and was cutting open the front of her dress, he decided he had better restake his claim.

As the man started back toward the others Hawkeye rose and came rushing from the trees, Killdeer in one hand and his knife in the other. The brave turned with a start and gave a cry of alarm as Hawkeye buried the knife in his belly and jerked it free. Despite the wound, the Huron managed to draw his own knife and flailed wildly at the dark apparition in front of him. But Hawkeye easily side-stepped the thrusts and swung the barrel of his rifle, striking him in the forearm and knocking his knife away. A second blow caught him on the side of the head, and he dropped to his knees, his head lolling groggily as he clutched his belly. With a sharp kick, Hawkeye knocked him out of the way and brought up his rifle.

The others were staggering to their feet now and snatching up their own weapons. Hawkeye sighted on the man nearest him—the one who had just begun to attack the clothed woman. But as he was about to pull the trigger, he saw one of the others bring his tomahawk down against the skull of the woman who already had been raped. With a piercing cry, the Huron jerked the 'hawk free and leaped at the second woman, raising the weapon high above his head. In one smooth motion, Hawkeye swung Killdeer toward him and fired, the bullet catching him in the side of the face. His body stiffened and jerked, then flopped lifeless to the ground.

Dropping Killdeer, Hawkeye dove to his side and

rolled just as a musket fired, the bullet smacking harmlessly into the trees. The two remaining braves rushed him, and he rose up with his pistols in hand and fired. One blast caught the lead Huron in the middle of the chest, stopping him in his tracks. But the other pistol misfired, and before Hawkeye could thumb back the hammer again, the second brave was upon him, swinging viciously with his 'hawk. The scout took a glancing blow across his shoulder, then barreled into the man, staggering him. But the brave caught his balance and came at him again.

Hawkeye stood his ground, shifting deftly from his left foot to his right to avoid the hatchet. He waited until the man lunged, and then he rushed him, throwing his left arm up to deflect the 'hawk. He felt the sting of the blade catching the edge of his forearm, but before the brave could bring the weapon back around, Hawkeye kneed him in the stomach, doubling him over. Grabbing the handle of the hatchet, he wrenched it free and jerked it upward, catching the man's jaw with the back of the blade and snapping his head backward. The Huron groped for the knife at his waist, but Hawkeye gave a furious oath and swung the 'hawk again. This time the sharp edge caught the man on the side of his head, and there was a sickening crunch of bone as the blade shattered his skull, took off his ear, and buried itself deep in the crook of his neck.

Hawkeye did not bother to remove the tomahawk from the body. Taking the Huron's knife, he cut off the man's belt and wrapped it around his left forearm to stop the bleeding, then retrieved the pistol that was still loaded and dashed across the clearing to where the women were lying. A quick glance confirmed that the first woman was dead, while the other one was sobbing through a cloth gag as she looked up at him with a mixture of hope and dread.

Putting down the pistol, Hawkeye cut away the thongs at her wrists. As she pulled her tattered dress around her he carefully undid the cloth gag, reassuring her that she was all right.

The woman gasped for breath, all the while moaning piteously, her body racked with sobs. Hawkeye reached out to her, and she threw her arms around him and pulled him close, holding on to him with all her remaining strength. She tried to speak, but she choked on the words, and he urged her to rest easy, to let herself cry.

A half hour later Hawkeye had dragged the bodies into the woods and then regathered and loaded his weapons, placing them close at hand. The woman had not yet spoken and was curled up under his bedroll beside the fire, at times silent and at other times sobbing gently. He had not dared ask yet, but he was fairly certain this was Rebekka Brower, since her breasts looked swollen with milk and she matched the description given by Astra Van Rensselaer.

Opening his pack, Hawkeye took out some dried meat and held it out to her. She seemed to stare right through it, then closed her eyes again.

"You should eat something," he said in as soft a tone as he could muster. She did not respond.

Sitting beside her, he took a bite of the meat and chewed it slowly, feeling it soften in his mouth. He kept looking down at the woman, wondering what to say, fearing that she was retreating into a place from which she might never return. Finally he decided that being direct might pull her out of her dark abyss.

"My name is Hawkeye," he began. "I'm a scout for the English, and it's no accident I'm here. I saw what the Frenchers did back at German Flats, and I tracked those Hurons to this campsite."

The woman's breathing changed, and he sensed that she was listening.

"I think I know your name. It's Rebekka, isn't it?"

Her eyes opened, then widened with fear as she stared up at him.

"Don't be afraid," he soothed, touching her arm. He felt her body go rigid, and he withdrew his hand. "I know a friend of yours . . . Astra Van Rensselaer."

"A-Astra—" she gasped, and he patted her arm.

"It's all right—I'm a friend. You *are* Rebekka Brower, aren't you?"

She gave a faint nod.

Hawkeye considered telling her that Astra had come to German Flats, but he did not want her worrying about her friend and decided to wait until she was feeling stronger. "I was on my way to Lake Oneida, and Astra asked me to check in on you. I arrived at German Flats only a few hours after the French. Do you know why they attacked?"

She opened her mouth to speak, then curled up tighter and shook her head.

"Probably as a warning to the English," he mused. "But I'd have thought they'd try to turn you to their cause."

"They . . . they did," she muttered, looking up at him.

"I thought as much. They sent some sort of emissary?" he asked, and she nodded. "And when you turned him away, they thought to make an example of you and send a shiver through the other settlers up and down the colony."

"I—" Her eyes welled with tears, and she sobbed again as she moaned, "Stefan! Oh, my God . . . Stefan!"

"I know," he said in a hush, not knowing what to do or say to ease her pain.

"My little boy!" she cried. She turned to him, her face a mask of agony, and he took her in his arms and held her close, rocking her gently. After a while she calmed somewhat and managed to stammer, "My little boy . . . they killed him."

"We gave him a Christian burial," he whispered as she clung to his neck.

"Jakob . . . my Jakob will never see him again."

Hawkeye stiffened at the mention of her husband. She must have sensed his reaction, for she pulled away slightly and looked up at him, her eyes narrowing with suspicion. "You know Jakob, don't you? You served with him?"

"No," he replied honestly, but he knew she could read a deeper truth in his expression.

"That's why Astra sent you, isn't it?" She pushed away from him and retreated deeper into the blankets. "You know something about my Jakob. . . ." Her voice trailed off, as if all the life were going out of her.

"Many were the militiamen who fell at Fort William Henry," Hawkeye said, his voice deepening with emotion. "Your husband died a hero among heroes."

It was as if all the tears had been wrung from her already. She fell back on the ground, her face wan and expressionless, a slight tremor of her lips the only sign that she understood what he had said.

He remembered Astra's dream and the message from Jakob Brower: *Tell her we are well. Tell her not to be afraid. Ease her journey home.* But he knew that nothing he could say just now would give her any comfort, so he merely whispered, "I'm sorry. . . ." He reached toward her, but she raised her hand to keep him back, then turned away and just lay there on her side, staring into the glowing embers.

Knowing she needed time to absorb all that had happened, Hawkeye moved away and sat by himself on the other side of the fire. For perhaps half an hour he busied himself tending the gash on his arm and then gathering additional wood for the fire. He arranged a sleeping place for himself, using some blankets of the Hurons, and was just getting ready to settle down for the night. Rebekka appeared to be asleep, perhaps overcome by emotion, and he decided it was best to let her sleep through the night. There would be time enough in the morning to tell her about Astra and to decide whether to take her to Lake Oneida or back to Albany.

Hawkeye had just climbed under the blankets when he saw Rebekka emerge from her bedroll. She moved around on the far side of the fire for a moment, then stood. Her face was reflected in the firelight, and for the first time he realized how strikingly beautiful she was—not in the fashionable way of the city but like a woman of the frontier. Her jaw was firm and strong, and her smooth skin had not yet been ravaged by the lines brought on by a life spent eking out an existence in the wilderness. Her figure was both lean and full, a woman who did not shrink from hard work.

He was about to ask if she was feeling better when she looked over at him and said, "If you'll excuse me a moment . . ." She gestured toward the trees, and he realized that she needed to tend to her toilet before going to sleep. He started to turn away so that she would not feel embarrassed, but she stopped him, saying, "I want to thank you

. . . for helping the way you did." She gave him the faintest of smiles, then headed toward the trees.

Hawkeye turned onto his side and pulled the blankets up higher. He listened to her footsteps recede across the clearing, then heard the snapping of twigs as she moved among the trees. It grew quiet, and he found himself thinking about another beautiful woman—one whose long hair blazed as brightly as the campfire flames. He wondered what Astra was doing just then and if she might be lying beside her own fire and thinking of him.

He grinned at such foolish thoughts. If Astra were thinking of anyone, it was probably the handsome English major. After all, he not only cut quite a figure in his scarlet uniform, but he knew what to do and say among the society folk back in Albany. And while Astra might be running away from all that right now, there was a part of her that would always remain close to society and its ways, no matter how far and fast she ran.

Hawkeye's reverie was broken by the sound of metal rasping against metal and the loud, distinct click of a hammer being cocked. Jumping up, he glanced over at his rifle and saw it lying undisturbed a few feet away. But farther beyond it, where he had left his pack of supplies, he saw only one pistol. He had left both of them on top of the pack, primed and loaded.

"Rebekka!" he shouted, running toward the trees. "No!"

He heard what sounded like a sigh, and then the hammer fell and the stillness exploded with a flash.

Chapter XIX

"I knew he was one of the cheats as soon as I laid eyes on him!" returned the scout, placing a finger on his nose, in sign of caution.
—*The Last of the Mohicans*, Chap. IV

Astra Van Rensselaer pulled her hand away from the young French officer, refusing his assistance as she stepped across the shallow brook and headed toward the winking lights ahead. In front of her, Major Horace Trevlayne did his best not to stumble on the forest trail despite having his hands tied in front of him. Glancing behind her, she saw Chingachgook walking proud and erect, his hands bound firmly behind his back and lashed to his neck with a loop of leather. She caught his eye, and he nodded slightly, as if to say that he had been in worse situations and would see her safely through this one.

The lights grew closer, and as they entered a broad, tree-lined meadow near the river, she saw about a dozen tents of white sailcloth. Pickets were posted around the meadow, and at the far end there stood a small Indian encampment.

The military detail led the prisoners past a row of light field cannon and a set of posts where horses were tied. Many of the soldiers were grouped around small campfires outside their tents, and as the procession went by they put down their tin dinner plates and approached to investigate. Astra spoke just enough French to realize that she was the primary object of their attention and that most of their remarks were not fit for genteel company.

The column came to a halt in front of one of the tents,

and the officer leading the group went inside. A moment later he returned and barked an order, and several of the grenadiers took the prisoners by the arm and escorted them inside. It appeared to be the headquarters, with half a dozen officers poring over maps that were spread on several tables off to one side. The officers looked up at their entrance, and one of them brought a pair of chairs to the middle of the tent and directed Astra and Major Trevlayne to sit down. Chingachgook, meanwhile, was forced to his knees at the far end of the tent. When Astra saw that they were tying him to a stake, she stood up to protest, but one of the officers gripped her wrist and forced her back onto the chair.

While Chingachgook stared into the distance, Trevlayne was looking all around, as though searching for a means of escape. Astra doubted he would find any, for just then eight armed grenadiers filed into the tent and took up positions, one pair at each corner. She expected someone to come over and start questioning them, but curiously, everyone went back to what they had been doing, the officers huddling over the maps and whispering to one another.

After a while the tent flap was thrust aside and a rather tall, middle-aged man strode in. He walked straight to where Astra and the English major were seated and doffed his hat, bowing with great dignity. "*Pardonnez-moi, monsieur et mademoiselle*. Please to excuse my *anglais*. I am Majeur Belêtre, at your service." He bowed again, then motioned for one of his underlings to untie Trevlayne. "I am most sorry, *Majeur*. It is *majeur*—ah, major—*non*?"

Trevlayne waited until he was released, then he stood and said perfunctorily, "Major Horace Trevlayne, late of General Webb's staff." He turned toward Chingachgook. "You will please release our guide as well."

"Oh, I am most sorry, but this is not possible. You must understand." He smiled graciously. "But won't you sit, *s'il vous plaît*, and we can speak?"

Trevlayne stared at him a long moment, then reluctantly resumed his seat. The French major signaled for another chair to be brought over, and he sat down facing Trevlayne and Astra.

"If I may say, mademoiselle, it is most unusual, most *agréable*, to see a woman of such—how do I say it?—" he waved a bony hand in front of his face, as if trying to snatch the proper words from the air "—of such fine breeding here in the middle of nowhere."

Astra fixed him with a withering gaze. "There were many such women in German Flats before you saw fit to burn it to the ground."

"I am so sorry about that bit of unpleasantness. But you are not German, *non*?"

"The Van Rensselaers are Dutch," Trevlayne put in.

"Ah, Mademoiselle Van Rensselaer! We have heard of your family."

"I'm afraid we've never heard of the Belêtres," she replied smugly.

"But of course not." He grinned.

Trevlayne leaned forward, his eyes narrowing. "And what did the poor folks of German Flats do to bring on the wrath of the Belêtres?"

"Me? But *non*, this is not so. I am but a humble soldier—what do I know of *la politique*? I only do as my *commandant* has decreed."

"And who might that be? Montcalm, perhaps?"

"Why, the Marquis de Vaudreuil, of course," he replied, naming the governor of New France, who was known to be Montcalm's chief rival. "But enough talk of all this unpleasantness. Now we must decide what to do with you and the good mademoiselle."

"All you need do is to let us be on our way."

"Ah, but to where?" He stroked his chin. "That is what we must find out. And may I presume you will not make this simple by telling me what an *Anglais* major and a woman *très élégante* are doing traveling west from German Flats?" When Trevlayne did not reply, Belêtre smiled grimly. "It is as I thought."

Standing, the Frenchman snapped his fingers, and a pair of grenadiers came over, grasped Trevlayne's arms, and jerked him up from his chair.

"You will come with me, *non*? We shall continue this interrogation where it will not be so *désagréable* to Mademoiselle Van Rensselaer."

He signaled the grenadiers, who dragged Trevlayne

from the tent. Astra jumped up to stop them, but two other grenadiers grabbed hold of her and forced her onto her chair.

"*Pardonnez moi, s'il vous plaît, mademoiselle,*" Belêtre said with a formal bow. "I do not think you would wish to be with the major just now."

He turned and strode from the tent.

Major Trevlayne was seated on a chair facing a make-shift desk that had been set up in one of the smaller camp tents. He had been left untied, but the armed grenadiers stood a few feet away on either side of him.

As Major Belêtre entered he barked an order at the two grenadiers, and they filed out. Sitting down at his desk, the officer looked up at his English counterpart and smiled. "*Bienvenu, monsieur le majeur,*" he began, continuing in French, "it is so good to see you again."

"I didn't think it would be so soon," Trevlayne replied in perfect French. "It was only last May—"

"June, I believe."

"Yes, of course. You were quite gracious during my visit to Fort Frontenac."

"I hope I can be as generous a host out here in the wilderness." Just then the tent flap opened, and a soldier entered carrying a tray that bore a crystal decanter and two glasses. Belêtre filled both glasses and handed one to Trevlayne, then motioned for the soldier to leave.

"A toast," Belêtre said, raising his glass. "To the Great Monarch—"

"Louis the Fifteenth!" Trevlayne completed, downing his brandy.

Belêtre poured a second drink, then reached into a drawer and took out a small leather purse, which he placed on the desk in front of Trevlayne. "A gift from the Marquis de Vaudreuil."

Trevlayne felt the weight of the gold coins but did not embarrass his host by opening the pouch to confirm the contents. "How did you know I was coming?" he asked, continuing to converse in French as he pocketed the purse.

Belêtre shook his head. "I didn't. It was one of the fortunate coincidences of this ruinous war. I had sent a representative to meet with the magistrate at German Flats, but they refused to support our cause. I'm afraid they gave me no choice but to read them a lesson their English friends will not soon forget. I sent most of the force ahead to Frontenac while I travel west to deliver prisoners to the English at Fort Herkimer."

"The prisoners are here?"

"Only twenty of them, including the magistrate. Another hundred or so are on their way to Frontenac. When this group is released, they'll soon spread word of our victory." He downed his glass. "But now let us talk about you. What in God's name brings you all the way out here?"

"The Oneida Prophet. Have you heard of him?"

The Frenchman thought a moment. "I don't believe so. Another of those fanatics?"

"Loudon thinks so. He's afraid this so-called prophet will turn the Oneidas against King George, so he sent me to assassinate the fellow and make it look like the handiwork of the French."

Belêtre chuckled. "But with you handling the job, it *will* be our doing."

"I'm only *half*-French," Trevlayne reminded him.

"Yes, but the better half." He offered his guest some more brandy, but Trevlayne declined. "And will you carry out this assignment for the Earl of Loudon?"

"Most certainly. Neither the English nor the French would want some crazed prophet stirring things up. So why not make a martyr of him, so long as the blame rests where it belongs—on the back of King George."

"And what of your woman?" Belêtre gestured in the direction of the tent where Astra Van Rensselaer was being held.

Trevlayne shook his head. "An unfortunate bit of business. We were escorting her to German Flats on our way to Lake Oneida when we came upon your handiwork. We couldn't very well leave her there by herself, and I was afraid we'd have to take her all the way with us."

"Perhaps there I can be of assistance."

Trevlayne shared Belêtre's smile. "I had the same thought. You could bring her to Fort Herkimer and release her with the others. But I want her handled with respect."

"Ah, might I presume that this young lady is of more than passing interest to you?"

Trevlayne's grin broadened. "Let's just say that when we get back to Albany, I intend to collect more than mere thanks for the many kindnesses I've shown her."

"Kindnesses?"

"Why, being her protector, of course. And it's my sincere hope, my dear Belêtre, that you will assist in that endeavor."

"I'd be delighted to help in any way I can," the Frenchman said graciously.

"Good, because I've worked out a plan."

"Ah, Major Trevlayne, we do not call you the 'cunning fox' for nothing. What is your plan?"

"I need to escape, and I need that Mohican guide. When you bring me back to their tent, you'll announce that in return for Miss Van Rensselaer's safe delivery to Fort Herkimer, I've confessed that my mission is to seek out this Oneida Prophet and win him to the British cause. Nothing must be said about an assassination, for that is known only to myself and the Earl of Loudon."

"I will tell no one but the Marquis de Vaudreuil himself."

"Good. Next, you send the Mohican and me under armed escort to Fort Frontenac and arrange for us to escape along the way."

"Delightful!" Belêtre slapped his hands on top of the desk. "I have just the man for the job. Captain Faillon can be trusted completely."

"One other thing—there's a second guide. He is called Hawkeye, but you may know him as La Longue Carabine."

Belêtre's eyes widened. "Yes, this Longue Carabine is well known to us. What has he to do with you?"

"He was with us but took off after some Hurons who captured a few women at German Flats."

The French officer frowned. "Some of the Indians could not be kept under control. Several war parties went off on their own, heading back to their homes for winter, I presume. Will this Hawkeye be coming after you?"

"If the Hurons don't kill him first."

"Well, there's not much he can do against a force as

large as ours. What shall I do with him if he falls into our hands?"

"It's of no importance to me," Trevlayne told him. "Just be sure our escape is convincing enough that the Mohican doesn't suspect anything."

"Will he understand what I say?"

"He speaks English."

"Then shall we get started?" Belêtre rose and gestured toward the tent flap.

Standing, Trevlayne rubbed his cheek. "Perhaps it would be more convincing if they saw that some force was applied."

"Force?" The Frenchman looked at him questioningly.

Trevlayne walked over to him and turned his head, presenting the left side of his face. "Is this suitable? Or would you prefer the other?"

"Forgive me, friend," Belêtre replied. Drawing his arm back, he swung his fist, catching Trevlayne just under the cheekbone.

The English major staggered slightly but stood his ground, shaking his head to clear it. "How does it look?" he asked, gingerly touching his face.

Belêtre rubbed his knuckles as he examined the reddish bruise, which was already quite puffy. "That should be sufficient—unless your right cheek is feeling left out." He smirked.

"One is enough, thank you. Of course, I could repay the honor, and we could pretend I put up a struggle."

Switching to English, sprinkled with a touch of French, Belêtre declared, "An *Anglais* getting the upper hand over a *Français*? No one would believe that!" He clapped Trevlayne on the back. "Come, *mon ami,* let our performance begin."

When Trevlayne was ushered back into the main headquarters, his hands were bound again and the bruise on his cheek was purplish. The grenadiers prodded him forward and shoved him into the chair beside Astra, who tried to tend to him but was pushed away roughly by one of the guards. Trevlayne signaled her that he was all right, then twisted around on the seat and looked back at Chingachgook, who remained tied to the stake, staring impassively ahead. The armed guards were still on hand, but the other officers had all left the tent.

Major Belêtre entered and walked over to where Astra was seated. With a curt bow, he said to her in English, "It seems, mademoiselle, as if you shall see Albany long before your friend Major Trevlayne—if, in fact, he ever sees Albany again."

"What did you do to him?" she demanded, rising to confront him.

He looked at her almost uncomprehendingly, then glanced over at the major. Waving a disinterested hand at Trevlayne's cheek, he said, "Oh, that . . . a small disagreement, but we convinced him to be more *agréable* and to admit where he was going—not to save himself, mind you. *Non*, the major is *très courageux* and would only acquiesce for the welfare of a woman. And a woman so very *jolie*, at that." He reached for her hand, as if to kiss it, but she pulled it away and dropped back down on the seat. He smiled and gave a slight bow. "Perhaps had we met under circumstances more *propices* . . ."

"You can be assured, Major, that there are no circumstances under which I would hold you under any but the lowest regard."

Belêtre clasped his breast. "You wound me, mademoiselle. And here I have most graciously agreed to the major's conditions in your regard."

Astra spun toward Trevlayne. "What does he mean?"

"Just that you will not be harmed."

"Good heavens, *non*," Belêtre assured her. "I shall see to it personally that you are delivered to the *Anglais* at Fort Herkimer. On this you have my sworn word."

"Is your word worth any more than the Marquis de Montcalm's at Fort William Henry?" she asked bitterly.

"Montcalm is an *imbécile*. I never would have made promises to English swine. But once my word was given, I would have backed it with my life. And so I shall with you, mademoiselle." He started to walk away, then looked back at her. "Might I suggest you and the major say your *adieux*? It may be a long time before you see each other again."

"What do you mean? Isn't he coming . . . ?"

"I am sorry, but that is not possible. The major and the *Peau-Rouge*"—he used the French term for redskin and gestured toward Chingachgook—"will be leaving at dawn for a rendezvous at Fort Frontenac, where perhaps they can be persuaded to tell us more about their mission to Lake Oneida—a mission we cannot allow them to finish."

"But that's unconscionable! You can't—"

"Un-con-shun . . . ?" he pronounced awkwardly, shaking his head. "*Je regrette,* but I do not know this word."

"*Peu scrupuleux,*" Trevlayne put in.

"Ah, the major speaks some *français,*" he commented, pretending to be surprised.

"*Un peu.*"

"A little or a lot—*peu importe.* At Fort Frontenac our *interrogateurs* speak your *anglais* as if they were native-born." He turned to Astra. "And I am sorry if you think me—I believe in your language you call it unscrupulous. I assure you, I bear no ill will toward your people but do only what the *nécessité* of war dictates."

"Such as killing the innocent women and children of German Flats?" Astra said pointedly.

"I assure you, mademoiselle, I take no pleasure in the death of innocents. Just as I will feel no joy if it comes to pass that the major and his *Peau-Rouge* companion do not survive their encounter with our *interrogateurs.* Of course, they need fear no such fate if they will only show their intelligence and answer fully all that is requested of them." He clasped his hands together. "Enough of this chatter. Say *adieu* to the major if you wish—it is of no concern to me. I go to arrange an escort to take him to Frontenac." He spun on his heels and exited the tent.

Astra turned to Trevlayne. "Fort Frontenac—that's at Lake Ontario. Why take you all the way there?"

Before replying, the major looked around at the armed guards to make sure they were not paying any attention. "To ensure your safe passage to Herkimer, I told him where we were headed, and he didn't seem particularly concerned about a lone English officer going in search of some little-known Indian prophet. But he realizes that his superiors will be quite interested in what I know about the strength and deployment of our forces throughout the north country. That's the real prize, and he aims to deliver it to the generals at Frontenac."

"What will you do?"

"Will I tell them?" His smile was smug and self-assured. "I was chosen for this mission because they knew that if captured, I could not be forced to say anything I didn't want—no matter how expert their *interrogateurs*."

She reached over and placed her hand atop his. "But they might—" She choked back the words.

"They won't kill me. I'm worth far more alive than dead." Despite his wrists being bound, he managed to take hold of her hand. "I promise I'll make it back to Albany. Will I find you there?"

She hesitated. "I . . . I'm no longer sure what I'll do."

"At least leave word with your friend—what was her name? . . . Miss Garrett, I believe?"

"Gerritsen. Christina Gerritsen."

"Yes, that's the one. If you're still intent on moving when you make it back to Albany, leave word with Miss Gerritsen where you've gone."

"I will—I promise."

Smiling, he lifted her hand to his lips and kissed her palm.

Chapter XX

"Arms and the clarion for the battle, but the song of thanksgiving to the victory! . . . Valiant and skilful hast thou proved thyself in the conflict, and I hereby thank thee . . . because thou hast proved thyself well worthy of a Christian's praise."

—*The Last of the Mohicans,* Chap. XII

Hawkeye lifted the small two-person canoe out of the water and lashed the paddles and his rifle between the center and bow thwarts. He unrolled his bedroll and laid it across his back to serve as padding, then hoisted the canoe and flipped it upside down onto his shoulders, using the paddles as carrying poles. It was just after dawn, and he had been traveling all night, carefully retracing his steps in the darkness from the place where Rebekka Brower had shot herself to the site of the German Flats massacre. He had buried Rebekka beside her son, then had found the canoe and started upstream in the first light of dawn, paddling for the better part of an hour before coming to this first portage.

As Hawkeye made his way around the small set of rapids, he watched the ground for signs that Chingachgook and his companions had passed this way. While there were no footprints or other markings, he detected one or two places where the Mohican might have covered their trail—nothing obvious and certainly not noticeable to any but the most astute observer.

Confident that the group he was following had passed that way the previous evening, Hawkeye headed for the riverbank on the upstream side of the rapids and prepared to launch his canoe. But as he lowered it to the ground he saw the marks of another canoe that had been carried up onto the shore, with moccasin prints all around it. The prints led to a set of bushes, and a full search of the area revealed a disturbing story written on the ground. Apparently Chingachgook had concealed his canoe there and taken Trevlayne and Astra to a nearby cove, then had returned to the canoe, where he was ambushed by a band of Indians. A small force of soldiers had taken the prisoners west on foot while the Indians took the captured canoe and followed on the river.

Hawkeye considered his options, then hurried back to the riverbank, where he double-checked the charges in his weapons and launched his canoe. He moved swiftly and silently over the surface of the water, pausing at every bend to scan the river ahead for any sign of the French soldiers or their Indian cohorts.

Astra Van Rensselaer was sharing a tent with six other captive women at Major Belêtre's encampment west of German Flats. They were under constant guard but were allowed to speak freely among themselves. Though most spoke German, they knew enough English and even some Dutch to converse with Astra, and she learned the full story of how Belêtre's force of three hundred French soldiers and Indians had launched their predawn raid and easily overpowered the sleeping residents. The small picket forts had been razed, and scores of men, women, and children had been either burned alive in their homes or butchered trying to escape. Those captured by the soldiers were the lucky ones; most could hope to be released after reaching Fort Frontenac or, at the worst, once the war was over. But countless others had been captured by roving Indian bands, who had either murdered them on the spot or carried them off into the wilderness, perhaps never to be seen again.

Astra inquired about her friend Rebekka, and though they all knew the young woman, none had any specific knowledge of her fate. It did not surprise them, however, to learn that her baby son had been killed and that Hawkeye and Chingachgook believed she had been taken into the Adirondacks by a Huron war party. It gave them some small comfort to know that Rebekka had killed at least one of her captors, and several confessed that they, too, had taken French or Indian lives defending their homes. That they would do so again was more a vow than a confession.

An hour after dawn Astra was allowed outside to watch her two companions being led away under armed guard to Fort Frontenac, far to the northwest. Again, Trevlayne's wrists were bound in front of him while Chingachgook's hands were held behind his back by a strip of leather looped around his neck. Astra was not allowed to approach or speak with them, but she managed to wave farewell and received a nod in reply from each of them.

At Major Belêtre's signal, Captain Pierre Faillon and a double column of twelve foot soldiers marched into position and started west across the meadow, six soldiers at the front and six to the rear of the prisoners. Belêtre then gave the order for the rest of his men to break camp. They would pull out within the hour and continue their journey to Fort Herkimer, where the prisoners would be turned over to the English as a show of good faith. If a suitable ransom was paid and other conditions were met, the one hundred prisoners taken ahead to Fort Frontenac would be released as well.

Astra was led back to her tent, but just before reaching it, she was confronted by Major Belêtre, who bowed and gave what passed for a smile. "Mademoiselle Van Rensselaer, you look well this morning." With a flick of the hand, he ordered the soldiers away, and they filed into the tent. "I trust my soldiers are treating you with respect?"

"Respect? If by that you mean they haven't tied me up, then yes, they're *très respectueux*," she said facetiously.

"Ah, mademoiselle, your friend the major warned me that your intelligence was exceeded only by your nerve. And your beauty, of course."

She eyed him suspiciously. "What exactly did Major Trevlayne say about me?"

Belêtre chuckled. "It is not what he said but the way

he spoke your name and looked at you. Yes, we *Français* understand this *langue d'amour*."

"*Langue de la mort* is more fitting, I'd say."

He laughed again. "The major was right about you. No wonder his tongue loosened when I threatened to have you executed." His smile was rigid and cold.

"You were going to kill me?"

"Do not look so surprised. Do you think an English major would reveal the purpose of his mission from only a bruise on the cheek?" His features softened slightly. "But do not worry. I would not have killed you, though had he not spoken, I cannot promise you would have left here as —how shall I put this?—as innocent as when you arrived."

Astra slapped him hard across the cheek, stunning him. Keeping her eyes fixed on his, she said without emotion, "*Au revoir, monsieur le majeur.*"

She turned to leave, but he grabbed her wrist and pulled her toward him. "Perhaps you are not so innocent after all."

She started to cry out, but he slapped her just as hard as she had done to him.

"Must I remind you that your *protecteur* is not here anymore?" Belêtre said, his jaw setting with menace. "Perhaps I will teach you to be more *gentille*."

As he dragged her across the encampment she tried to pull her arm free, but he jerked her along, stopping only to slap her again. She looked around wildly for some means of escape—for someone to come to her aid—but though quite a few soldiers were watching, none was about to interfere in the affairs of their commanding officer. Reaching his tent, Belêtre thrust aside the flap and shoved her inside.

"Much more *gentille*," he hissed, striding in after her.

Hawkeye tied the little canoe beneath some branches that hung over the river, left his bedroll and pack on board, and slipped ashore. Knife in one hand and Huron tomahawk in the other, he eased his way toward the landing area ahead. The French and Indian boats were guarded by three men—a pair of musket-bearing grenadiers and a young Abenaki brave, all of whom were making only the barest show of doing their jobs. The brave seemed more interested in catching up on his sleep, probably after a night of heavy drinking in celebration of the victory at German Flats, and he lay on his side near the edge of the water. The soldiers were smoking pipes and conversing, and occasionally one would make a circuit of the landing area along the riverbank while the other headed inland toward the French encampment to make sure all was well.

Waiting until the soldiers again made their rounds, Hawkeye moved swiftly through the trees, intercepting one of them as he neared the encampment. The man must have heard a faint rustle of leaves, for he turned just as the scout came hurtling out of the bushes. Hawkeye's knife glinted in the morning light, and then the blade sank into the man's chest and pierced his heart. Hawkeye clamped a hand over the man's mouth, stifling his death cry as he slid to the ground. Yanking the knife free, Hawkeye headed in search of the second man.

"*Hé!*" the soldier called as he returned to where the two men had been smoking their pipes. "Claude?"

He started to raise the barrel of his gun, but a tomahawk came whistling through the air and caught him between the shoulder blades, knocking the musket from his hands. His eyes wide with shock, he dropped to his knees, his fingers groping in front of him for the musket. He tried to yell, but a hand snapped his head back and a blade slid across his throat. His head lolled forward, his eyes fixed in death as he went sprawling across the dirt.

Hawkeye jerked the 'hawk from the man's back and spun around to find the Abenaki advancing on him, weapons in hand. The two men faced off, knife against knife, 'hawk against 'hawk, circling as they parried each thrust, the air alive with the spark of hatchet blade glancing off hatchet blade, the whoosh of knifepoints slashing at flesh.

The Abenaki jumped to his right and spun in a complete circle, swinging the 'hawk at Hawkeye's skull. The scout just managed to raise his own 'hawk, and the handles locked with a jolt. With his free hand, the brave thrust his knife upward, but Hawkeye tossed aside his own knife and caught the man's wrist. They stood locked in battle, Hawkeye slowly inching backward until it seemed as if he would fall under the brave's weapons.

Suddenly Hawkeye went tumbling backward, thrusting his legs upward and throwing the Abenaki into a somersault right over him. He sprang to his feet and, as the brave came back up, kicked the tomahawk from his hand and leaped at him. But the brave rolled to the side, and Hawkeye's tomahawk sank into the dirt beside his head. The brave was flailing with his knife, and Hawkeye released the 'hawk and grabbed his wrist with both hands.

The two men rolled and slid down the riverbank, tumbling over the edge and into the water. Hawkeye lost his grip, and they found themselves several feet apart in the knee-deep water, the brave still holding his knife, Hawkeye without any weapon but his wits. The Abenaki sensed that he had the upper hand and grinned malevolently as he closed in for the kill. Hawkeye just stood there, waiting for the final thrust. When it came, he met it with a deft kick that caught the man in the armpit and knocked the blade from his hand. He leaped to retrieve it, but Hawkeye was on him in an instant, knocking him off his feet and into the deeper water. The brave tried to squirm free, but Hawkeye worked one arm around his throat and drove his head under the water. The man flapped about desperately and managed to raise his head long enough to gulp some air, but Hawkeye forced him under again and again until the breath went out of him and his body stopped its jerking. Standing back up, Hawkeye watched as the river carried off the dead Abenaki.

Hawkeye climbed out of the water and retrieved his tomahawk from where it was still buried in the ground. Stepping back into the river, he found the canoe that had been taken from Chingachgook and the others and examined it closely, making sure it was in good condition. Then he started up the line of canoes, swinging his 'hawk and tearing great gashes in the rest of them.

Returning to the small canoe he had been using, he transferred his supplies to the larger one, then gathered up his rifle and guns from where he had hidden them and advanced on the French encampment.

Astra Van Rensselaer tried to remain calm as Major Belêtre followed her into his tent. She realized that she would have to use her wits if she were to have any hope of escaping with her honor or even her life intact, so she took a quick inventory of her surroundings. A makeshift desk and chairs stood near the center of the room, a few wooden trunks along the left wall, and a narrow cot on the right. The desk held an assortment of papers, and sticking out from beneath one of them was what looked like a metal letter opener—something, she thought, that might come in handy if she could maneuver herself over to it.

Belêtre grabbed Astra's left arm, and she turned to face him, all the while leading him ever so slowly toward the desk. Forcing a half smile, she said, "I'm sorry if I upset you. I didn't mean to be disagreeable, but you must admit you have me at a great disadvantage."

"Yes, I intend to have you." Stepping closer, he pinned her arm behind her back.

"This isn't necessary. I've apologized, and you've given Major Trevlayne your word."

He gave a curt laugh. "My word? I told him only that I would not hurt you. And if you do not struggle, there is no need for you to be hurt. You may even find yourself enjoying it."

With his free hand, he gripped her hair and yanked her head backward, then brought his lips down upon hers. She tried to pull free, but he pressed harder, bending her arm cruelly behind her back and twisting her hair to hold her in place. She struggled a few seconds more, then slowly forced her lips to soften and respond, until finally she was hungrily returning his kiss.

She could sense that Belêtre was excited by her unexpected passion, and she felt him ease his grip on her hair. She tried not to cringe as his hand traced the curve of her neck and slid along her shoulder down to her breast. She took a cautious step backward, and he moved with her, then a second and third step, until she felt the edge of the desk against the small of her back.

He released her arm, slid his hands down to her buttocks, and lifted her off the floor and onto the desk. Propping herself up with her hands behind her on the desk, she threw her head back, encouraging his lips to move down the front of her throat as she groped along the desktop, scattering papers and almost knocking over the reading lamp. And then she felt the cold metal, and she closed her fingers around the handle of the letter opener.

Her legs were wrapped around his hips, holding him to her. Balancing herself on the hand that held the letter opener, she reached up with her other hand and tugged at his waistband. Realizing what she was doing, he stood and began opening the buttons of his white jacket, grinning down at her. When the last button was undone, he pulled the coat back off his shoulders and let it slip to the floor. He was just reaching for his waistband when she tightened the grip of her thighs, grabbed his shirtfront, and pulled him down onto the blade of the letter opener. There was a slight tug, and then the sharp tip pierced his flesh beside the left nipple, sliding between his ribs and burying itself deep in his side.

Belêtre gasped, his body going momentarily limp. Then he jerked upright and staggered back from the desk, his eyes widening in shock as he groped for the handle protruding from the side of his chest. He started to cry out, but the sound caught in his throat as he dropped to one knee and, with a horrific moan, yanked the blade free.

Astra was already on her feet, and she dashed out of the tent. She had no plan—knew only that she had to get away from that place—and so she started for the nearest trees, hoping no one would pay her any attention. She had gone only about ten yards when she heard the tent flap being thrust open and Major Belêtre shouting in a pained voice, *"Arrêtez-la! Arrêtez-la!"*

She looked back and saw him leaning against the tent, holding his side with one hand and the bloody letter opener with the other. Beyond him, several soldiers had heard his cry to stop her. Some headed for Belêtre while three others took off after her, shouting for her to halt as they came.

Turning, she ran for the trees, knowing that in but a few moments she would be dragged back to a fate more terrible than what Major Belêtre had planned for her. That is, if they even bothered to take her alive, which she began to doubt when she heard a gunshot. She ducked instinctively but kept running. A second shot rang out, and she heard one of the Frenchmen scream in pain. She hazarded a glance behind her and was stunned to see that two of her pursuers were lying in the grass and that the third had pulled up short and was aiming his musket toward the trees a little to Astra's left. He fired, and she followed the path of the shot to where a man was standing about twenty yards from the edge of the forest. He was dressed in buckskin leggings and a green hunting shirt fringed in yellow.

"Hawkeye!" she shouted, racing toward him.

The scout had not been hit by the Frenchman's bullet, and he stood there calmly reloading his rifle. Then in one smooth motion, he raised the weapon to his shoulder and fired. There was a shriek, and another French soldier fell to the ground.

"Hawkeye!" she called again, running into his arms.

"Hurry!" he barked, pushing her toward the trees.

As she ran she caught a glimpse of the activity behind them. Soldiers were dashing all over the place, gathering up weapons and firing wildly into the trees as their officers tried to organize a defense against what they must have thought was a concerted attack by British forces. But their enemy was a lone scout armed only with a long rifle and a pair of pistols.

A moment later Hawkeye and Astra were in the relative safety of the woods. There was no time to rest, however, for it would be only a minute or so before the soldiers and their Indian allies were in pursuit. But Hawkeye had already marked a trail back to the river, and soon he and Astra were aboard their canoe. Together, they paddled upstream.

At the first sound of gunfire, Major Horace Trevlayne spun around and looked back along the narrow river trail toward Major Belêtre's encampment, about a half mile away. Several additional shots rang out, and he knew that something was wrong. A single word rose to his lips, and with a frown he whispered, "Hawkeye . . ."

He glanced at Chingachgook, who nodded in confirmation. Trevlayne did not doubt that the Mohican could pick out Hawkeye's long rifle from among the answering shots of what sounded like small-bore military muskets. What he did not know was whether the Indian would try to use the distraction as an opportunity to break free. That might disrupt the plans Trevlayne had carefully worked out with Captain Faillon, who was going to engineer their escape when they were near the Great Carrying Place.

At the head of the column, the captain gave the order to halt, then turned and came running back along the trail. Faillon was a ferret-faced man with a stringy black mustache and narrow-set brown marbles for eyes, which just now were darting about nervously in search of the source of the gunfire. He shouted a command for his men to ready arms and prepare for a possible attack.

"It's coming from the camp," Trevlayne said to the officer, who spoke a little English.

"*Oui*," he replied, his expression betraying his fear. "How many, you think?"

"It's probably just your Indians having a bit of sport," Trevlayne said, hoping the man's deferential tone had not raised suspicions in Chingachgook's mind.

Faillon shook his head. "I not think so." Drawing his sword and raising it above his head, he called out for his men to follow him back to the camp.

Trevlayne wanted to tell Faillon that their mission must come first, but he knew that any such comment would give him away to Chingachgook. Instead he decided to take advantage of the situation. As Faillon rushed off to lead their return march, the English major stooped down and palmed the knife that was secreted in his boot. He made sure Chingachgook saw what he had done, and as they started sprinting back to the camp, he cut through the rope around his wrists. Keeping his hands together, he maneuvered to a position slightly behind Chingachgook, and while they were rounding a bend in the trail he quickly slashed the strip of leather that was looped around the Mohican's neck.

Trevlayne started to cut away the rope at Chingachgook's wrists, but just then one of the soldiers behind them saw what was happening and gave a shout. Spinning around, Trevlayne rushed the man, knocking aside his musket and burying the knife in his stomach. Jerking it free, he plowed into the next man in line, knocking him off his feet.

As soon as Trevlayne launched his attack, Chingachgook dropped to the ground and deftly brought his bound hands under his feet. When he stood back up, his hands were in front of him, and he immediately launched himself at the nearest soldier, snatching his musket away and knocking him senseless with the butt. Twirling the gun around, he thumbed back the hammer and fired, catching another of the soldiers in the chest. Trevlayne also had a musket now, and he fired upon the last soldier in line, downing him just as the man got off his own shot, which went wide and struck one of his fellow grenadiers in the shoulder.

The rest of the column was in complete disarray. Men were diving off the trail, taking refuge from what they assumed was an ambush by an outside force. By the time Captain Faillon realized what had really happened, Trevlayne and Chingachgook had vanished into the forest. With great difficulty Faillon managed to regroup his men, but by then it was too late. The prisoners were gone.

"Damn!" the Frenchman cursed as he walked among the bodies lying on the trail. It was true that the Englishman was supposed to escape, but not at the cost of French lives. He considered hunting down Trevlayne, but then he heard additional gunshots from Belêtre's encampment. With a shrug of resignation, he ordered his remaining men to take up the dead and wounded and return to camp.

Hawkeye and Astra furiously paddled away from the landing area, where the Indian canoes sat submerged along the riverbank. The scout still heard an occasional gunshot and guessed that the officers would have gathered their men by now and would be launching an organized pursuit. It wouldn't take long to track them to the river, but he hoped the French would assume they had taken the faster route downstream toward Albany.

"Where are they holding Chingachgook and the major?" he called forward to Astra.

"They left a short while ago. They're being taken to Fort Frontenac by a column of twelve soldiers."

They paddled in silence a few minutes, and then suddenly Hawkeye sat bolt upright and cocked his head at the sound of a crow. Peering upstream, he saw a pair of men

scrambling down the riverbank into the water, each holding a musket over his head to keep it from getting wet.

Astra gasped with fear, but Hawkeye shouted, "It's
Chingachgook and the major!" Cupping his hand in front
of his mouth, he gave a return caw, then paddled toward
them. A minute later the canoe drew between the two
men, who tossed their muskets in and pulled themselves on
board. Trevlayne immediately set about cutting away the
rope that still bound the Mohican's wrists.

"Thank God you're all right!" Astra declared as
Chingachgook took the paddle from her and they switched
places.

"What happened to you?" Trevlayne asked, indicating the bruise on her cheek where Belêtre had slapped her.

"It's nothing," she replied, self-consciously covering it
with her hand.

"If someone—"

"Major," Hawkeye cut him off, "I put a couple more
paddles on board. I suggest we save our talk till we're
beyond the reach of those Frenchers."

With a brusque nod, Trevlayne found the extra paddles and handed one to Astra, who took it and turned to
Hawkeye. Her eyes held such hope and desperation that
Hawkeye knew she had finally summoned the courage to
ask the question that must have plagued her since their
escape from the French.

"Rebekka . . ." she began hesitantly. "Where is
she?"

The scout's expression did not mask the truth, and he
saw her eyes well with tears. "We'll talk of it later," he
replied, drawing his paddle through the water. "Now we'd
best put some distance between us and those varlets."

Major Belêtre grimaced as the surgeon jabbed the needle through his skin and tied off the last suture. A wet
plaster was applied, then a long strip of cotton tied around
his chest.

"That should fix you up in no time," the man said in
French, stepping back to admire his work.

"Get my jacket," Belêtre snapped, rising from the
chair in his tent.

"But you should lie down and rest—"

"Give it to me!" he bellowed, then snatched it from the surgeon's hands and wrapped it around his shoulders. Stalking across the tent, he threw aside the flap and stepped outside. There was a flurry of activity going on, with soldiers lining up in formation and small groups of Indians gathered around.

Spying the major, a junior officer broke away from the ranks and came over. With a smart salute, he announced, "We're ready for your orders, sir."

"What's the final count?" he asked. "How many did we lose?"

"Three here and another two down at the landing. Oh, yes, there was one Abenaki."

"Merde!" he cursed. "Can we keep them under control?"

"The Abenakis? I believe so. The poor fellow was not much liked, even by his friends."

"Good. I don't want them going off half-cocked and ruining everything."

"Ruining, sir?" The young man looked at him curiously.

"Never mind." Belêtre waved off the comment.

"Apparently there was only one of them—a frontiersman in buckskins."

"La Longue Carabine," he whispered, shaking his head in disdain.

"We believe he took her by canoe, but we're not certain if he went east or west."

"West," the major said with conviction.

"But we can't be sure—"

"West, damn it!"

"Yes, sir." The young man shifted uncomfortably on his feet. "There's one other thing, sir."

"Well, what is it?"

"Captain Faillon . . . it seems he lost his prisoners."

"Lost?"

"He ordered his men back to assist us, sir, and somehow during the confusion the Englishman and that Indian managed to break free. I'm afraid they killed three soldiers and injured two others during the escape."

"That idiot!" Belêtre exclaimed, looking around in anger. "Where is he?"

The young officer pointed toward a tent that served as a field hospital, and Belêtre saw Faillon and his men gathered in front of it.

"Tell him to wait in my quarters."

"What about the prisoners and that frontiersman, sir? How many troops shall we send in pursuit?"

Belêtre frowned bitterly as he stared out across the field of soldiers, then down at his bloodstained bandage. He considered what might happen if he sent his soldiers and those undisciplined Indians tramping through the forest in pursuit of a scout and a woman who didn't really matter anything in the larger scheme of things or a pair of prisoners who were meant to escape anyway. Belêtre would get his revenge, but he might inadvertently put their double agent at risk.

With an exasperated sigh, he looked up at the officer and muttered, "Dismiss the men."

"Excuse me?"

"Dismiss them!" he blared, pounding a fist into his palm.

"But the woman and—"

"She's no longer of any concern to us. I'll not jeopardize our mission for one woman or lose any more men to that rifle of his. As for those prisoners Faillon lost, he can answer to Vaudreuil when we get back." When the officer did not immediately react, Belêtre raised his eyebrows and hissed, "Didn't I give you an order?"

"Yes, sir!" The young man saluted and hurried back across the field.

Major Belêtre stormed into his tent and paced in front of his desk, pounding on it several times. *"Merde!"* he blurted, shaking his head in fury as he imagined the things he would like to do to Astra Van Rensselaer before killing her . . . the things he would have been able to do had it not been for Major Horace Trevlayne and his secret mission—and that damned scout, La Longue Carabine.

"Go!" he yelled. "Monsieur Trevlayne can have you —a present from Majeur Belêtre!"

Chapter XXI

"Softly, softly: we know our path; but it is good to examine the formation of things. This is my schooling, major; and if one neglects the book, there is little chance of learning from the open hand of Providence."
—*The Last of the Mohicans*, Chap. XXI

Hawkeye and his fellow travelers did not pause in their flight until they had put many miles between them and Major Belêtre's forces. When they finally landed their canoe in a calm inlet on the south riverbank, the sun was approaching its zenith and the day had grown warm. Chingachgook took one of the muskets in search of game, while the others rested in the shelter of a copse of birch trees beside the river. They did not risk a fire but made a quick meal of the last of the dried meat Hawkeye had with him.

The trio sat on the ground in silence, each lost in their private thoughts. Seeing that Astra had hardly eaten any of the meat he had given her, Hawkeye encouraged her to take some more, saying, "You have to keep up your strength."

She lifted the food halfway to her lips, then let her hand drop back onto her lap. She looked up at him, her green eyes reddened and swollen. "Was she . . . was she already dead?"

He had been expecting the question all morning and knew he could avoid it no longer. "We had a short while to speak before she . . ." He decided not to elaborate on the cause of her death.

"Then she knew about Jakob?"

"She knew she'd be reunited with him. She was at peace when I laid her to rest beside her son."

"You're certain of that?" she pressed, and he nodded.

Her shoulders slumped, and she shook her head in despair. "Why did they have to die?" She lowered her gaze and shook her head weakly. "It makes no sense—none of it. Those people were hurting no one. They didn't have to be killed."

"In the wilderness, many die with none to honor their passage. It's good that Rebekka Brower had a friend such as you to see her off on her next journey."

"Hawkeye is right," Major Trevlayne said, moving closer and taking her hand. "You proved yourself a friend to Rebekka to the end."

"What difference did that make?" she snapped, pulling back her hand. "They're gone—all three of them—and nothing I did was able to save them."

"It's not for us to decide who is and who is not to be saved," Trevlayne replied. "Our destiny is in God's hands."

"God . . ." she muttered as if it were a curse or a lie.

"I'm not a man of learning, like the major," Hawkeye put in. "And I cannot claim to be a man of God—at least not the kind who shuts himself up in your Sabbath-day churches. But from a life spent among his creatures, I'm convinced there's another world beyond the one we see, and when we leave this flesh, it's like a robe we're casting aside."

"Is that really true?" she asked earnestly.

"Of course it is," Trevlayne said, a bit patronizingly. "Doesn't the Bible tell us that life is more than meat and the body more than raiment?"

"But are you really certain, Hawkeye?"

The scout thought a moment before replying. "When I was a young man, Chingachgook took me to see an old, dying Mohican. He had me watch the man breathe his last, and when it was finished, he placed my hand upon the man's breast so I could feel his body cooling. 'What has changed within this man?' he asked me. When I couldn't say, he told me, 'His body is still the same flesh and blood and bones. Yet truly he is no longer with us, for what has departed is the Great Spirit that breathes life into all.'"

"Why are you telling me this?"

"Because we must honor the dead, but we need not mourn them. Everyone born to this earth will someday pass on, so why fight that which awaits us all, like sleep after a long march?"

Astra wiped a tear from her cheek. "But already I miss her so."

"There is no shame in mourning—but mourn our loss rather than her death, for Rebekka Brower has truly passed to a better world. For her, offer thanksgiving for the victory that was her life, no matter how short a time she walked upon this earth."

Astra nodded faintly.

Trevlayne merely looked annoyed, and he said to her, "Our friend the scout may speak wisely, but that won't lessen the pain of losing a friend. Time, however, will go a long way in that regard. Time . . . and revenge."

She looked up at him strangely. "Revenge?"

"Yes—revenge against those French scoundrels who laid waste to your friend's town and are threatening to do the same to yours."

Her eyes showed a new spark of animation. "What kind of revenge do you suggest?"

"We four are no army, able to strike the French at will. But we can choose our own time and place to hit them when they are unaware and perhaps turn the tide against King Louis."

"You're speaking of your mission to the Oneidas," she concluded.

"If we turn them from our enemies—if we secure their support for our cause—we shall strike a blow in the memory of German Flats and all those who have died at French hands."

"Yes," she whispered, nodding with conviction. "I'd like to do that."

"And you shall."

Just then, a shot rang out, causing Astra to jump with fear. Hawkeye stood and listened, then turned to the others. "It's Chingachgook," he announced. "He's caught some game." He headed toward where the canoe was tied.

"Good," Trevlayne declared. "Then we can continue our journey." Rising, he helped Astra to her feet and started from the trees.

She pulled away from him and walked ahead to where Hawkeye was standing beside the river. "I haven't thanked you," she said, reaching as if to touch his hand.

"There's no need." He clutched Killdeer to keep his hands busy.

"But you risked your life in going after Rebekka—and back there for me. I just want you to know—"

"I already know," he said, his words as gentle as the water lapping against the riverbank.

An hour later the group had loaded enough deer meat into the canoe for the next couple of days, and they paddled away from shore. They pushed deeper into the wilderness, the Mohawk River growing increasingly narrow and at times so shallow that they had to carry their canoe and supplies. For two days they followed the river, making camp at night among the trees or in the shelter of a rocky cove. Finally on the afternoon of the third day they reached the spot sixty miles west of German Flats known as the Great Carrying Place on the Mohawk River, which divided the waters that flowed to the Hudson from those that ran north to Lake Ontario.

One day, the city of Rome would rise there, but this day what greeted the travelers was little more than swampland and forest. Several portage trails followed the more solid ground, and Chingachgook chose one that took them five miles west to Wood Creek, where they made camp on the banks of the stream.

It was not a pleasant night. Not only was the air perpetually heavy and damp, but it was cloyingly pungent from the fetid rivulets of decaying matter that fed the creek from the surrounding marshes. Chingachgook promised that the next day would bring them to the clear waters of Lake Oneida. First, however, they had to navigate the creek, which was only ten miles long but a tortuous course of mudbanks, half-submerged tree trunks, and blanched and matted boughs. Fortunately, Hawkeye still had the tomahawk he had taken from the Hurons, and he spent much of the morning seated at the bow of the canoe, hacking away branches and pushing aside the barriers to their passage.

At length they rounded a sharp bend in the creek and paddled out of the shadows into the bright afternoon light that gleamed across the deep blue waters of Lake Oneida. Six miles wide and twenty miles long, the lake opened before them like a vast sea. As they paddled south, hugging the shore, Astra scanned the heavy stands of oak, maple, and white birch, searching for signs of the people who called this lake their home. But there was no evidence of the Oneidas or their village.

Hawkeye looked back at Astra from his place at the bow, and as if reading her thoughts, he said, "The Iroquois don't like to live too close to the water."

"Why is that?"

"Protection, no doubt. They usually place their villages a good ways inland. Oneida Castle is about eight miles south of the lake."

"Castle?" She seemed quite confused.

Major Trevlayne looked up at Astra and Hawkeye. "Isn't that a remnant from the early days of the Iroquois League, when they encircled their villages with stockades of sharpened logs?"

Hawkeye nodded. "Those were times of continual warfare. But the Iroquois grew so strong that none dared test them. They abandoned their stockades almost a hundred years ago."

Three miles south of Wood Creek, Chingachgook found the inlet of another stream and steered the canoe into it. The water was shallow but wide and clear running, and it followed a meandering southeasterly course through gently sloping hills and increasingly sparse trees as it traversed the miles between the lake and Oneida Castle.

Astra noticed how Hawkeye had begun to defer to Chingachgook here in the land of the Iroquois, much as the Mohican deferred to the scout among the colonists. This was no surprise, since she recalled his saying that Chingachgook was a figure of some renown among the Oneidas and spoke their language. Increasingly it was the Mohican who made decisions and called out directions to the others, though he didn't do so directly but through Hawkeye.

At one point Chingachgook said something in his native tongue to Hawkeye, who then told Astra and Trevlayne, "Undoubtedly word of our presence has already reached the village. Don't be worried if we find a delegation of braves waiting for us ahead."

Astra hunched lower in the canoe as they approached the landing area near the Oneida village. She thought she spied some movement ahead, and then she saw a row of overturned canoes lining a stretch of the left bank that had been cleared of trees and underbrush. A delegation had indeed gathered, though it was unclear whether the Oneidas were on hand to welcome the travelers or dispatch them.

As they paddled closer to the landing area Chingachgook called out something in the Oneida tongue, and a return voice shouted a reply. Hawkeye understood most of the Iroquois languages and told them, "He asked permission to put ashore and was welcomed as the sagamore of the Mohican people. They know who we are—who Chingachgook is, at least."

It quickly became apparent that they knew La Longue Carabine as well, for when he stepped ashore, he was surrounded by braves who seemed both admiring and wary. Though Astra had no idea what was being said, she noted that Hawkeye's rifle was an object of attention and renown. Likewise, Chingachgook was treated with great respect, as were Astra and the English major, due to their association with the Mohican and the scout. She could sense many eyes upon her, yet she felt safe, though she guessed she might feel otherwise without Chingachgook and Hawkeye present.

The canoe was carried onto shore, and the braves led them about a mile through the forest and up a slope to the broad plateau on which Oneida Castle was situated. Astra's first view of the village was something of a surprise. From Hawkeye she knew that the Iroquois tribes lived in longhouses rather than small individual lodges—in fact, the Iroquois called themselves the Hodenosaunee, or the People of the Longhouse. But she did not expect to encounter such impressive buildings. There were more than fifty dwellings, most twenty feet wide and sixty feet long. A few were even larger, with the great longhouse at the center of the village being close to two hundred feet in length. They were constructed upon a framework of upright posts planted in the ground, with horizontal poles lashed to the uprights and bent poles arched across the top to form a curved roof. The entire frame was sheathed in bark, with additional poles lashed to the outside to hold the bark in place.

The travelers were ushered into one of the larger longhouses. There were no windows, and it took a while for Astra to adjust to the light, which came primarily from the wide doors at each end of the structure and from square openings in the roof. Several low fires were burning in a series of stone pits situated along the central passage, with the smoke curling through roof vents above.

Astra stayed close to Hawkeye as they made their way down the central corridor of the longhouse. On either side of the ten-foot-wide corridor were raised platforms, each about ten feet long. Most were curtained off with blankets and skins, and as they passed an open one, Hawkeye explained that each was the living space for a family, with bunks for sleeping and with storage areas under the platform and in the rafters. Hanging from cross poles above the platforms were braided husks of corn, bundles of herbs, and strings of dried apples, pumpkins, and squash.

There were quite a few people in the longhouse, with children running up and down the corridor and their elders seated or reclining on reed and husk mats around the fire pits. Most retreated into their compartments as the visitors approached, but the bolder ones remained where they were or even came close to examine the Europeans and their curious garb. The brass buttons on Major Trevlayne's scarlet jacket were a source of great interest to the children, with the women taking particular delight in Astra's wide-brimmed straw hat with its blue ribbons and cream silk trim.

They were brought to one of the fire pits and given husk mats to sit on, while a simple wooden bench was provided for Astra. An older brave spoke briefly with

Chingachgook, then gave an order to one of the women and exited the longhouse.

"We're going to be fed before we meet with the elders," Hawkeye explained. "The Iroquois have one main meal a day, usually at midmorning. But they keep plenty of food warm, and anyone can eat whatever and whenever they want."

Astra sat in silence watching the Oneida women moving among the fire pits as they prepared what appeared to be a communal meal in a variety of metal and clay pots, which hung from wooden tripods or sat directly among the embers. The women wore loose-fitting broadcloth dresses and outer skirts with elaborate beadwork and fringes. The hems of the skirts came only to the calf and were slit to above the right knee, but their lower legs were covered with red wool leggings, fastened just above the knee and edged with yellow, blue, or white ribbon. Their hair was parted in the middle and worn with either one or two braids, and some of the younger women had added a touch of red vegetable dye along the part. All but the youngest girls were wearing cloth headbands with a slight crown in front. The bands were decorated with tiny beads, and each had a single feather rising straight up at either the back or front.

Leaning close to Hawkeye, Astra whispered, "Is there a reason all the younger women wear their feather in front?"

The scout glanced around, then smiled at Astra. "You're very observant. In front, the feather indicates that a woman is unmarried. So does a double braid; the married women wear only one."

"I see. And all the skirts are slit to the knee. That isn't to attract a husband, is it?"

Hawkeye looked a bit uncomfortable and gave a sheepish grin. "I don't think so. There . . . see?"

Astra looked where he gestured and saw a group of women kneeling near a fire pit farther down the corridor. One had pulled her skirt aside, revealing her bare right thigh. Astra was momentarily taken aback but realized the design of the dress served a functional purpose when the woman picked up a strip of some sort of vegetable fiber and began rolling it along her leg. Another woman took up a length of buckskin and proceeded to work it against her thigh.

Presently their meal was served in individual eating bowls made from maple knots dyed reddish black with hemlock root. The spoons were also maple, and each had an animal carved on the handle. Being a woman, Astra was served last and given a spoon bearing the likeness of an owl.

Hawkeye dipped his spoon into the stew. "We call this succotash, but the Iroquois say *ogansa ganonda*—at least the Seneca do; I know their dialect better than Oneidan. It's made from green corn and red beans, two of the three sisters."

"Sisters?"

"The three sisters of the Iroquois— corn, beans, and squash."

Astra tasted the warm succotash and nodded approvingly.

"A bit bland for my tastes," Trevlayne commented. "Could use some salt and a dash of pepper."

"Try the corn bread," Astra suggested. "It's delicious." She took another bite of the boiled bread.

As they ate, Astra and Trevlayne questioned Hawkeye about Iroquois customs and learned that, like most Indian tribes, the Oneidas lived a communal existence based on a notion of hospitality rarely found in white settlements. To them, the earth and all that it contained were gifts of the Great Creator and must be shared by all. "Everything is given in common to all men," Hawkeye told them. "Whatever lives on the earth or in the waters or grows out of the land does so not by the power of man but by that of the Great Creator, and everyone is entitled to his share."

After finishing the succotash, the guests were served roast venison, boiled applesauce, cranberry beans served in a squash shell, and finally something Hawkeye called *watatongwus odjiskwa*, which he explained was a pudding made with pulverized popcorn and maple syrup. The meal concluded when Chingachgook took the small portion of food that remained in his bowl and committed it to the ashes, both as an offering to the Great Creator and a sign that they had been served generously by their hosts.

* * *

At the conclusion of the meal the visitors were provided places to sleep within the longhouse, and then the three men were summoned before a council of elders, held in the largest of the buildings. There were a half-dozen men on hand, seated around the central fire pit. The oldest one was named Skenendowa, and he wore a beaded wampum sash and a special antler headdress, called *a-non-wao-re kio-na-ka-ron-ton,* which identified him as one of the fifty *rodiyanesho'o,* or lords, of the Iroquois League. These civil chiefs were nominated by the women of the *royaneh,* or noble families, and confirmed in office by councils of both men and women. When questions arose that affected the entire league, the *rodiyanesho'o* of each nation met to debate the issue, and a war chief carried their decision to the Onondagas, who were the firekeepers of the Iroquois. Only when all nations were in agreement did a decision become law.

Also on hand were several men known as *ehkanehdodeh,* or pine tree chiefs, who were given the honor of debating issues with the civil chiefs but were not allowed to vote. There was also one younger brave, who wore the scalp lock of a warrior and sat apart from the others, his expression a mixture of curiosity and disdain.

After introductions were made, Major Trevlayne explained that he had brought gifts for the Oneida people but that they had been lost when he was imprisoned by the French soldiers. With Chingachgook translating, he promised to return in the spring with cloth and metal goods and invited his hosts to send a delegation to Albany for additional gifts.

After acknowledging the Englishman's generosity, Skenendowa asked Chingachgook, "Why have you brought this man to our village?"

"We have heard stories of a great teacher who walks among your people," he replied in the Oneida tongue. "We would meet this prophet and hear what he has to say for our nations."

"The one of whom you speak . . . he has come to the People of the Standing Stone." The chief used the Oneida term for their tribe. The other Iroquois tribes were the People of the Flint, or Mohawk; the Hill People, or Onondaga; the People of the Great Pipe, or Cayuga; the People of the Great Mountain, or Seneca; and the Hemp Gatherers, or Tuscarora, who were not one of the founding five tribes but joined the league later. "He speaks to the *Ongwe-oweh*"—the original people, or Iroquois—"not to the Yengeese."

Hawkeye reached into the edge of the fire pit around which they were seated and grasped some of the warm ashes. As they sifted through his fingers he said, "If the people of the longhouse are the original men, then all the tribes of the earth—even the Yengeese—are their children, just as these embers are children to the fire that created them. Would not this prophet wish to speak with one of his children who has journeyed so far and across such dangerous lands?" He indicated the English major, who sat in silence, not understanding what was being said but aware that he was the object of their discussion.

Skenendowa's eyes narrowed, and he nodded approvingly. "Your tongue shoots as straight as your long rifle."

"Then you will take us to meet this prophet?"

"It is not for me to take you to Onowara."

For the first time they learned the name of the man others were calling the Oneida Prophet, and Chingachgook's eyes widened in surprise, for Onowara meant "turtle."

"We seek the path that leads to his fire," Chingachgook said, careful not to ask directly for the chief's assistance.

The old man clasped a fist to his breast. "The path lies here."

The Mohican nodded in understanding. "This path has brought us through the land of the People of the Flint. Along the way we passed Old Clearing, Overgrown With Bushes, Protruding Rocks, Between Two Places, Drooping Wing, Man Standing, Lake Bridge, Between Two Side Hills, Long Hill, Broken Branches Lying, Corn Stalks on Both Sides, Two Hillsides, and the Beast." He showed that he understood and honored their traditions by naming the places that Dekanawideh, founder of the Iroquois League, had visited two centuries earlier when bringing the Hymn of Peace to the five nations that first accepted *Ne' Gayanesha'gowa*—the Great Binding Law. Placing his own fist on his chest, Chingachgook continued, "This path has brought us to your longhouse. Perhaps Onowara may be found among your council fires."

The old chief looked around the circle, gauging the sense of the group. At last he said, "You have given us much to consider. We will smoke on this tonight."

Chapter XXII

"Men of the Lenape!" he said, in hollow tones
that sounded like a voice charged with some pro-
phetic mission; "the face of the Manitou is behind a cloud! His eye is turned from you; His
ears are shut; His tongue gives no answer. You
see Him not; yet His judgments are before you.
Let your hearts be open and your spirits tell no
lie. Men of the Lenape! the face of the Manitou is
behind a cloud."
—*The Last of the Mohicans*, Chap. XXXIII

*H*awkeye lay under a bearskin robe in the longhouse where they had eaten dinner. One of the compartments had been vacated for their use, and Astra and Major
Trevlayne were sleeping nearby under blankets and robes.
Only Chingachgook was not on hand, having risen and
gone outside a quarter hour earlier.

As he lay there listening to the sounds coming from
the other compartments, Hawkeye thought of the council
fire, where they had shared a pipe with Skenendowa and
the pine tree chiefs. He kept recalling the image of the
warrior with the scalp lock and the brooding expression.
Though the young man had neither said nor done anything
disrespectful, it was clear that he did not approve of Chingachgook having brought three whites to their village.
Hawkeye did not doubt that soon after they had left, this
warrior had made clear his displeasure and had counseled
against helping them to find the prophet named Onowara.
Whether or not the council heeded his advice would not be

known until the next day, when Chingachgook expected them to make their decision.

Hawkeye heard someone approaching along the corridor and assumed it was the Mohican. When the footsteps passed, he began to wonder what was taking his friend so long, and he decided to investigate. Climbing out from under the robe, he donned leggings, moccasins, and hunting shirt, then cinched his belt and tucked his knife behind it. As he made his way down the corridor he saw that the fires were low, but they provided enough light to reveal only a few people on hand. They gave him little notice as he headed from the longhouse.

There was a bit more light outside, for a large bonfire was burning near the center of the village. Hawkeye didn't hear any drumming or chanting, but he guessed that the Oneidas were gathering for some purpose.

Just then Chingachgook emerged from the shadows, and when Hawkeye asked where he had been, the Mohican replied in English, "I was returning for you."

"What's going on?" He motioned in the direction of the fire.

"He has come."

"Onowara?"

The Mohican nodded. "Let us listen to his words."

They headed across the village to the site of the fire. A large number of people had gathered, but they were walking away from the fire toward the distant trees. Chingachgook signaled for Hawkeye to follow, and together they joined the throng. There were some disapproving looks and hushed comments, but no one made any effort to stop them, and a number of the villagers smiled at them.

The crowd filed into the forest along a fairly wide, well-trod path, their passage illuminated by flaming brands that some of the men had taken from the bonfire. The path led about a quarter mile to a large clearing, at the center of which stood a second bonfire, onto which the braves tossed their makeshift torches. Beyond the fire, at the very edge of the trees, was a small round lodge.

The villagers gathered around the fire, their numbers increasing until there were perhaps two hundred on hand. They seemed unusually quiet and still, and they grew qui-

eter yet when their chief, Skenendowa, entered the circle
wearing his antler headdress and carrying a water drum.
Someone came forward with a bearskin robe and spread it
on the ground in front of the fire, and the chief placed the
drum on top of it. Sitting cross-legged with his back to the
fire, Skenendowa took up the drum beater and began to
play so softly that it sounded like a heartbeat. At one point
he glanced at the scout and the Mohican, who had joined
the circle, and though his expression did not change,
Hawkeye sensed a look of approval in his eyes.

Slowly the drumming quickened and intensified. The
people swayed gently and closed their eyes, and
Skenendowa began to chant:

> *"A-soh-kek-ne eh!*
> *A-soh-kek-ne eh!*
> *Ka-rih-wi-yoh!*
> *A-soh-kek-ne eh!"*

The crowd took up the song: "It is not yet done! It is
not yet done! Great tidings of peace and power! It is not
yet done!" They circled to the left, moving slowly as they
swayed to the rhythm of the drum. Even as they chanted
that the time had not yet come, their expressions betrayed
that they believed it already was at hand. Hawkeye and
Chingachgook found themselves caught in their midst, and
though they did not take up the song, they imitated the
shuffling gait.

As Hawkeye scanned the crowd he discovered one
brave whose eyes were not closed like the others. In fact,
he was staring directly at Hawkeye with a fierce look of
hatred. It was the young warrior with the scalp lock who
had been on hand earlier that evening at the longhouse
council. He was chanting, but his lips were tight and color-
less, and he seemed to be spitting out the words:

> *"Ka-rih-wi-yoh!*
> *A-soh-kek-ne eh!"*

Hawkeye looked back at the drummer. Skenendowa
was leaning over the drum, pounding furiously, his eyes
raised to the heavens. Suddenly he stood, raised his arms

high above his head, and cried out, *"Kwa-ah! Kwa-ah! Kwa-ah!"*

The gatherers came to an abrupt halt and looked to where their chief was standing over the drum, haloed by the leaping flames of the fire.

Again Skenendowa shouted the mourning cry reserved for when one of the *rodiyanesho'o* died: *"Kwa-ah! Kwa-ah! Kwa-ah!"* His right hand held the ornately carved drum beater, his left a simple string of black wampum. A final time he gave the mourning cry: *"Kwa-ah! Kwa-ah! Kwa-ah!"*

A hush came over the assembly, the silence broken only by the crackle of the fire. Skenendowa placed the drum beater on the robe, then reached into the quiver at his back and withdrew five arrows, representing the original Iroquois nations. He wrapped the wampum belt around them, forming the symbol of the league, and placed it beside the drum.

Turning to the fire, he backed away from it until he entered the circle about twenty feet to the left of where Hawkeye and Chingachgook were standing. All eyes turned in unison to a spot directly across from Skenendowa—to the very brave who only a few moments before had been staring at Hawkeye with such disdain.

Hawkeye began to wonder if this young warrior might in fact be the Oneida Prophet, when suddenly the brave and those around him moved aside, clearing a path for someone to enter the circle. The man who appeared was wrapped in a bearskin robe. His hair was long and loose, and he did not wear an antler headdress but only the common Iroquois cap of blue broadcloth, with a single eagle's plume rising from the tip of the crown. He had no other marks of distinction and in fact seemed to be clothed in the plainest of buckskin outfits, with an embroidered quill gorget on his chest.

Slowly the man circled the fire, three times to the right, three to the left, finally coming to halt in front of the robe where Skenendowa had left the bound arrows. He raised his head to take in the crowd, and even though at one point he looked directly at Hawkeye and Chingachgook, his features were shadowed by the blaze of fire behind him. From the little Hawkeye could discern, the man appeared to be in his twenties or thirties—not much older than the young warrior at the council fire.

"Everything is completed; we are now all assembled here," the man called out in the Oneida tongue. "We shall first give thanks to the Great Creator. We do this because our power is now complete. Each of us shall have a voice in the thanksgiving, and I shall be the first to lead." He raised his arms and cried, *"Yo-hen!"*

A voice echoed *"Yo-hen!"* and Hawkeye saw that it was Skenendowa. He was followed by the young warrior with the scalp lock. And then, one by one, the others took up the cry: *"Yo-hen!"*

As Hawkeye listened to their prayers overlapping and blending, one upon the other, he suddenly realized why the man's words had sounded so familiar. Many times he had heard the legend of the founding of the Iroquis League, and he now recalled that when Dekanawideh brought together the lords of each of the five nations to give them the Great Binding Law, he opened their council with almost precisely the same words and exclamation of thanksgiving that had just been used.

As the voices trailed off and the crowd grew quiet again, the man continued, "I bring you news of the Great Peace from one who is called 'He who has misplaced something but knows where to find it.'" He used the phrase *Hah-yonh-wa-tha*, which the whites erroneously translated as Hiawatha. Hahyonhwatha was the man who spread Dekanawideh's message and helped form the Iroquois League.

"Our fathers bound their arrows with those of the People of the Flint, the Hill People, the People of the Great Pipe, and the People of the Great Mountain," Onowara continued, moving slowly around the fire so that all could hear him. "And so the Great Peace was established. United we were strong, and our villages grew as corn upon the land. None dared oppose us—neither the Huron nor the Leni-Lenape nor even the Muhheconnuk."

As he said the name of the Mohicans he was facing Chingachgook. And then his shadowed gaze shifted to the white scout standing beside the sagamore.

"But we were not vigilant, and we allowed darkness to descend upon our land. When this darkness first stole upon us, it glittered and blinded us with its brightness. We had never seen such beauty, and we accepted it as a gift of the Above Father. It came in the form of pots and knives and muskets and shiny baubles and trinkets. Its givers were strange people who were not *Ongwe-oweh,* nor were they our red brothers who surround us. These men were pale, like the white buffalo that live below the earth, and we thought that surely they must be messengers of the Above Father, so powerful seemed the gifts they offered to share with us."

Onowara picked up the bundle of arrows at his feet and slowly untied the string of wampum holding them together.

"We were blind, and we allowed the darkness to creep into our villages and into our hearts. And today it threatens to extinguish each of the sacred fires."

One by one, he snapped the individual arrows and let them drop at his feet. When only one remained, he held it above his head, the tip pointing to the sky.

"People of the Standing Stone, I bring you news of the Great Peace. You have shut your eyes to the Above Father, and darkness has descended upon the land. We must dance the dances and sing the songs of our fathers, or surely the Great Peace will be no more!"

Turning, he flung the arrow into the flames.

"How are we to lift the darkness?" Skenendowa called out from his place in the circle. "Must we give up our muskets and our metal tools?"

Onowara continued to stare into the fire. "We used to hunt with bows and arrows. We used to plant our fields with hoes made from turtle shells or the shoulder blades of deer. And our longhouses were filled with meat and corn. The deer and the fish ran onto our spears, for they were a gift of the Above Father. The three sisters grew tall and gave their lives freely to us. We sang for the planting and the harvest, and we made sacrifices of tobacco and wampum."

"All this we do today," the chief declared. "Yet each day the game is less plentiful and the corn grows less tall."

"What shall we do?" a voice called out, and others echoed the cry.

"We must return to the old ways," Onowara replied. "We must be deaf to those who would untie the cord that binds our arrows."

"We must drive the whites from our lands!" shouted the warrior with the scalp lock as he stepped forward from the circle. He raised his arm and pointed at Hawkeye. "My name is Kahonwah, and I say we must drive the whites from our lands!"

Onowara turned to the young warrior. "How would you do this thing, Kahonwah? How would you drive them away?"

"The red-jacket soldiers are pushing onto the lands of our brothers, the Kanyenkehaka." He used the Iroquois name for the Mohawks, whose land lay between that of the Oneidas and the English. "The white jackets are pouring down from the Canadas and crowding in on our own lands each day. You say their weapons and gifts have blinded us, and we must throw them away. I say we must turn those weapons against them and drive them into their winged canoes and back across the salt lake!"

His declaration was greeted by the enthusiastic cries of a number of braves in the crowd. Hawkeye glanced around and realized that most doing the shouting wore the scalp lock of a warrior, like Kahonwah.

"Are our musket balls plentiful enough to hold back this tide?" Onowara asked. "I have been to the places where these Yengeese live. Their settlements along the river of the Kanyenkehaka are small and poorly defended, but closer to the salt lake they have great villages with lodges made of stone, whose people are more plentiful than lights in the night sky. If they come, our muskets will not hold them back."

"Then what would you have us do?" Kahonwah challenged. "Is it enough for us to be deaf to their voices? Must we not also cut out their tongues?"

"Kahonwah, you have heard my words these past days, and I have heard yours. Our voices fly to the Above Father. He hears our suffering and will not abandon us."

"You would have us sing and dance? You would have us destroy the whites with our songs?" Kahonwah folded his arms across his bare chest and sneered. "Our dance must be the war dance. We must sing with our guns." The other young warriors raised their fists and gave a keening cry.

Onowara waited until Kahonwah's followers quieted down. Then he bowed his head and said, "Truly, we must sing." He began to circle the fire, and as he did, he reached into a leather pouch hanging from his belt and tossed tobacco leaves upon the flames. In a low monotone, he chanted:

> "We throw tobacco upon the fire
> And give thanks to the Great Creator.
> The smoke carries our words to him.
> The smoke carries our words to him.
>
> "We thank him for our mother, the Earth,
> For our sisters—corn, beans, squash,
> For the Thunderers that bring rain,
> For creatures that walk and swim and fly.
>
> "Again we throw tobacco,
> Again we breathe smoke and listen.
> Hear our words, Great Creator.
> Lift the darkness from our eyes
> That we may see you,
> That we may see you."

Onowara ended his chant at the place in the circle where he had begun. Facing Kahonwah again, he said, "The Above Father has heard our voices. He will speak at our council fires, and our people will know the path they must walk."

Kahonwah nodded. "They will walk a path stained red with the blood of the Yengeese." Unfolding his arms, he stepped into the middle of the circle and turned in place to face the entire ring of villagers. Then he raised his hands toward the fire and boldly intoned the Iroquois war chant:

> "Now I am greatly surprised
> And therefore I shall use it—
> The power of my war song.

> *"I am of the Hodenosaunee*
> *And I give thanks to the Great Creator*
> *Who has raised up this army.*
>
> *"Our warriors shall be mighty*
> *In the strength of the Great Creator,*
> *For it was he who gave us this song,*
> *This war song that I sing."*

Turning, he pushed his way through the crowd and was gone. Some of the other young braves took up the chant and followed him into the night.

As their war cry faded into the distance Onowara looked up at the night sky and exclaimed, "The Above Father has heard our voices! He tells us to look for his sign. Then we shall know the path we must take."

"What sign will he send?" someone called, and others repeated the question.

His arms upraised, Onowara closed his eyes and moved closer to the fire, until he was almost on top of it. He was silent for a long while, the only sound being the crackling of the flames. When at last he spoke, his voice was deep and hushed and sounded almost as if it came from another man: "A warrior comes to our village who wears two masks and speaks with three tongues. A turtle crawls out from under a rock, seeking the sun." He hesitated a moment, then continued, "The eagle screams atop a tall and mighty tree. His chest is pierced, but the tree does not fall."

Several minutes passed in silence, until Skenendowa cried out, "What does this vision tell us? What are we to do?"

Onowara's hands dropped to his sides, and his shoulders slumped. Slowly turning around, he approached the chief. "I must smoke on these things," was all that he said. He started toward the spot from which he had entered the circle, but as he approached Hawkeye and Chingachgook he halted and looked up at them.

For the first time Hawkeye could clearly see Onowara's features in the glow of the fire, and for a moment he thought that what he was looking upon was a trick of the light. He stood transfixed as the flames danced across the young man's face and shimmered in his dark, familiar eyes. A strange cloud seemed to descend over Hawkeye, a dreamlike fog, and for what seemed like ages he was unable to move. But then Onowara looked past him to the Mohican, and Hawkeye found himself following his gaze.

Chingachgook was just as transfixed, his eyes wide with recognition and shock, his lips fashioning the name of the last in the line of the Mohicans: "Uncas . . ."

Onowara's smile was enigmatic. Lowering his head, he continued around the circle until he came to the place where Kahonwah had been standing. The crowd parted, and he passed through and headed across the clearing to the lodge beyond.

Chapter XXIII

"Think over your prayers," he whispered, as they
approached him; "for He to whom you make
them knows all tongues; that of the heart as well
as those of the mouth."
—*The Last of the Mohicans*, Chap. XX

*I*n darkness and silence, the Oneidas returned to their
longhouses. Hawkeye looked at Chingachgook, who stood
alone in the clearing, his back to the bonfire, his gaze fixed
on the lodge of Onowara. The scout wondered what his
friend would say to the young man—the very man he
would have killed when rescuing the soldiers near Ticonderoga had he not seen the mark of Unamis upon his chest.
A man who was so obviously a Mohican and the older half
brother of Chingachgook's son, Uncas.

Turning away, Hawkeye joined the line of Oneidas as
they entered the forest and headed back to the village.
When he emerged from the trees and started toward the
longhouses, he heard his name and saw Major Horace
Trevlayne walking toward him from the vicinity of some
small buildings near the edge of Oneida Castle.

"What was all that about?" Trevlayne asked as he
came over.

"They held a gathering."

"I know. That fellow with the bearskin robe—he was
the prophet, wasn't he?"

"You were there?"

"I heard the drumming and thought I'd investigate, so
I joined some stragglers heading to the bonfire. That was
him, wasn't it?"

Hawkeye nodded. "Onowara."

Trevlayne repeated the name, then commented, "From what I saw, it looks as if not everyone thinks him a prophet."

"Indians like to challenge their gods."

"When that young buck with the scalp lock challenged him and stalked away, he looked quite put out by the whole thing. I followed him and his friends over to there." He indicated the cluster of longhouses from which he had come. "I couldn't understand what they were saying, but none seemed too disposed toward their prophet."

"You followed him?" Hawkeye asked, looking genuinely surprised.

Trevlayne gave a smug grin. "I've spent my career spying for King George. I'm expected to go places I'm not invited."

"That's not always the wisest course of action in an Indian village."

"And certainly not the most productive when you don't speak the language. What was that Onowara fellow talking about, anyway?"

"If your generals are worried that he's fomenting war, they needn't be. He wants the Iroquois to return to the way of their fathers. It's that Kahonwah fellow they should be concerned about."

"The way of their fathers? But I've heard the early Iroquois were a dangerous lot—you either joined their confederacy or were killed."

"Some see it that way. But there was fighting all through this region before the league, and afterward there was relative peace—until we came along."

"So he's just another religious fanatic, eh?"

Hawkeye shrugged. "Naive, no doubt. He believes the old ceremonies will hold back the tide of settlers and keep their land safe for the *Ongwe-oweh*." Seeing Trevlayne's confused expression, he translated, "The original people—the Iroquois."

"And what if we keep coming? What will he do then?"

"His followers will turn to someone like Kahonwah." He motioned toward the buildings where the young warrior lived. "But for now, I'd say you don't have much to worry about from the Oneidas, though I doubt they'll heed Onowara's call to get rid of their muskets and the rest of our trading goods."

"He really called for that?" Trevlayne said incredulously.

"He believes the Iroquois are being corrupted by contact with whites and should adopt the old ways of the bow and arrow. It's a popular call among many, but nobody's going to throw away their pots and pans and guns."

Trevlayne glanced around. "Where's Chingachgook?"

"He'll be back," was all Hawkeye replied.

Chingachgook stood gazing upon the lodge of the Oneida Prophet. The only sounds were the crackling of embers and, off in the distance, the creek that led to Lake Oneida. The bonfire was dying down, and he could see a second fire, this one a faint orange glow at the heart of the lodge. It cast the shadow of a seated man upon the hide walls.

The sagamore slowly approached the lodge entrance and called out, "My name is Chingachgook. I bring news of your people." He said the words first in Mohican and then in the Oneida tongue.

The shadow rose upon the wall and moved toward the doorway. The blanket that served as a flap was pulled aside, and the shadow returned to where it had been. Chingachgook waited a moment, then ducked through the opening, pulling the flap closed behind him.

Onowara was seated on a blanket on the far side of the low-burning fire. With a wave of the hand he gestured for his visitor to sit across from him. For a time the two men did not speak, and then the younger one said in Oneidan, "You have come from the river your people call the Muhheconnuk."

For a moment Chingachgook was unable to speak. Though this man was a few years older and somewhat thinner than Uncas had been, everything about him spoke of the tall, powerful warrior who had been Chingachgook's son. Forcing out the words, he said, "My people are no more."

"But the river still runs."

"The river of my people has run its course. Even the Muhheconnuk has been given a new name—the white man's Hudson River. I watched the last child of Unamis fall at the hands of a Huron dog, and with him I thought the line of the Mohicans had come to an end." He struck a fist against his chest. "But I have seen the mark of Unamis upon the chest of a warrior of the People of the Standing Stone. I have been searching for that man, and tonight I have found him again. It is you who wears the sign of the turtle. You are the Mohican I saw that day."

Onowara stared at him with curiosity. "We have met?" He sounded genuinely confused.

"You don't remember me?"

"It is true that in my dreams I saw one such as you coming. Was it also in the land of dreams that you saw me?"

Chingachgook shook his head. "I was the one who raided your encampment near Horican"—he used an Indian name for Lake George—"and set free the red-jacket soldiers. We fought, and I almost killed you, but I stayed my hand when I saw that mark upon your breast." He gestured toward Onowara's chest. "The last I saw, you were running into the forest." He allowed himself a faint smile. "But tonight I have found you again."

Onowara closed his eyes in thought. Opening them finally, he let out his breath in a sigh. "It was not Onowara you saw but Oweya."

"Oweya?" Chingachgook repeated. The word meant "wing."

"My brother."

Taken aback, Chingachgook stammered, "But he looked exactly like—"

"Oweya entered this world clutching my heels."

Chingachgook's eyes widened in understanding and surprise. "Where is your twin now?"

Onowara's features hardened. "We no longer speak of him. He died to us the day he turned his back on the Great Peace of our fathers and set his face against our nation. You saw nothing more than a mission Indian—neither Muhheconnuk nor Ohnenyohdehaka." He used the Oneidas' name for themselves.

Chingachgook looked at him a long moment, weighing his words before saying, "How did you come to wear the sign of my people?"

Onowara's reply was in the Mohican tongue: "My mother taught me the language of your people. She once lived along the banks of the Muhheconnuk, and her path was long and troubled before she found a home here among the People of the Standing Stone."

"Then you and your brother *are* Muhheconnuk," Chingachgook declared, more a statement than a question.

"I am Muhheconnuk. I am Ohnenyohdehaka. I am Potawatomi. I am Huron. All these I am, yet I am none."

"As a young woman, your mother was called Two Feathers by my people, but she took the white name Hannah."

Onowara's eyes narrowed, and he seemed to be reaching back for some forgotten memory. "She has been gone these many years. I knew her as Yegowaneh." The term meant "great woman," and it was unclear whether that was her Oneidan name or simply a title of respect. "Did you know my mother?"

Chingachgook nodded. "Before she accepted the cross and went away with the Potawatomis."

Onowara frowned. "Yegowaneh found nothing but trouble in their village. When we were born, she cast aside their cross and ran away. She was returning to her people but was captured by the Hurons. A chief of the Ohnenyohdehaka rescued her and brought her to this village. He raised me as his son."

"But you have another father."

"Today I have but the Above Father."

"You have a father who still walks these forest paths. And you had a younger half brother who fell at the hands of the Hurons. His name was Uncas, and like you and Oweya, he wore the sign of Unamis. So did his father . . . your father." Chingachgook raised his hunting shirt.

Onowara stared in wonder at the blue turtle emblazoned upon Chingachgook's chest. His hand reached for his own chest, but then he pulled it away.

"Two Feathers was to be my wife. She gave you this mark so you would know your true father and your true people."

Rising, Onowara turned away from Chingachgook

and the fire. He faced the shadows, his arms folded across his chest, and said in a hush, "I am Onowara. My father is the Above Father. My people are the Huron, the Potawatomi, the Ohnenyohdehaka, the—"

"You are Muhheconnuk, the last hope for our people," Chingachgook declared, standing and lifting a hand toward his son.

Slowly, the young prophet turned to the sagamore of the Mohicans. "I have heard your words. I will smoke on them." He sat back down and closed his eyes.

Chingachgook watched him for a time, saw the way the light of the fire played across his mouth and cheeks, and remembered the many lodge fires he had shared with Uncas. He raised his hand again to speak, then spun around and walked from the lodge. As he started toward the Oneida village he heard Onowara chanting the Iroquois song for the dead—a song for the passing of his people.

Chingachgook had only gone about a hundred yards along the forest path back to the Oneida village when he heard approaching footsteps. Darting among the trees, he peered out at the dark trail and caught a glimpse of someone making his way to Onowara's lodge. He could not be certain, but the silhouette appeared to be that of a brave with a scalp lock and a musket. He waited until the man had passed, then slipped back out onto the trail and followed.

Arriving back at the clearing, Chingachgook saw in the shadows cast upon the hide walls of the lodge that the man had entered and was standing over Onowara, who was still seated at the fire. Chingachgook eased closer until he could hear their conversation.

"I want only what is best for our people," Onowara was saying. "Just as you do, Kahonwah."

"You have tricked half the village, but not me. You would make us weak with your talk of peace, when you know it does nothing but play into their hands."

"The hands of the red jackets? The white jackets? Or the Above Father?"

"There is no difference between the red and the white.

They will kill each other, and whoever is left standing will turn against us. Today the red jackets send their soldier to convince us that we must take up arms in their defense. Tomorrow it will be the white jackets. They are the same, and they are our enemies."

"Is what we want so different, Kahonwah? I tell our people that we must not align ourselves with the red jackets or the whites. And you—"

"I would have us fight any who dare set foot upon our land, while you would make us dogs to our women, without guns or bullets and with only our songs and our dances to hold the enemy at bay."

"The Above Father will protect and provide for our people, if only—"

"Your Above Father is a lie!" Kahonwah blared, and Chingachgook saw him raise a fist as if to strike the seated man. "He is not the Great Creator of our fathers. He is not the one who gave us the Great Peace."

"You would turn your back on the Great Creator of our people?"

"Never! But I spit on the false god that you serve! Our Great Creator taught us to stand strong, six nations bound by one law. He taught us to fight and to drive out of our lands all who did not accept the Great Peace. And now you would have us cast aside the very weapons that can make us strong again."

"The gifts of the white man will never make us strong." Onowara's voice was calm and even.

Kahonwah paced across the lodge, then back to the fire. "I did not come to argue with you. I came to warn you."

There was a long pause before Onowara replied, "What does Kahonwah want to warn me about?"

"I know you, *Onowara*." His tone dripped with contempt. "I used to hunt with you and your brother. I was there when your brother almost died and you boasted of your first vision. I saw how the praise of our elders made your heart swell with pride. I know that it is because of you that Oweya became infected with the teachings of the black robes and ran off to the mission."

"You did not come to speak of Oweya," Onowara

said without emotion. "What have you come to warn me about?"

"There are those among our people who would see you dead."

"Are you one of them?"

"I would be your friend."

Onowara laughed. "You have not called me friend since we were boys."

"I would call you that again," Kahonwah declared. Listening outside, Chingachgook sensed both cunning and sincerity in the young warrior's voice. "I have seen how our people listen to your words. But you speak to them of dreams, when they need a call to action. Our brothers, the Kanyenkehaka, guard our eastern door, and the Yengeese are already upon their lands. It is time for our war chiefs to gather the nations and push back the enemy, before we are so few and so weak that there are none to strike the war drum and give the cry."

"You are a pine-tree chief, Kahonwah. You can speak to the council, and if they agree, they will send runners to Onondaga—"

"The council is blinded by the medicine of your tongue. They believe that when the whites hear your words, they will return to their homes across the salt lake. You and I know that this will not be."

"And now it is your wish that I use my medicine to lead our people on the path of war. And if I do not, you will kill me?"

"The life of one brave is unimportant, whether he is Kahonwah or Onowara."

"My medicine comes from the Above Father. It is his words that I speak, not my own."

"Then ask him to counsel our people not to allow the enemy upon our lands."

"I do not tell him what to speak. I do not ask. I simply wait and listen."

"Do not wait too long, Onowara."

"I have heard many voices tonight. Tomorrow I go in search of the voice of the Above Father. When I return, we shall speak again."

"Do not oppose me, Onowara. Stand beside me, and

we will be strong for our people. Apart, you will not be standing for long."

"We shall speak again," the young prophet repeated.

In the shadows cast upon the lodge wall, Chingachgook saw Onowara rise from his place on the ground. The Mohican retreated into the trees and watched as Kahonwah left the lodge and headed back to the village. He waited a few minutes, then turned to follow. As he started down the trail he heard Onowara again begin to chant the Iroquois song for the dead:

> *"Jatthontenyonk,*
> *Jatakweniyosaon!*
> *Jatthontenyonk,*
> *Jatakweniyosaon!"*

Chapter XXIV

"Yes," muttered the Indian, in his native tongue;
"the pale-faces are prattling women! they have
two words for each thing, while a redskin will
make the sound of his voice speak for him."
—*The Last of the Mohicans,* Chap. X

*C*hingachgook was gone from the longhouse before
dawn. When Astra Van Rensselaer and Major Horace
Trevlayne arose and asked what had become of him,
Hawkeye said only that he would be back before too long.
In truth, the scout knew only that his friend would not
return to the Oneida village until he was certain that
Onowara was in no danger. Until then he would follow at
a distance as the young shamen journeyed in search of the
voice of the Great Creator.

The major spent the morning wandering on his own
through the village, striking up conversations with several
of the braves who knew some English. Astra remained in
the longhouse, quite exhausted from the journey and
wanting to rest. She seemed particularly quiet and reserved, but Hawkeye did not think much about it until the
midmorning meal, when he noticed that she ate practically
nothing. Trevlayne had not returned for the meal, so
Hawkeye and Astra ate alone in awkward silence.

After they finished and offered a portion of the food
to the fire, Hawkeye suggested they go for a walk, and she
somewhat reluctantly agreed. She was still very quiet as
they made their way across the village plateau, and finally
Hawkeye summoned the nerve to say, "You're thinking of
Rebekka, aren't you?"

She hesitated, then gave a curt nod. "My brother, also. I . . . I thought it would affect me more, but . . ."

"What do you mean?"

"They're all dead—Pieter, Rebekka, even Jakob and little Stefan. But I've hardly cried. And each morning I rise and go about my daily affairs, as though nothing's happened." They had just passed beyond the outer ring of longhouses, and she came to a halt at the edge of a large field that held the last of the winter corn. "What's the matter with me?"

"Nothing," he said, reading the pain in her expression as she stared out across the field. "We do these things—we go on—because we have to. It's what they'd want us to do."

She shook her head bitterly. "I don't believe that. They're gone. They have no idea what we're doing down here. They don't even care."

"They care, and so do you." He grasped her shoulders and turned her toward him. "In time you'll realize—"

"Do you know what I was really thinking about? It wasn't Rebekka. Not even my brother. I was worrying about what my father will do to me when I get home."

"Then you *are* going home?"

She shrugged. "What does it matter? My brother, my best friend are dead, and all I can think about is what kind of trouble I'll be in when I return. You'd think I were a little schoolgirl."

"You're judging yourself too harshly. Give yourself some time."

She pulled free and walked several feet away. "He'll never forgive me. He . . . he'll be furious."

Hawkeye came up behind her. "Are you worried he'll strike you again?"

"He may try, but . . . I don't care about that. It's just . . ." Her shoulders slumped, and she shook her head in frustration.

"What is it?"

"I . . . I'm so worried about him."

"The way he's treated you, I should think you wouldn't care anymore."

She spun around and grasped his forearms. "Hawkeye, you don't understand. Father wasn't always like this . . . like the way you saw him. When we were younger . . ." A half smile played across her lips. "Pieter was such a rogue, and he loved to cause trouble. But Father never minded—encouraged him, in fact. Said it built character. That was why I was surprised how badly he took it when Pieter ran off to join the militia."

"He didn't like being disobeyed," Hawkeye commented.

"No, it wasn't that. Father encouraged us to disobey him. At least he used to. But then he started to have these rages—uncontrollable at times. He never hit me—not back then—but he smashed things. I'd never seen him like that. I think it frightened him as much as me."

"Perhaps there's something wrong with him. Has he seen a doctor?"

"You don't know Father. He's never been sick a day of his life—at least not that he'd admit. I tried to get him to go, but he refused." She frowned. "And to think of the way I've treated him . . . I'm so ashamed." She turned away again.

"Astra, you're being foolish." He walked around her, forcing her to look back up at him. "He's the one who struck *you*. He's the one who's been unreasonable—and violent."

"That wasn't Hendrik Van Rensselaer," she said emphatically. "I'll never believe that the man who hit me was my father."

Hawkeye hesitated, then reached up and touched her cheek where the bruise from her father's hand had been. "He struck you. Don't ever forget that."

"Forget?" she blurted, her eyes welling with tears. "Forget that he hit me? Or forget the way I abandoned him?"

"He drove you away."

"He *needed* me, and what did I do? Just thought of myself, as always. What kind of a daughter am I, running off at the very moment he needed me?" She started to sob.

Pulling her toward him, Hawkeye folded her into his arms.

*   *   *

"Merci beaucoup de cet excellent repas," Major Trevlayne said as he put aside his bowl. *"Quelque chose pour vous."* He reached into a pocket of his jacket and removed the leather purse that had been given him by Major Belêtre. Opening it, he removed two gold coins, making sure that the others in the purse were visible. Leaning forward, he placed the coins on the blanket in front of his host.

"Merci," Kahonwah replied, continuing in poor but passable French, "But what is gold to an Oneida?"

"Gold buys muskets and gunpowder." Trevlayne placed a third coin beside the others. Being careful to speak slowly and clearly, he continued, "Gold can buy the Oneidas the things that will make them strong."

Kahonwah eyed him suspiciously. "Why would you have us strong?"

The major was about to reply when a woman entered the longhouse to take their bowls and spoons. It was one of the smaller buildings in the village, with only a single fire pit and four compartments.

"You may speak in front of her," the warrior assured him. "Few here know the language of the Great Monarch." To the Indians who spoke French, *le Grand Monarque* was Louis XV.

"And where did Kahonwah learn his French?"

With a sneer of contempt, the young man replied, "At Caughnawaga," naming the Christian mission set up for Indians near Montreal. "To defeat an enemy, one must first wear his moccasins." Not knowing the French word for moccasin, which itself was Algonquin, he used the Iroquois word, *a-ta,* and pointed at his feet.

Trevlayne nodded with respect. "You speak like a great general. But our own generals are fools. They march through your woods as if crossing an open field. They kill their own men with their stupidity. If a leader such as you had enough muskets and ammunition, you could drive our generals back to the salt lake."

Kahonwah thought on the major's words for a long moment. The woman reappeared at the longhouse entrance, but he brusquely waved his hand, dismissing her. Alone again he leaned toward Trevlayne. "Of which generals do you speak? The red jackets or the white?"

The major smiled. "Is there any difference?" he asked, repeating what Kahonwah had said many times before.

"You wear the uniform of the red jackets, yet you speak the language of the Great Monarch."

"I speak both English and French. I, too, know the value of walking in my enemy's shoes."

"But who is your enemy?" Kahonwah pressed. "Who would you have us fight?"

Trevlayne's smile hardened. "Who is your greatest enemy?"

"They are both the same," the young man replied with a wave of the hand.

"No," the major said emphatically. "Neither the English nor the French are your greatest enemy."

Kahonwah looked at him with uncertainty.

"The greatest enemy is always found lurking in one's own camp," Trevlayne continued. "It is the one who would weaken the spirit of your warriors—the one named Onowara."

"Onowara . . ." the warrior muttered with disdain. "But he is no concern of yours. He is like a dog to the women." He shook his head. "Onowara will never take to the warpath against your people."

"You are wrong, Kahonwah." Dipping into his purse, he dropped yet another coin onto the blanket. "Onowara is my sworn enemy. I have come to Oneida Castle to kill him."

There was a long silence as Kahonwah absorbed what had been said, his expression revealing intrigue and distrust. Finally he picked up one of the coins and examined it.

"If you will help me do this thing, Kahonwah, I will fill the longhouses of your people with muskets and gunpowder and ammunition. You will be able to drive your enemies far beyond the salt lake."

The young man clutched the coin in his fist. "Which enemy would you have me drive away?" His eyes locked with the major's and did not waver, as if he were reading the other man's innermost thoughts.

Trevlayne merely shrugged.

"You do not care whether we fight the red jackets or the white?" Kahonwah said incredulously.

"I care only that I complete my mission."

"To kill Onowara . . ."

"Yes, to kill Onowara."

"And why should I help you do this thing?"

"He is your enemy, too, is he not? You wish to see him dead, but you fear making him a martyr and yourself an outcast among your people. If *I* kill him, he will still become a martyr, but one you can use for your purposes."

Kahonwah turned away and stared into the embers of the fire. "This is an evil thing of which we speak. I have no wish to see the life of Onowara come to an end."

"Is it evil for a warrior to kill his enemy?"

"Onowara is my brother."

"But he is *my* enemy. If there is any evil in this act, it will be upon my shoulders, not yours."

Kahonwah looked up at him. "What would you have me do?"

"Onowara has left the village seeking a vision."

"How do you know this?"

"The Mohican is following him. Chingachgook fears that you will harm his son."

Kahonwah's eyes widened. "Son?"

Trevlayne nodded. "Perhaps you have seen the sign of a blue turtle on Onowara's chest." He saw in the warrior's expression that this was so. "Chingachgook has this same sign on his chest. He came here searching for his son."

"Yes . . . Muhheconnuk." From the way he said the word, it was apparent that he knew something of Onowara's background and might have suspected that the mother of the twins was a Mohican. "But what does the Mohican have to fear from me?"

"When he returned from the gathering last night, he said that he heard you speaking with Onowara . . . that you threatened Onowara's life."

Kahonwah's jaw tightened, but he betrayed no emotion. "And now you will kill Onowara for me," he stated.

"You must let me know when Onowara returns from his journey, and I will kill him. All you have to do is to help me get away."

"And what of your friends?"

"I have no friends," Trevlayne said coldly.

"The people will demand blood for the life of Onowara."

"Let them have the blood of his Mohican father and the one known as the Long Rifle."

"And what about the woman?"

"Do with her as you wish."

Trevlayne emerged from the longhouse and stood looking at the village. In many ways it was more impressive than he had expected. Before coming to the Colonies, he had imagined the Indians as wild, nomadic people who ate with their hands and killed without reason. But Oneida Castle was a well-designed, orderly community that operated quite efficiently despite the close living conditions. He knew that all this would soon come to an end—that this land that had been theirs for centuries would pass to the English or the French—and for a fleeting moment he was almost sorry for them.

England or France? he thought. In many ways he hated them both. The son of an Englishman of lesser nobility and his French mistress, Horace Trevlayne had lived with his father since birth and had not known his real mother until he was in his early teens. Later, after his father had died penniless, his mother's French husband had introduced him to certain political figures willing to provide gold for the information that Trevlayne, then a young army officer, could provide.

Secure in the knowledge that they had an effective spy within the English military, the French had paid often and paid well, and they had taken particular pleasure when Trevlayne had been promoted to major and sent to the Colonies. But the move had been a calculated one on the part of his English superiors, whom he kept fully informed about his secret dealings with the enemy.

England or France? Trevlayne himself did not know for whom he was really working, nor did he care, so long as each thought he was on their side and continued to pay for his services. As for this current business with the Oneida Prophet, his only concern was to kill the man and get away, and he did not much care which enemy the Indians ended up blaming for his death. Either way, he would have no trouble concocting a suitable story for each of his masters.

Masters, he thought ruefully. In fact, he had come to scorn both of them equally. And now that he had spent time in the Colonies, he sensed a third power in the making, for it had grown apparent that the colonists would not long suffer being under the control of what they increasingly considered foreign powers. If they ever tried to throw off that yoke, a man like Trevlayne would be in a unique position to profit from all sides.

As the major started back across the village he considered ways he might curry friendships among the leaders of the various provincial militias. So intrigued was he at the thought of this new opportunity for profit that he didn't notice Hawkeye standing with Astra Van Rensselaer less than a hundred yards away, watching with suspicion as he walked from Kahonwah's longhouse.

Later that evening Astra stood alone, gazing up at the night sky outside the longhouse where she was staying.

"Have you been out here long?" a voice said from behind, startling her.

Spinning around, she made out the figure of Major Horace Trevlayne in the moonlight and let out a sigh of relief. "Oh, it's you, Horace."

"I didn't mean to frighten you, but I thought you might be cold." Smiling, he held open a small Iroquois blanket.

"Why, thank you."

She turned her back to him, and as he placed the blanket around her shoulders, she noticed that he let his hands linger there awhile. It made her somewhat uncomfortable, so she moved away slightly.

"The moon's so bright, you can hardly see the stars," he commented, coming up beside her.

"Yes, it's beautiful."

They stood a moment staring up at the sky above Oneida Castle. Around them, most of the fires had burned down, and few Indians remained outside.

"Perhaps we should go in," Astra said when the silence grew awkward. "I don't want to worry Hawkeye."

"I think he's relieved to have a few minutes alone. He seemed a bit edgy tonight. I suppose he's concerned about his Mohican friend."

"Yes. I think he expected Chingachgook back by now." Astra looked toward the dark line of trees in the distance. "Where do you think he could be?"

"Probably sitting around a campfire swapping tales with that Onowara fellow and having a good laugh at our expense."

"Do you think it's true? Could the Oneida Prophet really be Chingachgook's son?"

Trevlayne shrugged. "The way these Indians change families and allegiances, how could anyone be sure?"

"We change our families, too," she pointed out. "Women go off to live with their husbands."

"That's true. But they're married."

"Indians get married."

"Yes, but they don't place the same value on it that we do. It's not as if they're married in the eyes of God."

"Perhaps not *our* God," she conceded. "But Hawkeye says they have a marriage ceremony and take vows in their own way."

"If you can call it that. From what I hear, the man simply brings a deerskin to the father of the girl he wants. If her family doesn't object to the marriage, she sits down on the skin, and they're married."

"Oh, there's much more to it than that. Hawkeye told me that a herald announces the impending marriage, and then gifts are exchanged and a great feast is held, with singing and dancing. There's even a man who preaches to the couple about the duties of marriage. Hawkeye says that it's just as solemn and joyous an occasion as our weddings—and that the bride and groom take their vows just as seriously."

"Hawkeye said all that, did he?" Trevlayne's tone was cynical, which surprised her. "He's been telling you a lot about the Iroquois, I see."

"He's only trying to be helpful," she replied a bit defensively.

"Has he told you about some of their other customs? Not just the way they behave among themselves, but the things they do to outsiders who fall among them?"

"I don't care to hear it," she said tersely, starting back to the longhouse.

"I'm sorry, Astra." He came up behind her and took her arm.

Pulling free, she turned to him and said quite sharply, "I should think that after what happened at German Flats, you'd keep such talk to yourself."

"You're right—I was terribly thoughtless. Please forgive me."

She looked down and gave a slight nod.

"I'm afraid I must confess to a dose of jealousy."

"Jealousy?" She looked genuinely surprised. "Whatever could you be jealous about?"

"What do you think?"

She wanted to say that she had no idea, but she knew it would be a lie. "Hawkeye?" she finally said. "But why?"

"I see how solicitous he's being—and how responsive you are."

"Hawkeye is a dear friend."

"Is that all he is?"

"Good heavens, Major . . ."

"Horace," he reminded her.

"Do you seriously think I have intentions toward Hawkeye?"

"It's crossed my mind."

"Is that why you've been acting so strangely?" she asked, looking up at him curiously.

"Have I?"

"Yes. I've noticed it ever since we escaped from the French."

"How do you mean?"

"Well, you've been more . . . distant is the only way I can put it. More aloof."

"Believe me, I don't intend to be aloof." He moved a few inches toward her.

"I thought it was me, at first—what with the ordeal and learning about . . . about Rebekka." Her voice caught, but she drew in a breath and continued, "The last few days I realized it isn't just me. Something about you has changed as well."

"I . . . I'm sorry. I don't know what to say."

"Oh, please don't apologize," she said, feeling a rush

of sympathy. "We've been through so much, and if you've wanted to be by yourself—"

"I haven't. I just . . ."

"What is it?" she asked in concern.

"It's just . . ." He hesitated only a moment. "Just this." Pulling her close, he kissed her full on the lips.

Astra was shocked by the brazen strength of his kiss. She was equally amazed at her reaction. There was a time when she had fantasized about this moment, but now that it had come, she only wished that it hadn't. Pushing against him, she broke his grip and backed away several steps. "Horace, I'm sorry if I've led you to believe—"

"Didn't you want to be kissed?" he said boldly, moving toward her. "If I'd thought you didn't want it, I never would have—"

"I don't," she said simply, pulling the blanket more tightly around her.

"Are you so certain of that?" He moved yet a step closer. "It's been my experience that a woman often won't admit what she really wants. Not even to herself."

"I know what I want, and it isn't this. Now, if you'll excuse me . . ."

She started past him, but he took her arm and turned her toward him, saying, "Is it Hawkeye? Is that what you want?"

She looked up into his eyes, and even in the faint glow of the moon, she was able to see that they possessed a dangerous, unsettling light. She tried to twist her arm free, but his grip tightened.

"You're hurting me, Horace."

"I don't want to leave it like this," he declared.

She could not tell from his tone whether he was apologizing or simply did not want to leave unfinished what he had started. An instant later it became clear, for he pulled her closer and tried to kiss her again. When she jerked her head away, he hungrily kissed her neck, his hands searching her back and buttocks.

Summoning all her strength, she pressed against his chest, breaking his grip. She staggered back a few steps, and when he came toward her again, she lashed out and slapped him hard across the cheek. He drew up short and looked at her with the most curious expression, almost as if he did not understand why she was upset.

Astra rushed past him into the longhouse. She heard him calling after her, but she didn't stop running until she was back at the compartment and safely under her robes. Only then, as she lay there, did she let the tears come, softly at first and then with increasing emotion.

"What is it, Astra?" a voice whispered. It was a soothing voice—the voice of a friend.

"I . . . I'm all right," she muttered, burying her face in the robes.

She felt a hand upon her shoulder and cringed at the touch. But the hand was gentle, almost hesitant, and she reached up and took hold of it, clutching it as if she would drown.

"Is there something I can do?" Hawkeye asked a bit uncertainly.

"Hold me. . . ." she murmured. "Just hold me."

She raised up slightly and wrapped her arms around his waist, clinging desperately to him. Ever so tenderly, ever so innocently, he caressed her hair.

Chapter XXV

"He has the religion of the matter, in believing what is to happen will happen."
—*The Last of the Mohicans*, Chap. V

Onowara sat cross-legged on the hard-packed earth, unmoving, silent beneath the stars. He had been there since late afternoon, dressed only in a loincloth, his buckskin clothes piled in front of him as if an offering to the Great Creator. He had smoked and given gifts of corn, tobacco, and an eagle's feather, and now he waited and listened for a voice or even a sigh. But still he was alone, and he feared he would remain that way, for he knew that the Great Creator came and went in his own time.

The young man whom some called a prophet knew he was being watched—perhaps by the Great Creator, but also by the Mohican who claimed to be his father. Onowara had sensed someone following him that morning when he had left Oneida Castle and hiked to this grassy promontory overlooking the lake of his people. At first he had thought it might be Kahonwah, intent on doing him harm. But he saw before his eyes the image of the blue turtle, and he knew that it was Chingachgook.

Onowara had chosen not to confront his shadow, and so he continued to sit, offering up his prayers and songs, awaiting a voice over which he had no control—a voice that had failed him only once, on the day that his brother had gone away.

Oweya . . . The name rose through him like mist off the lake, and the image of his brother appeared full-formed, in all his terrible beauty. Onowara had hardly thought of his twin since the morning Oweya had abandoned Oneida Castle for the promise of salvation in Canada. But that was before the Mohican had come asking disturbing questions and telling troublesome tales of the days before the twins were born.

"Oweya . . ." he whispered, the word floating out across the still, dark waters of Lake Oneida. He opened his eyes and blinked against the faint glimmer of moonlight on the surface of the water. And there, out in the middle of the lake, he saw the young warrior rising, a bow in his left hand, a cross in his right, water dripping from the long tendrils of his hair. *Brother!* he called with his inner voice, wanting to walk out to him, wondering what message Oweya had come to bring.

Excited by the vision, Onowara's muscles tensed, and immediately Oweya began to slip beneath the waters. Onowara forced calm into his thoughts, but still the image faltered and faded. He felt a moment's panic, then realized that it was his fear that was chasing the voice away. Smiling ever so faintly, he let the water wash over him, easing his arms and legs and back. Closing his eyes, he opened his heart.

Onowara . . . his brother called, moving toward him across the lake. *I am coming home.*

"But why? Why did you go away?"

You followed one voice, I another.

"Did you find the one you were seeking? The warrior on the cross?"

If he was there, I did not see him. I saw only sickness and death. It is a path that holds darkness for our people. And so I have come home.

Onowara did not move, yet he felt himself walking out to greet Oweya, the brother who had been lost and now was found. The water was soft yet firm, and it cradled his feet, supporting him as it drew him slowly under, until it was lapping at his knees. He faltered, and the lake rose up to his waist, tugging ever so gently, yearning to embrace him.

Take my hand, Oweya urged, moving closer and raising an arm toward him.

Onowara looked up at his brother—looked into eyes

that mirrored his own—and reached for his hand. "I . . . I'm frightened," he heard himself saying.

I will hold you, Oweya promised. *As you once held me.*

Onowara *had* held his brother. It had happened on the morning the voice first spoke to him, when they were in the first blush of manhood. The voice had come as a single word—his brother's name. And instantly he had known that Oweya was in trouble. He had run from the village, racing down off the plateau and through the forest as fast as his legs would carry him. He had found the small canoe shattered in the rapids and had plunged into the creek to drag his brother from where he was pinned among the rocks below the surface of the water. That day Onowara had promised to serve the Great Creator if only he would breathe the spirit back into Oweya's lifeless body. And when at last Oweya revived, Onowara had kept his promise, shunning the life of a warrior, hunter, or husband and seeking the shaman's path.

I will hold you, his brother repeated, grasping his arm as he had once grasped Oweya.

Even as he felt himself being pulled from the water, he saw his brother sinking, taking his place.

"No!" Onowara gasped, trying to pull him up. But Oweya was like a stone, slipping below the surface of the lake, smiling up at him.

I must return, Oweya called to him, releasing Onowara's hand. *It is my time, and I must return.*

Onowara looked down into the water and saw his brother, hardly yet a man, lying wedged among the rocks. "No!" he heard himself shout, even as the life flowed out of Oweya in a final sigh that rustled through the leaves overhanging Lake Oneida.

Onowara wanted to lie down in the water and join his brother, but he soon found himself seated back upon the hard earth, alone in the darkness, the only sound the cool night wind. He realized that his eyes were open, and he considered standing, speaking, shouting. But as he started to move, the silence was shattered by a crack of thunder— no, the retort of a musket. There was the flapping of wings, the pained squawk of a bird tumbling from its perch high above.

The noise ceased, as though the bird had vanished in midair, and Onowara looked up to see a tiny glowing light come drifting through the trees. It floated on the air, spinning gentle circles as it settled to the ground in front of him. It was a single eagle's feather, and Onowara picked it up and held it before him. At the tip of the feather was a spot of blood, and as he touched it to his lips he heard the voice he had been seeking.

The eagle screams atop a tall and mighty tree. His chest is pierced, but the tree does not fall.

Onowara stared at the feather, which glowed with moonlight. His vision clouded over, and he saw the feather hanging from the hair of his brother, but then it fluttered to the ground as the young man ran into the trees. A hand picked up the feather, and Onowara saw the Mohican tie it in his own hair and go walking away.

As Onowara clutched the feather in his fist he saw a musket barrel peeking through the leaves, heard its report, and saw the Mohican fall. Onowara ran toward him, rolled him over, but it was not Chingachgook but his brother who lay there dying, blood pulsing from a hole in his chest. Or were these his own eyes that stared up at him? he thought as he shook off the vision and rose to his feet.

Onowara stretched, then looked down at his hand and saw not a feather but a handful of earth. Letting it slip through his fingers, he gazed out across the lake. The light had softened, turning the faintest orange as the first hint of dawn touched the eastern sky.

"Oweya," he whispered, thinking first of his brother and then of the man who was their father. He tried to understand the vision he had been given, but his thoughts were tangled with confusion. Yet there was one feeling he could not shake, one truth from which he could not escape: Someone was going to die.

Onowara knew that all was in the hands of the Great Creator and that not a single feather fell from the wings of a bird that the Creator did not ordain. *What is to happen will happen,* he told himself, even as he felt the dull pain of a bullet buried deep in his chest.

Picking up his clothes, the Oneida Prophet turned away from the lake and headed into the forest.

*   *   *

Major Horace Trevlayne checked his musket a third time, making sure the powder in the pan was still dry, as he crouched among the reeds beside the creek that led from Lake Oneida. Satisfied, he raised the barrel and sighted down the path that ran alongside the water. The path made a turn about fifty yards away, and he would have a clear shot at whoever came around that bend. If Kahonwah was correct, that person would be the Oneida Prophet.

Kahonwah had sought out Trevlayne a couple of hours after dawn and had informed him that Onowara had been sighted returning alone to the village. The major had waited until Hawkeye and Astra were away from the longhouse, then he had gathered up a few supplies for the journey back to Albany, along with one of the muskets taken from the French, and had slipped away into the woods. Now he sat, hidden in the underbrush near where the trail turned from the creek and headed up toward the village on the plateau, ready to take down the prophet and fulfill his end of the pact he had made with Kahonwah. In return, Kahonwah would assist Trevlayne in getting away and would make sure that Chingachgook and Hawkeye did not interfere. To that end, he had dispatched half his men throughout the village to keep an eye on Hawkeye and the rest along the approaches to Oneida Castle to watch for the Mohican.

Trevlayne heard footsteps and pulled the hammer of his musket to full cock, shielding the mechanism with his jacket sleeve to muffle the sound. Again he raised the barrel, taking care to keep it hidden among the reeds as he trained the sights on the point at which Onowara would emerge.

A few seconds later the young Oneida came into view, walking resolutely toward his village. He was dressed in winter buckskins and looked somewhat more gaunt than Trevlayne had remembered, but there was no mistaking the strong features and piercing eyes. As he approached he was staring directly at the spot where the major crouched, and for a moment Trevlayne hesitated. But then the young man looked away.

It was the moment Trevlayne was awaiting, and he

held his breath and squeezed the trigger. The hammer smacked against the pan with a loud snap, causing the brave to jerk his head around. He seemed to realize what was happening, but before he could react, the charge ignited and the lead ball went straight into his chest, knocking him back off his feet and onto the ground.

Trevlayne quickly reloaded, then rose from his hiding place and cautiously stepped out onto the trail. Shouldering the musket, he thumbed back the hammer. He could see the arms and legs of the young man jerking spasmodically, and he did not want to take any chance that the Oneida Prophet would survive. Walking over to where he was lying, Trevlayne aimed the barrel at his head and coldly pulled the trigger. The hammer struck, but the spark failed to set off the charge. Muttering an oath under his breath, Trevlayne opened the flashpan and reached for his powder horn. Glancing down, he saw that his victim was indeed still alive and was trying to speak, but all that could be heard was the gurgle of blood.

"*Au revoir,* Onowara," Trevlayne said without emotion, pouring some additional gunpowder into the pan.

Trevlayne was just thumbing back the hammer when he heard a whooshing sound and felt something smack into the back of his leg. A stab of pain shot threw him, and he knew without looking that he had been struck by an arrow. Going down on one knee, he spun around, expecting to see Chingachgook, and fired the musket at a brave in full war paint who stood about fifty feet away. But his shot went high as a second and then a third arrow came from opposite directions and thudded into his chest and back. His eyes wide with shock, he clawed at the musket, which had slipped from his hands and was lying a few feet away. He tried to pick it up, but his fingers would not close around it.

One final arrow struck him in the back, and he fell forward onto his hands. He was dizzy with the pain and felt himself gagging, and he had to force his eyes to stay open as he looked up at the brave who was approaching along the path.

"K-Kahonwah . . ." he stammered, then slid forward onto the ground, snapping the arrow from his chest.

"*Au revoir,*" were the last words that he heard.

"Good-bye," Kahonwah repeated, this time in the Oneida tongue as he kicked the English major onto his side and confirmed that he was dead. Looking back up, he raised a hand, and a half-dozen braves emerged from the trees and walked over to where the young shaman lay writhing on the ground. One had his tomahawk out and was about to give the coup de grâce and finish the job started by Trevlayne's musket, but Kahonwah signaled him to wait.

"We will take Onowara back to the village," he said, motioning for two of his men to pick up the mortally wounded Indian. "Before he dies, he can tell who it was who shot him and how Kahonwah avenged his death."

As he picked up the musket the other two braves grabbed Trevlayne's body by the ankles and dragged it toward the Oneida village.

Weaving among the trees as he raced down off the plateau, Hawkeye pulled the stopper from his powder horn with his teeth and poured a measure down Killdeer's barrel. Letting the horn drop to his side, he snatched a ball from his pouch and pushed it into the muzzle. Still running, he slid out the ramrod and set the ball against the powder, then replaced the rod and primed the pan.

The shots had come from the vicinity of the creek. There had been two of them, both from a musket that sounded far more powerful than the usual Indian trading gun. Hawkeye was certain it was one of the rifles Chingachgook and Major Trevlayne had taken when they escaped from the French—and that meant that one of them might be in trouble.

Nearing the creek, Hawkeye heard voices and pulled up short, ducking behind a tree and shouldering his rifle. A moment later a pair of Oneida braves came into view, dragging an arrow-riddled body by the legs. The victim was facedown, but the moment Hawkeye saw the scarlet jacket, he knew who it was. The scout drew a bead on one of the braves and started to pull the trigger, then held back. He had no idea what the major might have done to provoke such an attack or even if these two men had killed him. It could even be possible, though Hawkeye thought it unlikely, that some other band of Indians had attacked Trevlayne and that the Oneidas had driven them off and recovered the body.

Lowering his rifle to his side but keeping it trained on the braves, he stepped from behind the tree and into their path. They halted abruptly, and one of them let go of Trevlayne and went for the tomahawk on his belt. As he jerked it out and drew it back, Hawkeye pulled the trigger, knocking him off his feet and across the trail. The second brave already had his knife in hand, and he leaped at the scout. The blade sliced the air near Hawkeye's cheek, and he swung the butt of the rifle upward, knocking the man's hand and sending the knife hurtling through the air.

The two men locked arms and fell to the ground. The brave landed on top of Hawkeye, who brought a knee up and threw him to the side. But the momentum broke Hawkeye's grip, and the brave was able to lunge at the knife. Closing his fingers around the handle, he gave a triumphant cry and dove at Hawkeye, who deflected the knife with one hand and jabbed upward with the other. The brave's cry became a strangled groan as he landed on the tip of the knife Hawkeye had managed to draw from his belt. The blade sank deep into his belly, twisted upward, and pierced his heart.

Hawkeye rolled the brave away and jumped to his feet. He heard others coming and knew he had no time to reload Killdeer, so he yanked the knife from the brave's body and snatched up the tomahawk from where it had fallen. Spinning around, he faced the next of his adversaries—two more braves who raced up the trail. One brandished a pair of tomahawks, the other was nocking an arrow onto his bow as he came.

Bracing himself, Hawkeye drew back his 'hawk and let it fly. It spun twice through the air and struck the bowman in the center of his chest with a thud, staggering him and then dropping him face forward on the ground. The other brave threw one of his tomahawks, but Hawkeye dove clear. Unwilling to throw his remaining weapon, the brave swung at Hawkeye's head as he closed in. Hawkeye feinted to the left and right, slashing out with his knife and laying several gashes across the man's forearm.

Hawkeye heard hurried footsteps behind him, and he

jumped back from the 'hawk-wielding brave and twirled around. He caught a glimpse of a warrior with a scalp lock, then heard the whoosh of a musket being swung through the air. The barrel struck a glancing blow on the side of his head, stunning him. Momentarily blinded, he swung wildly with his knife, but the barrel then connected full force on his shoulder and knocked him off his feet.

Hawkeye found himself on his hands and knees, groping in the darkness for the knife. He heard voices, struggled to clear his vision, and glimpsed a pair of moccasins in front of his face. Following them upward, he saw Kahonwah leering down at him in victory. The warrior took a half step backward, raised Major Trevlayne's musket in his hands, and brought it smashing down against Hawkeye's skull.

Chapter XXVI

"When the white man dies, he thinks he is at peace; but the redmen know how to torture even the ghosts of their enemies."

—*The Last of the Mohicans*, Chap. X

Astra Van Rensselaer managed with great effort to thread a bone needle that one of the Oneida women had given her so that she could repair some of the many tears in her blue jacket and linen skirt. Hearing hurried footsteps that halted just outside her longhouse compartment, she looked up and called, "Is that you, Hawkeye?"

The blanket curtain was thrust aside, and she found herself confronted by a pair of braves in full war paint, the one in front wearing a scalp lock and brandishing a long hunting rifle that she immediately recognized as Hawkeye's Killdeer.

"What's going on?" she exclaimed as the second man jerked her to her feet and then clamped a hand over her mouth. She was hauled off the platform and down the long corridor, drawing a crowd of Indians who emerged from their compartments and crowded the longhouse entrance to find out what was happening. She tried to break away or at least twist her head free, but he gripped her all the more violently until she thought she would pass out. Finally she surrendered and let her body go limp, and he eased the pressure on her mouth just enough for her to breathe.

It appeared as if the entire community had gathered outside, and many were shouting what Astra could only assume were imprecations as she was half dragged, half carried through their midst toward the center of the village. Some of the bolder youth ran up and grabbed at her dress, further ripping it, before the brave carrying Killdeer chased them away. Every now and then he glanced back at her, his face revealing a curious mixture of hatred and indifference.

The shouting grew louder as the villagers pressed in around her, blocking their passage. And then something struck the side of her head—a club or a rock—and everything went black.

When she regained her senses, Astra was on her knees with her arms wrapped around a wooden post in front of her. She felt a harsh tug at her wrists and realized that the brave who had been carrying her was now lashing her hands around the post. She shook her head to clear it and felt something warm and moist running into her left eye and down her cheek. As it touched her lips she tasted her own blood.

"Leave her be!" a voice shouted, followed by the stinging sound of a man being struck. She forced her head to the left and, blinking against the blood, saw Hawkeye standing with his back against a second post, his hands tied behind it, his face gashed and bruised. The brave who had led Astra from the longhouse was in front of him, taunting him with words and with Hawkeye's own rifle. When the scout defiantly turned to Astra and started to speak, the brave swung Killdeer's barrel into his belly, doubling him over. He slid down the post onto one knee, then struggled back up.

"Stop it!" she shouted, standing as she fought the leather cords lashed around her wrists.

The brave with the scalp lock stalked over to her and jammed the muzzle of Hawkeye's rifle under her chin. He shouted something that she guessed meant, "Shut up," then turned to face the encircling crowd. He began a long harangue that effectively whipped the crowd into a fever. Astra had no idea what he was saying, but she knew that somehow this warrior had turned the villagers against them. She did not recall having seen him before but guessed that he was the one Hawkeye and Major Trevlayne had said was named Kahonwah—the one who stood in opposition to the Oneida Prophet and to all whites.

Thinking of Trevlayne, she realized that she had not seen him for the past few hours. Despite her unpleasant encounter with him the night before, she hoped that he was in hiding and had not fallen into their hands. She also prayed that Chingachgook and the prophet would return soon and would find a way to free them—for somehow she knew that Kahonwah did not intend to let them live more than a few minutes longer.

Astra saw both of her prayers crushed when the crowd parted and two bodies were brought forth. The first was dragged facedown through the dirt and deposited at Hawkeye's feet. With a gasp of shock and fear, Astra gazed upon the bloody, arrow-riddled form of Major Horace Trevlayne. The second body was laid out in on a litter borne by two braves, who placed it on the ground not far from where she was tied. Though she had not yet seen the Oneida Prophet, she knew that this must be the man they called Onowara.

Dead! Both dead! She felt her stomach roil and thought she would pass out. But just then there was a groan, and she saw the prophet's head move. He was still alive, though bleeding profusely from his chest.

Several of the village elders crowded around the litter, examining the wound and talking to the prophet, who nodded several times but seemed unable to speak. They conferred among themselves, then signaled for the litter to be carried away.

Realizing that no one was paying any attention to her just then, Astra turned to Hawkeye, who was listening intently to what was being said. She spoke his name, and when he looked over at her, she called to him, "What's happening? Why did they kill them?"

He shook his head and mouthed the word *Trevlayne.*

"Horace?" she said, not fully comprehending.

"He shot Onowara."

"But he—"

"Shhh . . ." he breathed as he strained to hear what the Oneidas were saying.

Astra stared down at the body of the English major. Could it be true? she asked herself. Could Horace

Trevlayne really have shot the Oneida Prophet and been killed for his treacherous act? She could not comprehend it, yet somehow she knew that it was so. And for some unfathomable reason, she was not at all surprised.

Now they will kill us. . . .

She shuddered as the image of German Flats flooded her senses . . . the charred, smoking ruins, the stiffened carcasses of cows and horses, the body of an infant boy. The throbbing pain at her temple swelled, and her head grew dizzy. She eased herself down the post to her knees and closed her eyes, fighting against the tears. They could kill her, but she would not let them see her cry.

Kahonwah walked away from Skenendowa and the elders and followed after the pair of braves who were carrying the litter to Onowara's lodge. People pressed around them, trying to touch the feet and hands of the man they called a prophet. The warrior allowed them this moment of mourning; he knew that it would pass, for he would see to it that their grief was transformed to rage. And he would wield that rage in a manner that Skenendowa and the elders had been unwilling to do.

They stopped near the edge of the village, and Kahonwah raised Killdeer and ordered the crowd back. Slowly they complied, and when he was certain he could not be overheard, he told his men to put down the litter. Kneeling beside it, he placed a hand on the chest of the mortally wounded young man.

"You will soon be dead," he said, not bothering to mask his delight. He waited until Onowara's eyelids fluttered open, then continued, "It was not a red-jacket soldier who killed you. He pulled the trigger, but I brought him there and sent his bullet into your heart. And when you are dead, I will sing of you as a great chief and teacher. I will lead our people away from your path of shame and onto the true path of war."

The dying man's eyes widened, and he reached up and pawed at the beaded gorget around Kahonwah's neck. He tried to twist it, but his fingers slipped and his hand fell back at his side.

"You have lost, Onowara. Your time is past. It is the

day of the warrior." Standing, he drew his knife and handed it to one of the braves. "When you get to the lodge, kill him—if he isn't dead already."

As the braves carried the litter into the woods, Kahonwah headed back toward the crowd, smiling at how well this day had turned out.

Hawkeye felt the urge to fight the cords binding his wrists; yet he knew that would only tighten them further. Even were he to break free, there was no chance of escape. Kahonwah's braves would be on him before he was half-way across the few feet that separated him from Astra. The only thing he would accomplish would be to hasten their deaths—perhaps a blessing. From what he had heard Kahonwah and the others say, it was apparent that he and Astra were considered accomplices in the shooting of Onowara and would suffer a punishment reserved for the Oneidas' most bitter enemies: They would be burned alive at the stake. The only reason that they hadn't yet been put to the torch was because Onowara was still clinging to life. Once he was gone—in a matter of minutes, no doubt—the villagers would turn their full attention and wrath on any-one who might have had a hand in murdering their prophet.

Bastard! Hawkeye seethed, forcing himself not to curse aloud at the blood-drenched body of Horace Trevlayne. At first, Hawkeye had assumed that Kahonwah had done away with his Oneida rival and then killed Trevlayne in order to pin the blame on him. But Skenendowa had put the question directly to the mortally wounded prophet, who had confirmed with a nod of the head that his murderer was the man in the scarlet uniform. Hawkeye still suspected that Kahonwah was involved, per-haps having encouraged or assisted Trevlayne, but such fine points no longer mattered. Kahonwah had succeeded in turning Onowara into a martyr whose blood he would avenge first here at the stake and then on the warpath against all whites.

The only chance Hawkeye had of stopping him was to convince Skenendowa and the other elders that he and Astra had known nothing about the assassination and that

Trevlayne had acted without the knowledge of his military superiors. It would require quite a bit of bluster, for Hawkeye's every instinct told him that this brutal act was in fact the true reason the Earl of Loudon had sent Trevlayne on this mission.

There was one other source of hope—Chingachgook —but Hawkeye did not see what the lone Mohican could do against so many. Undoubtedly Kahonwah had his men scouring the woods for him, and they would show no mercy.

Hawkeye turned to Astra, who was kneeling against her post, her eyes closed as if in prayer. He did not doubt that she understood the seriousness of their situation, yet he knew that he could not tell her the fate that awaited them. He could hope only that if he did not obtain her freedom, he could at least convince Skenendowa to make her death quick. He had some reason to think he would succeed, for it was unheard of for the Iroquois to burn a woman at the stake. That kind of barbarity was left to the civilized Europeans, who had a long history of meting out such punishment equally upon men, women, and even children.

Several minutes passed, and then Kahonwah returned and approached the prisoners. His expression was a smug mask of victory as he jabbed Killdeer toward Hawkeye's chest and declared in the Oneida tongue, "Do you know what we do to our enemies, Yengee?"

"I am not your enemy," the scout replied in a strong, confident tone. His words were directed not at Kahonwah but at the village chief, who stood nearby but seemed either unwilling or unable to intercede.

"Was this the act of a friend?" Kahonwah challenged, sweeping his arm toward Trevlayne's body.

"Today the Englishman has proved himself no friend of mine or of his people. We came here in peace, but I see now that his heart was black."

"Kahonwah has made sure that his heart will beat no longer. Nor shall the hearts of the Yengee dogs who brought him among our people and asked us to call him a friend."

"Skenendowa," Hawkeye called out. "I ask you to hear what I say. You know that La Longue Carabine speaks as straight as his rifle, and I tell you that we did not do this thing. The sagamore of the Mohicans has long been a friend of the People of the Standing Stone, and—"

"Your sagamore has abandoned you," Kahonwah cut him off. "Even now he is running away through the forest like a frightened rabbit."

"Chingachgook is no rabbit, though Kahonwah would shoot him like one so that the truth of his words cannot be heard." He turned again to Skenendowa. "Have Kahonwah call off his men, and the Mohican will show that he is not afraid to stand before you and speak the truth."

"A Mohican's truth is not our truth," Kahonwah countered. "And the voice of a Yengee is as twisted as the creek that feeds our valley. Feed us no more of your lies."

"La Longue Carabine speaks the truth," Hawkeye again declared, and he sensed in Skenendowa's expression that the old man was not in full accord with the hotheaded warrior. It was equally apparent, however, that the rest of the village was.

"And tell me, white man, will you speak these words at the stake? Or will you yelp and beg like the dog that you are? Perhaps then Kahonwah will show you mercy from the barrel of your rifle." He raised Killdeer high above his head and presented it to the crowd.

Hawkeye spoke but could not be heard above the shouts and cries for revenge. He tried to get the attention of the chief, but Skenendowa had turned away and was looking at his people. The old man glanced back at the two whites tied to the posts, then lowered his head and walked off, disappearing into the mob.

"Kahonwah!" Hawkeye called. "Don't do this! Don't—"

The young warrior spun around and struck Hawkeye across the cheek, stunning him.

"The—the woman . . ." he said groggily, shaking his head to clear it. "Don't do this to the woman. . . ."

Stepping closer, Kahonwah raised Hawkeye's chin. "Die like a warrior and show us you are not a dog. Then perhaps I will let the woman taste the lead of your rifle before we feed her to the flames." With a smile of utter victory, he walked away, the crowd parting and then swallowing him up. Hawkeye turned to Astra, who looked up at him with fear, but also with resignation. As he struggled for words to bring her comfort, he felt something scrape his leg—a branch dropped at his feet by a young brave who leered up at him and scurried away. Others surged forward, tossing branches and brush as they chanted the name of the prophet who had been taken from their midst.

Chapter XXVII

"Now let my brother show his power."
—*The Last of the Mohicans*, Chap. XXV

*Y*oung Ganishando was pushed and prodded by his friends, and so he made a show of snatching up one of the larger branches from the pile and dragging it to where the white maiden was lashed to the stake. As the boy added it to the ones around her feet, he tried to meet her eyes. But he saw her defiance and pride, and it so filled him with shame for what his people were doing that he had to look away. He wanted to reach out to her, but his friends were dancing and shouting and calling for the burning to begin. Everywhere drums were sounding, and in the distance he could hear the chant of the condolers as they sang of the passing of their great, fallen prophet:

> *"Jatthontenyonk,
> Jatakweniyosaon!
> Jatthontenyonk,
> Jatakweniyosaon!
> Jatthontenyonk,
> Jatakweniyosaon!"*

> Continue to listen,
> Thou who wert ruler!
> Continue to listen,
> Thou who wert ruler!
> Continue to listen,
> Thou who wert ruler!

A bonfire was blazing nearby, and several of the bolder braves ran up to it and snatched brands from the flames. They went running through the crowd, torches raised high as they danced wildly around the man and woman tied to the stakes. Never had Ganishando seen a woman treated so cruelly, and he could only think that she must be less than human. Yet she had the form and grace of a woman, and in her eyes he had seen the same hunger for life.

"Jatthontenyonk, Jatakweniyosaon!" the mourners cried, their voices echoed by the death shouts of the crowd.

The warrior Kahonwah pushed through the circle and snatched a brand from one of the braves. Ganishando drew closer to where his mother was standing, watching with repulsion and fascination as the dancers came to a halt and waited for their new leader, who had killed the red-jacket soldier and would be afforded the honor of starting the blaze that would consume his accomplices.

Ganishando saw that the white prisoner was speaking to the woman, but it was a strange language he did not understand. The woman said something in reply, then closed her eyes as if praying to the Great Creator. The boy made a silent prayer of his own—that her pain would be brief and that she would then be reunited with the spirits of her ancestors—and he found himself wondering if the whites went to the same place as the *Ongwe-oweh* and whether they all lived there in peace.

Kahonwah was just approaching the pile of brush and branches that had been heaped around the feet of the man known as La Longue Carabine, when the drummers and chanting condolers suddenly went silent and a lone voice could be heard crying out, *"Ka-rih-wi-yoh! Ka-rih-wi-yoh!"*

All eyes turned toward the trees at the far end of the village. A man was running from the path that led to Onowara's lodge, his arms raised as he continued to shout joyously, "Great tidings of peace and power! Great tidings of peace and power!"

Kahonwah started across the field, his eyes blazing like the brand still clutched in his fist. The warriors and elders followed, with Ganishando and the other boys breaking away from their mothers and taking off in close pursuit.

"*Ka-rih-wi-yoh!*" the man proclaimed, running up to Kahonwah and waving his arms wildly toward the trees. "He is coming! He has come!"

Kahonwah looked across the clearing, and the brand slipped from his hand and was smothered in the dirt at his feet.

Ganishando saw him then, walking resolutely from the woods, his powerful arms bearing the limp body of an Oneida warrior. He wore only moccasins and a loincloth, and where the red jacket's bullet had pierced his breast, there was now only the small blue tattoo of a turtle.

Almost in unison, Ganishando and the villagers whispered his name: "*Onowara!*"

The Oneida Prophet didn't even glance at Kahonwah as he moved past the young warrior and proceeded toward the place where the pyres had been built. The crowd pulled back, gaping in silence as he walked up to the body of the red-jacket soldier and dropped the dead Oneida brave beside it. They saw then that it was one of the men who had been carrying the litter—and that the handle of a knife was protruding from the side of his chest.

Turning, Onowara raised his arm and pointed at Kahonwah, who stood alone across the field. "You would have me dead," he declared in a deep, firm voice that betrayed no evidence of the wound he had suffered—the wound that had magically disappeared. "Why would you have me dead?"

The people turned in wonder toward Kahonwah, who slowly approached, shaking his head in disbelief.

Onowara swept his hand over the body of Major Trevlayne. "You sent this warrior to shoot me on the trail —this warrior who speaks with three tongues—that of the red jackets and of the white jackets and of Kahonwah. And then you told your brave"—he indicated the dead Oneidan at his feet—"to finish the work in my lodge."

"I . . . I did not kill you," Kahonwah stammered, at last finding his voice. "They are the ones. . . ." He indicated Hawkeye and Astra.

"It was you. I heard these things from your own lips, and now you are betrayed by your own treachery." He bent down and jerked the knife out of the brave's chest. "With your own knife you ordered him to kill me, but it was not my day to die. I am the turtle who crawls out from under the rock, seeking the sun." He clasped his fist against the blue symbol on his chest. "In my place, two of your brothers have made the journey; one lies here, the other lies dead outside my lodge."

"You speak lies!"

"With your own hand you have pierced the chest of the eagle." He referred to the legend that Dekanawideh had placed an eagle atop the Tree of the Great Peace to serve as a guardian and sentry for the Iroquois League. "But the tree does not fall; the Great Peace will not be broken."

"These words are lies! Your voice is that of an evil spirit!"

As Kahonwah tried to convince the people that this was not Onowara but some ghost who had come to delude them, the young boy named Ganishando slipped through the crowd until he was standing only a few feet away from the prophet. He gazed at the bloody knife in Onowara's hands, saw the taut muscles of his arms and neck. There was no sign of the gunshot wound—not even a scar disfigured the mark of the turtle on his chest. Ganishando knew that this truly was a man of spirit, but also one of flesh.

Kahonwah seemed to sense that his words were without power and that the crowd had now turned against him. When at Onowara's command several of Kahonwah's followers began to untie the white man and woman from their stakes, it became apparent that the traitorous warrior would soon be forced to take their place, and so he raised Killdeer and aimed it at Onowara. But the young prophet just stood there without moving, as if challenging him to pull the trigger.

Kahonwah did not accept the challenge but instead kept the rifle trained on Onowara as he backed toward the trees. There he would be beyond their musket range but could still reach Onowara with the big hunting gun. And once in the safety of the forest, there was no one in the village who could outrun him.

Young Ganishando stepped from the crowd and placed himself in front of the prophet, determined to take the bullet if it was fired. Onowara saw what the boy was doing and lunged at him just as the air was shattered by the report of not one but two guns. Neither the boy nor the prophet was struck, and as they looked across the field they saw Kahonwah drop the rifle he had just fired and crumple forward into the grass. About twenty feet away, an Indian strode out of the forest, the barrel of his gun still smoking from the bullet he had sent into Kahonwah's back.

"Chingachgook!" a voice shouted, and the white man and woman went running across the field to embrace their Mohican companion.

Ganishando felt strong arms hugging him, and he looked up into the Oneida Prophet's smiling face.

Chingachgook was strangely silent as he and Onowara led the way to the prophet's lodge in the woods. When finally they came into the clearing, he motioned for Hawkeye and Astra to remain outside while they went in. A few minutes later he emerged looking quite solemn as he declared in English, "It is finished. My son is gone."

"But . . . but we just saw him," Astra said, looking quite confused. "He was fine."

"Onowara?" Hawkeye asked, then nodded with understanding. "Oweya."

Chingachgook held aside the door flap, and as they entered the lodge they saw Onowara seated beside the fire, cradling his dead twin brother in his lap.

"He was returning home," Onowara said in the Oneida tongue. "He died among his people."

Chingachgook explained in halting English how Oweya had been mistaken for his twin brother and had been shot by Major Trevlayne. Chingachgook and Onowara had arrived back at the lodge in time to overpower Kahonwah's braves, and Oweya had managed to tell them what was happening in the village. Onowara had gone at once to confront Kahonwah, while Chingachgook had said his final good-byes to the son he had never known and then had taken up his gun and followed. While they were gone Oweya had made his journey to the land of the spirits.

There were tears in Onowara's eyes as he clutched his brother to him and looked up toward the heavens, chanting the song of mourning to the Great Creator:

> *"Jatthontenyonk,*
> *Jatakweniyosaon!*
> *Jatthontenyonk,*
> *Jatakweniyosaon!*
> *Jatthontenyonk,*
> *Jatakweniyosaon!"*

It was not yet dawn as Oweya was placed into the bottom of the very canoe that had brought his murderer to Oneida Castle. No one had seen Chingachgook and Onowara carry the buckskin-shrouded body down off the plateau to the landing place on the creek. Indeed, no one in the village even knew that it was Oweya and not Onowara who had been shot. Instead they had spent the night celebrating the miraculous recovery of their prophet and the demise of the traitor who had tried in vain to kill him. Even Hawkeye and Astra were heralded as agents of the miracle, and though Skenendowa had urged them to stay on as guests of the community, they had gathered up their few belongings and the gifts given them by the Oneida elders and had gone to Onowara's lodge for the night. Now they were seated in a second canoe, smaller and swifter than the one bearing the slain Oneidan.

Onowara and Chingachgook took their positions in the larger canoe, and the two vessels slipped away from shore and headed down the creek toward Lake Oneida. Hawkeye could have easily kept pace with the Indians on his own, but Astra insisted on doing her share of the paddling, and as she knelt at the bow of the canoe, Hawkeye could not help but admire her strength and spirit. And her beauty. He had always been captivated by that beauty, but never more so than this morning as the first light of dawn touched her hair. She wore it Oneida style, with the double braids of an unmarried woman. And as he watched her draw the paddle through the water, he could not help but admire her figure beneath the beaded outfit the women of the village had given her. She seemed neither Iroquois nor European yet somehow embraced both.

Forcing his concentration back to the task at hand, Hawkeye guided the canoe around some shallows just in time to keep from scraping bottom. The creek was low as winter approached, and he sensed in the brisk air that the winds were shifting and would soon carry the snows across the great lakes to the north and west.

It was good to be back on the trail again, but he wondered if he would feel the same way by the time he and Astra reached Albany—for it would be a long, slow passage without Chingachgook. The Mohican had not spoken of his plans as yet, but Hawkeye already knew he would not be making the return journey. He had found one son and was about to bury another; he would not leave without Onowara at his side. And there was much yet for Onowara to do here among his adopted people.

This was as it should be, Hawkeye told himself. Perhaps after he saw Astra safely reunited with her father, he would return to winter with Chingachgook and the People of the Standing Stone.

The sun was climbing above the hills to the west as the canoes paddled out onto Lake Oneida and put ashore on a sandy stretch just north of the inlet. It was Onowara who spoke first, in the Oneida tongue. "We will bury my brother among the birches on that rise." He indicated a small promontory that jutted over the water about a half mile to the south. "It is where I go to listen—where I saw my brother coming home."

"I must make this final journey with my son," Chingachgook announced solemnly in Mohican.

"And we must make our own," Hawkeye replied.

Chingachgook nodded, and the two men grasped forearms. When the sagamore again spoke, it was in English: "My people are your people. My path is yours."

"So it shall be."

Without further words between them, Hawkeye returned to the small, two-person canoe that they would use for the return journey. He and Astra climbed aboard, and as Chingachgook pushed them away from shore they raised their paddles in farewell. Hawkeye glanced back a final time at his Mohican friend, then turned the canoe north along the shore toward Wood Creek.

*   *   *

Chingachgook removed the eagle feather from his hair and placed it upon the grave of his son. Closing his eyes, he listened as Onowara chanted the song of mourning:

*"I will make the sky clear for you
so you will not see a cloud.
I will make the sun shine upon you
so you can look upon it peacefully as it goes down.
Yea! the sun shall hang over you,
and you shall look upon it peacefully as it goes down.
Now I have hope that you will see the pleasant days.
This we say and do, your brother and your father."*

As Onowara ended his song Chingachgook looked out upon the reflection of the sun as it set upon Lake Oneida and said, "Your brother walks with Two Feathers now."

Onowara's reply was in the Mohican language of his mother and father. "When we were boys, we would take our canoes out upon the lake and imagine we were going to meet our father. Two Feathers told us he was a great chief among his people and that we must be strong if we are to wear his symbol." He touched a hand to his breast. "My heart is glad that before he made his final journey, my brother met his father . . . and that my father has at last found his son."

"My son . . ." Chingachgook whispered, clasping Onowara's shoulders. "Let us walk this day together."

Chapter XXVIII

A hunter would be her companion, who knew how to provide for her smallest wants; and a warrior was at her side who was able to protect her against every danger. . . . That she was of a blood purer and richer than the rest of her nation, any eye might have seen; that she was equal to the dangers and daring of a life in the woods, her conduct had proved.
—*The Last of the Mohicans,* Chap. XXXIII

*I*t was late on a blustery autumn afternoon when Hawkeye and Astra eased their canoe between the blackened pilings of what had once been the German Flats dock. It had been an uneventful passage thus far, and they had passed only a few stray Mohawks en route to their winter quarters. Hawkeye wanted to continue downriver and make camp several miles from the ruins of the settlement, but Astra insisted they spend the night right there, among the ghosts and the memories of her friend.

At this time of year the people of German Flats would generally be busy preparing for the coming storms, but that was before the treacherous attack by the French and their Indian accomplices. Astra steeled herself for the shock of again seeing the devastation they had wrought, but as the canoe touched land and Hawkeye helped her ashore, the shock came from the sound of hammers and saws. Already the people of German Flats were returning. A few, it seemed, had escaped into the forest during the attack, while others had been released by the French and were already rebuilding their destroyed homes.

Hawkeye and Astra walked out into the community and were heading toward the place where Rebekka and Stefan Brower were buried when they came upon a pair of men and a woman who were constructing a lean-to shelter out of what could be salvaged from their burned-out home. The two men were struggling to free some roof beams from the rubble, and Astra encouraged Hawkeye to help, saying she would just as soon wait awhile before visiting her friend's gravesite.

The men were brothers, and though they spoke English, few words were said as Hawkeye set to work helping them. Astra, meanwhile, assisted the middle-aged woman in preparing a simple meal of boiled venison and roots. The woman also seemed curiously disinterested in who these two strangers were, and she only asked, in broken English, whether they brought news from Albany. When Astra explained that they had come from deeper in the frontier, the woman simply nodded and resumed her work.

Periodically Astra tried to make conversation, but she did not get past the simplest of pleasantries. While she learned the woman was named Dorothea Hesse and was the wife of one of the brothers, nothing was mentioned about the tragedy that had befallen the people of German Flats. At first Astra thought this was due to the shock of recent events, but as they worked together she began to sense something far more simple and basic. There was no past for these people. With so much pain behind them, they could only look forward, as if their lives had just begun this day.

As the sun went down they took their meal, after which Hawkeye went to scout the area. When he returned, he told Astra that about fifty people had come back to German Flats, with another fifty or so having decided to move on. Hawkeye had found shelter for them on a neighboring farm, which had weathered the attack somewhat better, and they took their leave of the Hesse family and headed across the fields to the ruins of a once spacious farmhouse. The front end of the structure was largely intact, though half of the roof was gone. But one of the chimneys was still standing, so Hawkeye built a fire in the remaining fireplace, and they spread their bedrolls in what had been the parlor.

They were just settling in when a voice called out, *"Guten Abend! Kann ich mich hersetzen?"*

They looked up to see the face of an elderly man reflected in the firelight. He was smiling as he stepped through the archway where a door once hung and gestured toward a half-crushed chair in the corner of the room.

"Please," Astra replied, standing and motioning for him to sit.

"Sprechen Sie Deutsch?"

"Ich spreche nur ein wenig . . . only a little," she replied uncertainly. *"Sprechen Sie Englisch?"*

"Ja, Englisch. A little." He wiped some rubble off the chair and sat down awkwardly, steadying himself in case it collapsed.

"This is Hawkeye, and I'm Astra Van Rensselaer."

"Ja, Van Rensselaer!" Apparently he had heard of the prominent Dutch family. *"Mein Name ist Karl Rittner."* His grin widened. "Do you like German Flats?"

Astra looked at him curiously. "It . . . it was quite beautiful."

"Ja! Beautiful!" He looked around the room. *"Mein Frau . . .* my wife, she died here."

"Oh, I'm so sorry. You must be—"

"Nein," he said with a wave of the hand. "It was two years ago—in this very chair." His expression softened as he gazed around the room. "She was happy here."

"This was your home?" Astra said, then turned in surprise to Hawkeye.

"Ja."

"Please excuse us. We didn't realize. . . ." She began to pick up their bedrolls.

"Nein! Nein! You sleep here. I am staying with my daughter. Her husband is gone, and I help with the child."

"I truly am sorry."

He shook his head. "My grandson is what matters. You come back next year, you will see that we survive . . . that we prosper." Standing, he started for the doorway, then turned and gestured at the two of them. *"Haben Sie Kinder?"*

"Children?" She looked at Hawkeye and blushed. "No, we don't have any."

"You must make children. There must be new life." With a nodding smile, he ducked through the doorway and was gone.

Astra lay beneath her blanket, watching the glowing embers, listening to Hawkeye's slow, steady breath.

The word played through her: Children . . .

She thought of Chingachgook, reunited with the son he had not realized that he had. And of little Stefan, buried out there beside the mother he hardly had a chance to know. And of Pieter . . .

Rolling over, she gazed at Hawkeye, lying beside her. He looked somehow different at night, in the glow of a fire or touched by the cool, soft moonlight. During the day he was handsome—magnificent, in fact—in an untamed, almost dangerous way. Perhaps that was why he had seemed so uncomfortable that night of the Ten Eycks' party. She had sought to contain his wild spirit, but if she or anyone else ever succeeded, that spirit would surely wither and die. Yes, during the day, out here in the wilderness, Hawkeye was magnificent—a man few could equal and none could best. But at night, when he didn't realize that she was looking at him, Astra saw another man. No, a boy, she realized. A child filled with tenderness and love and even a hint of awkward fear. That was the Hawkeye she envisioned when she closed her eyes. That was the man who had held her in his arms.

"*Both of you*," she whispered. "*I want both of you. . . .*"

Hawkeye stirred and opened his eyes. It took a moment for him to focus on her, and when he started to speak, she reached over and touched his lips. It startled him, and as she caressed his cheek he took her hand. She felt both the power of a man and the innocence of a boy and knew that she yearned to be touched by both.

As Hawkeye gazed into her eyes Astra sensed his struggle and his desire. She drew his hand toward her, opening it against her mouth, kissing the palm, placing it against her throat so he could see how her pulse raced. As he lifted his blanket and moved toward her, she ran her finger along the white ridge where a bullet had once creased his side, then pressed the taut muscles of his chest and felt the surging beat of his heart. He took her in his arms then, and she lifted her blanket over them, caressing the child as she gave herself to the man.

Hawkeye finished pounding a crude wooden cross into the ground. A few feet away Astra unfastened a white ribbon from her hair and placed it on top of her friend's grave. "Good-bye, Rebekka," she whispered.

As Astra stood back up Hawkeye placed a hand on her shoulder. "Once this town is back in shape, we can return and give her and Stefan a proper headstone."

"Yes, I'd like that."

"Do you want a few minutes alone with her?"

She shook her head. "Rebekka knows what's in my heart." She glanced up at the eastern sky. "I'm ready now. We'd best get started."

They returned to their canoe and set off down the river. The next few days provided a swift, easy passage back to Albany, marred only by an afternoon's soaking rain, during which they took shelter beneath the overturned canoe. At night they slept in each other's arms but did not again make love—nor did they speak of that night in German Flats. This was not due to any shame on their part but rather the fear that soon they would have to part, each to a world in which the other did not really fit.

It was early on a Thursday afternoon when they finally put in at the army dock on the Hudson River just north of Albany. There were several officers on hand, and Hawkeye presented them with Major Trevlayne's effects, including his torn, bloodstained jacket. He also gave them a note for the Earl of Loudon, which Astra had written out for him using a small writing kit the major had carried on his belt. The terse message read:

> *Any threat from the Oneida Prophet has been removed, but at the cost of Major Trevlayne's life and England's honor.*

Climbing back into the canoe, Hawkeye and Astra paddled south down the Hudson River to the Van Rensselaer estate. Astra wanted to face her father alone, but Hawkeye insisted on escorting her to the house and waiting nearby, in case Hendrik went into a rage.

As they walked up the drive Astra took off her straw hat and tucked it under her arm. This was the first time since leaving the Oneida village that she had worn her customary clothes, and they felt strangely unfamiliar and uncomfortable. And these were only a simple wool jacket over a linen skirt and blouse. She looked up at the manor and shuddered at the thought of the silk stockings, hooped skirts, and whalebone corsets that awaited her.

They stopped at the front steps, and just as Astra was turning to speak to Hawkeye, she was startled by the sound of the front door being jerked open and a woman calling out, "Juffrouw Van Rensselaer!"

"Clarice!" Astra exclaimed. "What are you doing here?"

"Thank God you're all right!" The young maid came rushing down the steps. "Thank God you're home!"

Clarice started to curtsy, but Astra grabbed her hands and embraced her. Blushing, the maid glanced over at Astra's companion, as if not knowing what to say.

"You remember Hawkeye, don't you?"

Clarice was about to reply when another voice called Astra's name. It was also a woman, and Astra turned to see her father's mistress standing in the doorway. Marthe Cryn was wearing a plain dressing gown and looked older and more haggard than Astra had remembered.

"What's wrong?" Astra blurted as Marthe came down to greet her. "Is Father all right?"

Marthe hugged the young woman and kissed each of her cheeks. "We were so worried about you," she said, touching Astra's face to make certain she was not dreaming. "If anything had happened to you, I never would have forgiven myself."

"I'm fine—really I am. Hawkeye took good care of me."

"Yes . . ." Marthe said a bit distractedly as she led Astra up the steps.

"How's Father? Has something happened?"

Marthe patted her hand. "I'm so sorry I didn't tell you. Perhaps if you had known . . . but he was so insistent that I keep it a secret."

Astra stopped just inside the doorway and turned Marthe to her, saying firmly, "Tell me what's going on. What happened to Father?"

Marthe abruptly broke into tears, and Astra found herself comforting the woman. Looking back at Clarice, she whispered in confusion, "What is it? Has he died?"

"Oh, no, *juffrouw*. He . . . he's upstairs."

Clarice took charge of Marthe, and Astra headed across the foyer. But Marthe dashed over to her and grabbed her hand.

"I'll be all right," Astra said. "I *want* to see him."

"B-but you don't . . . you don't understand," Marthe stammered. "Your father isn't well."

"His stomach again?"

Shaking her head, she started crying again but forced back the tears. "It . . . it's his mind."

Astra looked at her curiously, then turned to Clarice, who held her head down but nodded. "His mind? I don't understand."

"Your father is dying," Clarice said simply. "The doctor says it's bad blood."

"Blood?"

"The French disease," Clarice added, her voice a hush.

Syphilis! Astra pulled away from Marthe and started up the stairs.

"He . . . he may not recognize you," Marthe called after her.

Astra gained the top of the stairs and hurried down the hall to Hendrik's bedroom. The moment she opened the door and looked in at her father, she could sense the presence of death. It wasn't just the odor of the various chemicals that had been used to rub him down or the cloying smoke from the censer Marthe had placed in the room. It was the utter helplessness of his expression as he stared with vacant eyes at the stranger in his doorway.

"Father?" she said cautiously as she approached his bed. *"Vader? Het es jouw dochter, Astra. . . ."*

Hendrik did not respond, his only movement the palsied shaking of his hands. When she came up beside him and pulled the blanket over his chest, he stirred slightly, his eyes following her movements and then gazing beyond her at some uncertain point in the distance.

"Oh, Father, what has happened to you?" she whispered, fighting back her tears as she looked down at him. She wanted to ask him about this disease—how long had he known about it, and had he had passed it on to his mistress?—but even if he were lucid, she would never have been able to ask.

She had heard stories of the so-called French disease. In its early stages it caused chancres and sores, and if treated aggressively with mercury ointments and pills, there was every hope for an eventual cure. But sometimes the disease did not make itself known—or the sufferer was too proud to seek help—until it reached the later stages. And then it could rob the victim of his faculties and ultimately his life.

"He's been like this almost since you left," Marthe Cryn said, entering the room and going over to the bed. "Sometimes he recognizes me and even speaks. But usually he just lies there." Reaching over, she tenderly patted his hand. "It's a blessing, I suppose."

"A blessing?" Astra said incredulously.

"Dr. Coeymans calls it brain syphilis. He says it has progressed quite quickly. First headaches and insomnia, then confusion and rage. Now this." Her voice caught with emotion, and she bent down and kissed Hendrik's hand. "At least he seems at peace now."

As Astra looked at her father's lover she saw a different woman from the one who had been crying downstairs, and she suddenly realized how strong Marthe really was. She had been denied a life with the man she loved, just as she denied herself any tears or pity in his presence.

Marthe turned to her and smiled gently. "He loves you very much, you know. And he loved Pieter. It wasn't your father but the sickness that made him treat Pieter the way he did. And it wasn't his hand that hit you." She gingerly touched her own cheek, and Astra knew that Hendrik had struck her as well.

"Why didn't he tell me?"

"Your father is a proud man. And a generous man. Remember him that way . . . not like this."

"I . . . I said some terrible things when I left. Do you think he . . . ?"

"Your father knows that you love him. He was angry when you left, but later the rage passed. He got weaker, but he saw things more clearly. He knows you love him and that you weren't trying to hurt him."

"How can I be sure?" Astra whispered, taking her father's hand. He just stared toward the ceiling.

"He can hear you." The older woman tenderly touched Astra's arm. "Tell him how you feel."

Marthe backed across the room and stepped out into the hall. Beside the bed, Astra dropped to her knees and buried her face in her father's hand.

Hawkeye propped Killdeer just inside the doorway and looked across the foyer to the staircase. He had heard enough of the women's conversation to understand Hendrik Van Rensselaer's condition, and he feared what Astra had found when she entered his room.

"You needn't worry about her," Clarice said, closing the door behind him. "He won't hurt her. He isn't the same man he was when she left."

"I saw the way he treated her."

"Yes. We all had a taste of his anger." She crossed the foyer and looked up the stairs. "I was ready to leave, myself, thanks to the *juffrouw*'s generosity, but then Mijnheer Van Rensselaer collapsed, and we had to call the doctor. He sent for Mevrouw Cryn, and she explained what was happening. He was unconscious for two days, and ever since then he's passed in and out." She shook her head in resignation. "The end will come soon now, the doctor says. I'm just glad that the *juffrouw* got home in time. Perhaps in his death, he can make up for the many sins of his life."

"It's never easy to lose a father—or a friend."

"Even one who treated his own kin so poorly. I know it was the sickness, but there's something devilish at work when a man sends outlaws to hunt down his own daughter. I don't see how she could ever forgive him, sickness or no."

"Hunt her down? What do you mean?"

She looked surprised at his question. "Why, the ones you dispatched, of course. We knew nothing of it until that odious man came riding up asking for Mijnheer Van Rensselaer, just a couple of days after you'd left. It was plain to see he'd been shot, and when I told him the *mijnheer* couldn't take visitors, he barged right in and confronted the poor man in his sickbed. He railed on about how you'd killed his partners and demanded payment in full, despite having failed to bring Juffrouw Van Rensselaer home."

"This man—do you know his name?"

Clarice's lips tightened as she hissed, "Marcus Dent. I'll not soon forget a fellow such as that."

"Dent . . ." Hawkeye repeated beneath his breath, recalling the last word spoken by one of the ambushers who had attacked them on the river. "Is this Marcus Dent from around these parts?"

She nodded. "When he realized how sick the *mijnheer* was, he told me to send word to the Proost Huis as soon as he was better."

"Is that a tavern?"

"Yes. Over on Handelaer Street."

"Thank you." He walked back across the foyer and picked up his rifle.

"Will you be leaving now?" she asked in concern. "What shall I tell the *juffrouw*?"

"I won't be gone long. Just tell her I had some business to attend in town." He opened the door, then looked back. "And please don't mention anything of this Marcus Dent fellow to Miss Van Rensselaer. She doesn't know her father was involved, and now isn't the time to upset her further." He gave a polite bow and headed from the house.

"Why are you crying?" a voice whispered, and Astra looked up in surprise at her father. He had turned toward her, his eyes drifting to the left and right as he spoke.

"Father!" she exclaimed, touching his sweat-matted brow. "It's me—Astra. I've come home."

Hendrik's eyes narrowed, then fluttered closed and back open again. "Pieter and I have been searching everywhere. Your mother's been heartbroken with worry."

"Mother always worries too much," she replied with conviction, even though her mother had died shortly after Astra was born.

"She loves you so much."

"I know."

"So does Pieter."

"Yes, Father." She smiled as she caressed him. "And you. . . ."

His hands trembled, and he started to turn away.

"Don't go yet, Father."

"I . . . I—"

"I love you, Father. . . ."

He raised his head slightly and looked back at her, and there was a flash of understanding in his eyes. "I . . . I'm sorry, Astra."

"Shhh . . ." she breathed, kissing his hand. "I know you love me, Father. I know."

"Tell her I'm sorry. . . ."

She looked at him curiously, then said, "Marthe?"

"Tell her I . . . I love her."

His head lolled back on the pillow. Astra spoke to him, told him how much she loved him, tried to get him to say anything in reply. He was still there, gazing up at the ceiling. He was there, but already he was gone.

Chapter XXIX

"The law of the Manitou is just. It is so; while the rivers run and the mountains stand, while the blossoms come and go on the trees, it must be so."

—*The Last of the Mohicans*, Chap. XXX

*H*endrik Van Rensselaer was laid beside his wife and son in the family plot behind the manor. Only his closest friends were on hand, including the Ten Eycks and Marthe Cryn. Astra treated Marthe as though she were part of the family, for indeed she had been closer to Hendrik than anyone. Her husband, Colonel Reinold Cryn, sent Astra his condolences and apologized that he could not leave his posting in the north to attend the funeral. Hendrik's relationship with Marthe and her husband had been a curious one, no less so in death than in life.

As Willem Ten Eyck spoke a few words over the grave, a second ceremony was taking place several miles away, this one without any pretense of formality. Other than a pair of grave diggers, a single minister was the only one in attendance, and he had been rousted from Humphrey's Tavern out near the fort. They stood in a muddy field in Albany Rural Cemetery, the minister taking an occasional nip from a bottle of *jenever,* a popular Dutch gin.

As the diggers finished their work the minister corked the bottle and stuffed it back into his jacket pocket. "What's his name?" he muttered.

One of the men shrugged, but the other said, "Marcus Dent."

"How'd he die?"

"Tavern brawl, I suppose. He was found in the alley behind the Proost Huis."

"Gunshot?"

"Knife."

"Did they catch the man who did it?"

"Not likely they will. Those that frequent the Proost are an idle and dissolute lot. Not like at Humphrey's," he quickly added.

The minister nodded. Stepping forward, he held a hand over the grave. "Well, Marcus, it looks as if there's only us to see you off." Clearing his throat, he intoned, "Earth to earth, ashes to ashes, dust to dust, in sure and certain hope of the Resurrection unto eternal life . . ."

Astra sat in the study of the Van Rensselaer manor, trying to concentrate on the task at hand as Willem Ten Eyck pored over her father's papers, which were spread out on top of the large oak desk.

"We really should take care of this one right away," he commented as he handed her one of the documents. "And of course there's the question of the bank. Your father left Andries Van Bergen in charge, and he's been doing a fine job. But if you prefer someone else—"

"No, no," she blurted, shaking her head. "Andries was always loyal to my father. I want him to continue."

"Good. Now, there are several other matters that really must be cleared up." He tapped his finger on the paper in front of him. "Here, for instance . . ."

There was a knock, and Astra turned to see Hawkeye standing in the doorway. "Excuse me," he said, taking a step forward. "I wanted to say good-bye."

"You're leaving? But I thought you'd—"

"I have to go to the fort. Lord Loudon wants a full report on what happened at Oneida Castle."

"And you'll give it to him?" she asked, somewhat surprised.

"I don't want him getting any ideas about sending another envoy out there. If I can convince him the major completed his mission, perhaps he'll leave the Oneidas in peace." He glanced beyond her to Willem. "Good day to you, sir."

"Will I see you later?" Astra asked, standing and walking over to him.

"Not tonight. I'll be staying at the fort."

"Tomorrow, then." She embraced him.

He awkwardly returned her embrace, then nodded to Willem and said, "Thank you for taking such good care of Miss Van Rensselaer."

"I'm only sorry it isn't under more pleasant circumstances," the older man replied.

"Good-bye, Astra." Hawkeye raised her hand to his lips, then turned and headed down the hall.

Astra returned to her seat and stared somewhat absently through the window.

"We were discussing your father's affairs," Willem said.

"What? Oh, yes, the papers. Where were we?" She took the document Willem was holding out for her.

Just then Marthe Cryn breezed through the doorway. "There will be plenty of time for that later," she declared, snatching the paper from Astra's hands. "Aren't you going to see him off?"

"But he's only going to the fort."

"Fort? Is that what he told you?" She led Astra to the window. Outside, Hawkeye had Killdeer tucked under one arm and his travel pack slung across his back as he strode down the drive toward the Hudson River. "That fool man is honorable to a fault."

"Honorable? I don't understand."

"He's not going to the fort. He's leaving for the frontier. He thinks he wouldn't fit into your life, and he's too blind to realize you just might fit into his." She gripped Astra by the shoulders. "Well, would you?"

"I . . . I'm not sure. . . ."

"Perhaps you should find out. Don't make the same mistake your father and I did. Nothing is worth it—not even all of this." Her gesture took in the entire manor.

"But . . . where is he going?"

"Does it matter?"

Astra turned back to the window and watched as Hawkeye disappeared down the drive. "My God, he's really leaving, isn't he?" She clutched Marthe's hand. "I've got to stop him."

"You can't stop a man like that. It would be like trying to stop your own heart."

"But what can I do?"

"I think you know." Pulling away from Astra, she moved to Willem's side.

Astra looked a final time out the window, then down at her stiff bombazine mourning dress, her gaze finally settling on the desk full of documents. "Do you think you could . . . ?"

"Don't worry about any of this," Willem said, smiling. "Marthe and I will take care of everything."

An eager light came into Astra's eyes, and she hurried over to Willem, kissed him on the cheek, and hugged Marthe. As she ran from the room she heard Marthe call after her, "Just send word where you've gone!"

Hawkeye pushed against his paddle, steering the canoe around the sandy shallows. The water was so low that passage was almost impossible, and he prepared himself for yet another portage through the icy waters of the creek. The bitter December wind found any opening in his deerskin robe, and he knew they should have taken to winter quarters before now. *Yet she's never once complained,* he mused, smiling.

Astra raised her paddle and turned to face him. "I have something to tell you," she announced, a hint of mischief in her voice. When he did not immediately reply, she said, "Aren't you interested?"

He eyed her suspiciously. "What is it?"

She whispered something he could not hear above the din of the water.

"What was that?" he asked, momentarily putting up his paddle.

"So you want hear it again, do you? Well, if you insist . . ." She grinned broadly as she intoned in the Oneida tongue, *"Konolonkwa."*

Hawkeye blushed.

"You don't have to say it. I hear it in your heart." She turned back around and resumed paddling.

A few minutes later, as they rounded a familiar bend in the creek, Astra called over her shoulder, "They probably already know we're here." She was answered by the cry of a crow. "Chingachgook!" she breathed in excitement as Hawkeye gave a return call.

Ahead, they saw the landing area just below the Oneida village. A delegation of braves was on hand, and at the front stood the Mohican and his son, Onowara. Hawkeye and Astra pulled for shore, gaining speed with each stroke, and Chingachgook stepped out into the water to meet them. Grabbing hold of the prow, he pulled the canoe up onto land, then reached to help Astra to shore. But she had already leaped into the water, and she embraced him.

"Welcome home, sister," he said in English.

"Yes . . . it's good to be home."

Chingachgook turned to greet his friend. "My people are your people."

"Our path is yours," Hawkeye replied, clasping forearms with the sagamore of the Mohicans.

So it shall be.

Afterword

A special thanks is due literary agent Ethan Ellenberg, who first envisioned a sequel to *The Last of the Mohicans* and came to me with the idea. His active participation in this project, from inception to finished manuscript, has been instrumental, and he has my eternal gratitude. I am also indebted to G. Gregory Tobin, vice president and editorial director of the Quality Paperback Book Club, for steering Ethan to my door, and to Bantam editor Tom Beer for his insights and suggestions and for being such a pleasure to work with.

I would also like to thank Linda Ronstadt for introducing me to the armonica, or glass harmonica, on her album *Winter Light*. This curious, beautiful instrument was extremely popular in the eighteenth and nineteenth centuries but fell in disfavor because of the discomfort and nervous agitation suffered by the players. While at the time it was attributed to the intense vibrations produced by the rotating cylinders, modern science has unearthed a more disconcerting cause: The cylinders were made of leaded glass, and prolonged playing invariably resulted in lead poisoning.

Finally, *Konolonkwa,* Connie. You are my constant support and inspiration, my Great Peace. Thank you for sharing the beauty that lives on in Oneida Castle, New York.

Bibliography

In writing *Song of the Mohicans,* I drew heavily upon the works of James Fenimore Cooper. The following is a partial list of other books that were invaluable in my research for this novel:

Baumgarten, Linda. *Eighteenth-Century Clothing at Williamsburg.* Williamsburg, VA: The Colonial Williamsburg Foundation, 1986.

Bruchac, Joseph. *Return of the Sun: Native American Tales From the Northeast Woodlands.* Freedom, CA: The Crossing Press, 1990.

Castle, Thomas. *A Manual of Surgery.* London: E. Cox, 1831.

Cornplanter, Jesse J. *Legends of the Longhouse.* Philadelphia: J. B. Lippincott, 1938. Reprinted 1986 by Iroqrafts Ltd., Ohsweken, Ontario.

The Encyclopaedia Britannica. Ninth Edition (1875-1889) and Eleventh Edition (1910-1911). Cambridge, England: The University Press.

Fenton, William N. *Masked Medicine Societies of the Iroquois.* Washington, D.C.: Smithsonian Institute Annual Report, 1940. Reprinted 1984 by Iroqrafts Ltd., Ohsweken, Ontario.

Frazier, Patrick. *The Mohicans of Stockbridge.* Lincoln, NE: University of Nebraska Press, 1992.

Gabor, Robert. *Costume of the Iroquois.* St. Regis Reservation: Akwesasne Mohawk Counselor Organization. Reprinted 1980 by Iroqrafts Ltd., Ohsweken, Ontario.

Gifford, Stanley M. *Fort William Henry, A History.* Lake George, NY: 1955.

Hale, Horatio E. *The Iroquois Book of Rites and Hale on the Iroquois.* Ohsweken, Ontario: Iroqrafts Ltd., 1989. *The Iroquois Book of Rites* was originally published in 1883 as No. 2 of Brinton's Library of Aboriginal American Literature.

Jaeger, Ellsworth. *Wildwood Wisdom.* New York: The Macmillan Company, 1945. Reprinted 1987 by Iroqrafts Ltd., Ohsweken, Ontario.

Johnson's Universal Cyclopaedia (eight volumes). New York: A. J. Johnson Co., 1874.

Kimm, S. C. *The Iroquois: A History of the Six Nations of New York.* Middleburgh, NY: Press of Pierre W. Danforth, 1900. Reprinted by J. C. & A. L. Fawcett, Inc., Astoria, NY.

Lyford, Carrie A. *Iroquois Crafts.* Washington, D.C.: U.S. Bureau of Indian Affairs, 1945. Reprinted 1982 by Iroqrafts Ltd., Ohsweken, Ontario.

Nevins, Allan. *The Leatherstocking Saga.* New York: Pantheon Books, 1954.

Parker, Arthur C. *Parker on the Iroquois.* Reprint edition of three works: *Iroquois Uses of Maize and Other Plant Foods* (1910); *The Code of Handsome Lake, the Seneca Prophet* (1913); *The Constitution of the Five Nations* (1911). Syracuse, NY: Syracuse University Press, 1981.

Parkman, Francis. *Montcalm and Wolfe*, Volumes I, II, and III. New York: Little, Brown, and Company, 1897.

Peterson, Scott. *Native American Prophecies: Examining the History, Wisdom, and Startling Predictions of Visionary Native Americans.* New York: Paragon House, 1990.

Potts, Charles S., M.D. *Nervous and Mental Diseases.* Philadelphia: Lea & Febiger, 1908.

Sharpe, Samuel. *A Treatise on the Operations of Surgery.* London: G. Robinson, 1782.

Smith, Erminnie A. *Myths of the Iroquois.* Washington, D.C.: U.S. Bureau of American Ethnology, Second Annual Report, 1883. Reprinted 1983 by Iroqrafts Ltd., Ohsweken, Ontario.

Tehanetorens. *Tales of the Iroquois, Volumes I and II.* Rooseveltown, NY: Mohawk Nation Akwesasne Notes, 1976. Reprinted 1986 by Iroqrafts Ltd., Ohsweken, Ontario.

Waugh, F. W. *Iroquois Foods and Food Preparation.* Ottawa: Government Printing Bureau, 1916. Reprinted 1991 by Iroqrafts Ltd., Ohsweken, Ontario.

Weed, Susun S. *Healing Wise.* Woodstock, NY: Ash Tree Publishing, 1989.

Weiner, Michael A. *Earth Medicine—Earth Food.* New York: Fawcett Columbine, 1991.

PAUL BLOCK was born in Manhattan and raised in Glen Cove on Long Island. He attended the State University of New York and received his degree in creative writing in 1973. Block has worked as an apartment manager, cappuccino maker, fish cleaner, and newspaper and book editor, and since 1993 he has been writing full-time. His previous novels include *San Francisco, The Deceit, Beneath the Sky,* and *Darkening of the Light.* Block lives with his family in upstate New York.